D1616652

TKO STUDIOS

SALVATORE SIMEONE - CEO & PUBLISHER

TZE CHUN - PRESIDENT & PUBLISHER

CARA MCKENNEY - TALENT RELATIONS

SEBASTIAN GIRNER - EDITOR-IN-CHIEF

JEFF POWELL - PRODUCTION MANAGER

ROBERT TERLIZZI - DIRECTOR OF DESIGN

POUND FOR POUND #1-6.
Copyright © 2019
TKO Studios, LLC. All rights reserved.
Published by TKO Studios, LLC.
Office of Publication: 450 7th Ave., Suite 2107. New York, NY 10123.
All names, characters, and events in this publication
are entirely fictional. Any resemblance to actual persons
(living or dead), events, or places, without satiric intent,
is unintended and purely coincidental. Printed in the USA.
ISBN: 978-1-7327485-6-9

TKOPRESENTS.COM

TKO PRESENTS A WORLD BY:

NATALIE CHAIDEZ
WRITER

ANDY BELANGER
ART

DANIELA MIWA
COLOR ART

SERGE LAPOINTE
LETTERER

SEBASTIAN GIRNER
EDITOR

ANDY BELANGER
COVER ART

JARED K FLETCHER
TITLE & COVER DESIGN

JEFF POWELL
BOOK DESIGN

POUND FOR POUND

CHAPTER 1

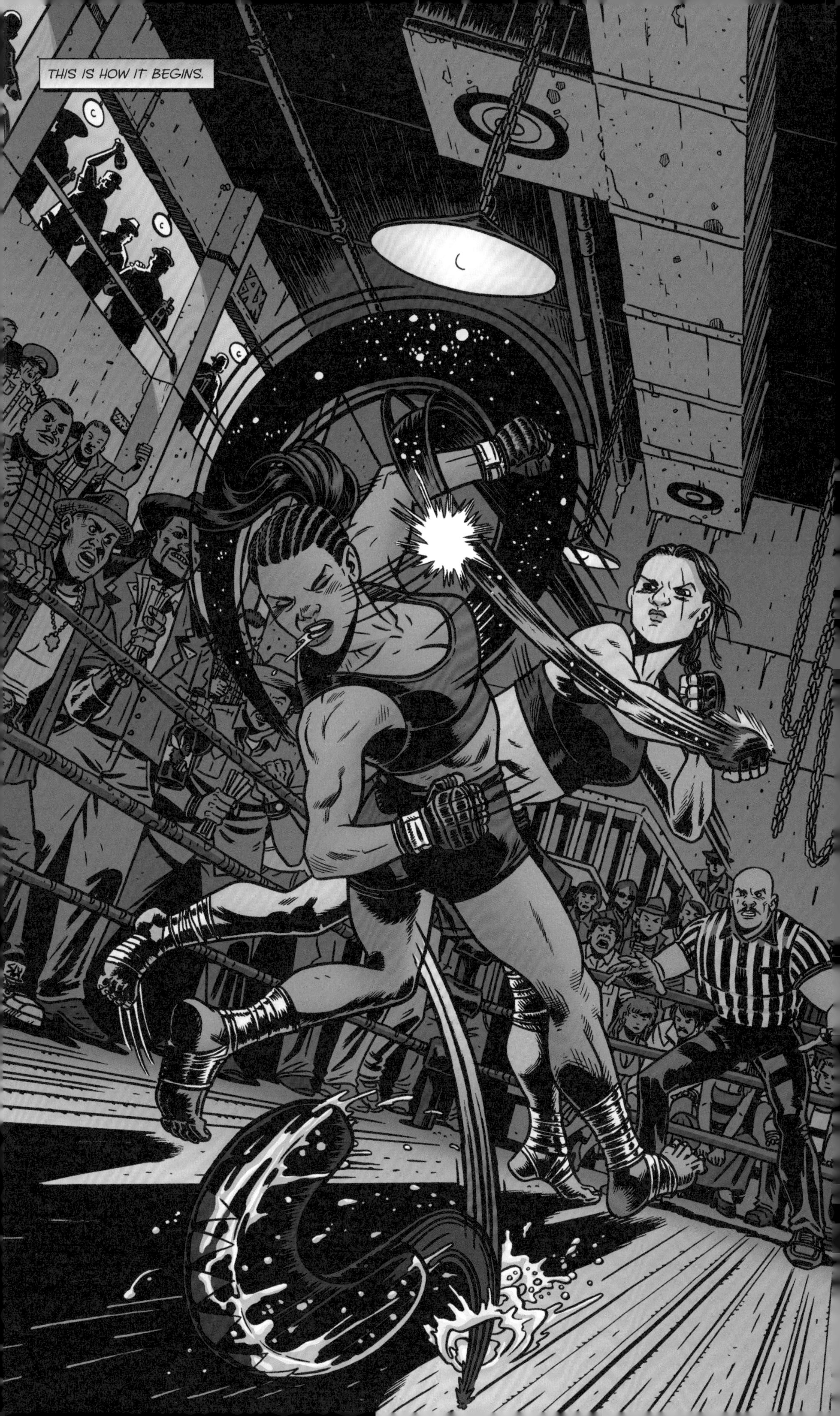
THIS IS HOW IT BEGINS.

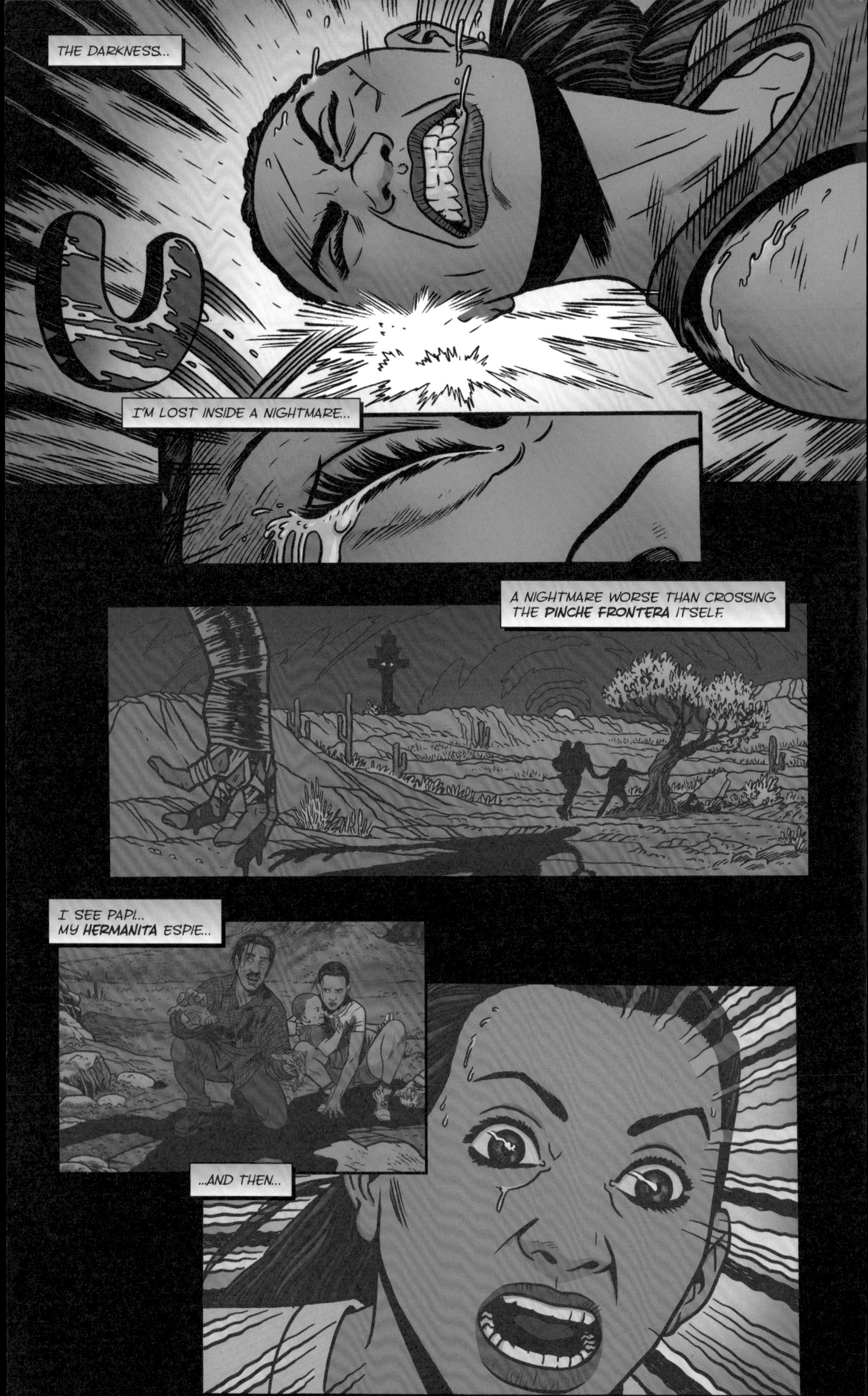
THE DARKNESS...
I'M LOST INSIDE A NIGHTMARE...
A NIGHTMARE WORSE THAN CROSSING THE **PINCHE FRONTERA** ITSELF.
I SEE PAPI...
MY **HERMANITA** ESPIE...
...AND THEN...

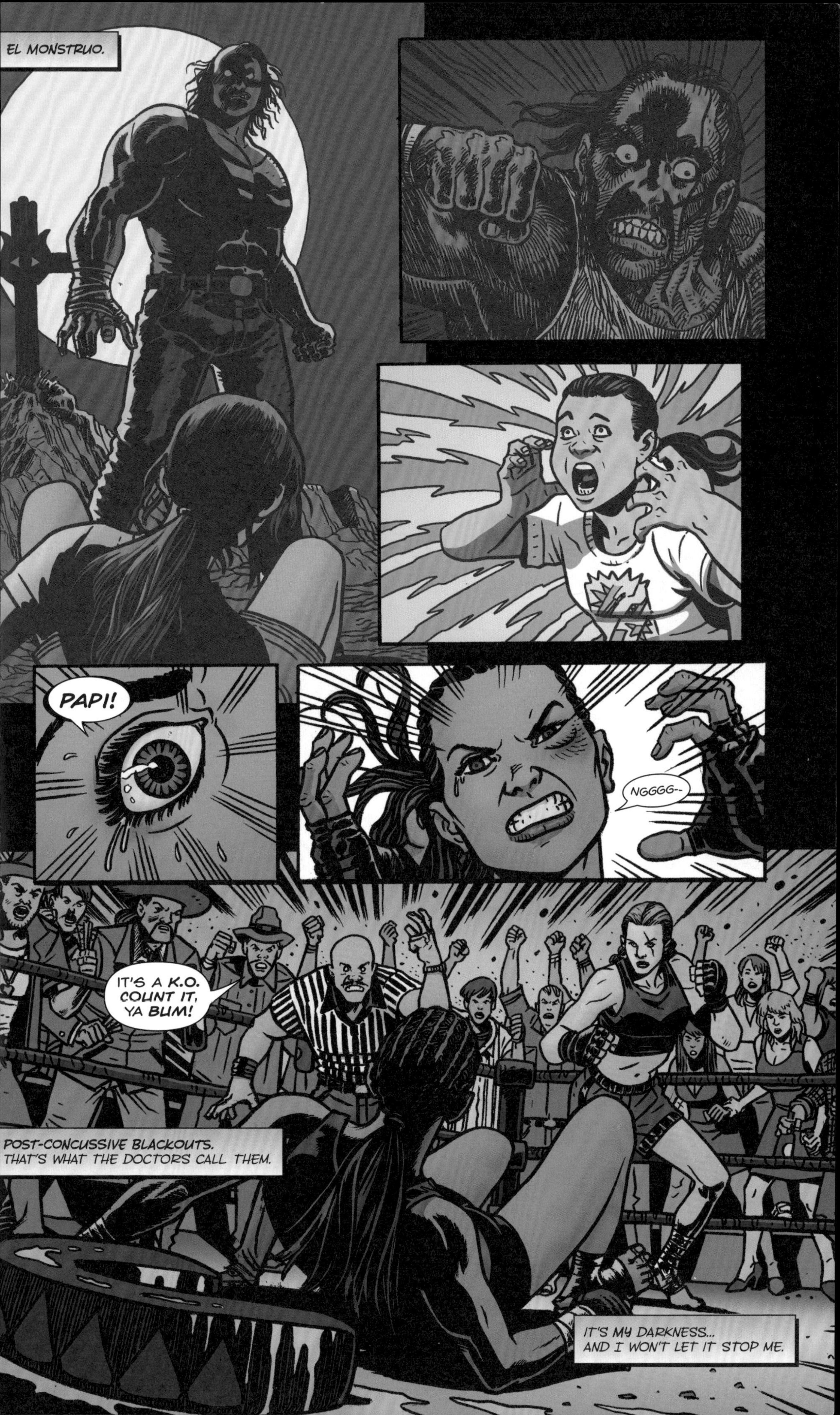
EL MONSTRUO.
PAPI!
NGGGG--
IT'S A K.O. COUNT IT, YA BUM!
POST-CONCUSSIVE BLACKOUTS. THAT'S WHAT THE DOCTORS CALL THEM.
IT'S MY DARKNESS... AND I WON'T LET IT STOP ME.

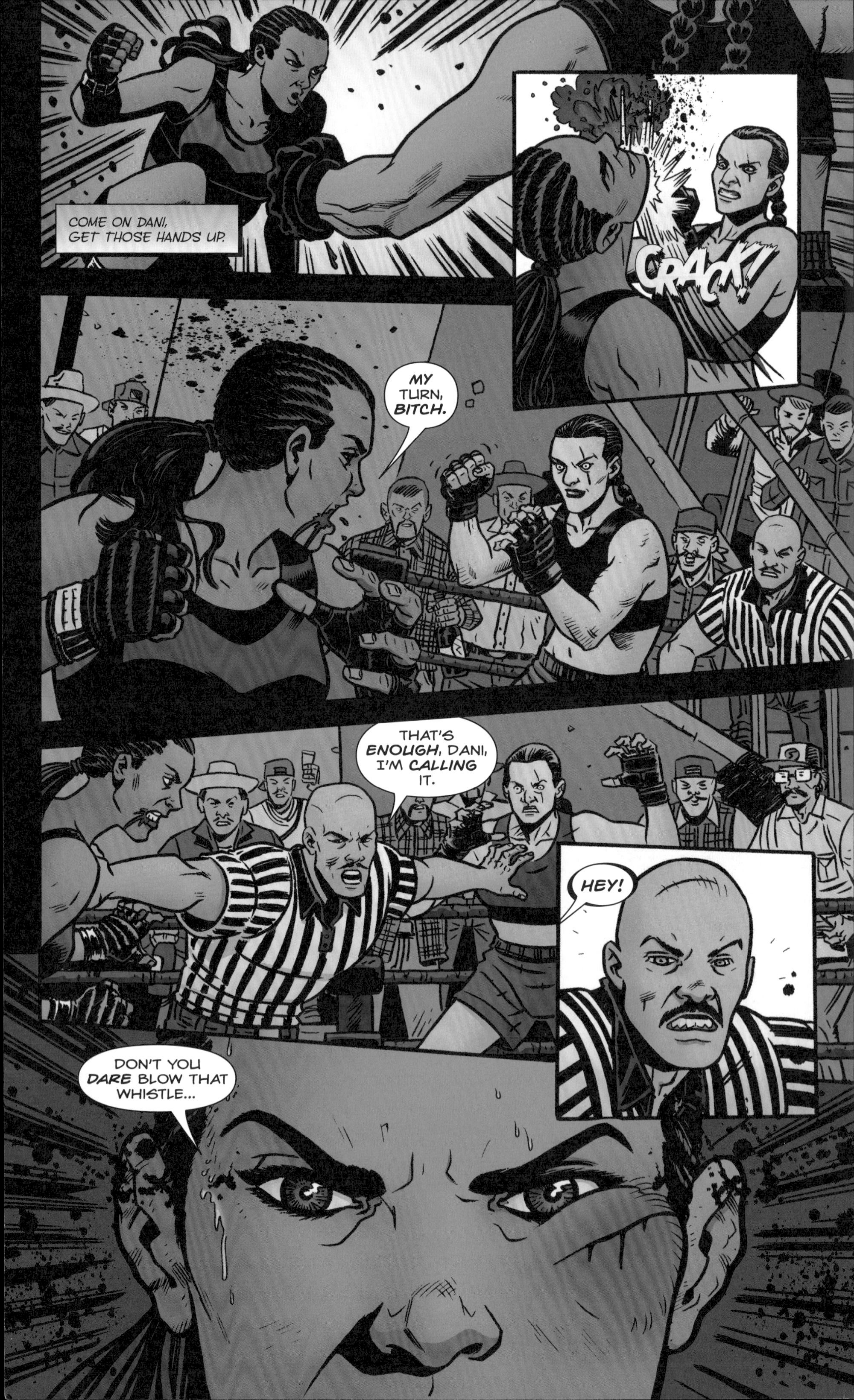
COME ON DANI,
GET THOSE HANDS UP.
CRACK!
MY TURN, BITCH.
THAT'S ENOUGH, DANI, I'M CALLING IT.
HEY!
DON'T YOU DARE BLOW THAT WHISTLE...

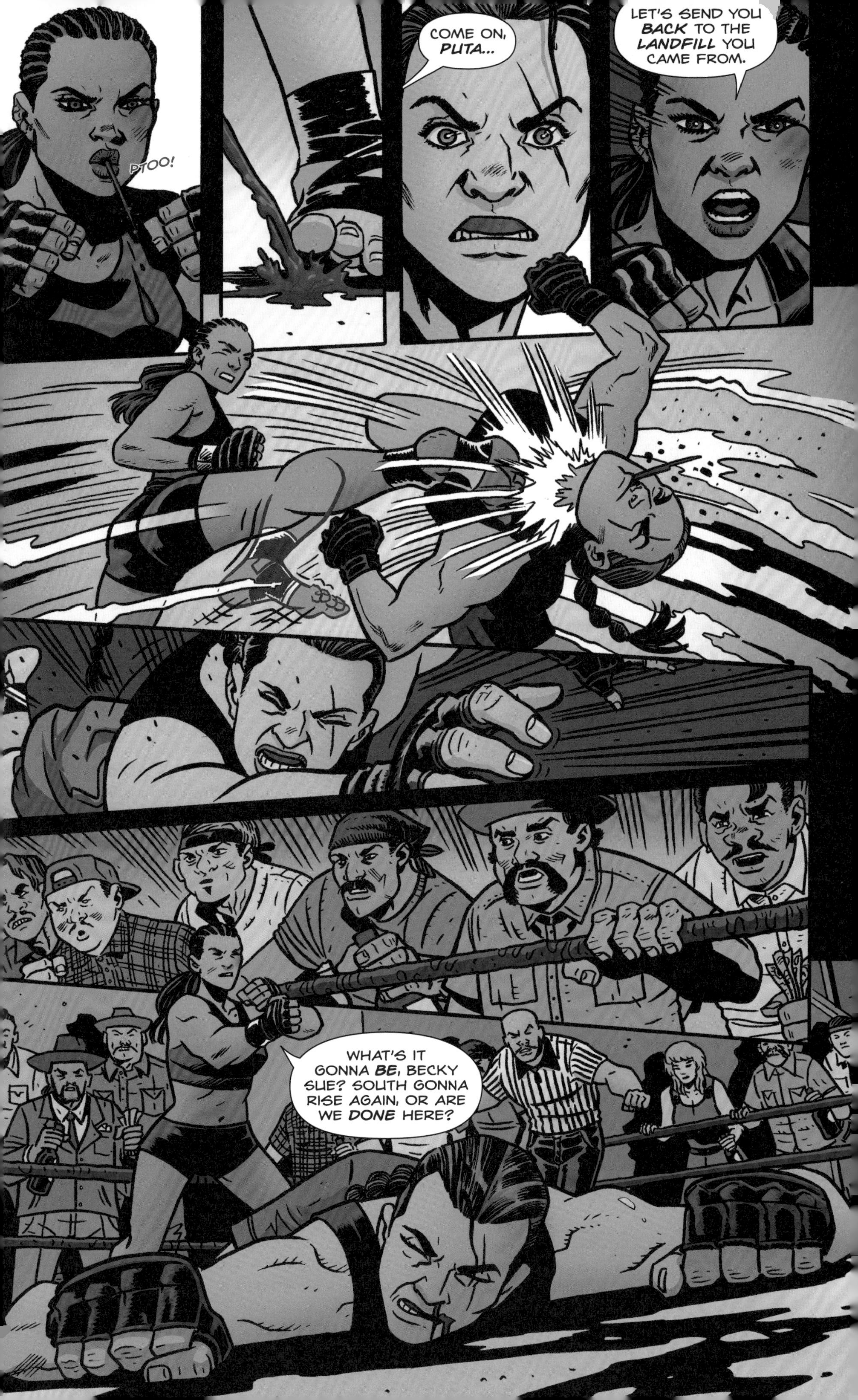
PTOO!
COME ON, PUTA...
LET'S SEND YOU BACK TO THE LANDFILL YOU CAME FROM.
WHAT'S IT GONNA BE, BECKY SUE? SOUTH GONNA RISE AGAIN, OR ARE WE DONE HERE?

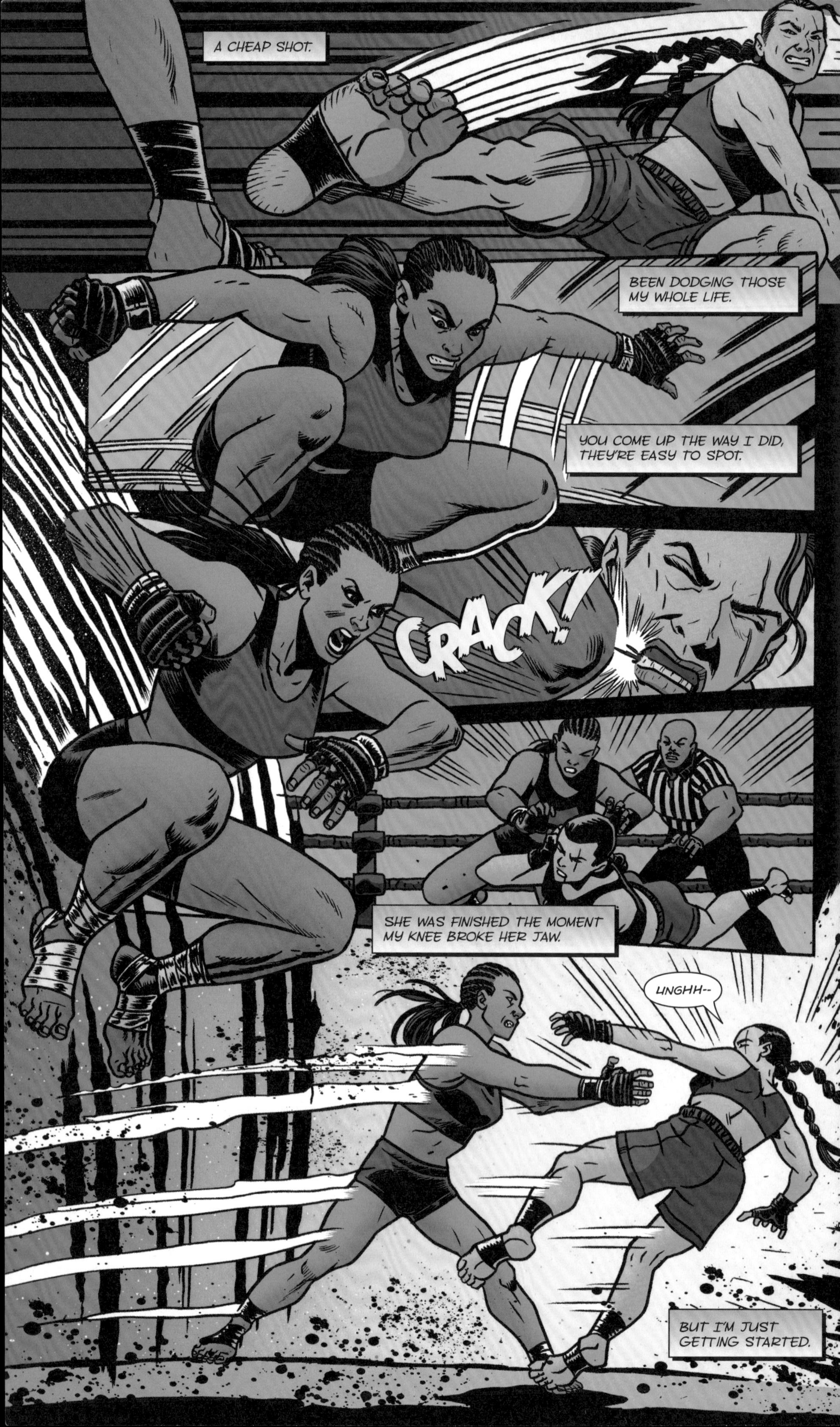
A CHEAP SHOT.
BEEN DODGING THOSE MY WHOLE LIFE.
YOU COME UP THE WAY I DID, THEY'RE EASY TO SPOT.
CRACK!
SHE WAS FINISHED THE MOMENT MY KNEE BROKE HER JAW.
UNGHH--
BUT I'M JUST GETTING STARTED.

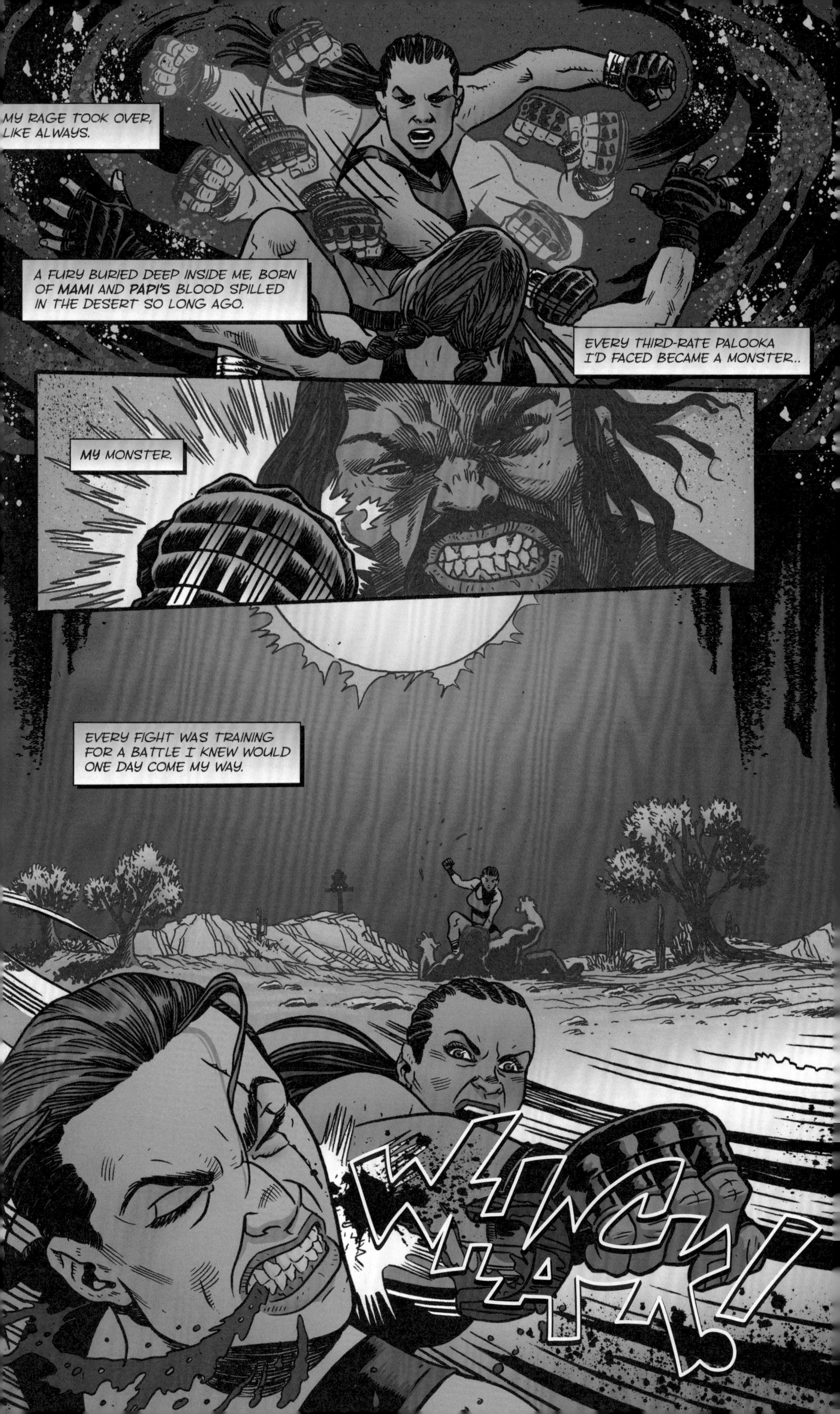
MY RAGE TOOK OVER, LIKE ALWAYS.
A FURY BURIED DEEP INSIDE ME, BORN OF **MAMI** AND **PAPI'S** BLOOD SPILLED IN THE DESERT SO LONG AGO.
EVERY THIRD-RATE PALOOKA I'D FACED BECAME A MONSTER..
MY MONSTER.
EVERY FIGHT WAS TRAINING FOR A BATTLE I KNEW WOULD ONE DAY COME MY WAY.
WHACK!

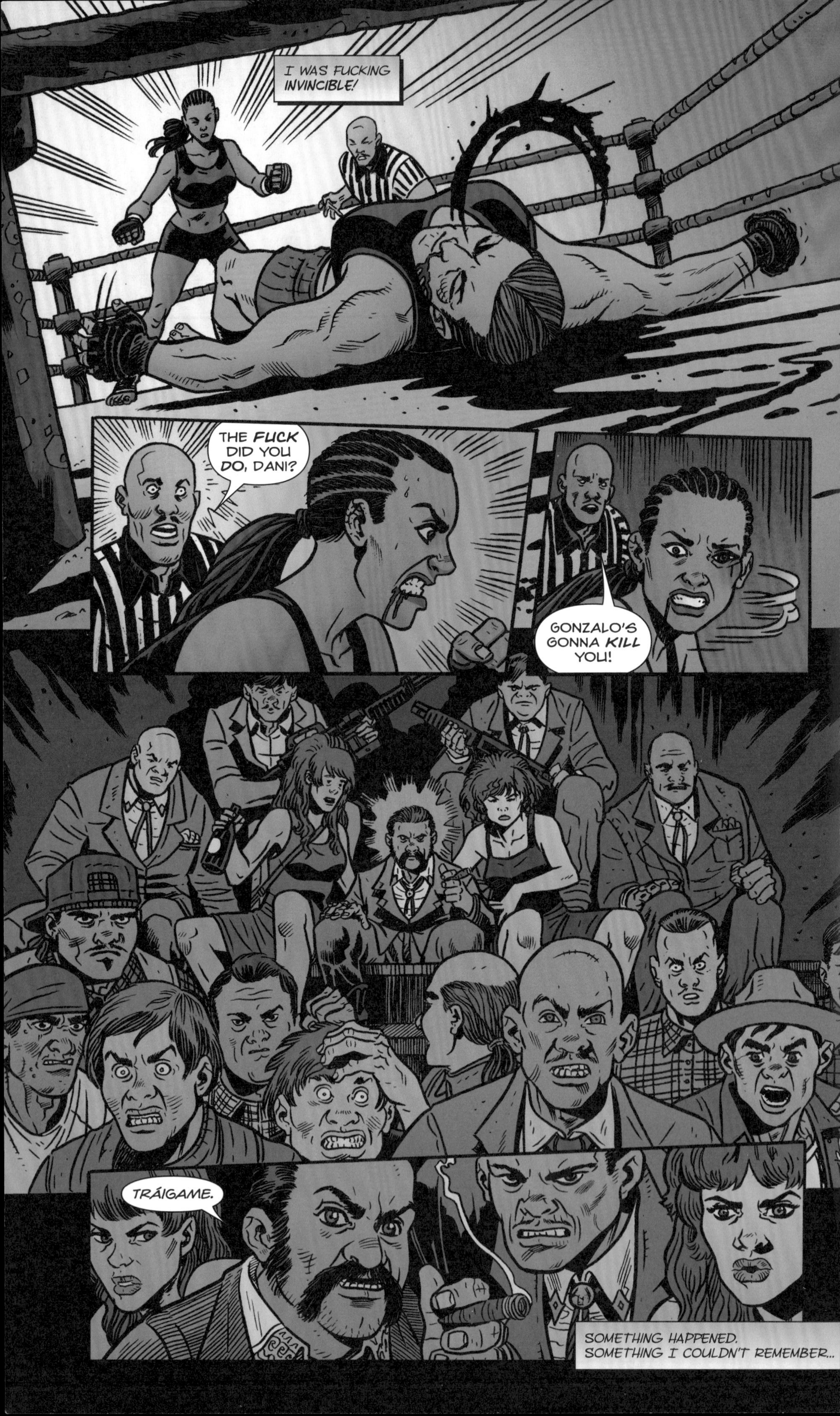

I WAS FUCKING INVINCIBLE!
THE FUCK DID YOU DO, DANI?
GONZALO'S GONNA KILL YOU!
TRÁIGAME.
SOMETHING HAPPENED.
SOMETHING I COULDN'T REMEMBER...

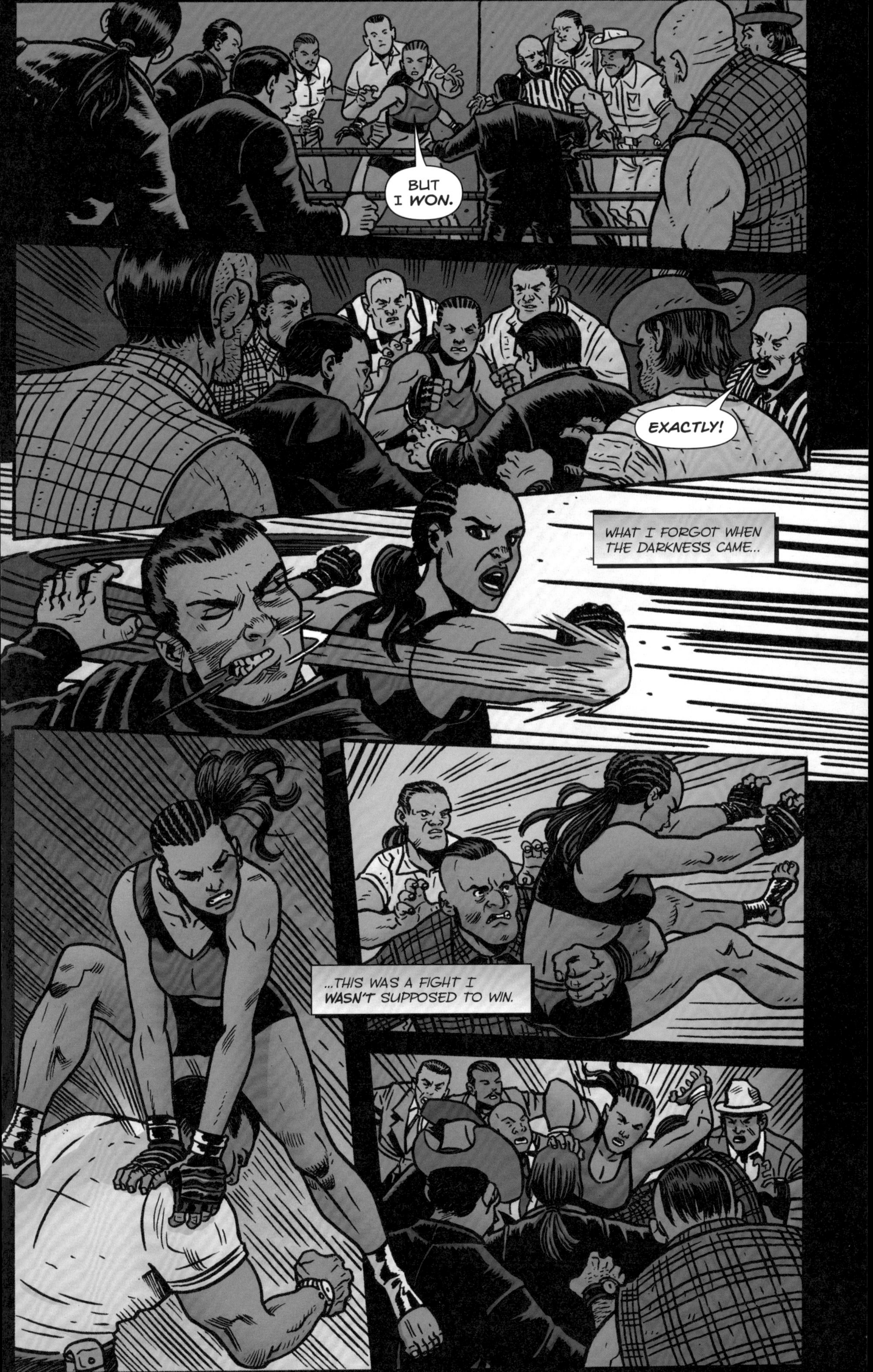
BUT I WON.
EXACTLY!
WHAT I FORGOT WHEN THE DARKNESS CAME...
...THIS WAS A FIGHT I WASN'T SUPPOSED TO WIN.

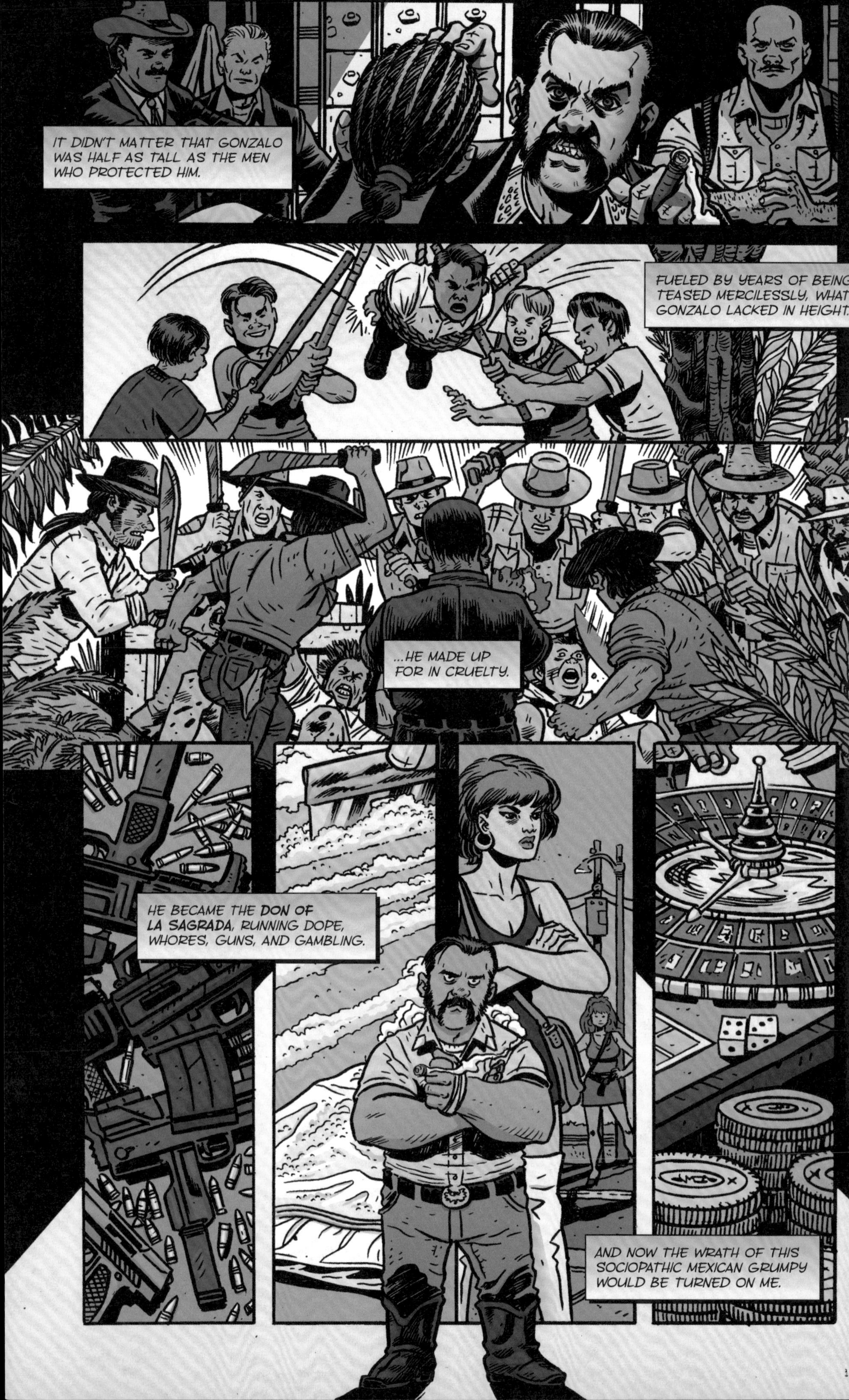
IT DIDN'T MATTER THAT GONZALO WAS HALF AS TALL AS THE MEN WHO PROTECTED HIM.
FUELED BY YEARS OF BEING TEASED MERCILESSLY, WHAT GONZALO LACKED IN HEIGHT...
...HE MADE UP FOR IN CRUELTY.
HE BECAME THE DON OF LA SAGRADA, RUNNING DOPE, WHORES, GUNS, AND GAMBLING.
AND NOW THE WRATH OF THIS SOCIOPATHIC MEXICAN GRUMPY WOULD BE TURNED ON ME.

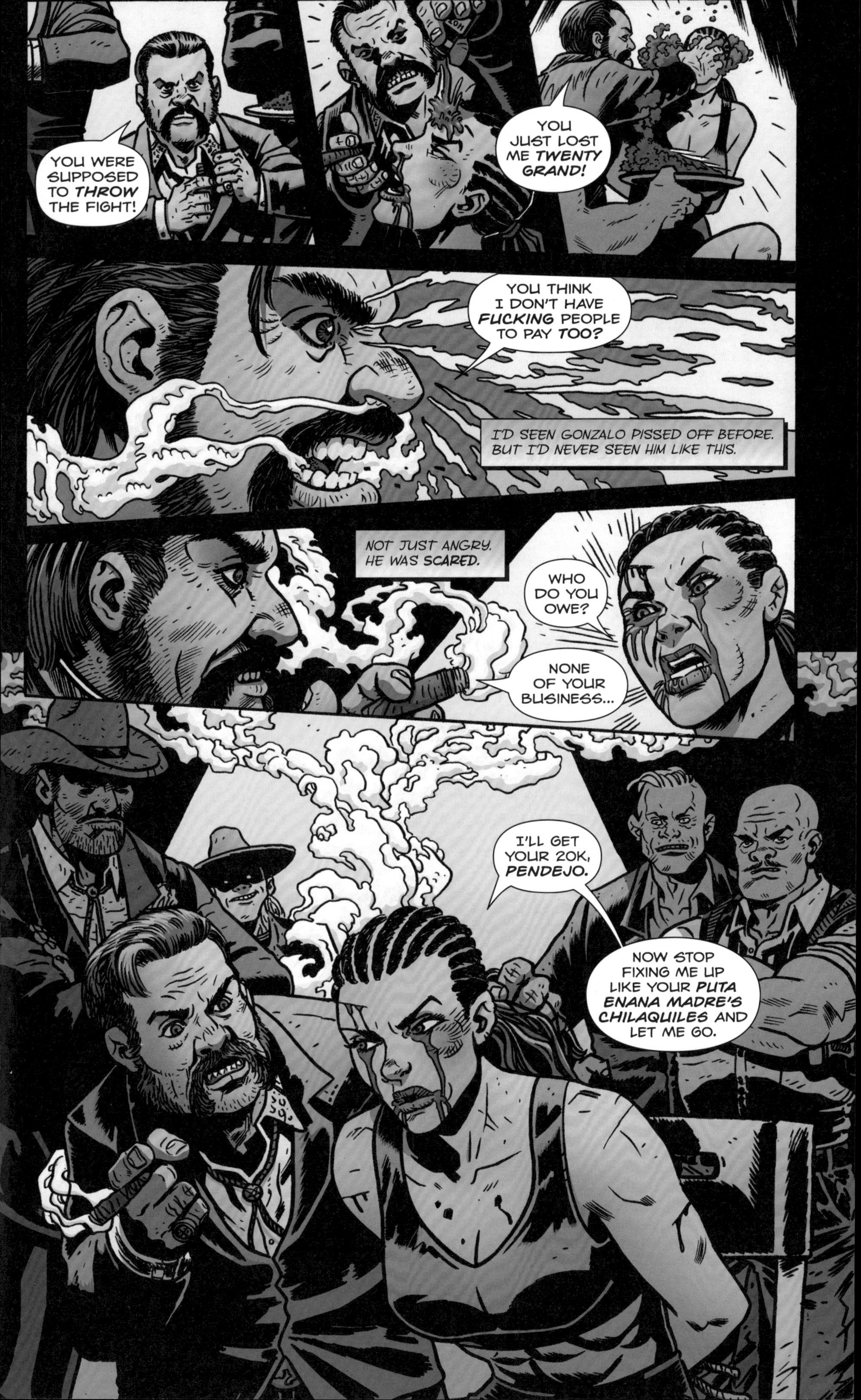
YOU WERE SUPPOSED TO THROW THE FIGHT!
YOU JUST LOST ME TWENTY GRAND!
YOU THINK I DON'T HAVE FUCKING PEOPLE TO PAY TOO?
I'D SEEN GONZALO PISSED OFF BEFORE. BUT I'D NEVER SEEN HIM LIKE THIS.
NOT JUST ANGRY. HE WAS SCARED.
WHO DO YOU OWE?
NONE OF YOUR BUSINESS...
I'LL GET YOUR 20K, PENDEJO.
NOW STOP FIXING ME UP LIKE YOUR PUTA ENANA MADRE'S CHILAQUILES AND LET ME GO.

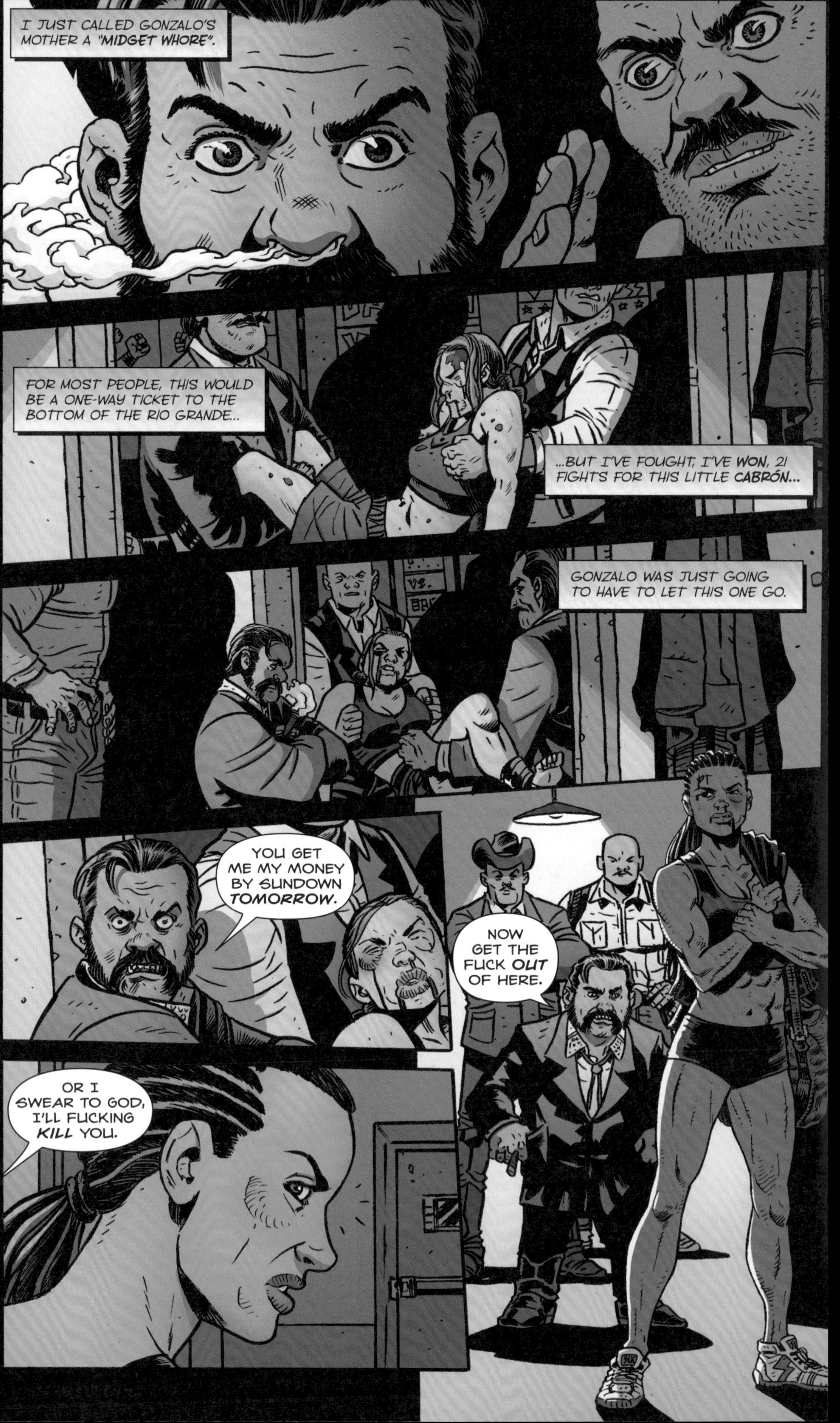

I JUST CALLED GONZALO'S MOTHER A "MIDGET WHORE".
FOR MOST PEOPLE, THIS WOULD BE A ONE-WAY TICKET TO THE BOTTOM OF THE RIO GRANDE...
...BUT I'VE FOUGHT, I'VE WON, 21 FIGHTS FOR THIS LITTLE CABRÓN...
GONZALO WAS JUST GOING TO HAVE TO LET THIS ONE GO.
YOU GET ME MY MONEY BY SUNDOWN TOMORROW.
NOW GET THE FUCK OUT OF HERE.
OR I SWEAR TO GOD, I'LL FUCKING KILL YOU.

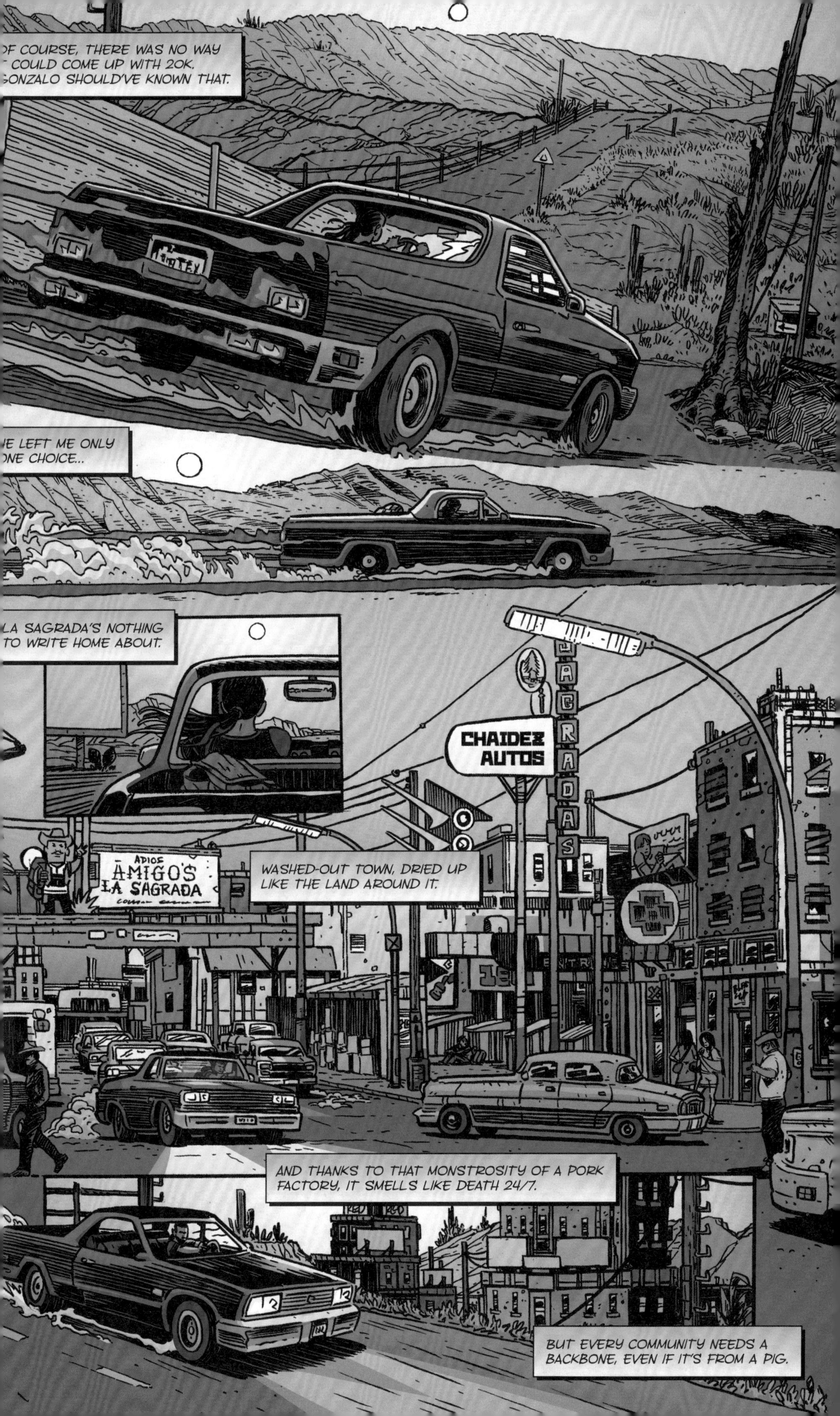

OF COURSE, THERE WAS NO WAY I COULD COME UP WITH 20K. GONZALO SHOULD'VE KNOWN THAT.
HE LEFT ME ONLY ONE CHOICE...
LA SAGRADA'S NOTHING TO WRITE HOME ABOUT.
LA SAGRADA
CHAIDEZ AUTOS
ADIOS AMIGO'S LA SAGRADA
WASHED-OUT TOWN, DRIED UP LIKE THE LAND AROUND IT.
AND THANKS TO THAT MONSTROSITY OF A PORK FACTORY, IT SMELLS LIKE DEATH 24/7.
BUT EVERY COMMUNITY NEEDS A BACKBONE, EVEN IF IT'S FROM A PIG.

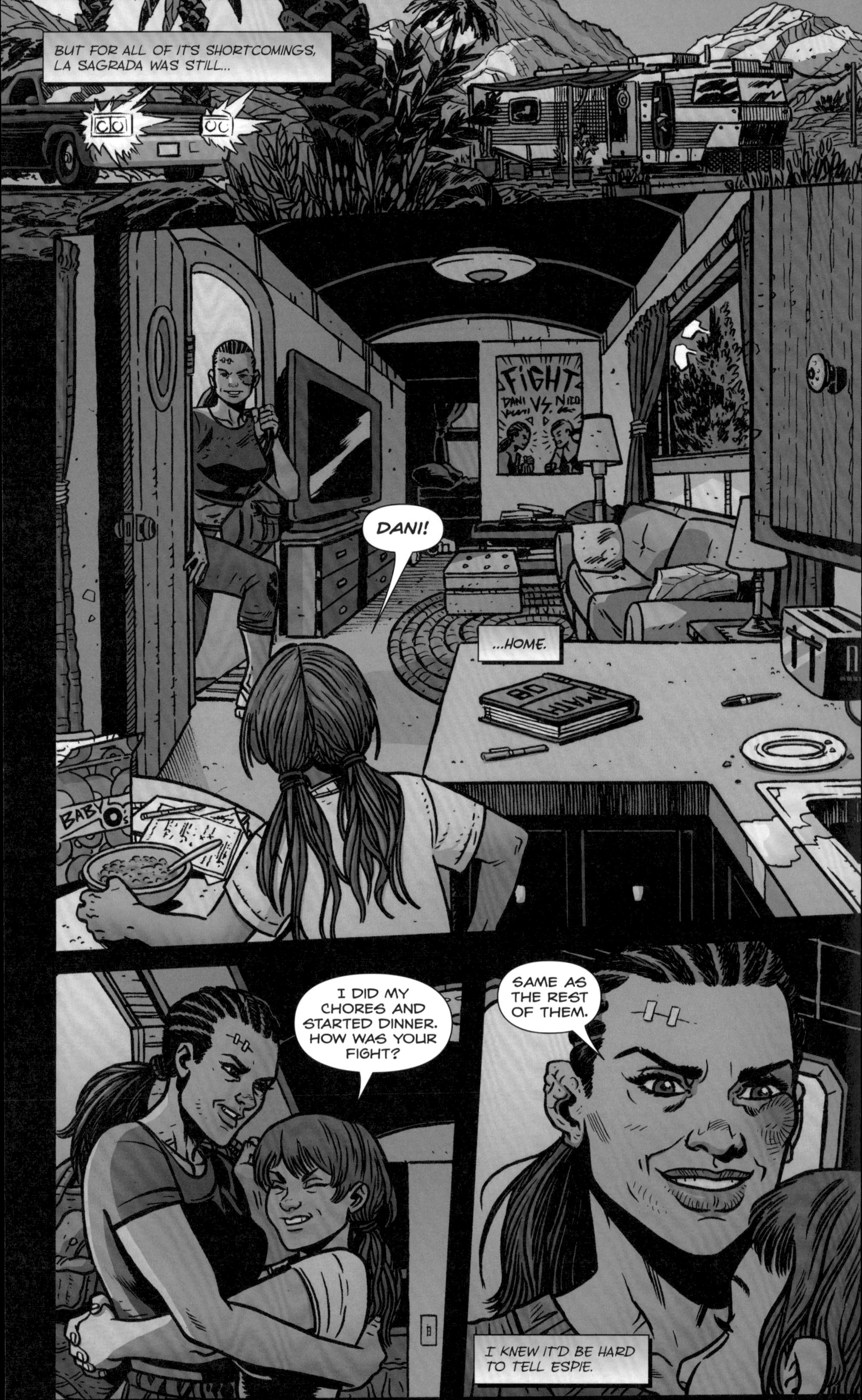
BUT FOR ALL OF IT'S SHORTCOMINGS, LA SAGRADA WAS STILL...
FIGHT
DANI VS. NICO
DANI!
...HOME.
MATH 8D
BABY
I DID MY CHORES AND STARTED DINNER. HOW WAS YOUR FIGHT?
SAME AS THE REST OF THEM.
I KNEW IT'D BE HARD TO TELL ESPIE.

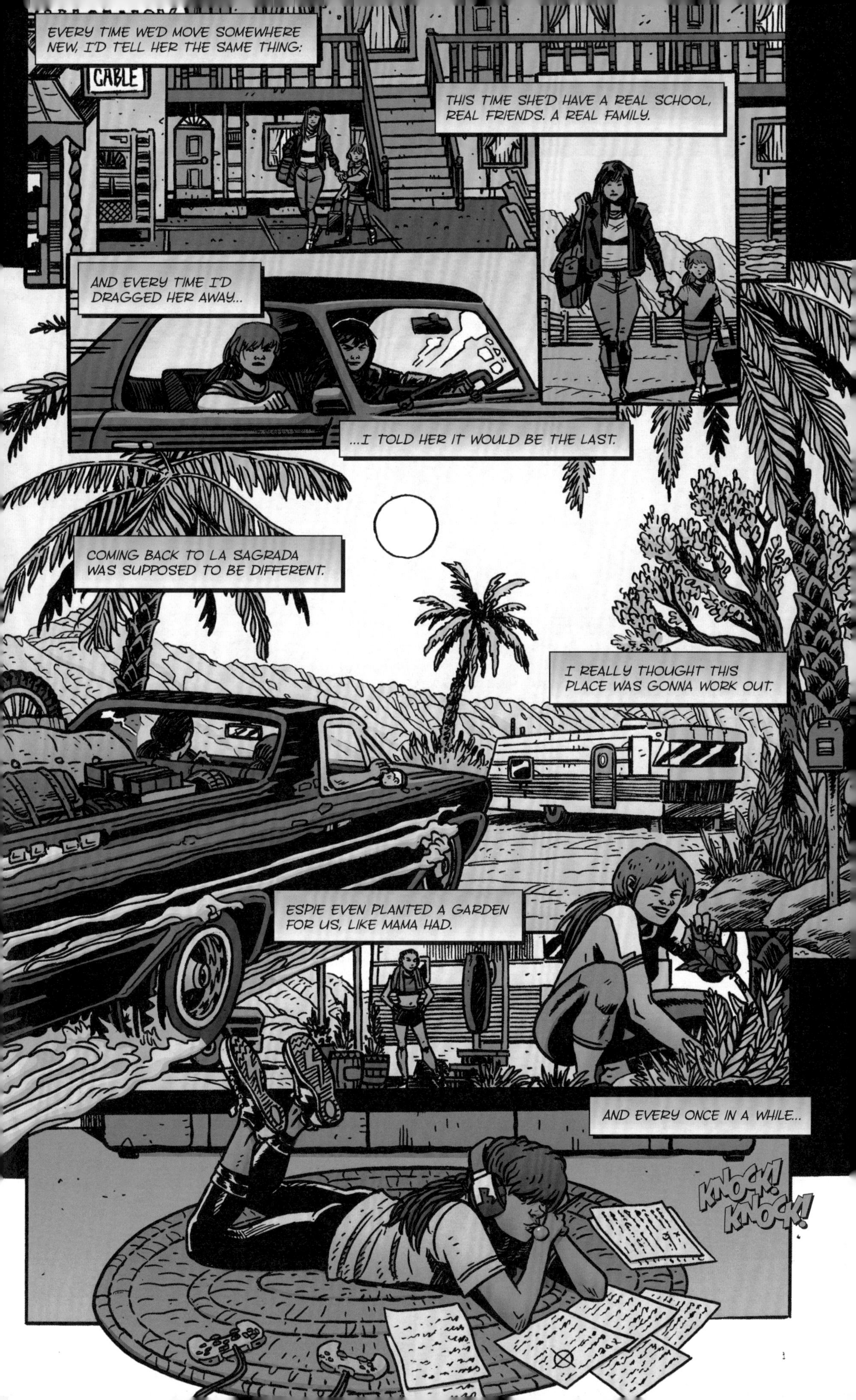
EVERY TIME WE'D MOVE SOMEWHERE NEW, I'D TELL HER THE SAME THING:
CABLE
THIS TIME SHE'D HAVE A REAL SCHOOL, REAL FRIENDS. A REAL FAMILY.
AND EVERY TIME I'D DRAGGED HER AWAY...
...I TOLD HER IT WOULD BE THE LAST.
COMING BACK TO LA SAGRADA WAS SUPPOSED TO BE DIFFERENT.
I REALLY THOUGHT THIS PLACE WAS GONNA WORK OUT.
ESPIE EVEN PLANTED A GARDEN FOR US, LIKE MAMA HAD.
AND EVERY ONCE IN A WHILE...
KNOCK! KNOCK!

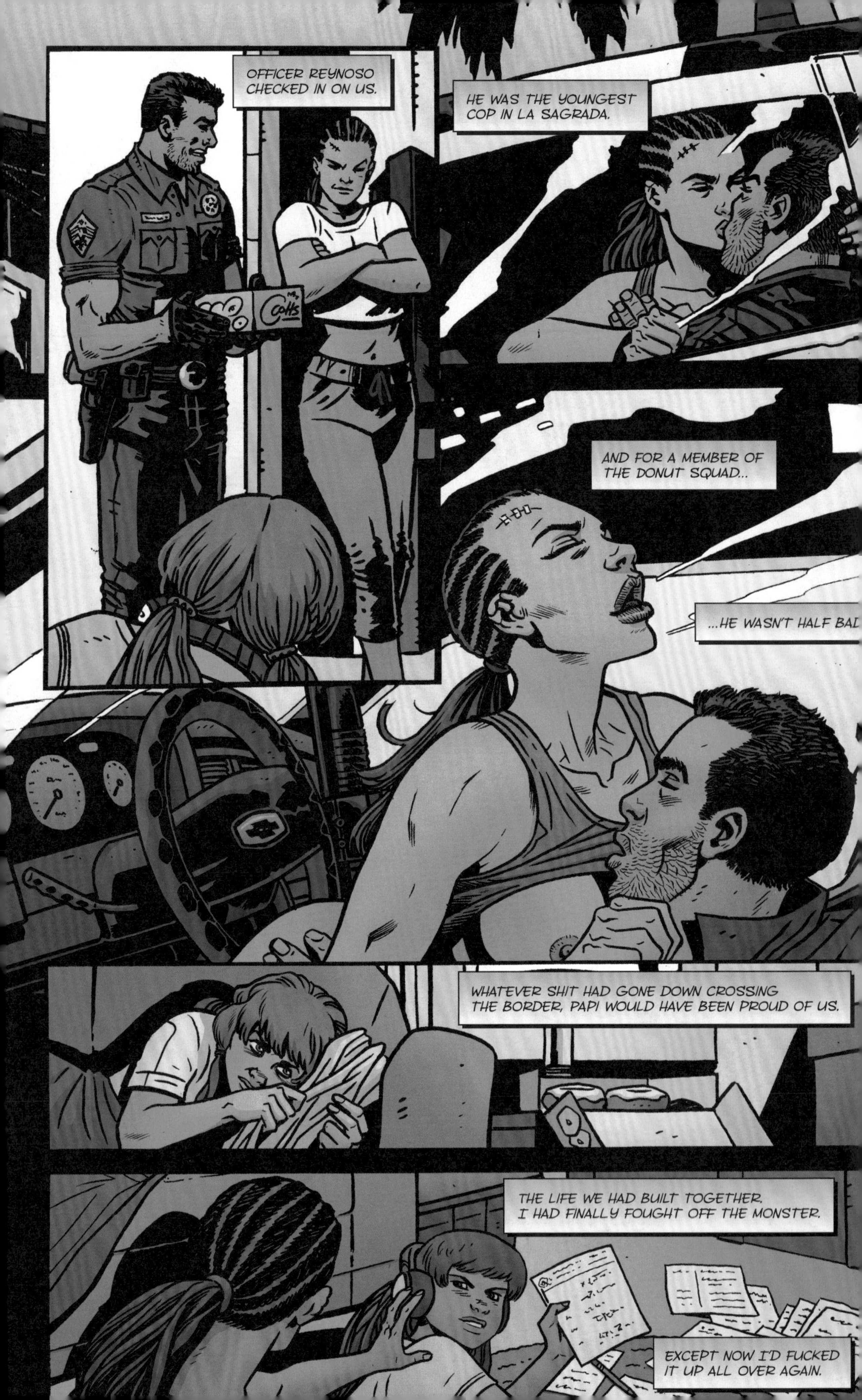
OFFICER REYNOSO CHECKED IN ON US.
HE WAS THE YOUNGEST COP IN LA SAGRADA.
AND FOR A MEMBER OF THE DONUT SQUAD...
...HE WASN'T HALF BA
WHATEVER SHIT HAD GONE DOWN CROSSING THE BORDER, PAPI WOULD HAVE BEEN PROUD OF US.
THE LIFE WE HAD BUILT TOGETHER. I HAD FINALLY FOUGHT OFF THE MONSTER.
EXCEPT NOW I'D FUCKED IT UP ALL OVER AGAIN.

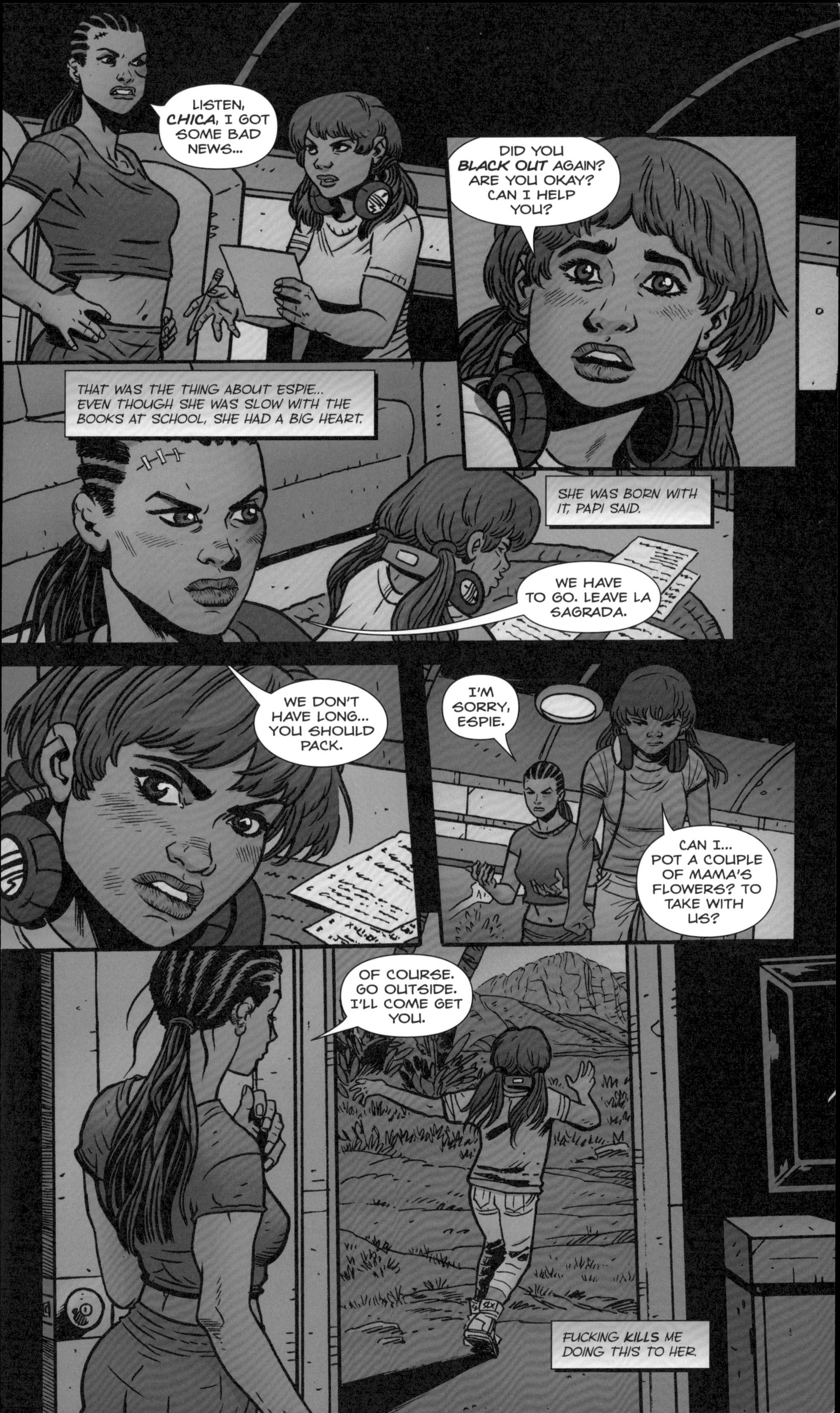

LISTEN, CHICA, I GOT SOME BAD NEWS...
DID YOU BLACK OUT AGAIN? ARE YOU OKAY? CAN I HELP YOU?
THAT WAS THE THING ABOUT ESPIE... EVEN THOUGH SHE WAS SLOW WITH THE BOOKS AT SCHOOL, SHE HAD A BIG HEART.
SHE WAS BORN WITH IT, PAPI SAID.
WE HAVE TO GO. LEAVE LA SAGRADA.
WE DON'T HAVE LONG... YOU SHOULD PACK.
I'M SORRY, ESPIE.
CAN I... POT A COUPLE OF MAMA'S FLOWERS? TO TAKE WITH US?
OF COURSE. GO OUTSIDE. I'LL COME GET YOU.
FUCKING KILLS ME DOING THIS TO HER.

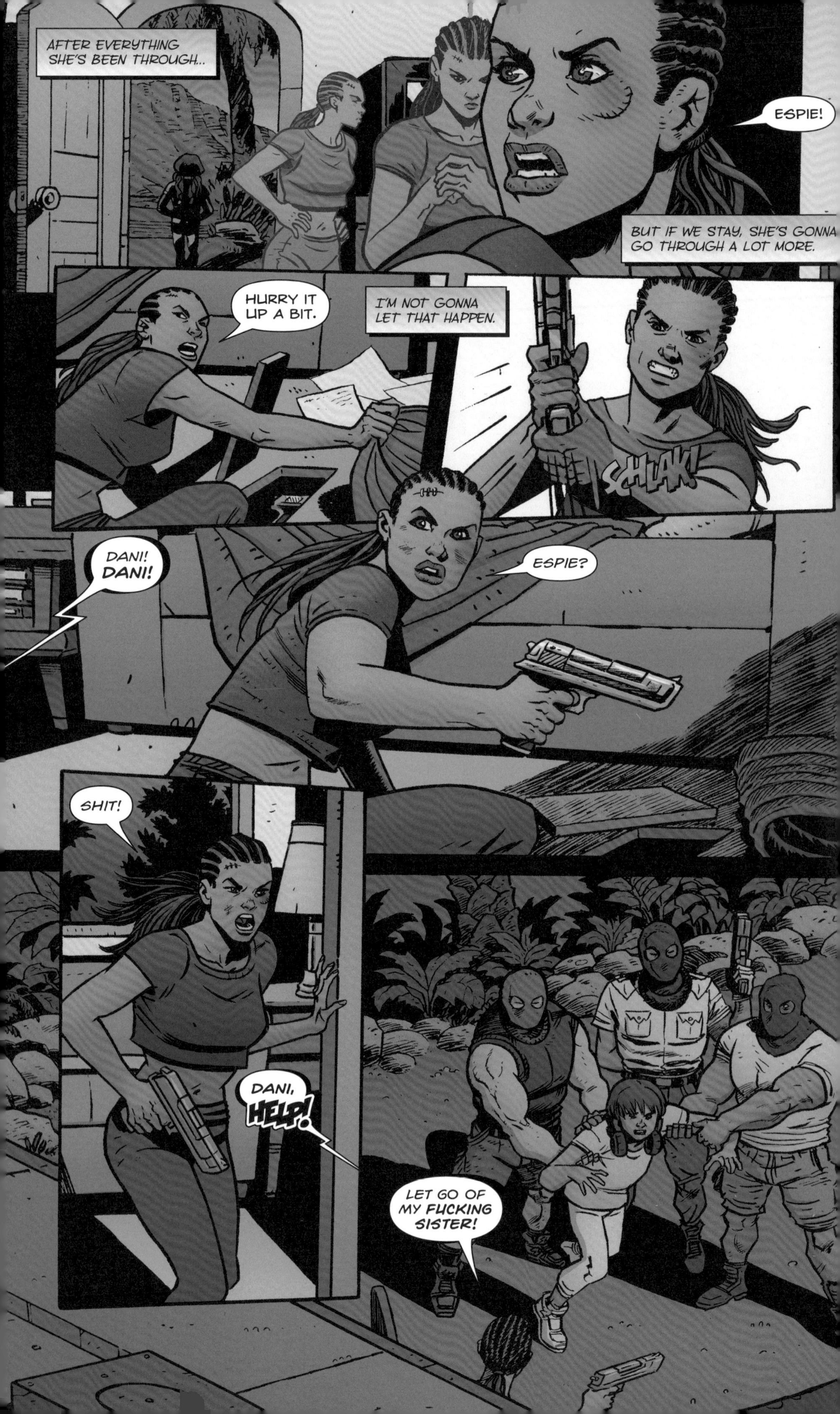

AFTER EVERYTHING SHE'S BEEN THROUGH...
ESPIE!
BUT IF WE STAY, SHE'S GONNA GO THROUGH A LOT MORE.
HURRY IT UP A BIT.
I'M NOT GONNA LET THAT HAPPEN.
SCHLAK!
DANI! DANI!
ESPIE?
SHIT!
DANI, HELP!
LET GO OF MY FUCKING SISTER!

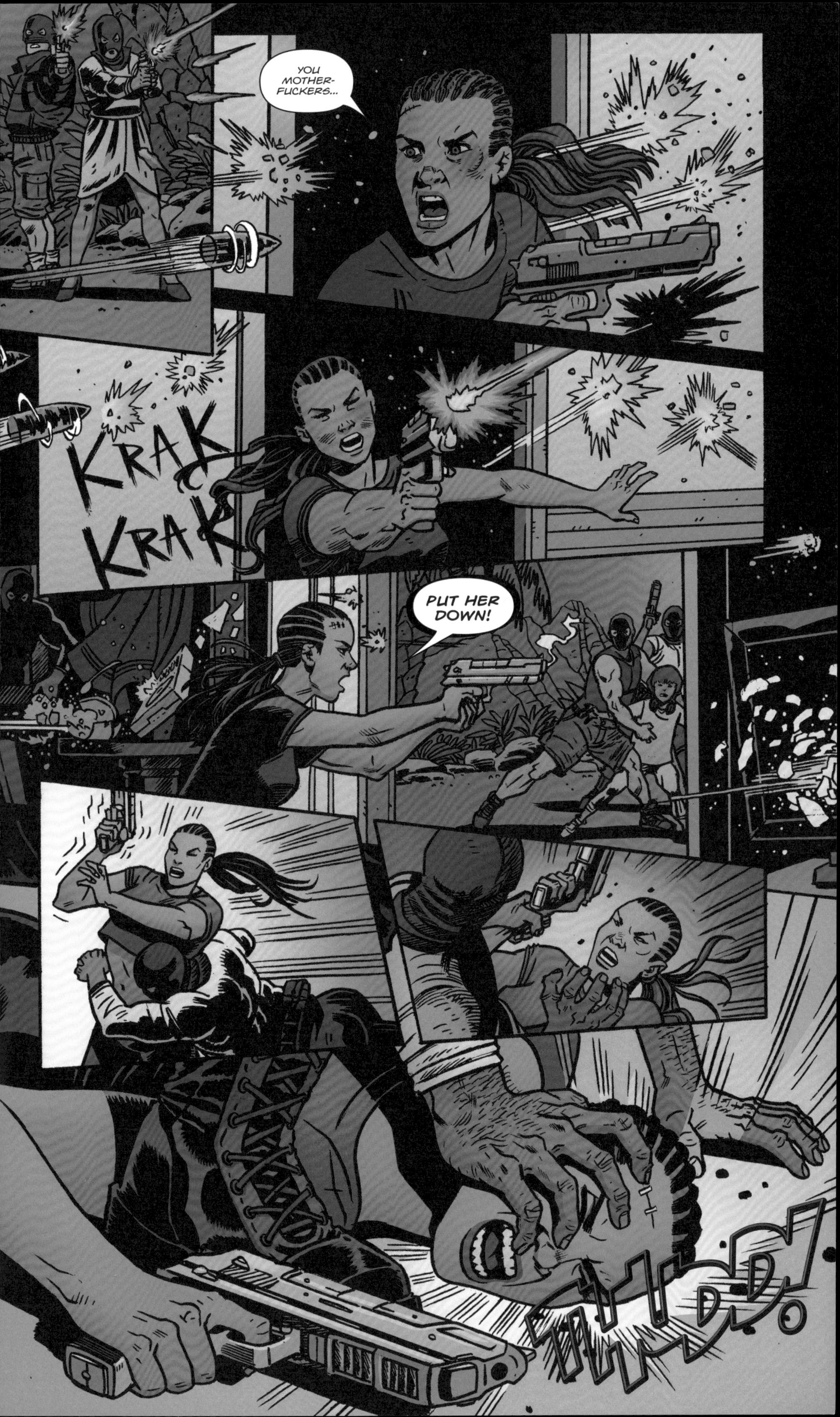
YOU MOTHER-FUCKERS...
KRAK KRAK
PUT HER DOWN!
THUDD!

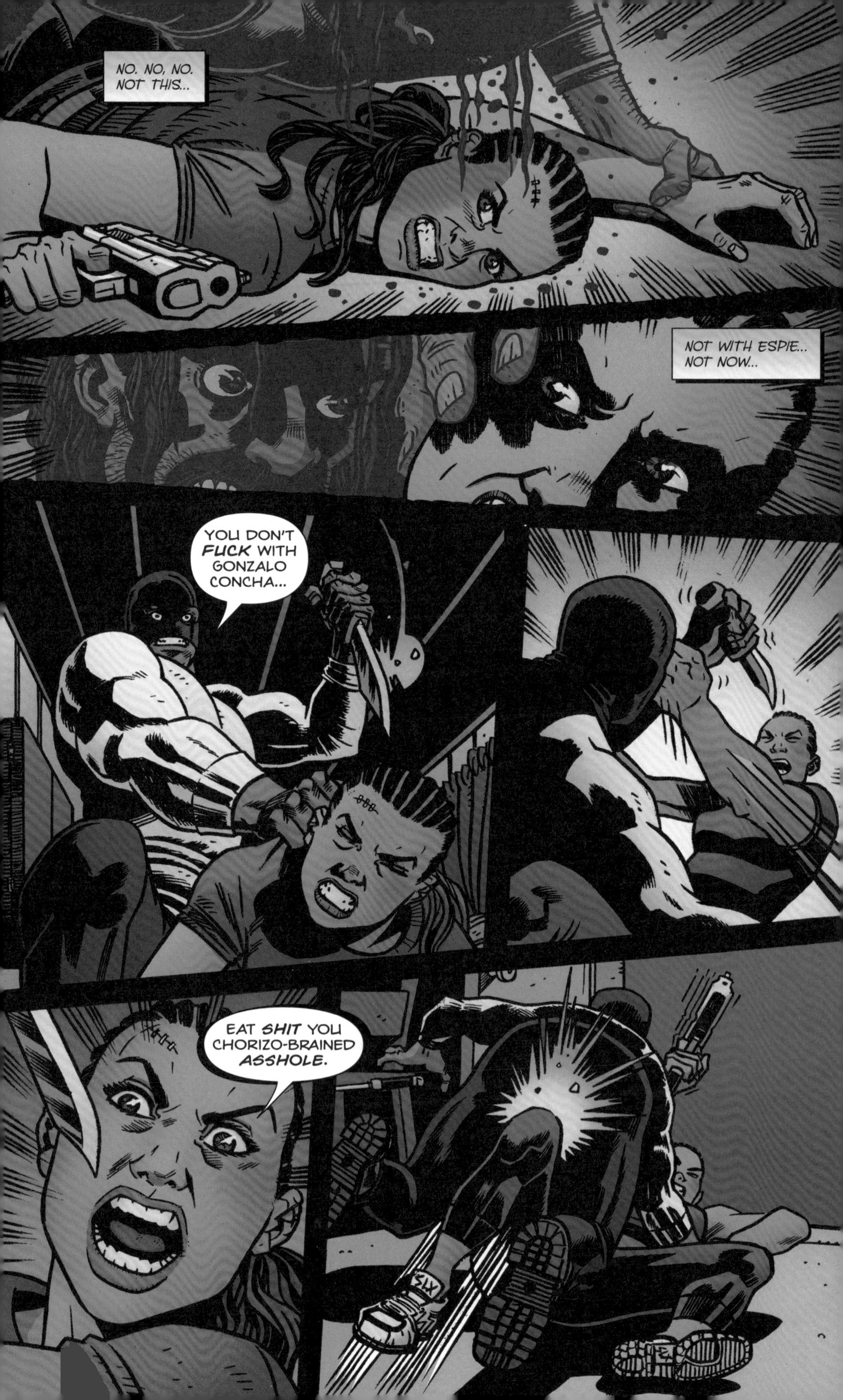
NO. NO, NO. NOT THIS...
NOT WITH ESPIE... NOT NOW...
YOU DON'T FUCK WITH GONZALO CONCHA...
EAT SHIT YOU CHORIZO-BRAINED ASSHOLE.

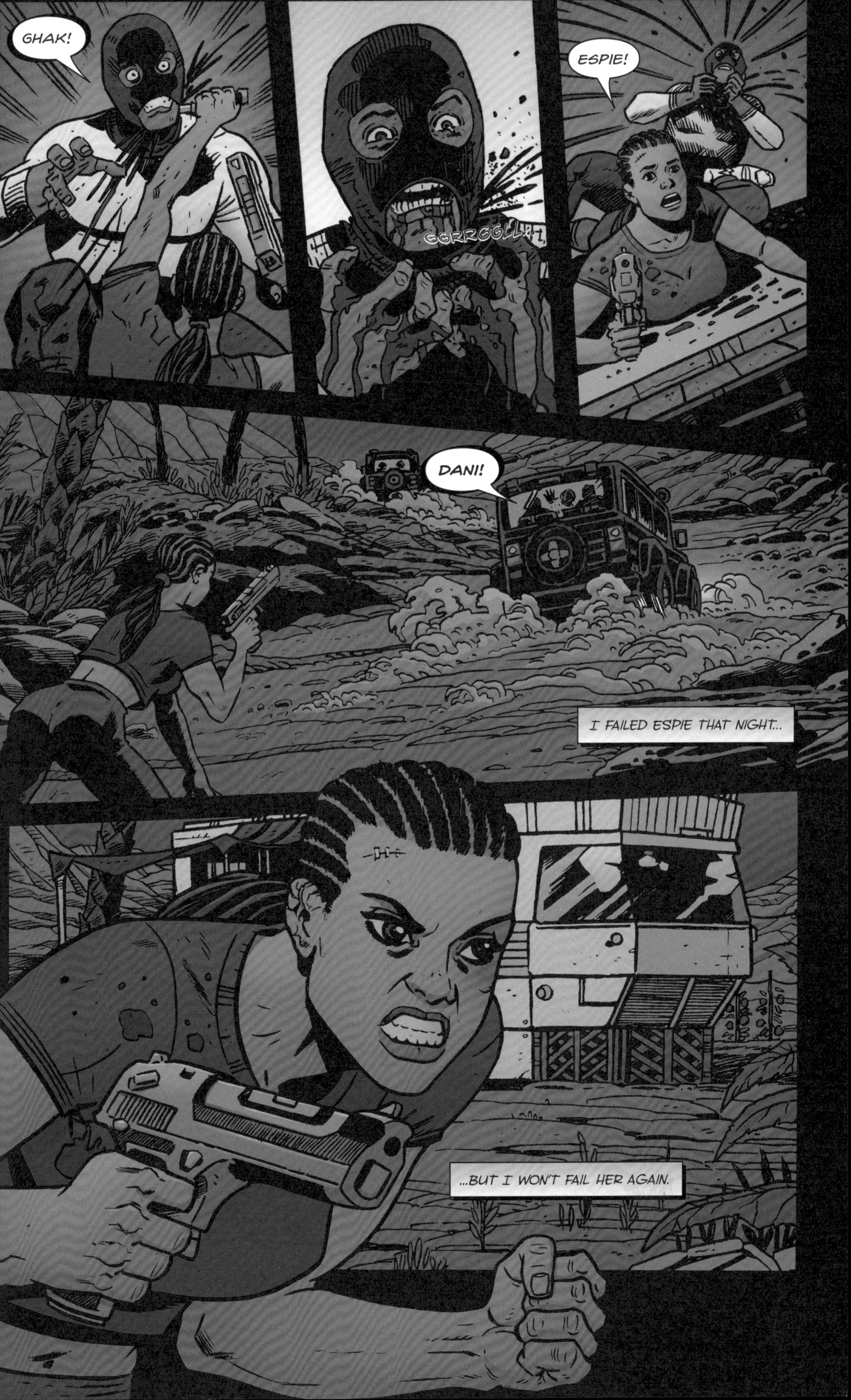
GHAK!
GGRRGGLL...
ESPIE!
DANI!
I FAILED ESPIE THAT NIGHT...
...BUT I WON'T FAIL HER AGAIN.

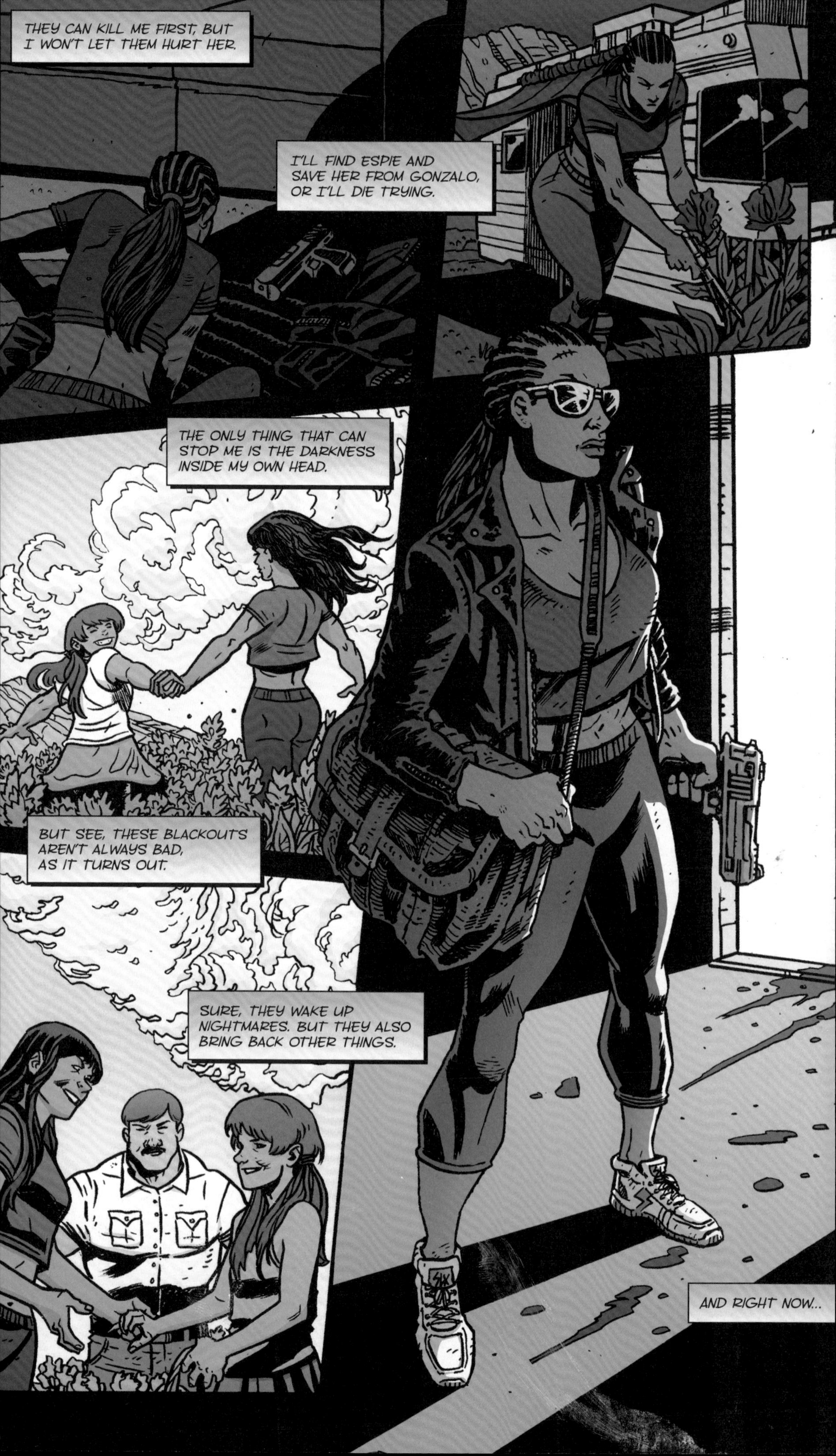
THEY CAN KILL ME FIRST, BUT I WON'T LET THEM HURT HER.
I'LL FIND ESPIE AND SAVE HER FROM GONZALO, OR I'LL DIE TRYING.
THE ONLY THING THAT CAN STOP ME IS THE DARKNESS INSIDE MY OWN HEAD.
BUT SEE, THESE BLACKOUTS AREN'T ALWAYS BAD, AS IT TURNS OUT.
SURE, THEY WAKE UP NIGHTMARES. BUT THEY ALSO BRING BACK OTHER THINGS.
AND RIGHT NOW...

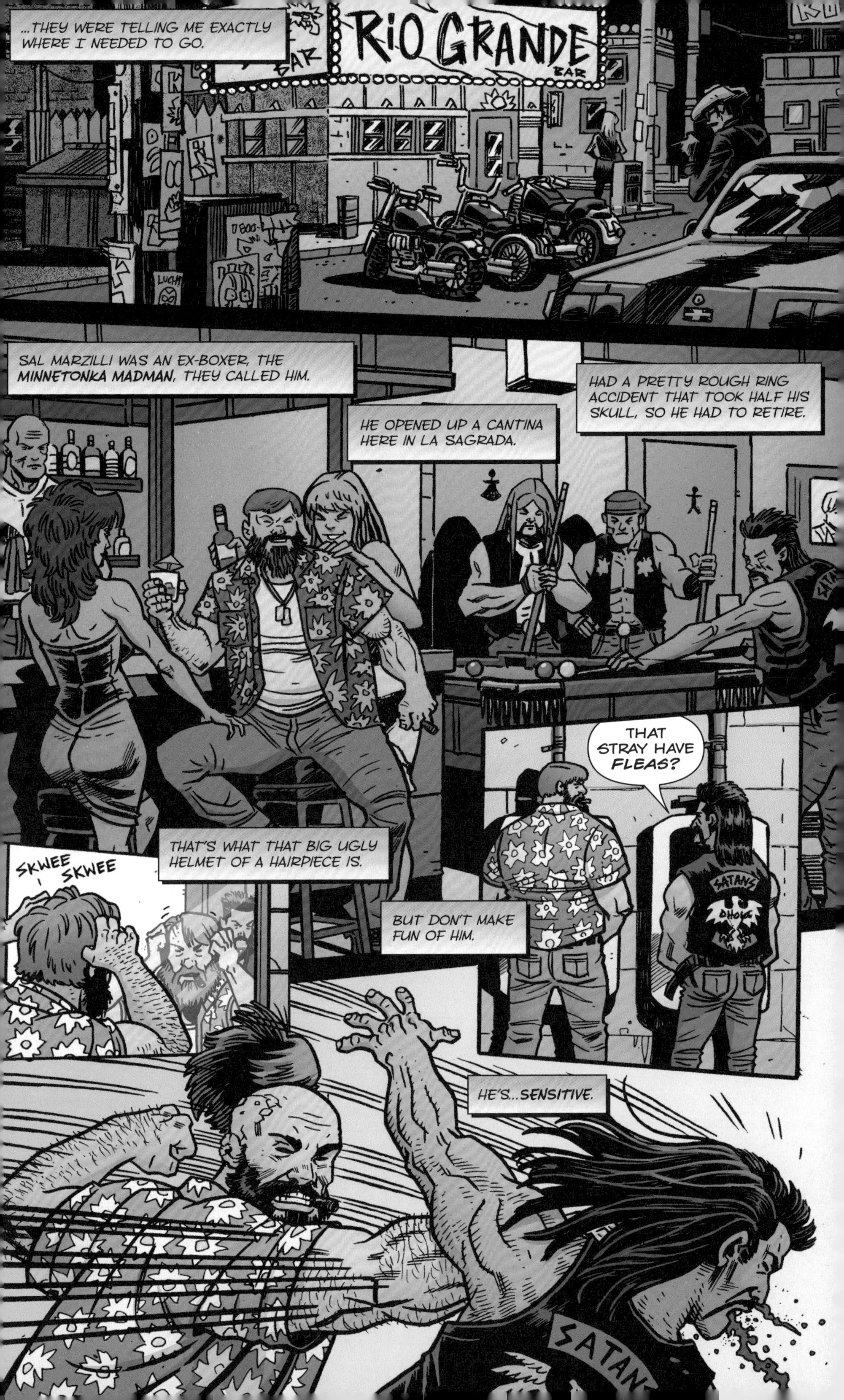

...THEY WERE TELLING ME EXACTLY WHERE I NEEDED TO GO.
RIO GRANDE
BAR
SAL MARZILLI WAS AN EX-BOXER, THE MINNETONKA MADMAN, THEY CALLED HIM.
HE OPENED UP A CANTINA HERE IN LA SAGRADA.
HAD A PRETTY ROUGH RING ACCIDENT THAT TOOK HALF HIS SKULL, SO HE HAD TO RETIRE.
THAT STRAY HAVE FLEAS?
THAT'S WHAT THAT BIG UGLY HELMET OF A HAIRPIECE IS.
SKWEE SKWEE
BUT DON'T MAKE FUN OF HIM.
SATANS
HE'S...SENSITIVE.
SATAN

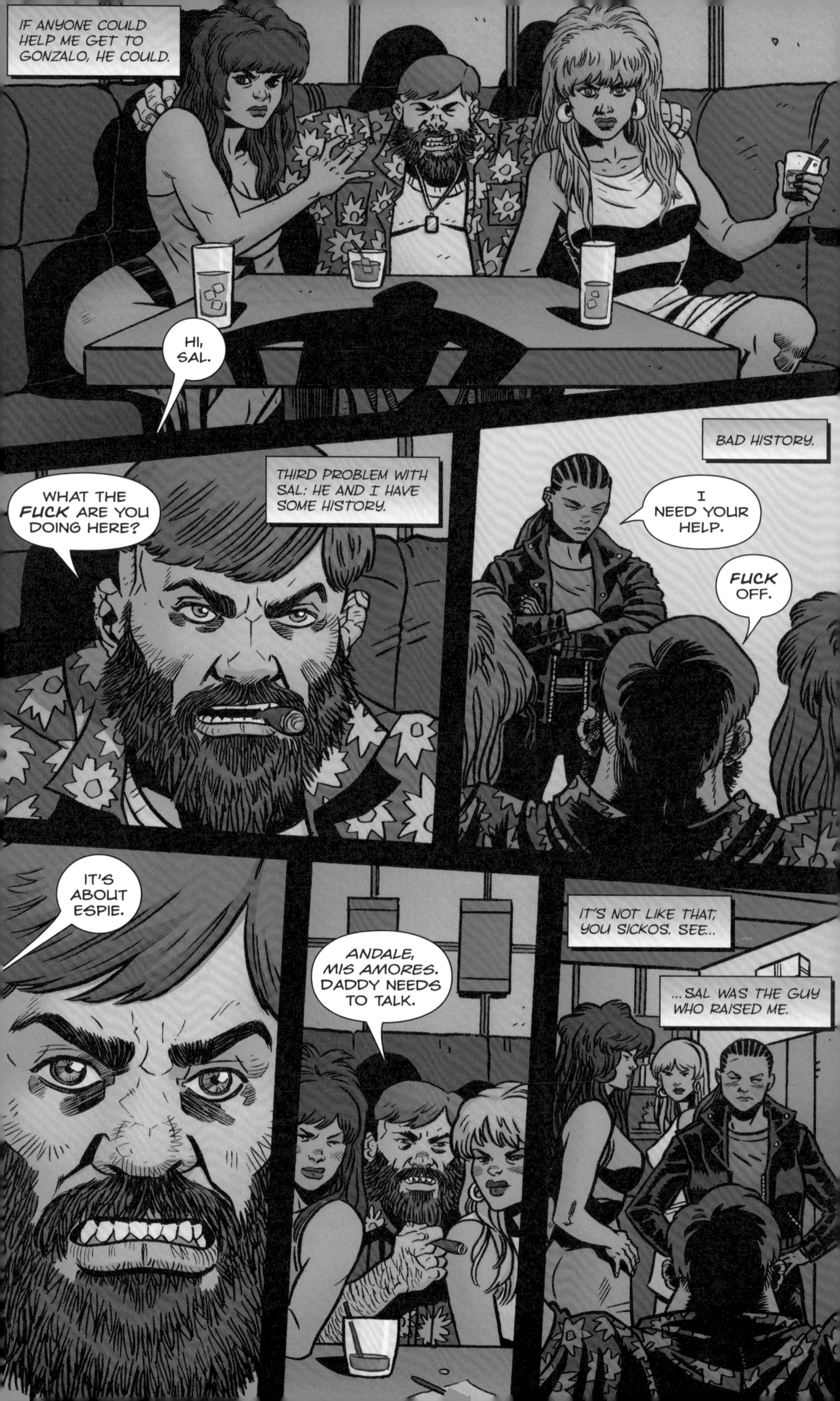
IF ANYONE COULD HELP ME GET TO GONZALO, HE COULD.
HI, SAL.
WHAT THE **FUCK** ARE YOU DOING HERE?
THIRD PROBLEM WITH SAL: HE AND I HAVE SOME HISTORY.
BAD HISTORY.
I NEED YOUR HELP.
FUCK OFF.
IT'S ABOUT ESPIE.
ANDALE, MIS AMORES. DADDY NEEDS TO TALK.
IT'S NOT LIKE THAT, YOU SICKOS. SEE...
...SAL WAS THE GUY WHO RAISED ME.

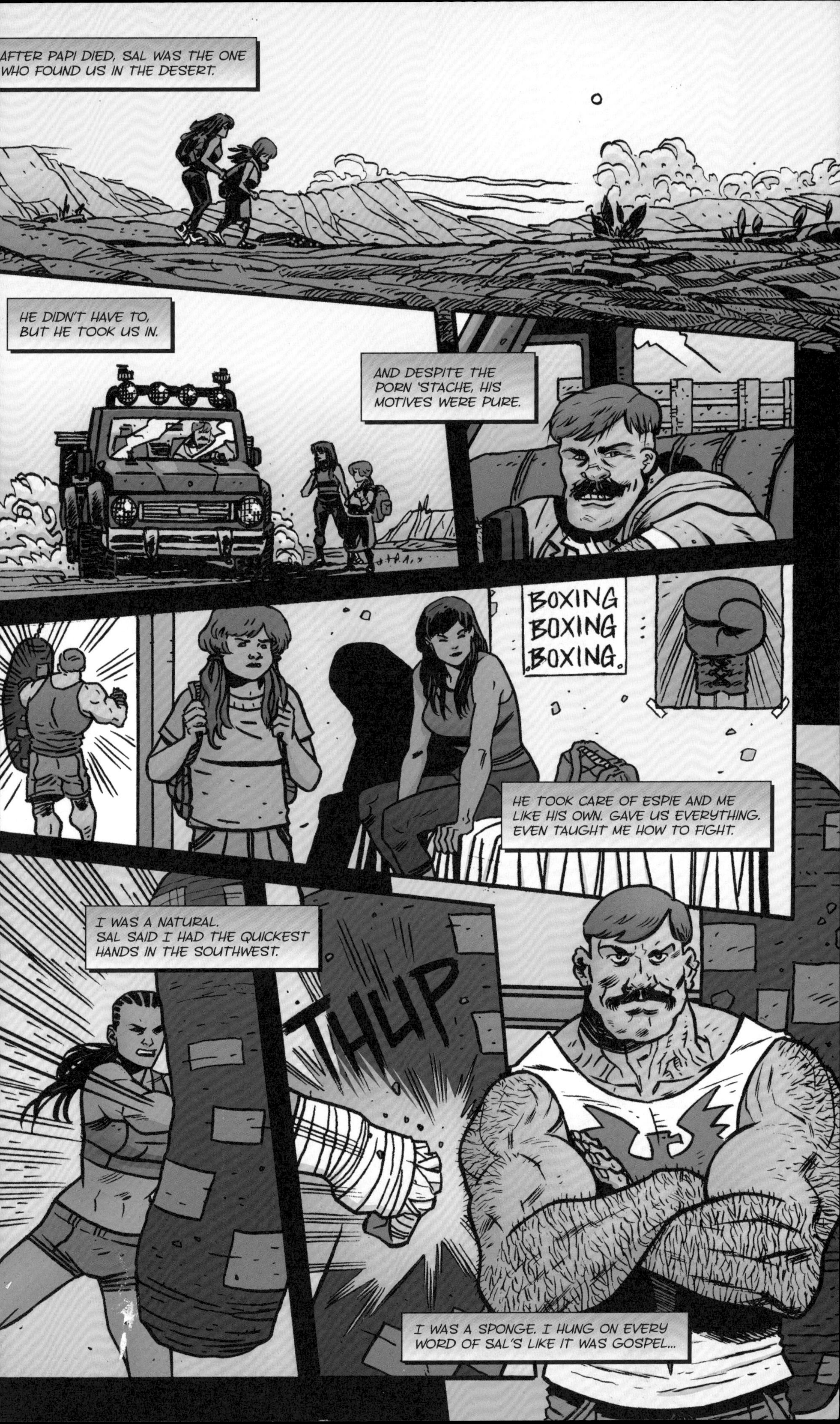
AFTER PAPI DIED, SAL WAS THE ONE WHO FOUND US IN THE DESERT.
HE DIDN'T HAVE TO, BUT HE TOOK US IN.
AND DESPITE THE PORN 'STACHE, HIS MOTIVES WERE PURE.
BOXING BOXING BOXING.
HE TOOK CARE OF ESPIE AND ME LIKE HIS OWN. GAVE US EVERYTHING. EVEN TAUGHT ME HOW TO FIGHT.
I WAS A NATURAL. SAL SAID I HAD THE QUICKEST HANDS IN THE SOUTHWEST.
THUP
I WAS A SPONGE. I HUNG ON EVERY WORD OF SAL'S LIKE IT WAS GOSPEL...

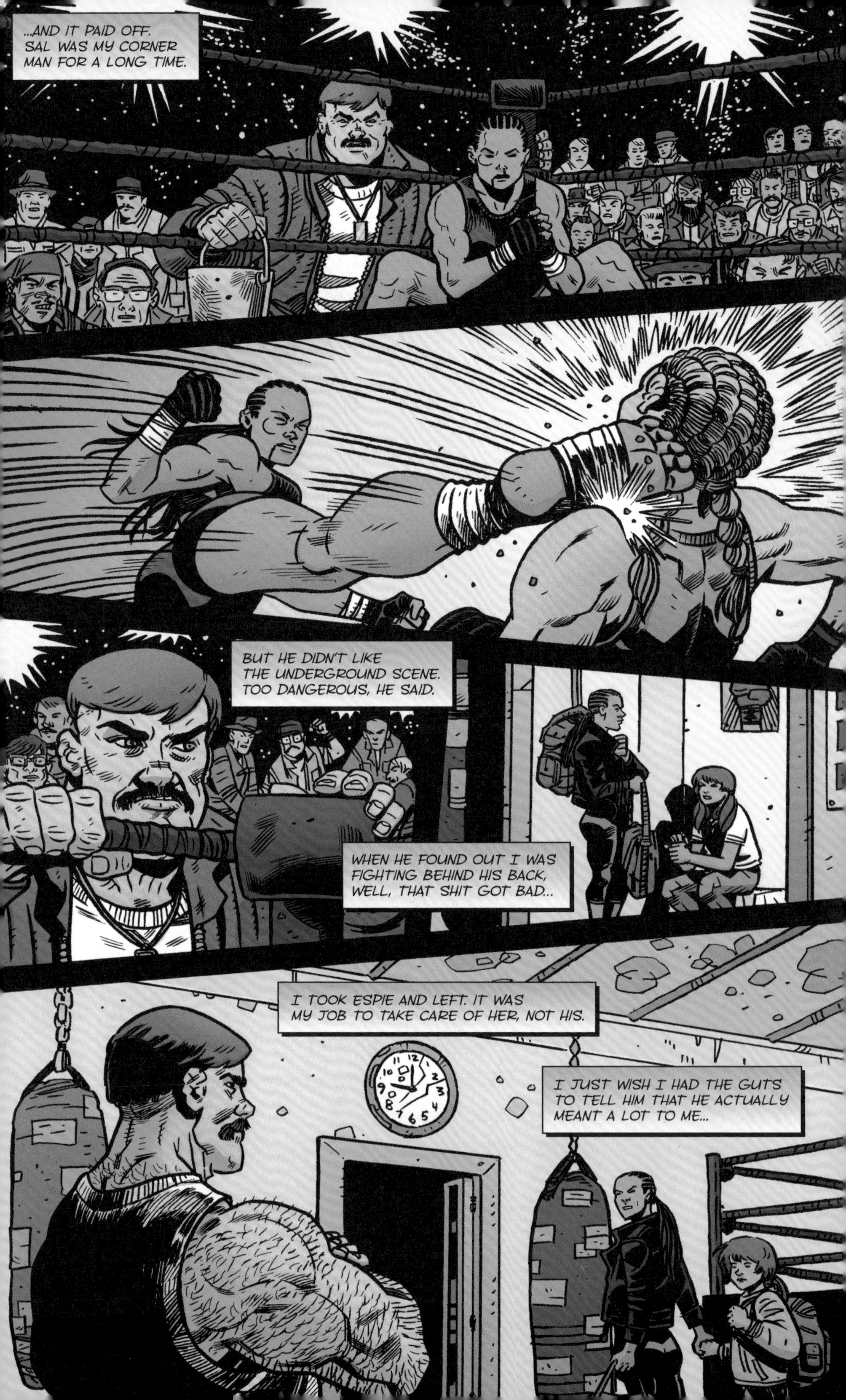
...AND IT PAID OFF. SAL WAS MY CORNER MAN FOR A LONG TIME.
BUT HE DIDN'T LIKE THE UNDERGROUND SCENE. TOO DANGEROUS, HE SAID.
WHEN HE FOUND OUT I WAS FIGHTING BEHIND HIS BACK, WELL, THAT SHIT GOT BAD...
I TOOK ESPIE AND LEFT. IT WAS MY JOB TO TAKE CARE OF HER, NOT HIS.
I JUST WISH I HAD THE GUTS TO TELL HIM THAT HE ACTUALLY MEANT A LOT TO ME...

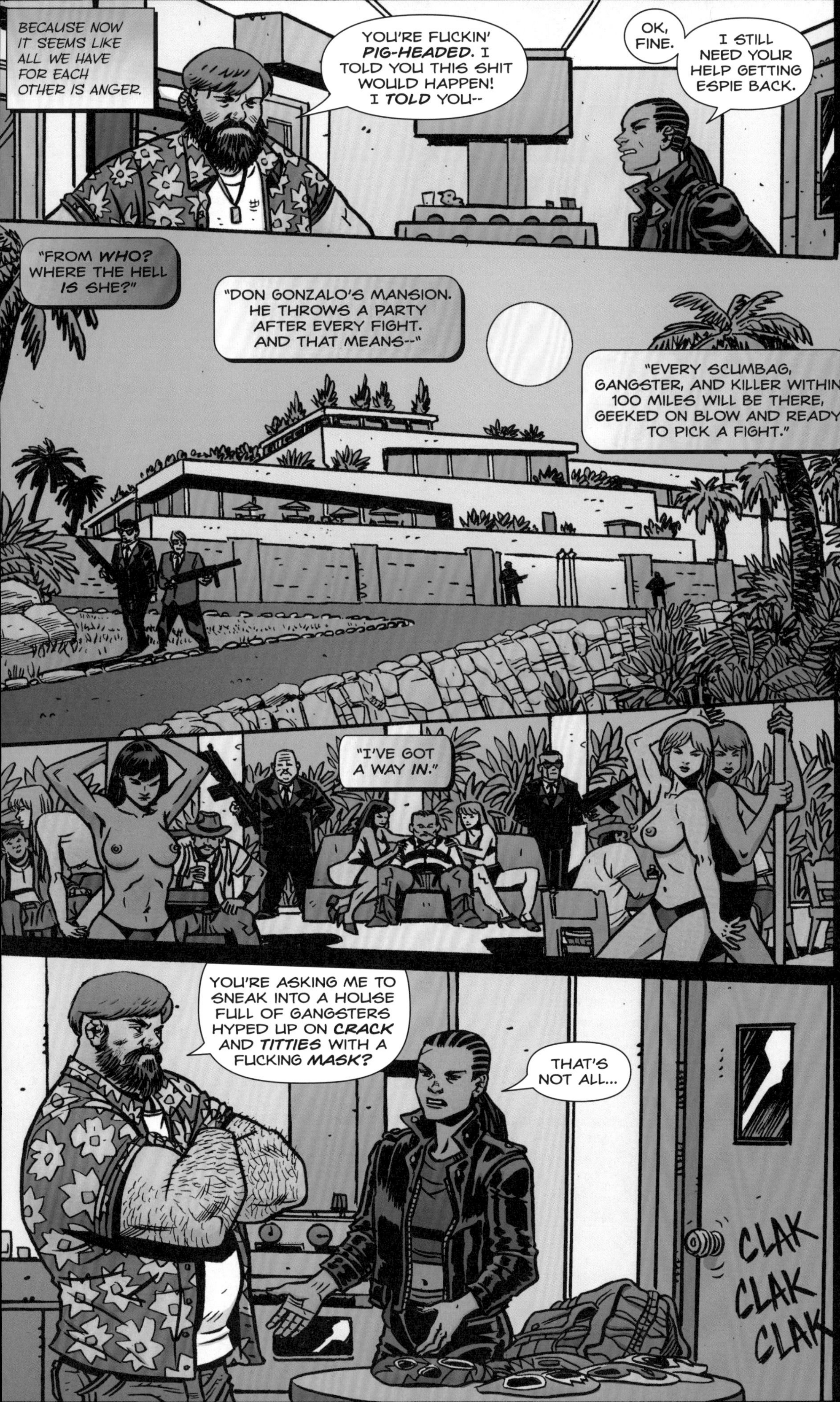
BECAUSE NOW IT SEEMS LIKE ALL WE HAVE FOR EACH OTHER IS ANGER.
YOU'RE FUCKIN' PIG-HEADED. I TOLD YOU THIS SHIT WOULD HAPPEN! I TOLD YOU--
OK, FINE.
I STILL NEED YOUR HELP GETTING ESPIE BACK.
"FROM WHO? WHERE THE HELL IS SHE?"
"DON GONZALO'S MANSION. HE THROWS A PARTY AFTER EVERY FIGHT. AND THAT MEANS--"
"EVERY SCUMBAG, GANGSTER, AND KILLER WITHIN 100 MILES WILL BE THERE, GEEKED ON BLOW AND READY TO PICK A FIGHT."
"I'VE GOT A WAY IN."
YOU'RE ASKING ME TO SNEAK INTO A HOUSE FULL OF GANGSTERS HYPED UP ON CRACK AND TITTIES WITH A FUCKING MASK?
THAT'S NOT ALL...
CLAK
CLAK
CLAK

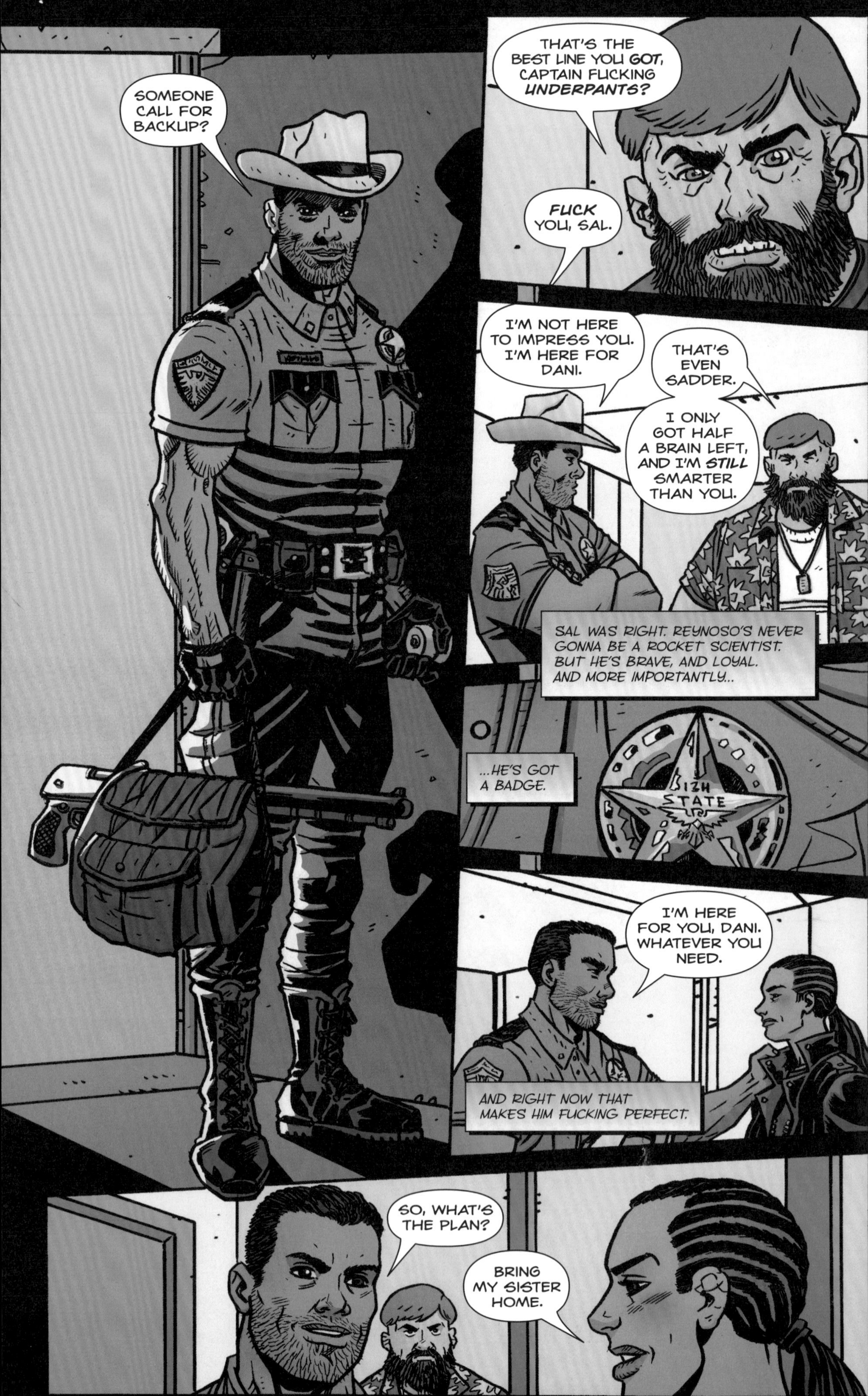
SOMEONE CALL FOR BACKUP?
THAT'S THE BEST LINE YOU GOT, CAPTAIN FUCKING UNDERPANTS?
FUCK YOU, SAL.
I'M NOT HERE TO IMPRESS YOU. I'M HERE FOR DANI.
THAT'S EVEN SADDER.
I ONLY GOT HALF A BRAIN LEFT, AND I'M STILL SMARTER THAN YOU.
SAL WAS RIGHT. REYNOSO'S NEVER GONNA BE A ROCKET SCIENTIST. BUT HE'S BRAVE, AND LOYAL. AND MORE IMPORTANTLY...
...HE'S GOT A BADGE.
I'M HERE FOR YOU, DANI. WHATEVER YOU NEED.
AND RIGHT NOW THAT MAKES HIM FUCKING PERFECT.
SO, WHAT'S THE PLAN?
BRING MY SISTER HOME.

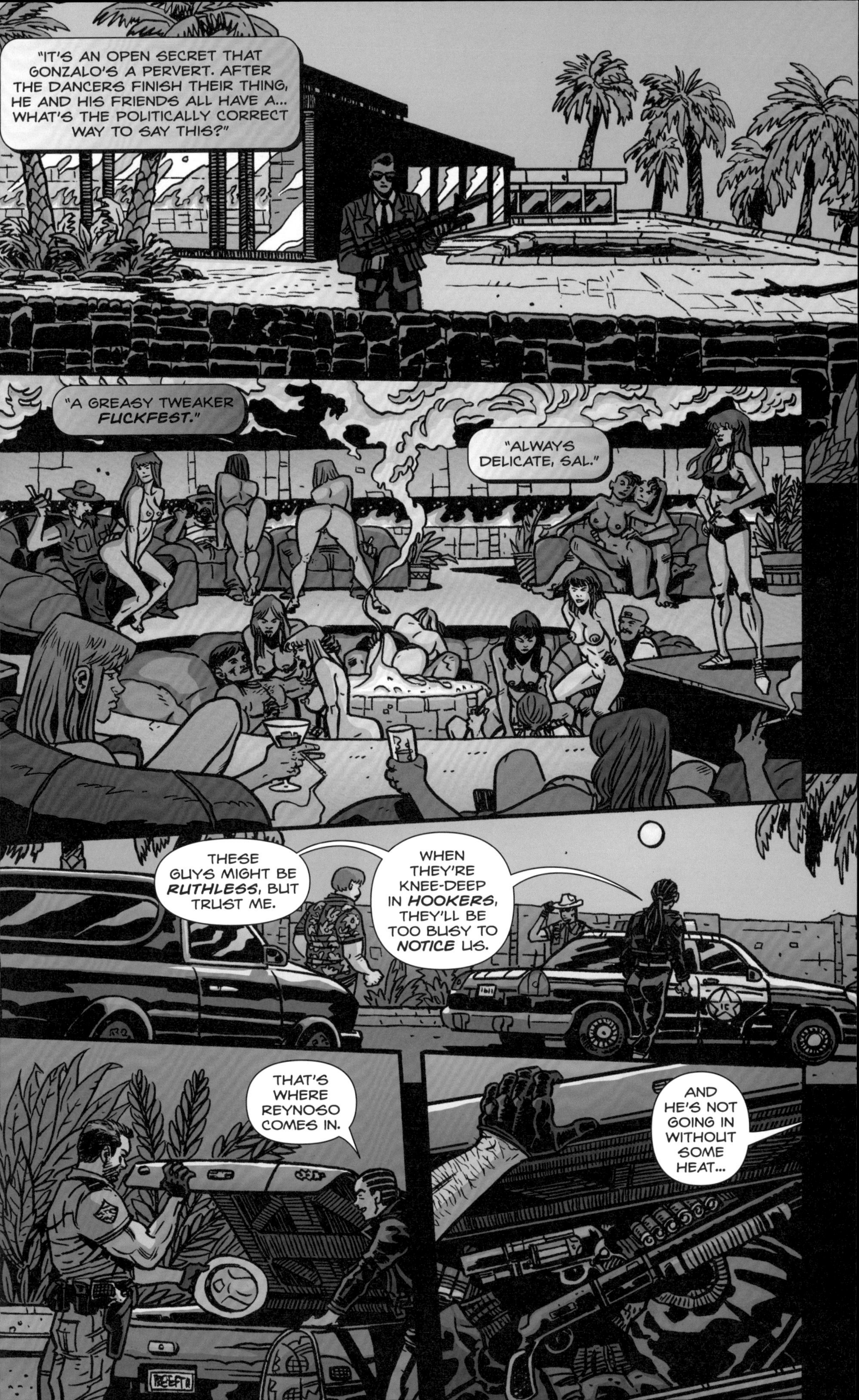
"IT'S AN OPEN SECRET THAT GONZALO'S A PERVERT. AFTER THE DANCERS FINISH THEIR THING, HE AND HIS FRIENDS ALL HAVE A... WHAT'S THE POLITICALLY CORRECT WAY TO SAY THIS?"
"A GREASY TWEAKER FUCKFEST."
"ALWAYS DELICATE, SAL."
THESE GUYS MIGHT BE RUTHLESS, BUT TRUST ME.
WHEN THEY'RE KNEE-DEEP IN HOOKERS, THEY'LL BE TOO BUSY TO NOTICE US.
THAT'S WHERE REYNOSO COMES IN.
AND HE'S NOT GOING IN WITHOUT SOME HEAT...

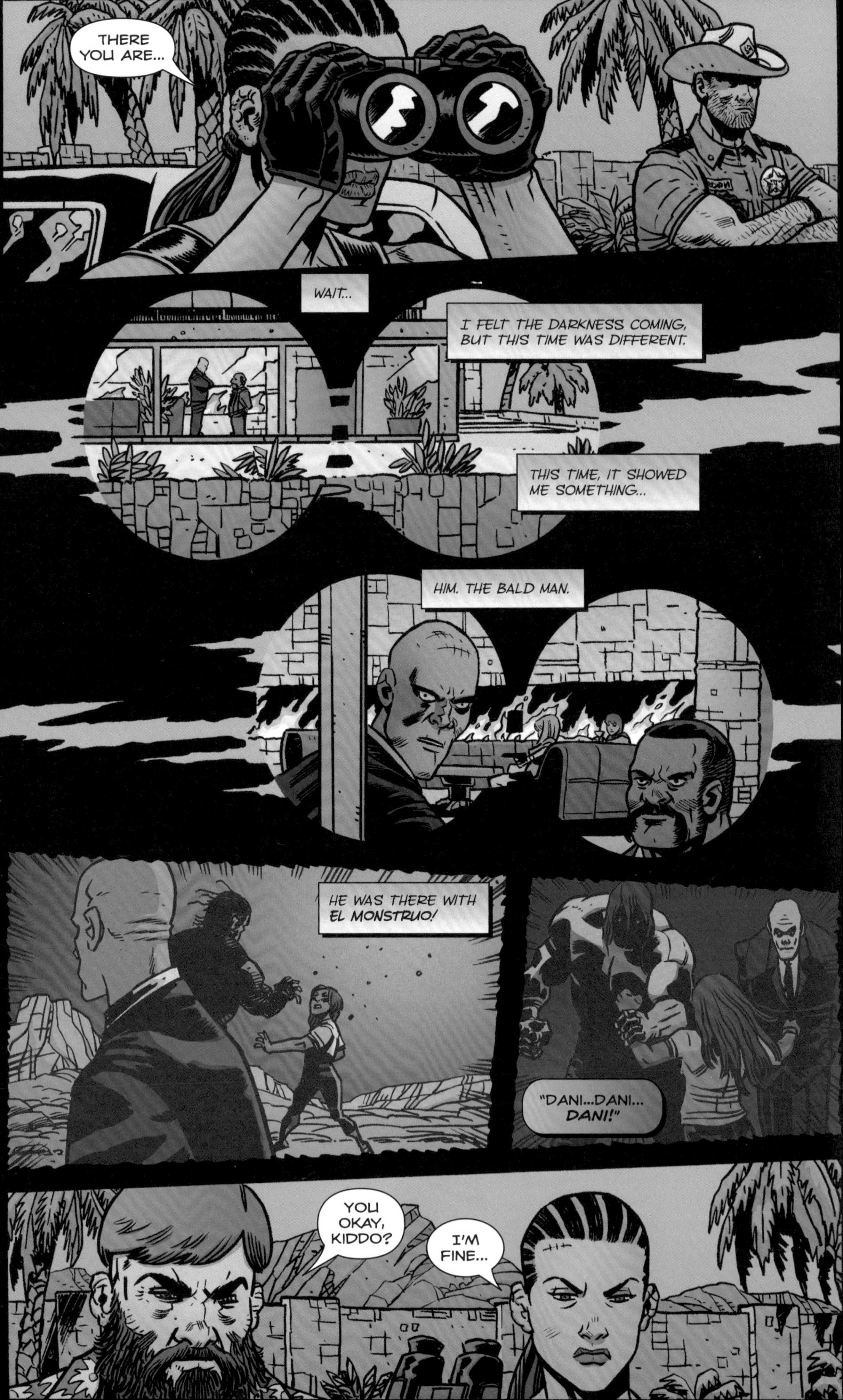
THERE YOU ARE...
WAIT...
I FELT THE DARKNESS COMING, BUT THIS TIME WAS DIFFERENT.
THIS TIME, IT SHOWED ME SOMETHING...
HIM. THE BALD MAN.
HE WAS THERE WITH EL MONSTRUO!
"DANI...DANI... DANI!"
YOU OKAY, KIDDO?
I'M FINE...

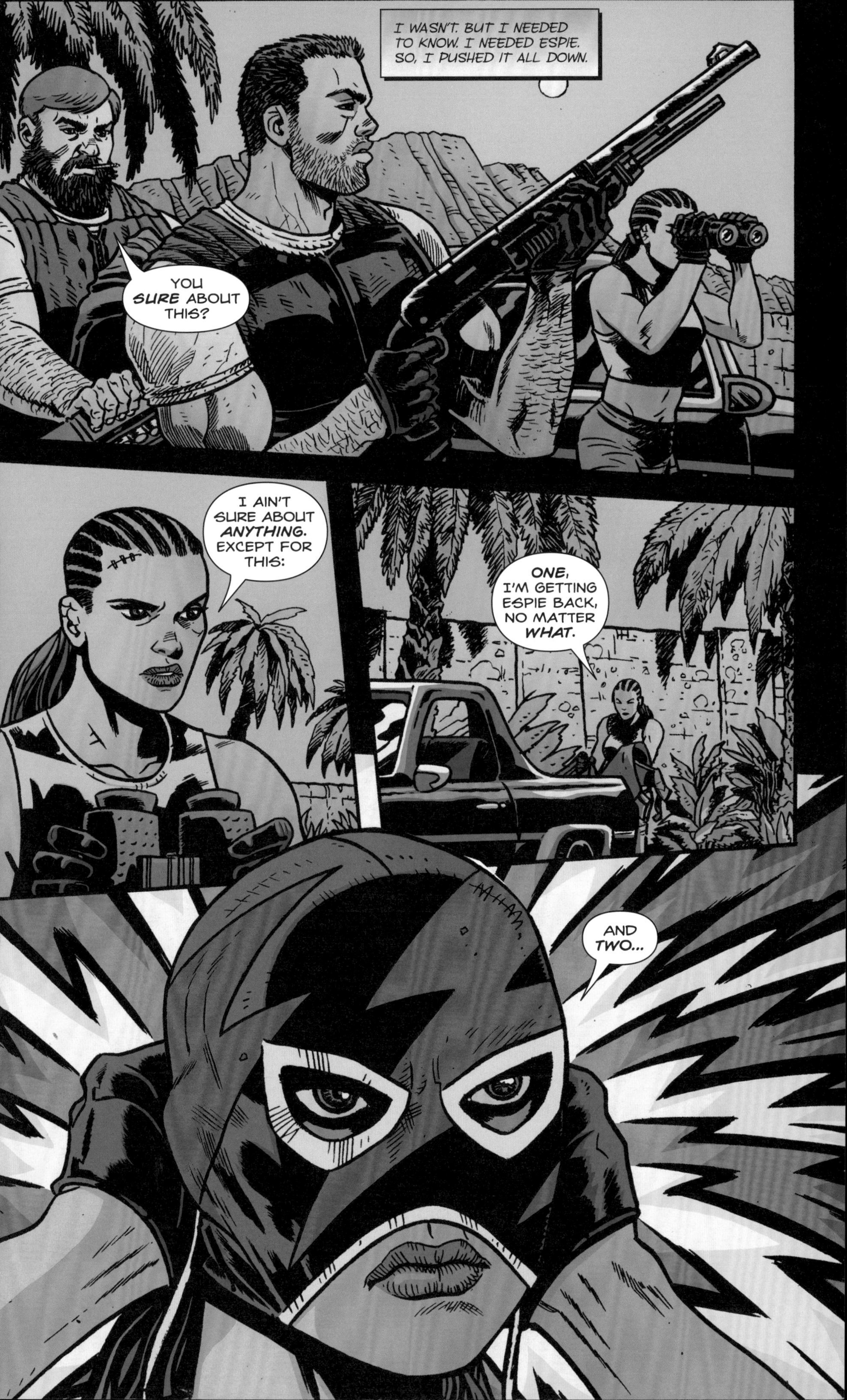

I WASN'T. BUT I NEEDED TO KNOW. I NEEDED ESPIE. SO, I PUSHED IT ALL DOWN.
YOU SURE ABOUT THIS?
I AIN'T SURE ABOUT ANYTHING. EXCEPT FOR THIS:
ONE, I'M GETTING ESPIE BACK, NO MATTER WHAT.
AND TWO...

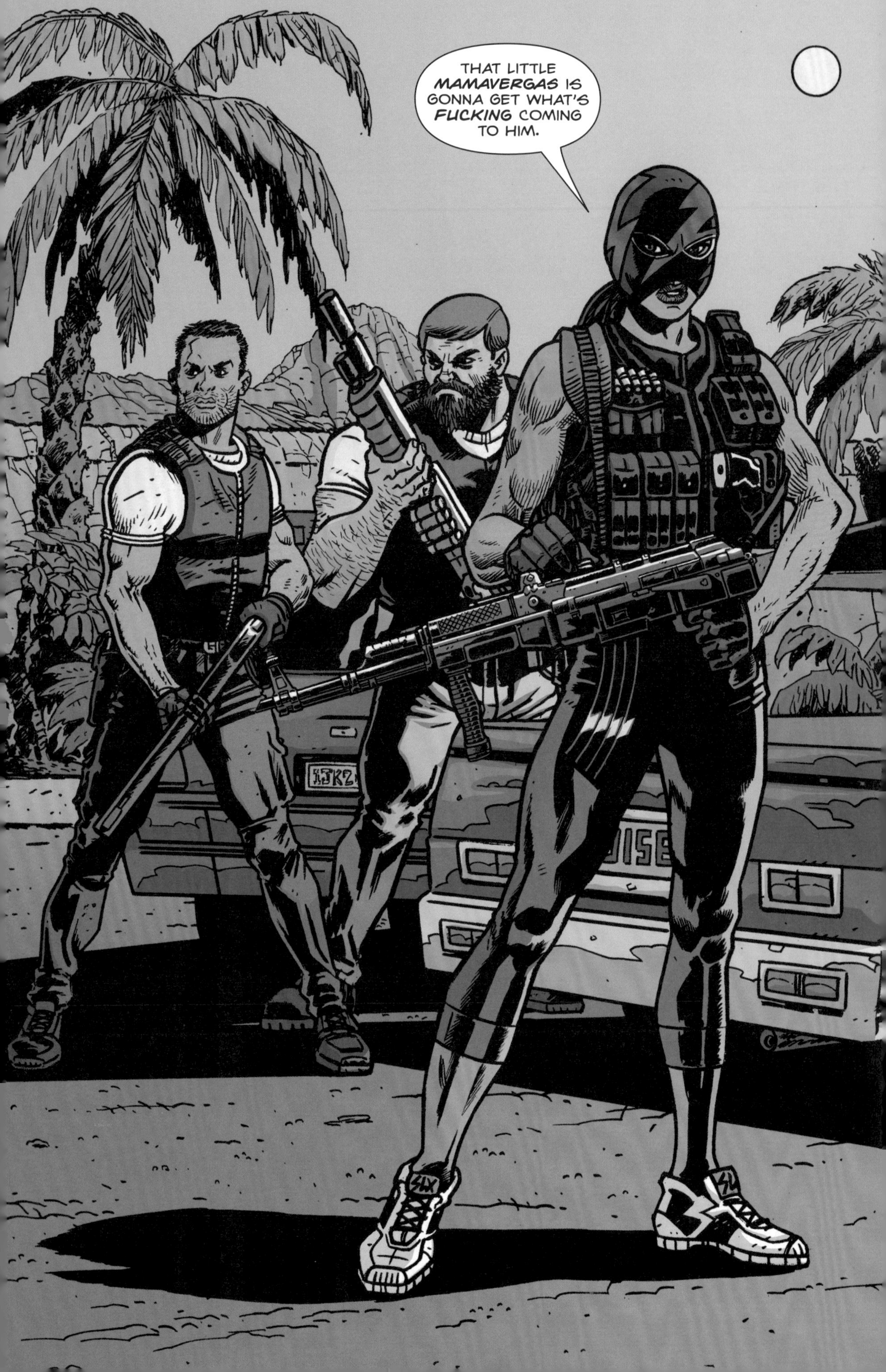
THAT LITTLE *MAMAVERGAS* IS GONNA GET WHAT'S *FUCKING* COMING TO HIM.

CHAPTER 2

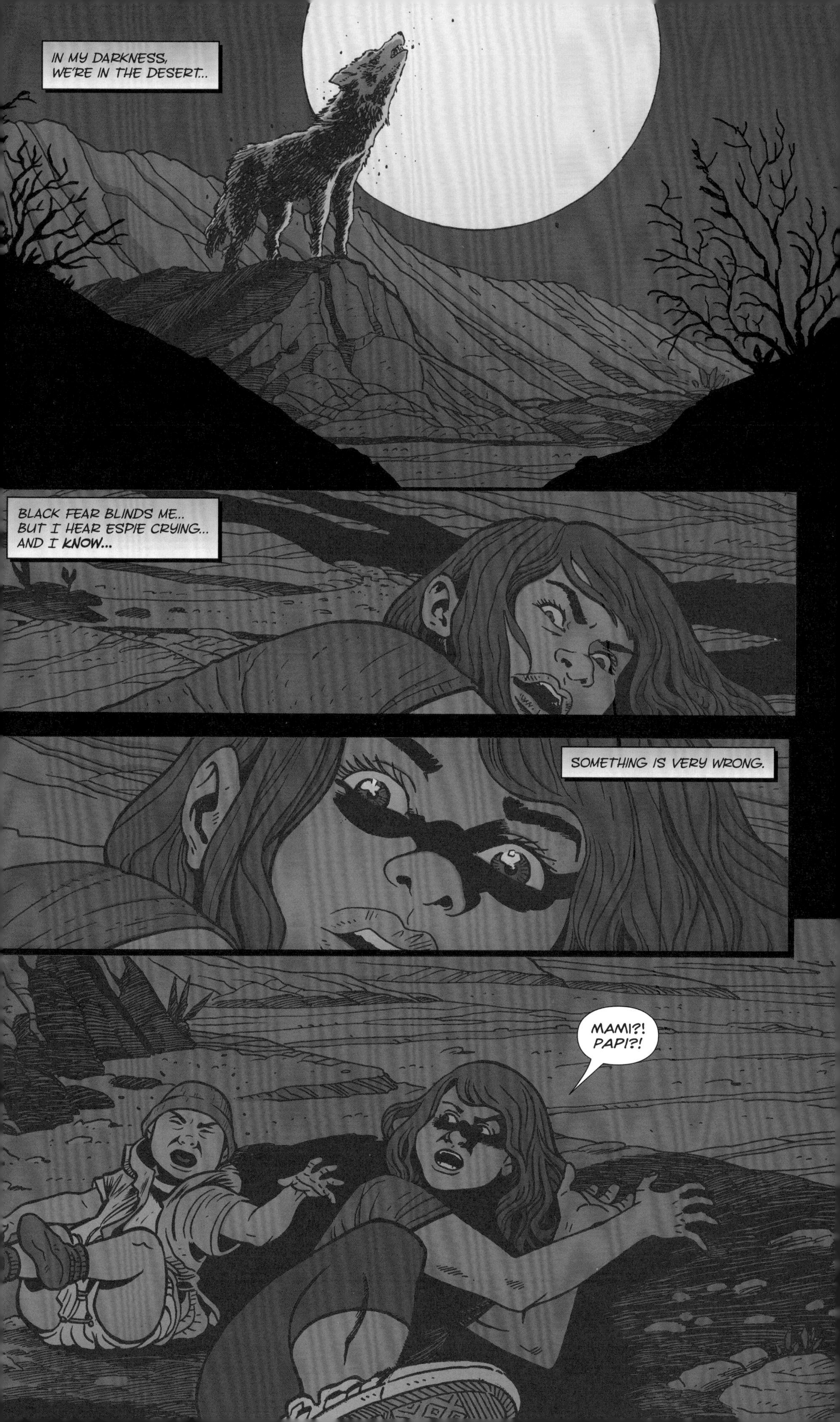
IN MY DARKNESS, WE'RE IN THE DESERT...
BLACK FEAR BLINDS ME... BUT I HEAR ESPIE CRYING... AND I KNOW...
SOMETHING IS VERY WRONG.
MAMI?! PAPI?!

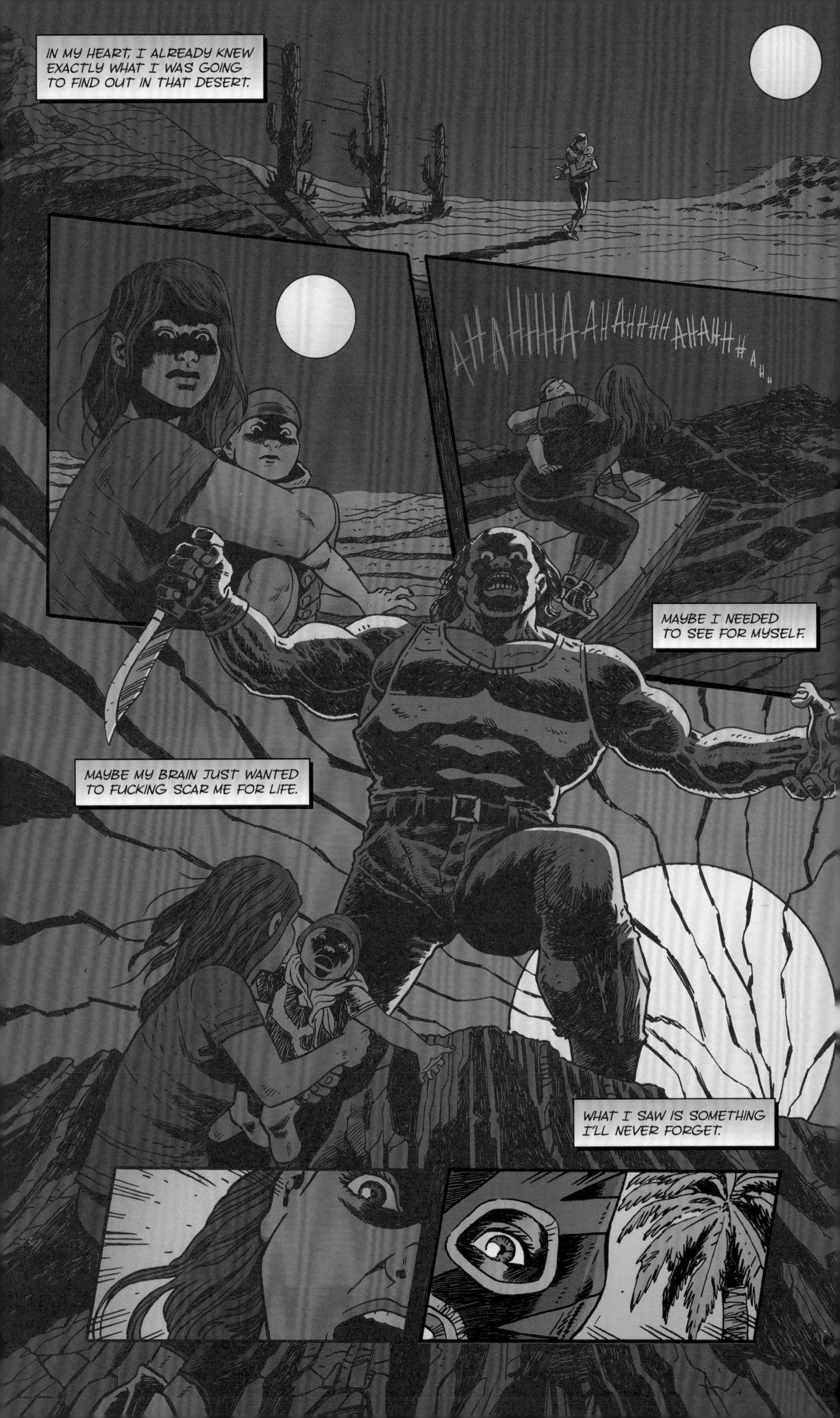
IN MY HEART, I ALREADY KNEW EXACTLY WHAT I WAS GOING TO FIND OUT IN THAT DESERT.
AHAHHHAAHAHHHHAHAHHHAH
MAYBE I NEEDED TO SEE FOR MYSELF.
MAYBE MY BRAIN JUST WANTED TO FUCKING SCAR ME FOR LIFE.
WHAT I SAW IS SOMETHING I'LL NEVER FORGET.

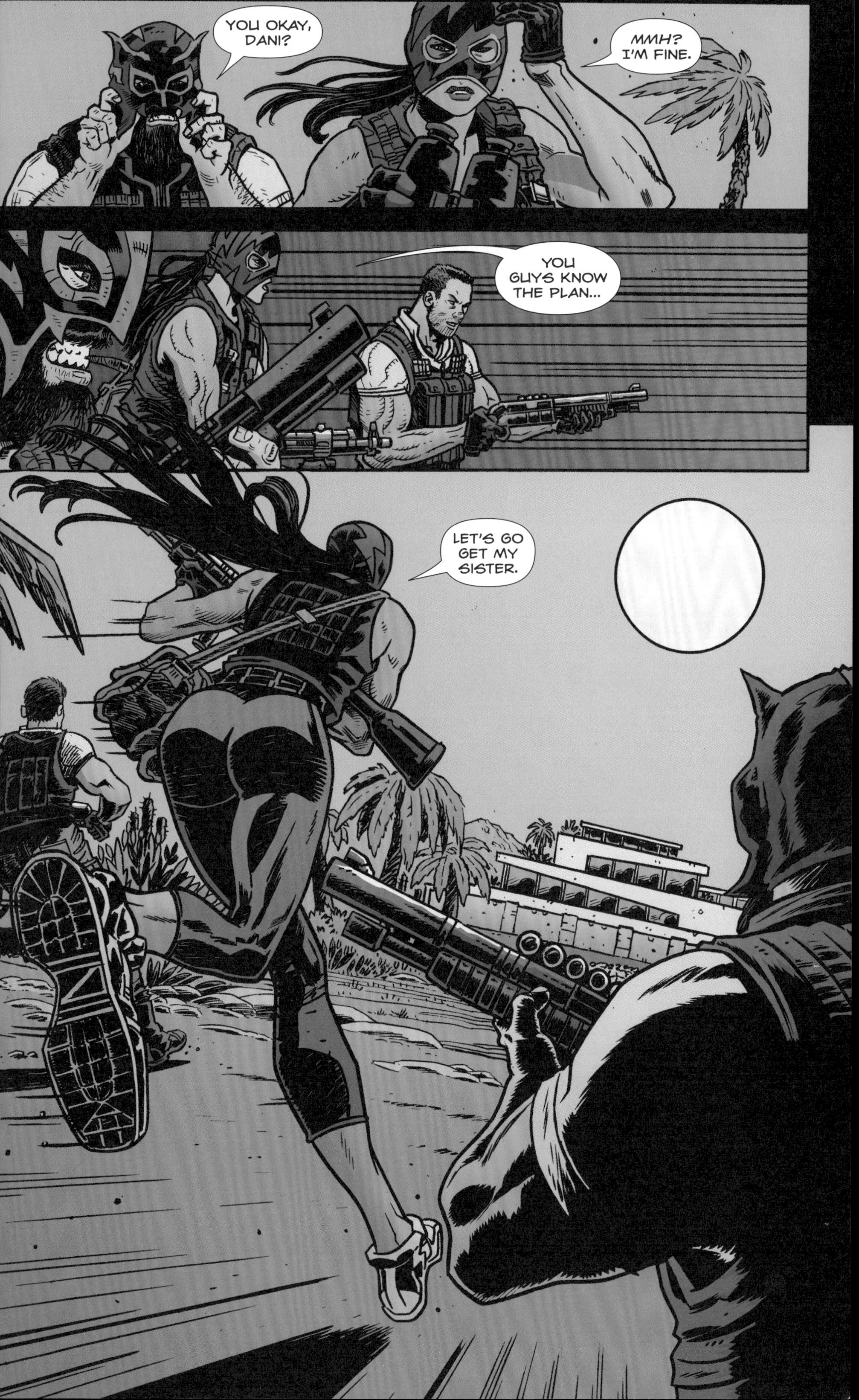
YOU OKAY, DANI?
MMH? I'M FINE.
YOU GUYS KNOW THE PLAN...
LET'S GO GET MY SISTER.

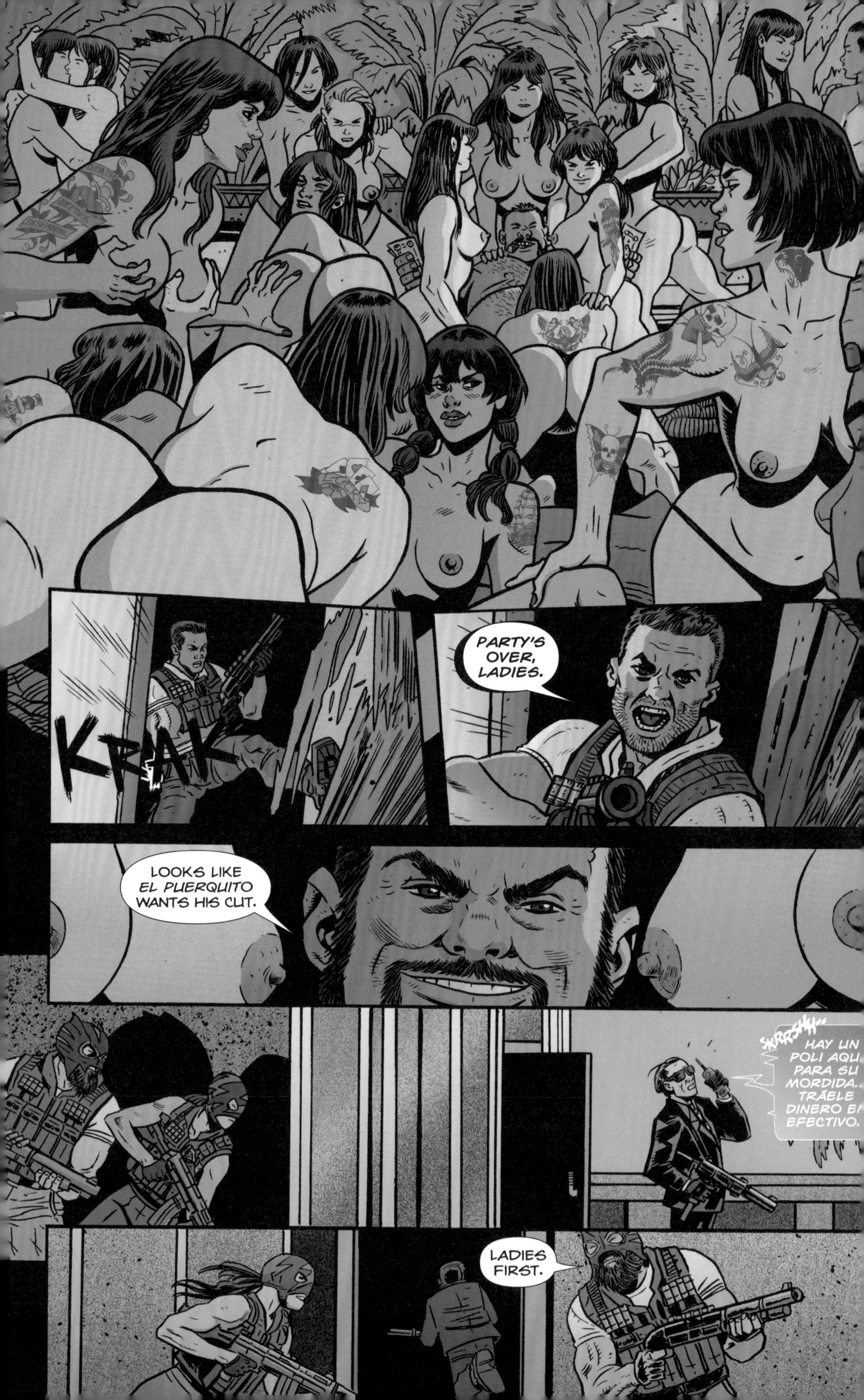
KRAK
PARTY'S OVER, LADIES.
LOOKS LIKE EL PUERQUITO WANTS HIS CUT.
HAY UN POLI AQU
PARA SU MORDIDA.
TRÁELE DINERO E
EFECTIVO.
LADIES FIRST.

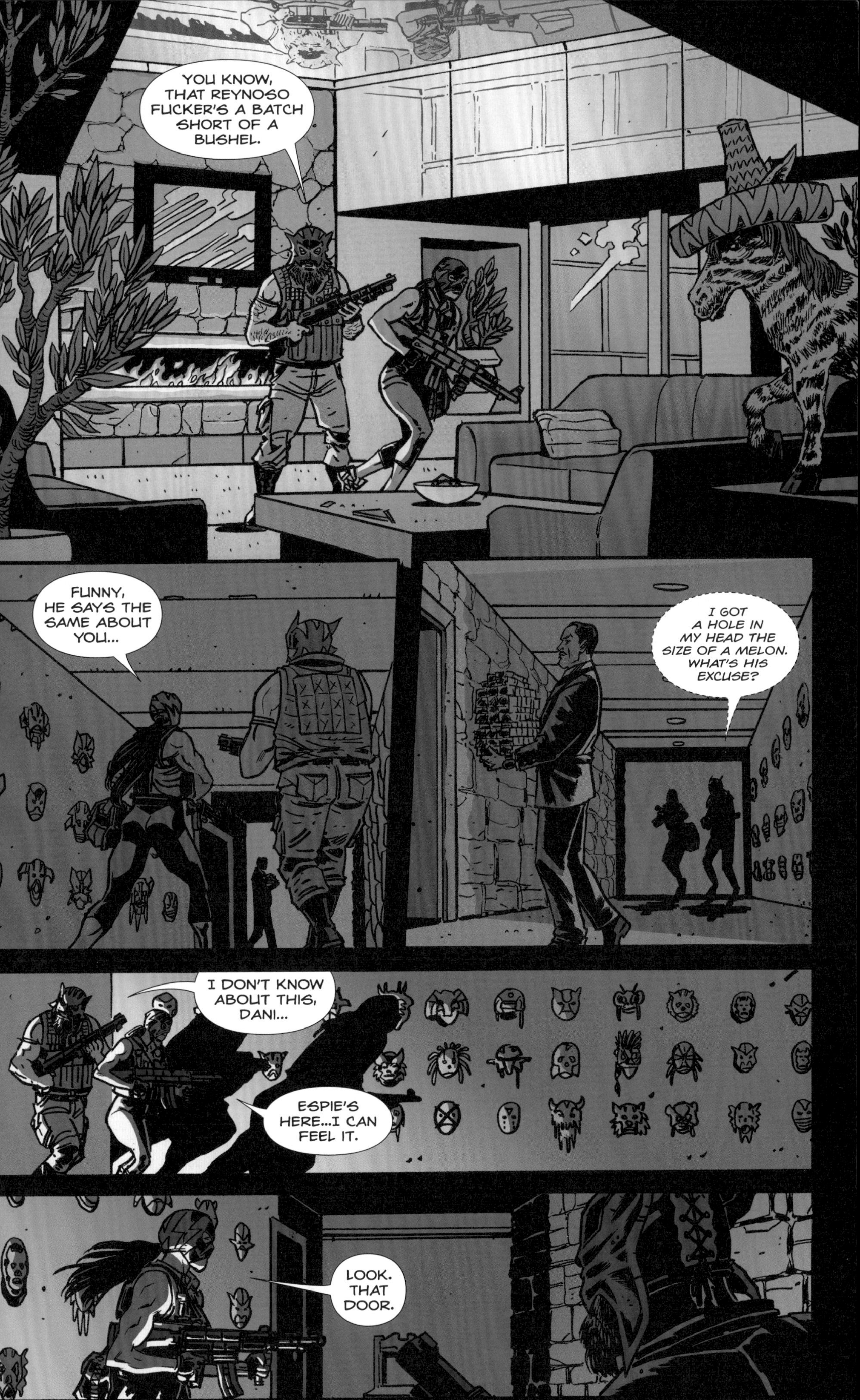
YOU KNOW, THAT REYNOSO FUCKER'S A BATCH SHORT OF A BUSHEL.
FUNNY, HE SAYS THE SAME ABOUT YOU...
I GOT A HOLE IN MY HEAD THE SIZE OF A MELON. WHAT'S HIS EXCUSE?
I DON'T KNOW ABOUT THIS, DANI...
ESPIE'S HERE...I CAN FEEL IT.
LOOK. THAT DOOR.

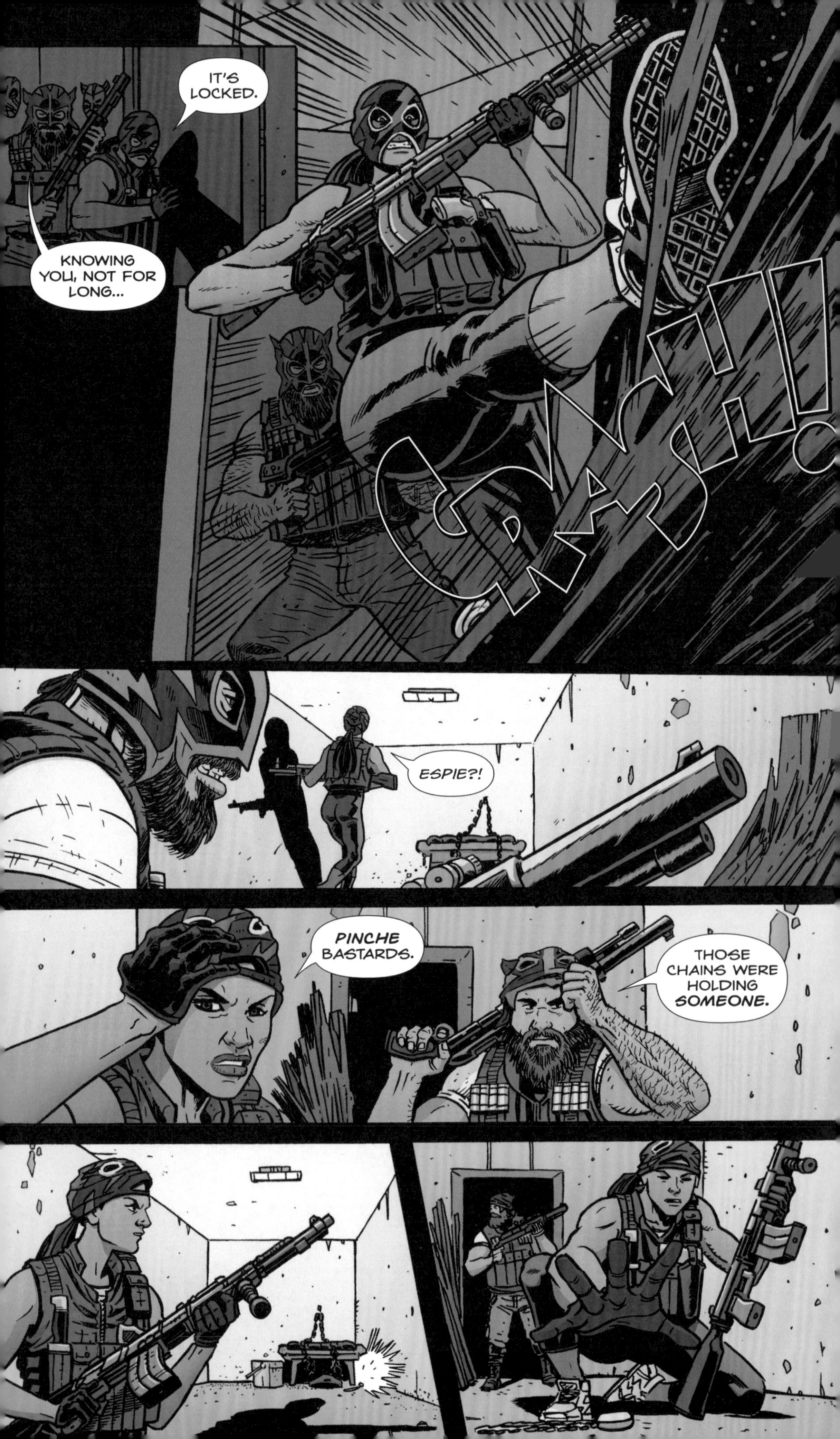
IT'S LOCKED.
KNOWING YOU, NOT FOR LONG...
CRAASH!!
ESPIE?!
PINCHE BASTARDS.
THOSE CHAINS WERE HOLDING SOMEONE.

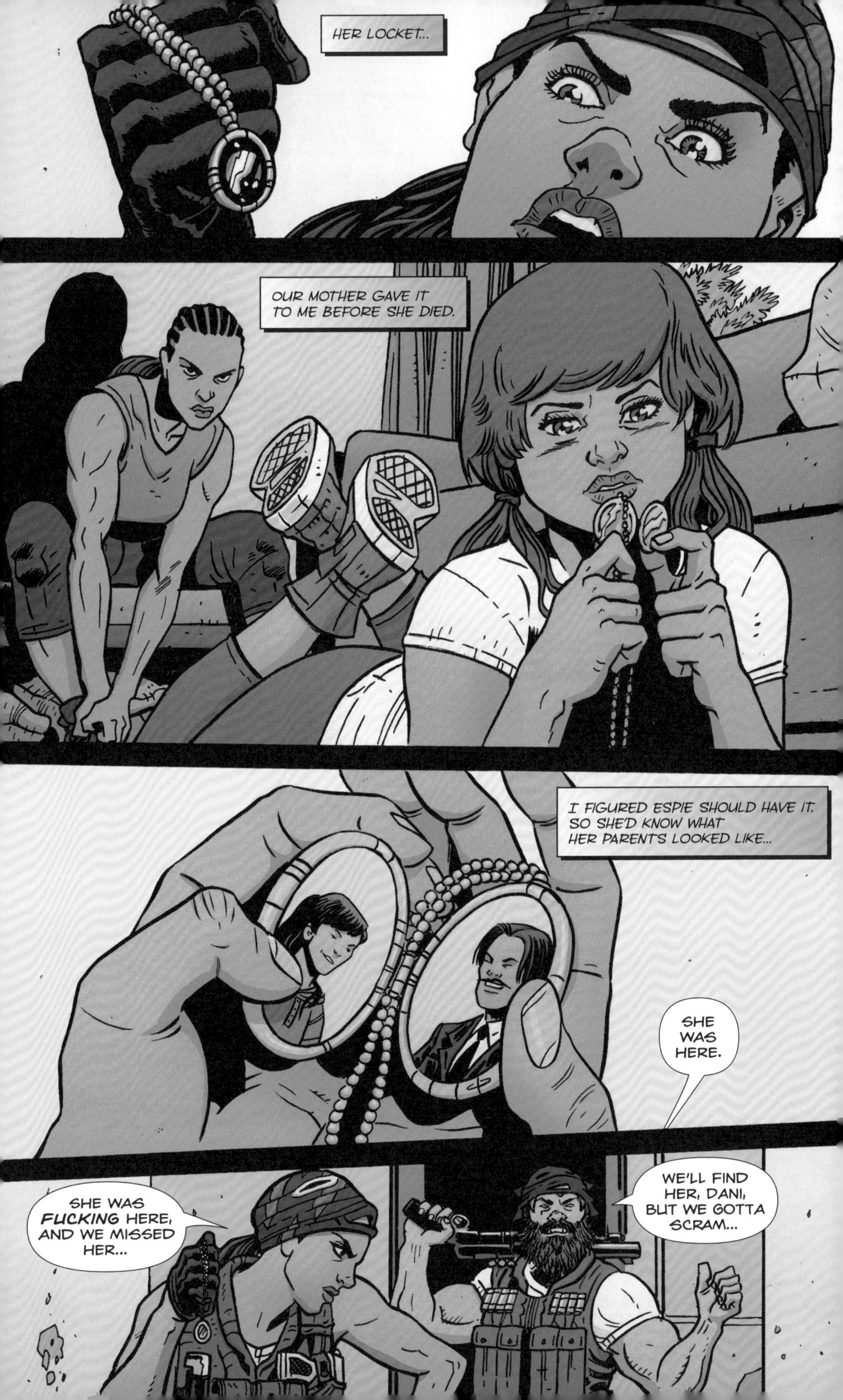
HER LOCKET...
OUR MOTHER GAVE IT TO ME BEFORE SHE DIED.
I FIGURED ESPIE SHOULD HAVE IT. SO SHE'D KNOW WHAT HER PARENTS LOOKED LIKE...
SHE WAS HERE.
SHE WAS FUCKING HERE, AND WE MISSED HER...
WE'LL FIND HER, DANI, BUT WE GOTTA SCRAM...

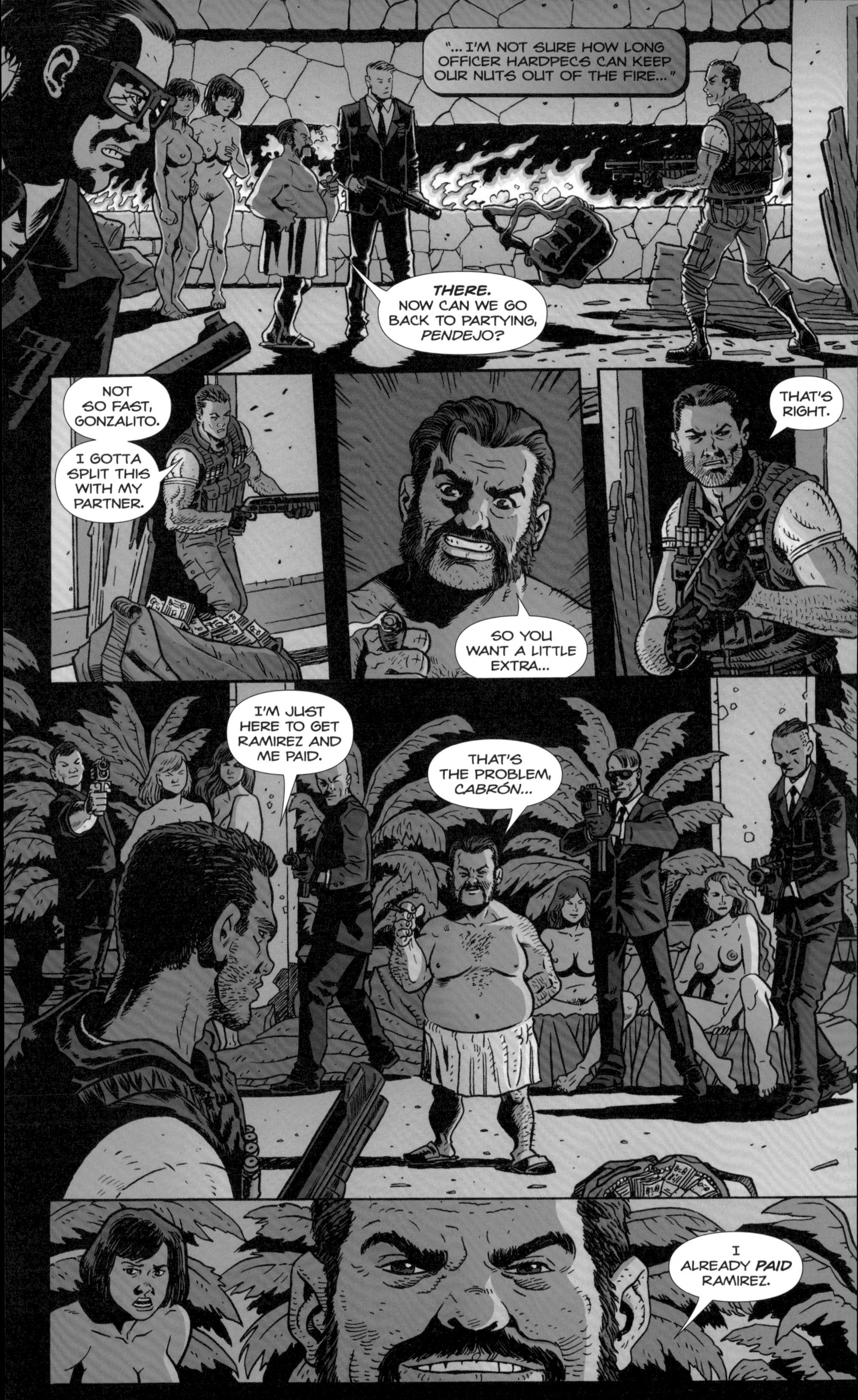
"...I'M NOT SURE HOW LONG OFFICER HARDPECS CAN KEEP OUR NUTS OUT OF THE FIRE..."
THERE. NOW CAN WE GO BACK TO PARTYING, *PENDEJO?*
NOT SO FAST, GONZALITO.
I GOTTA SPLIT THIS WITH MY PARTNER.
SO YOU WANT A LITTLE EXTRA...
THAT'S RIGHT.
I'M JUST HERE TO GET RAMIREZ AND ME PAID.
THAT'S THE PROBLEM, *CABRÓN*...
I ALREADY *PAID* RAMIREZ.

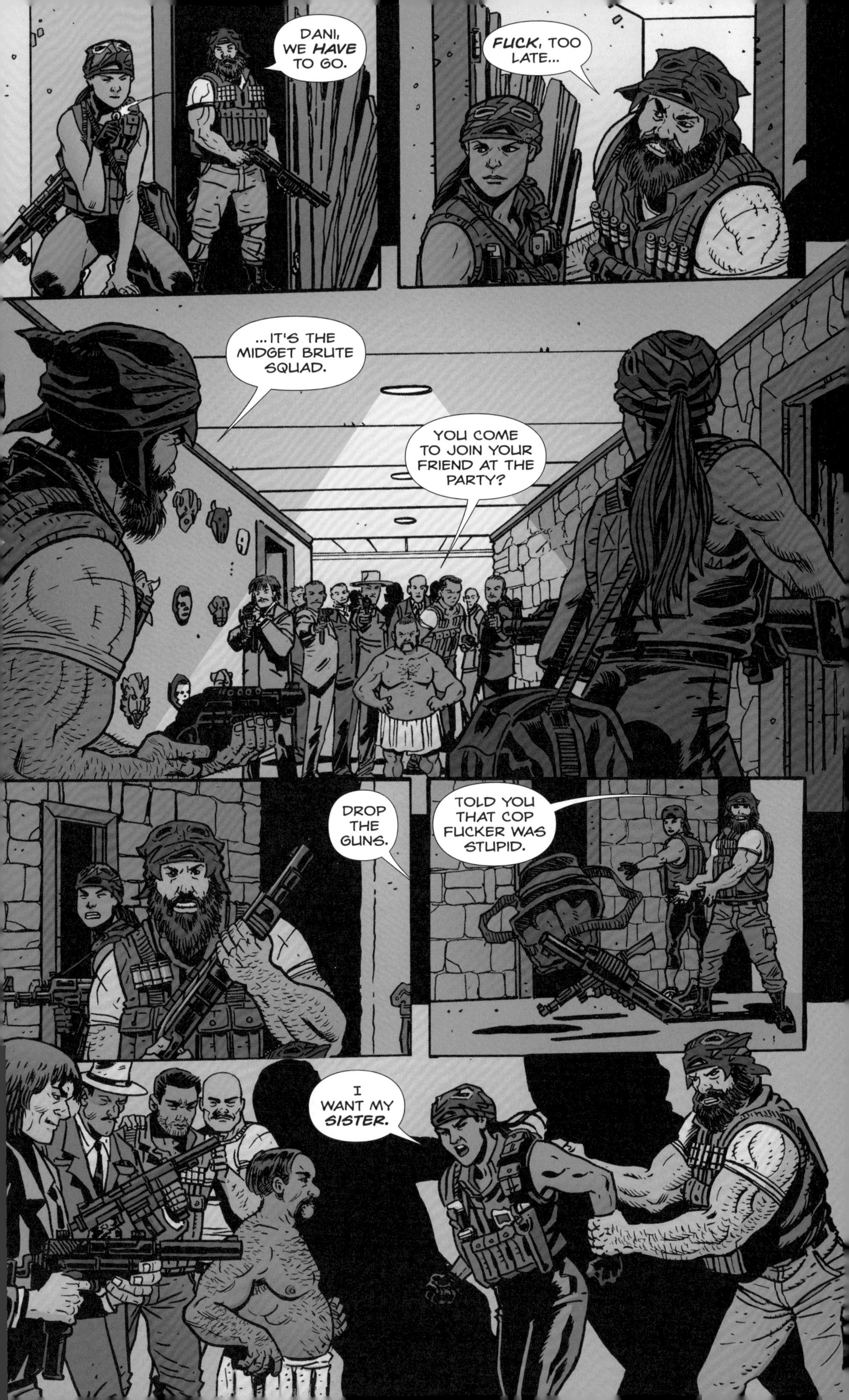
DANI, WE *HAVE* TO GO.
FUCK, TOO LATE...
...IT'S THE MIDGET BRUTE SQUAD.
YOU COME TO JOIN YOUR FRIEND AT THE PARTY?
DROP THE GUNS.
TOLD YOU THAT COP FUCKER WAS STUPID.
I WANT MY *SISTER*.

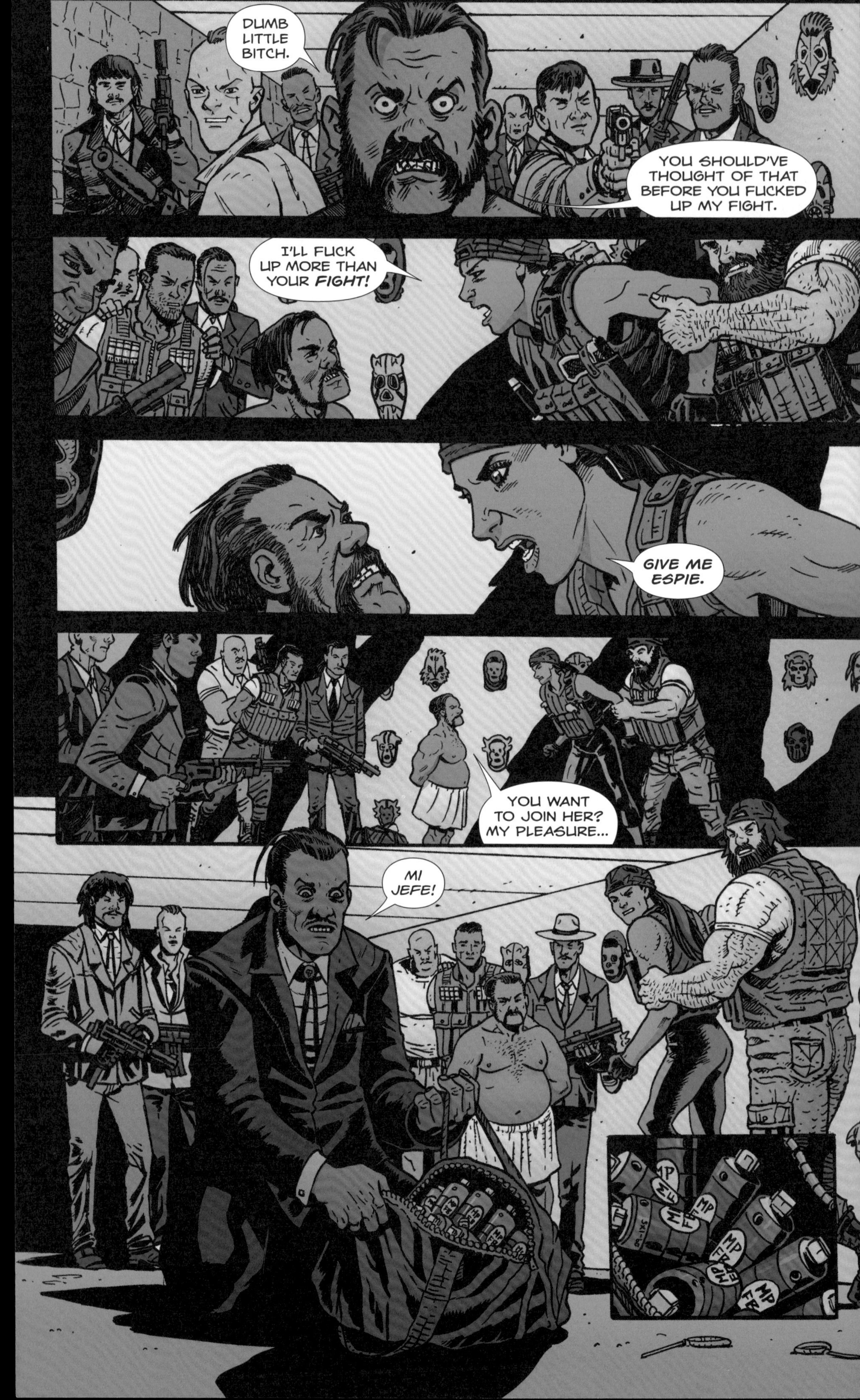
DUMB LITTLE BITCH.
YOU SHOULD'VE THOUGHT OF THAT BEFORE YOU FUCKED UP MY FIGHT.
I'LL FUCK UP MORE THAN YOUR *FIGHT!*
GIVE ME ESPIE.
YOU WANT TO JOIN HER? MY PLEASURE...
MI JEFE!

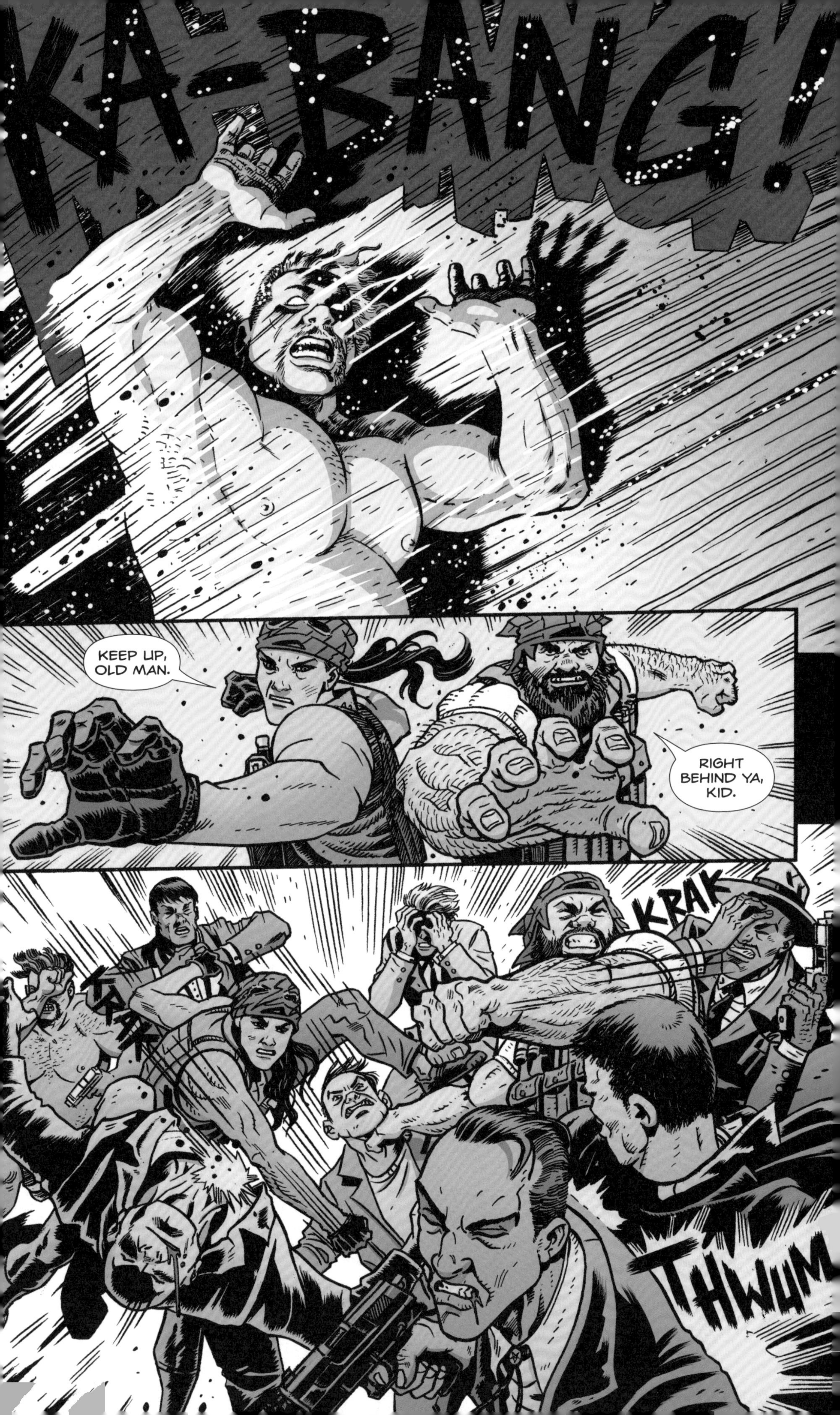
KA-BANG!
KEEP UP, OLD MAN.
RIGHT BEHIND YA, KID.
KRAK
KRAK
THWUM

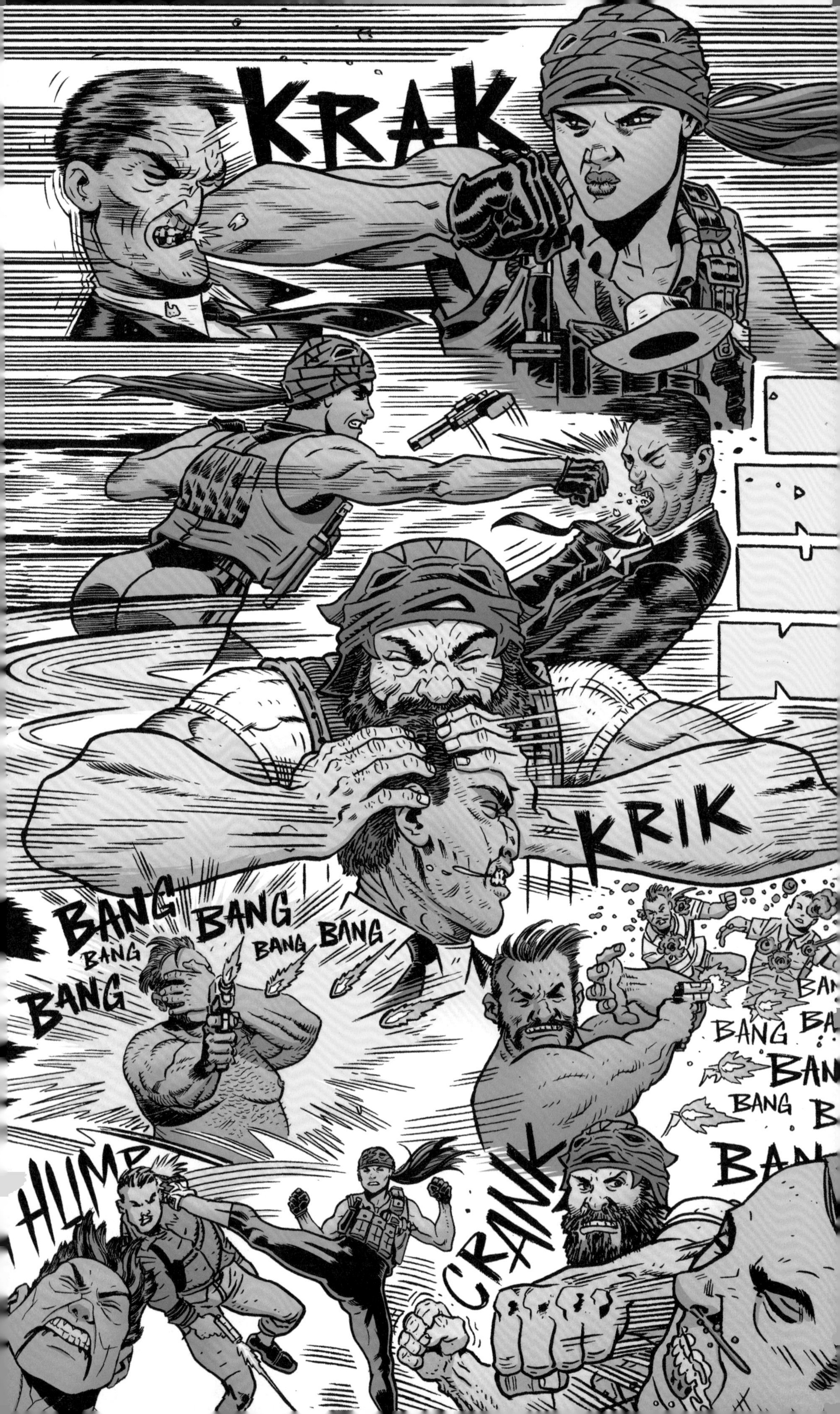

KRAK
KRIK
BANG
BANG
BANG
BANG
BANG
BANG
BANG
BANG
CRANK

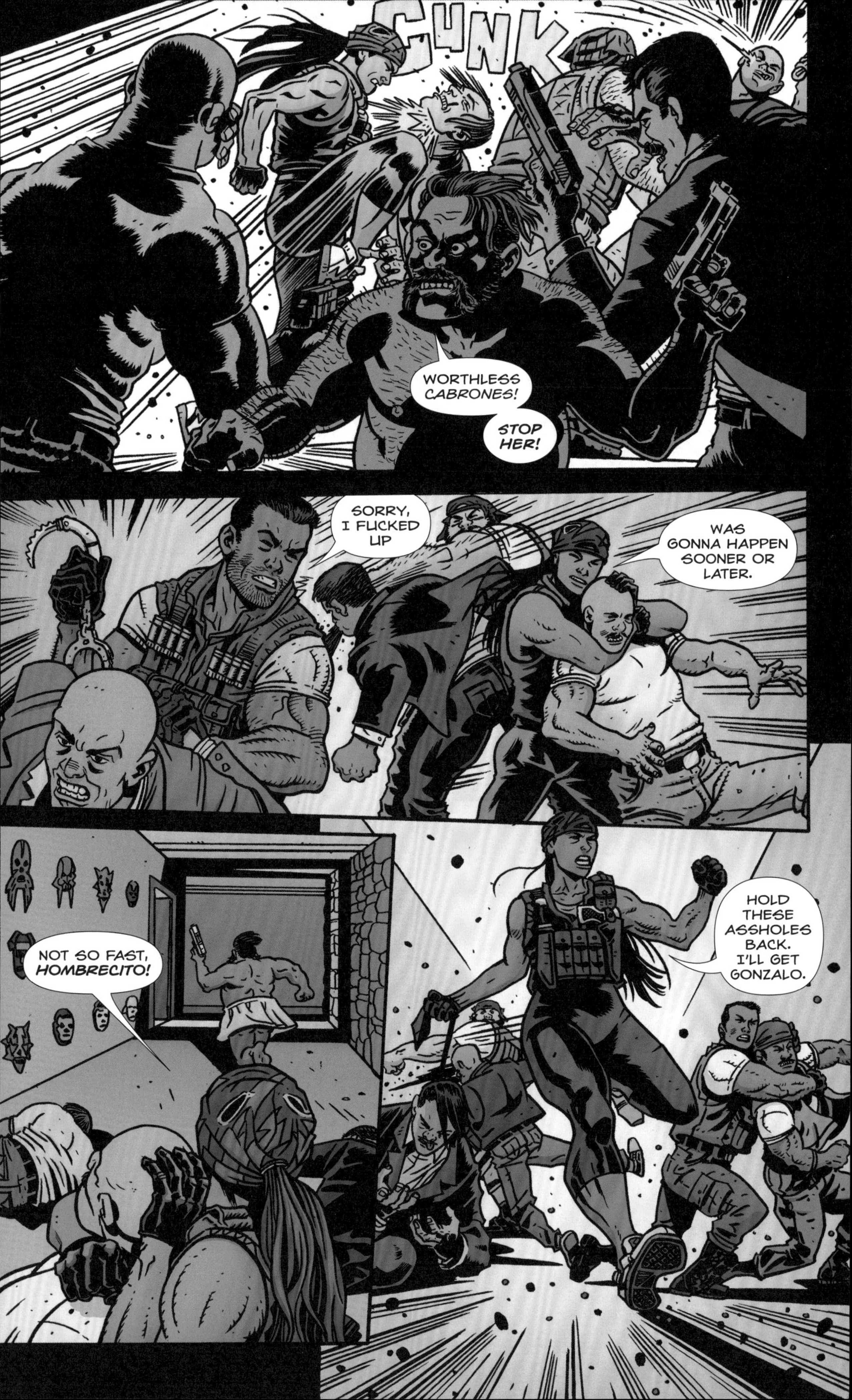
GUNK
WORTHLESS CABRONES!
STOP HER!
SORRY, I FUCKED UP
WAS GONNA HAPPEN SOONER OR LATER.
NOT SO FAST, *HOMBRECITO!*
HOLD THESE ASSHOLES BACK. I'LL GET GONZALO.

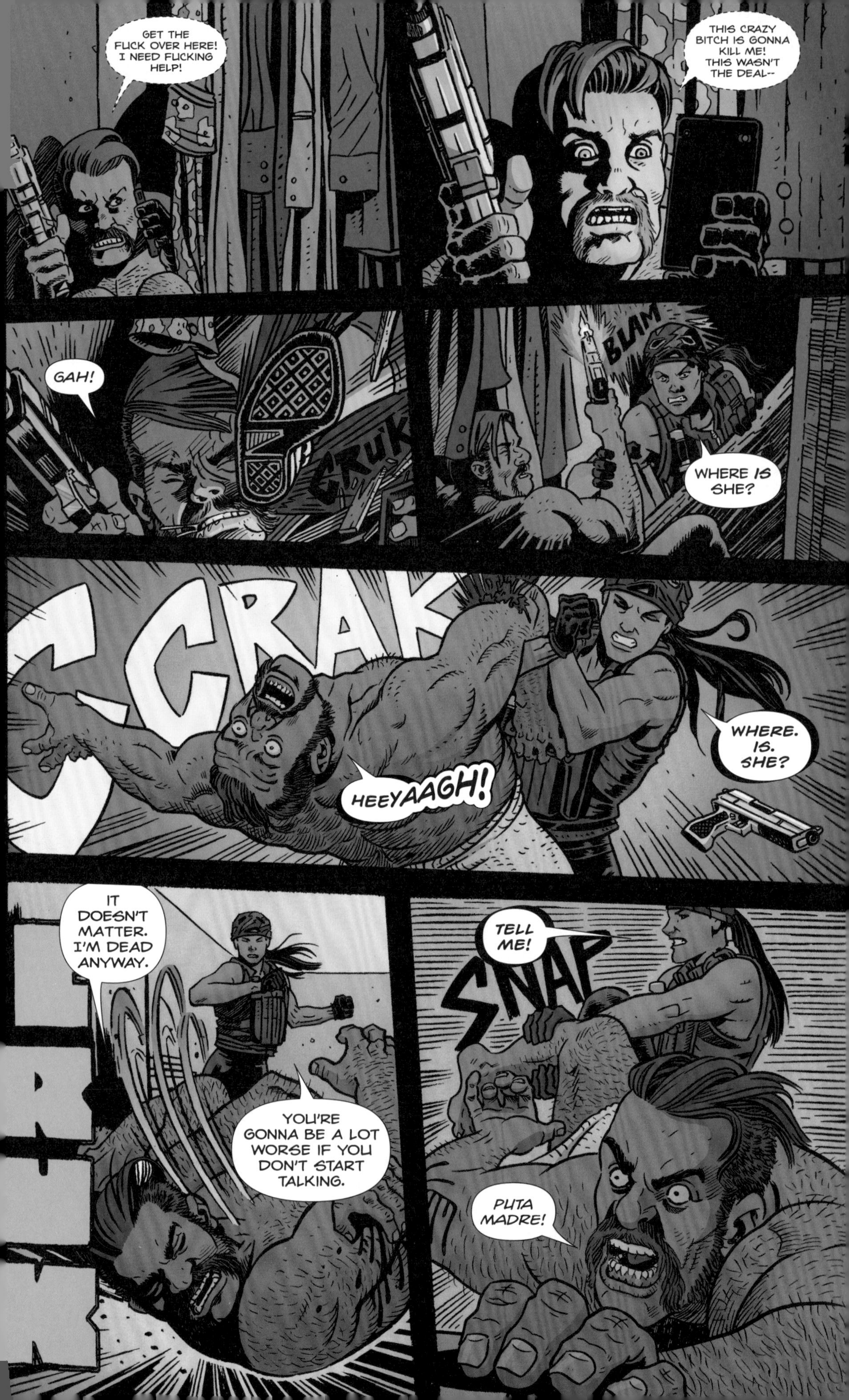
GET THE FUCK OVER HERE! I NEED FUCKING HELP!
THIS CRAZY BITCH IS GONNA KILL ME! THIS WASN'T THE DEAL--
GAH!
CRUK
BLAM
WHERE IS SHE?
CRAK
WHERE. IS. SHE?
HEEYAAGH!
IT DOESN'T MATTER. I'M DEAD ANYWAY.
YOU'RE GONNA BE A LOT WORSE IF YOU DON'T START TALKING.
TELL ME!
SNAP
PUTA MADRE!

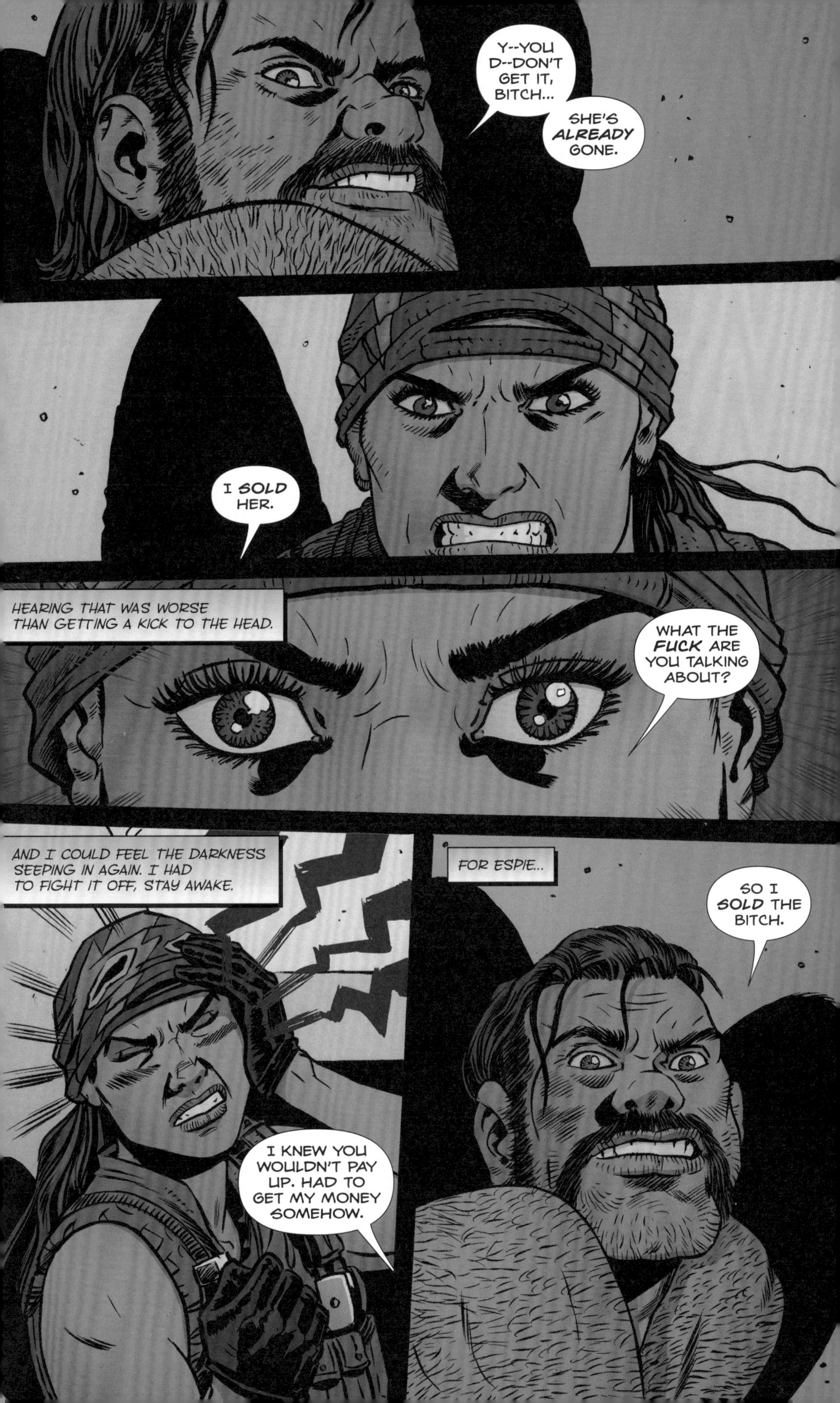

Y--YOU D--DON'T GET IT, BITCH...
SHE'S ALREADY GONE.
I SOLD HER.
HEARING THAT WAS WORSE THAN GETTING A KICK TO THE HEAD.
WHAT THE FUCK ARE YOU TALKING ABOUT?
AND I COULD FEEL THE DARKNESS SEEPING IN AGAIN. I HAD TO FIGHT IT OFF, STAY AWAKE.
I KNEW YOU WOULDN'T PAY UP. HAD TO GET MY MONEY SOMEHOW.
FOR ESPIE...
SO I SOLD THE BITCH.

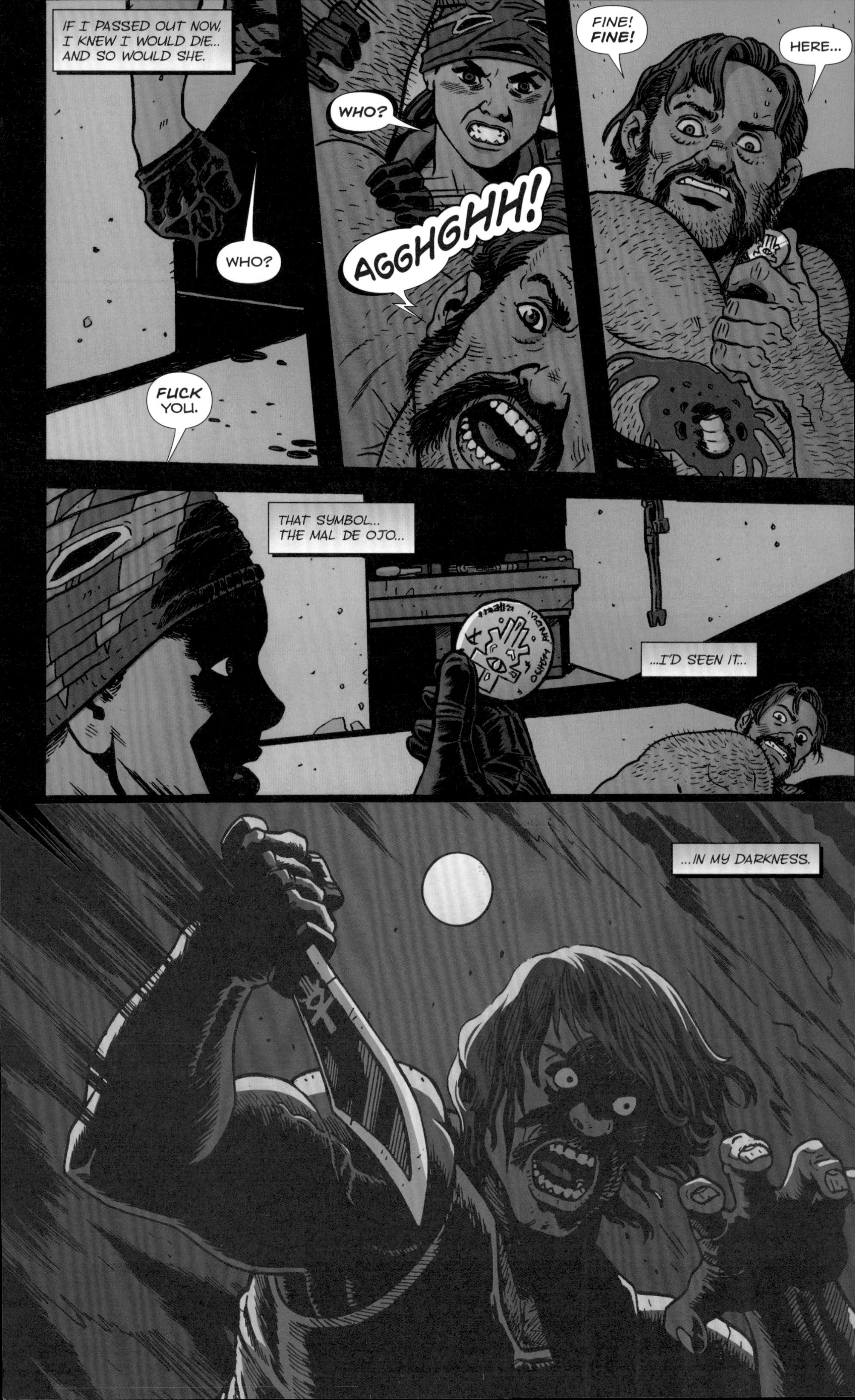
IF I PASSED OUT NOW, I KNEW I WOULD DIE... AND SO WOULD SHE.
WHO?
WHO?
FUCK YOU.
AGGHGHH!
FINE! FINE!
HERE...
THAT SYMBOL... THE MAL DE OJO...
...I'D SEEN IT...
...IN MY DARKNESS.

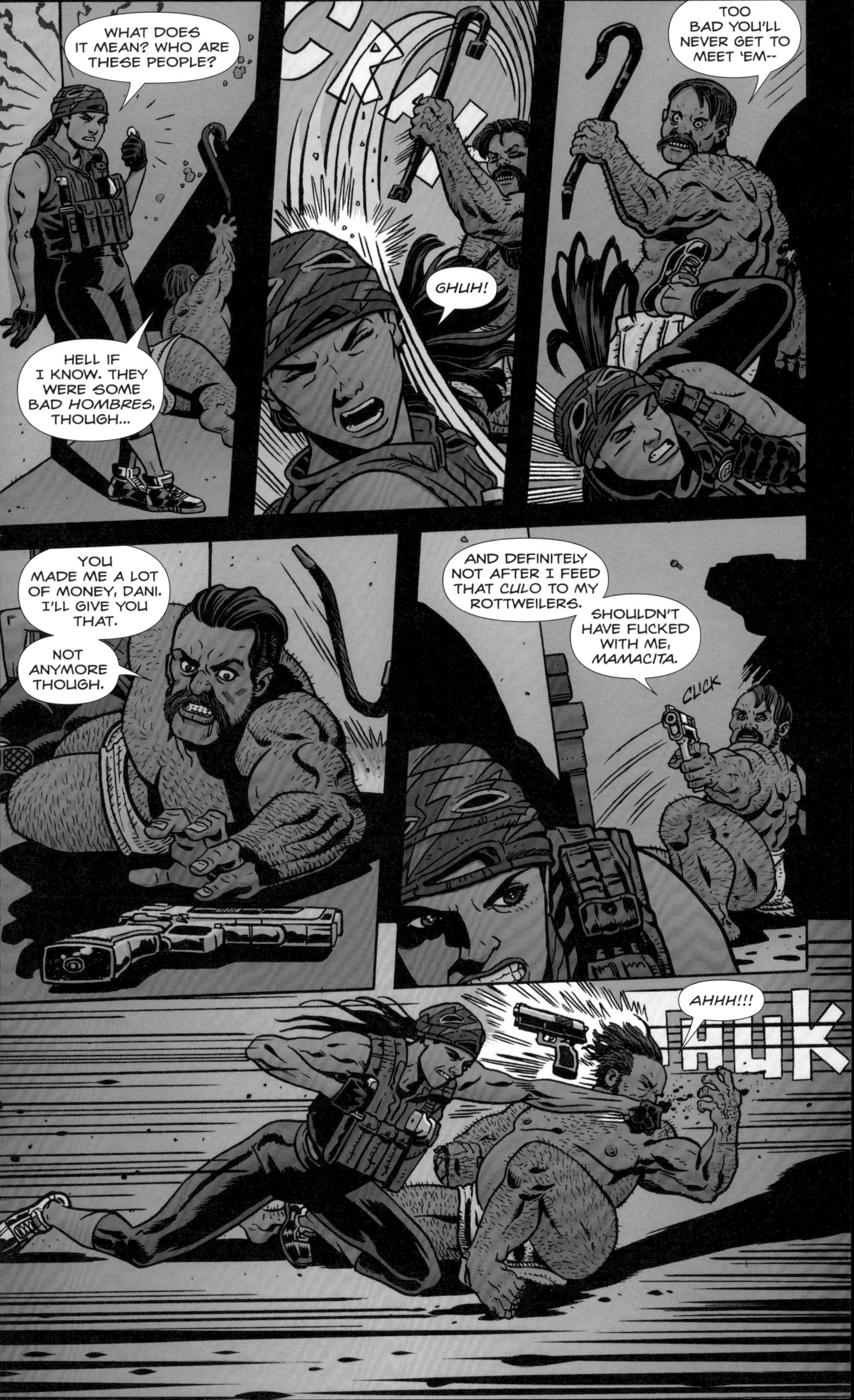
WHAT DOES IT MEAN? WHO ARE THESE PEOPLE?
HELL IF I KNOW. THEY WERE SOME BAD HOMBRES, THOUGH...
GHUH!
TOO BAD YOU'LL NEVER GET TO MEET 'EM--
YOU MADE ME A LOT OF MONEY, DANI. I'LL GIVE YOU THAT.
NOT ANYMORE THOUGH.
AND DEFINITELY NOT AFTER I FEED THAT CULO TO MY ROTTWEILERS.
SHOULDN'T HAVE FUCKED WITH ME, MAMACITA.
CLICK
AHHH!!!
THUK

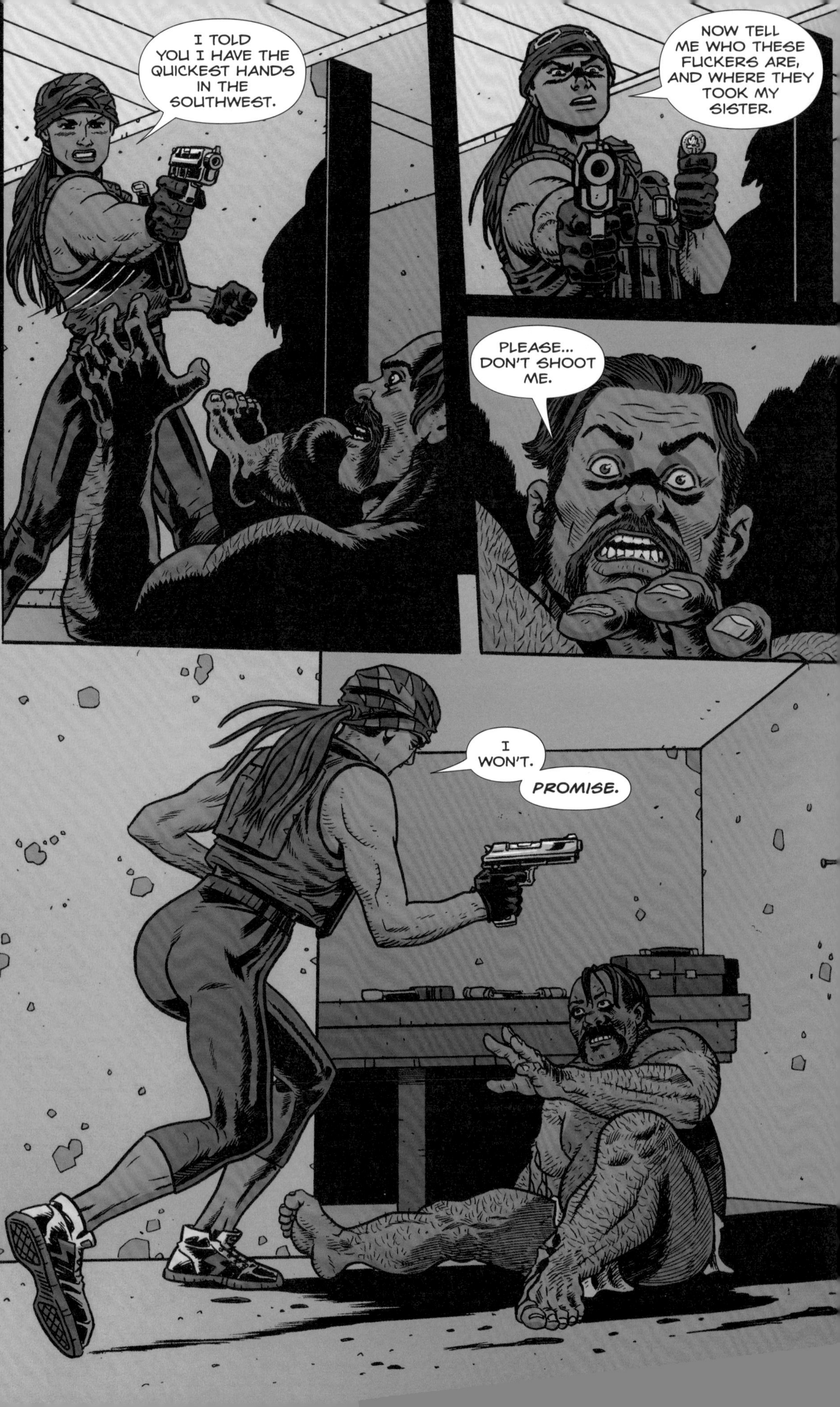
I TOLD YOU I HAVE THE QUICKEST HANDS IN THE SOUTHWEST.
NOW TELL ME WHO THESE FUCKERS ARE, AND WHERE THEY TOOK MY SISTER.
PLEASE... DON'T SHOOT ME.
I WON'T.
PROMISE.

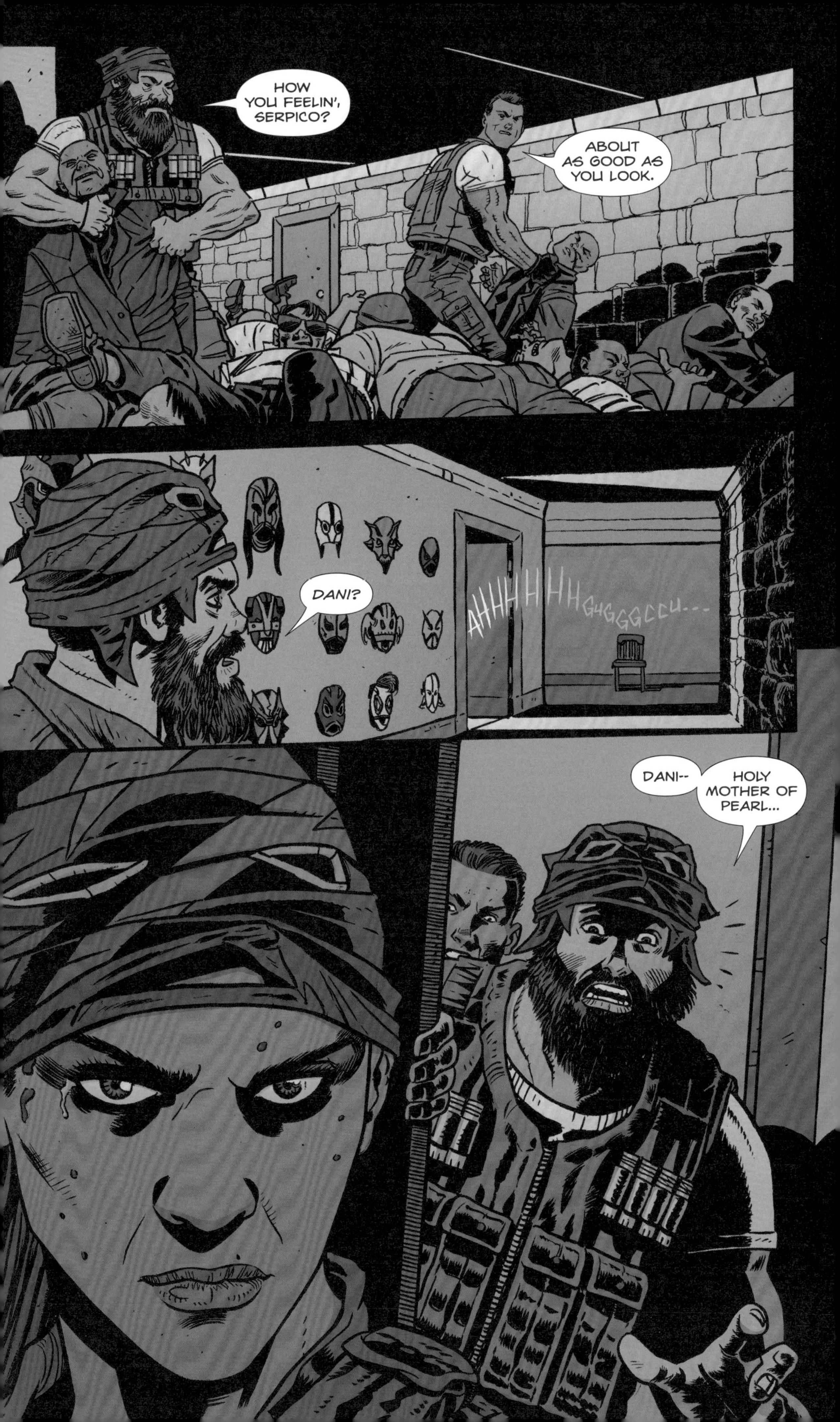

HOW YOU FEELIN', SERPICO?
ABOUT AS GOOD AS YOU LOOK.
DANI?
AHHHHHHHGUGGGCCU...
DANI--
HOLY MOTHER OF PEARL...

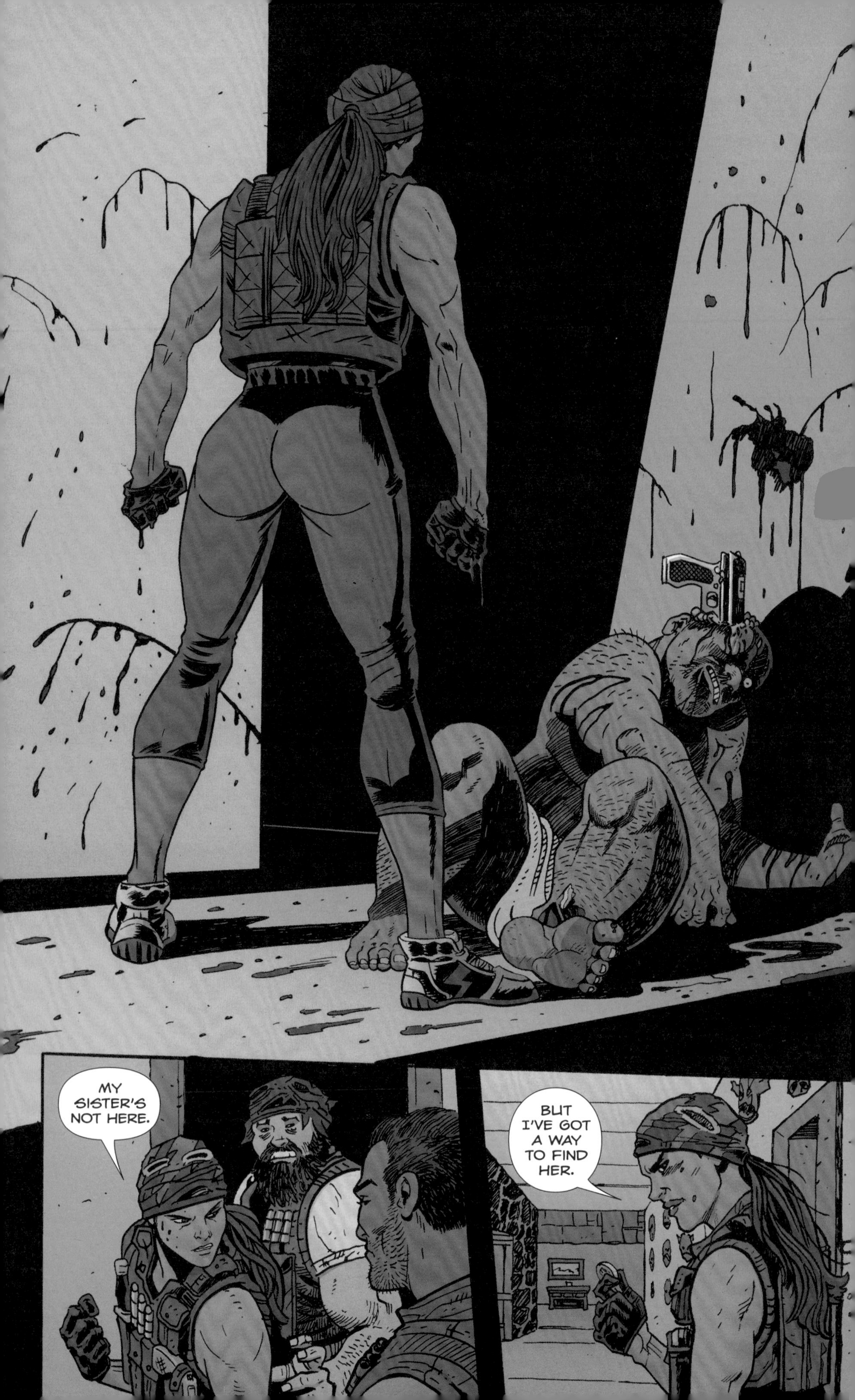
MY SISTER'S NOT HERE.
BUT I'VE GOT A WAY TO FIND HER.

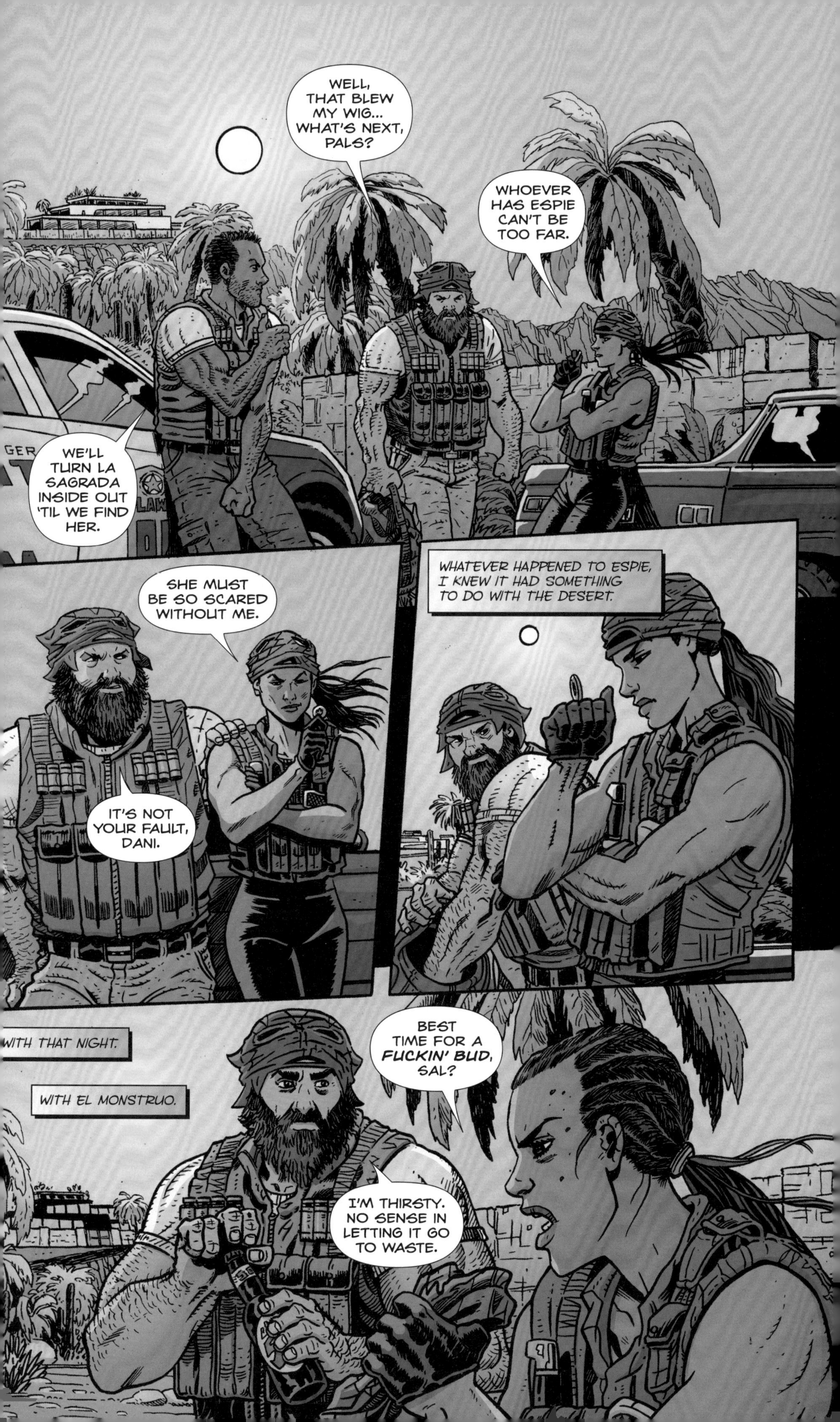
WELL, THAT BLEW MY WIG... WHAT'S NEXT, PALS?
WHOEVER HAS ESPIE CAN'T BE TOO FAR.
WE'LL TURN LA SAGRADA INSIDE OUT 'TIL WE FIND HER.
SHE MUST BE SO SCARED WITHOUT ME.
IT'S NOT YOUR FAULT, DANI.
WHATEVER HAPPENED TO ESPIE, I KNEW IT HAD SOMETHING TO DO WITH THE DESERT.
WITH THAT NIGHT.
WITH EL MONSTRUO.
BEST TIME FOR A FUCKIN' BUD, SAL?
I'M THIRSTY. NO SENSE IN LETTING IT GO TO WASTE.

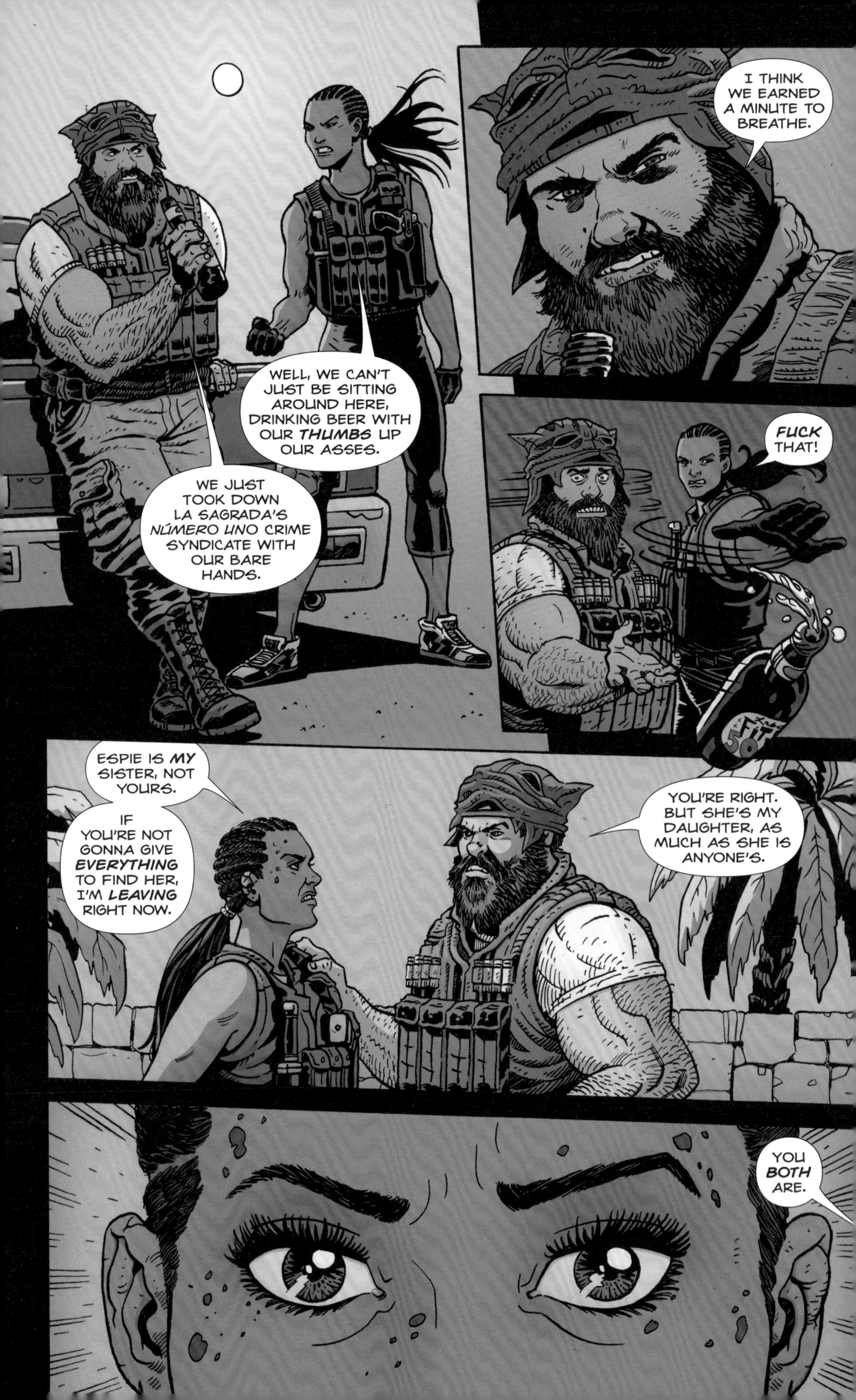
WE JUST TOOK DOWN LA SAGRADA'S NÚMERO UNO CRIME SYNDICATE WITH OUR BARE HANDS.
WELL, WE CAN'T JUST BE SITTING AROUND HERE, DRINKING BEER WITH OUR THUMBS UP OUR ASSES.
I THINK WE EARNED A MINUTE TO BREATHE.
FUCK THAT!
ESPIE IS MY SISTER, NOT YOURS.
IF YOU'RE NOT GONNA GIVE EVERYTHING TO FIND HER, I'M LEAVING RIGHT NOW.
YOU'RE RIGHT. BUT SHE'S MY DAUGHTER, AS MUCH AS SHE IS ANYONE'S.
YOU BOTH ARE.

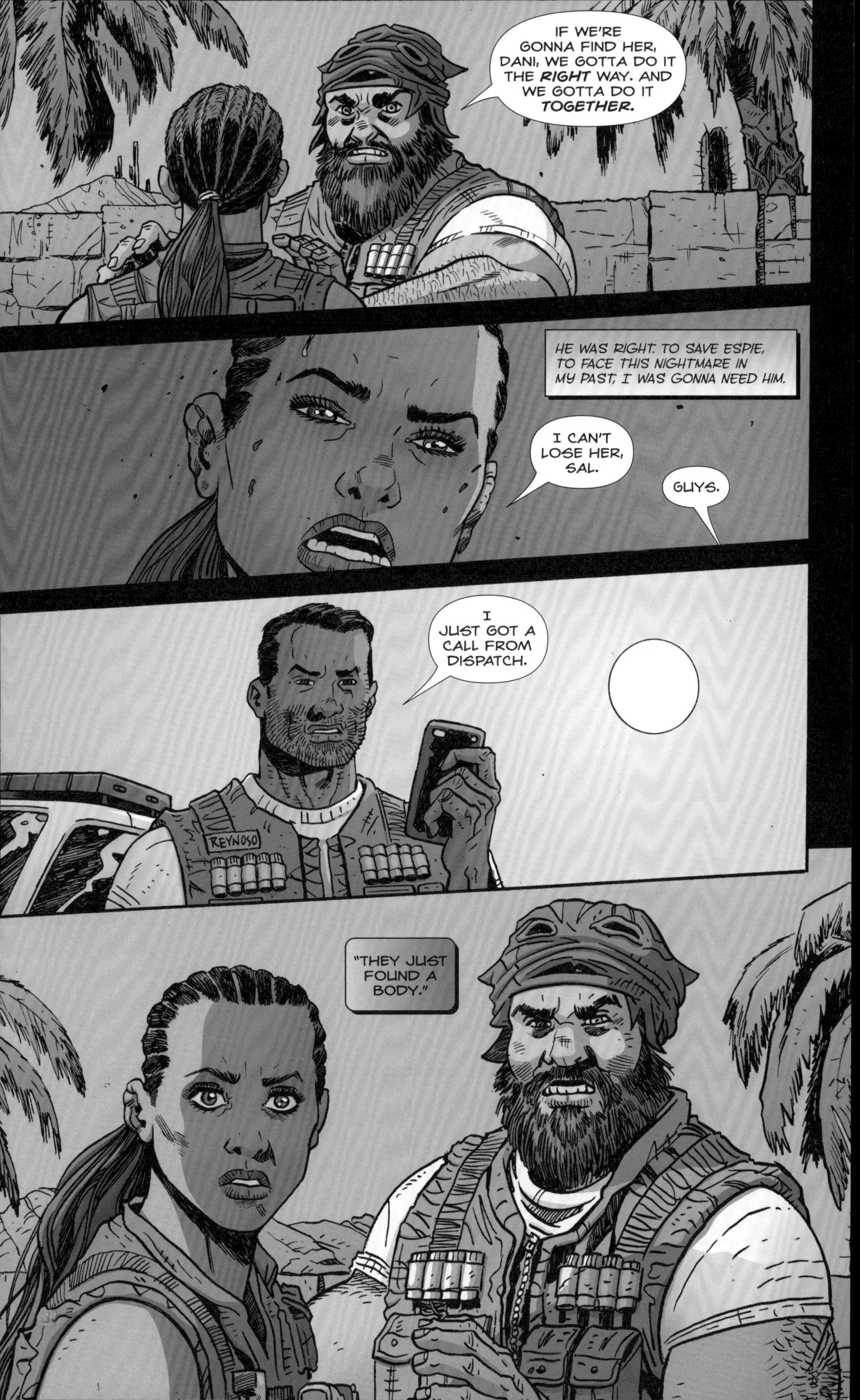
IF WE'RE GONNA FIND HER, DANI, WE GOTTA DO IT THE *RIGHT* WAY. AND WE GOTTA DO IT *TOGETHER.*
HE WAS RIGHT. TO SAVE ESPIE, TO FACE THIS NIGHTMARE IN MY PAST, I WAS GONNA NEED HIM.
I CAN'T LOSE HER, SAL.
GUYS.
I JUST GOT A CALL FROM DISPATCH.
REYNOSO
"THEY JUST FOUND A BODY."

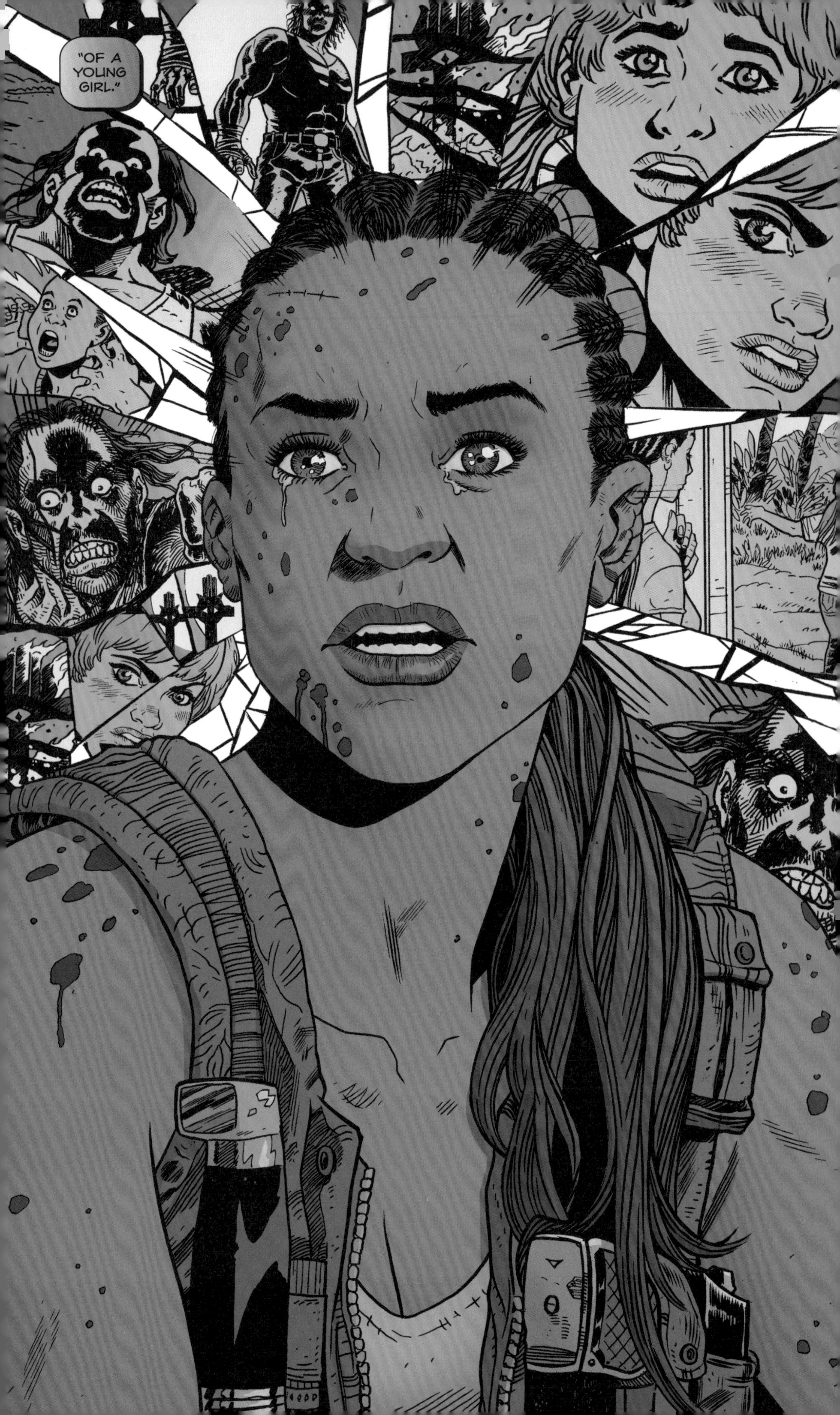
"OF A YOUNG GIRL."

CHAPTER 3

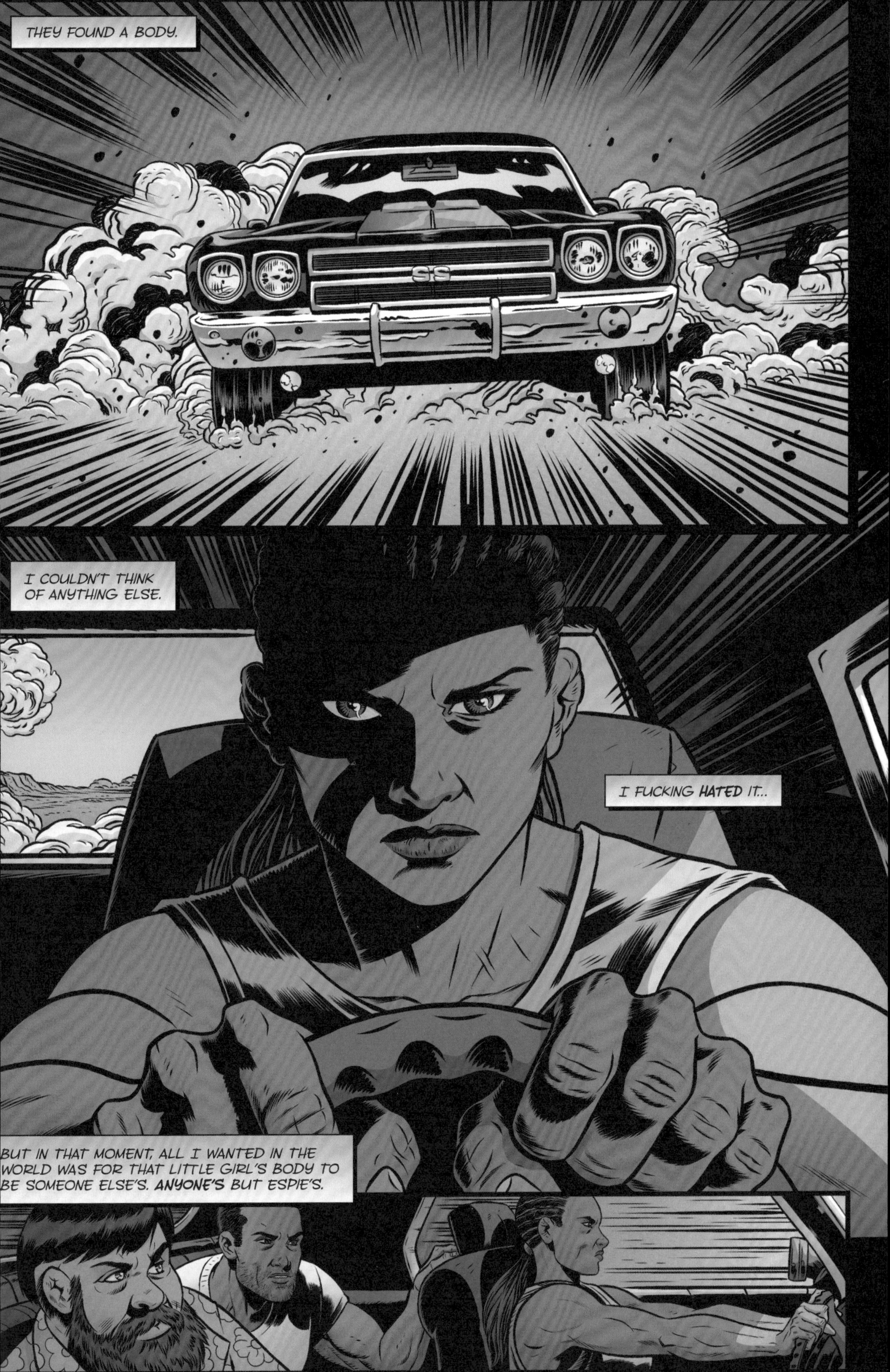
THEY FOUND A BODY.
I COULDN'T THINK OF ANYTHING ELSE.
I FUCKING **HATED** IT...
BUT IN THAT MOMENT, ALL I WANTED IN THE WORLD WAS FOR THAT LITTLE GIRL'S BODY TO BE SOMEONE ELSE'S. **ANYONE'S** BUT ESPIE'S.

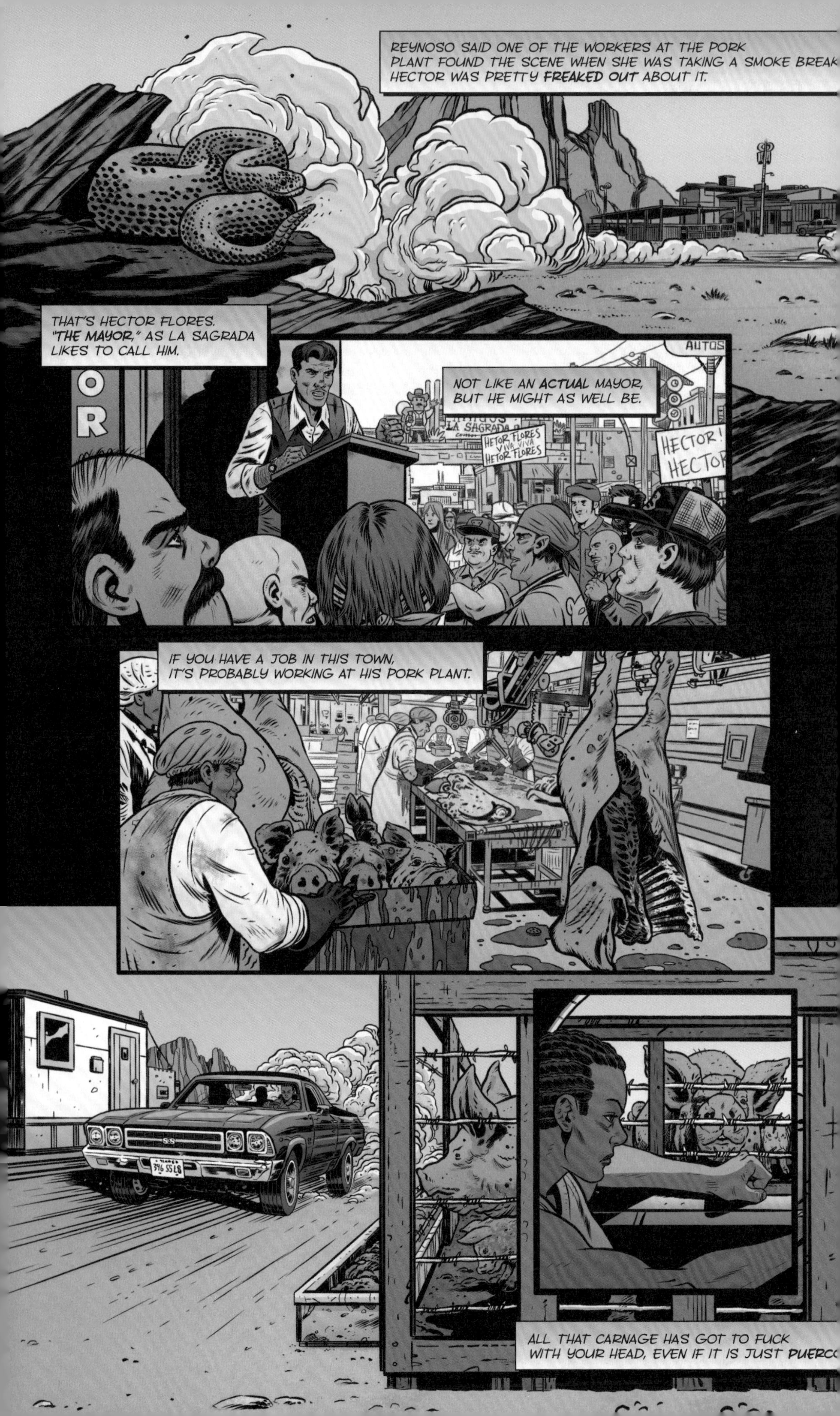
REYNOSO SAID ONE OF THE WORKERS AT THE PORK PLANT FOUND THE SCENE WHEN SHE WAS TAKING A SMOKE BREAK. HECTOR WAS PRETTY **FREAKED OUT** ABOUT IT.
THAT'S HECTOR FLORES. **"THE MAYOR,"** AS LA SAGRADA LIKES TO CALL HIM.
AUTOS
NOT LIKE AN **ACTUAL** MAYOR, BUT HE MIGHT AS WELL BE.
LA SAGRADA
HECTOR FLORES VIVA VIVA HECTOR FLORES
HECTOR! HECTOR
IF YOU HAVE A JOB IN THIS TOWN, IT'S PROBABLY WORKING AT HIS PORK PLANT.
SS
ALL THAT CARNAGE HAS GOT TO FUCK WITH YOUR HEAD, EVEN IF IT IS JUST **PUERCO**

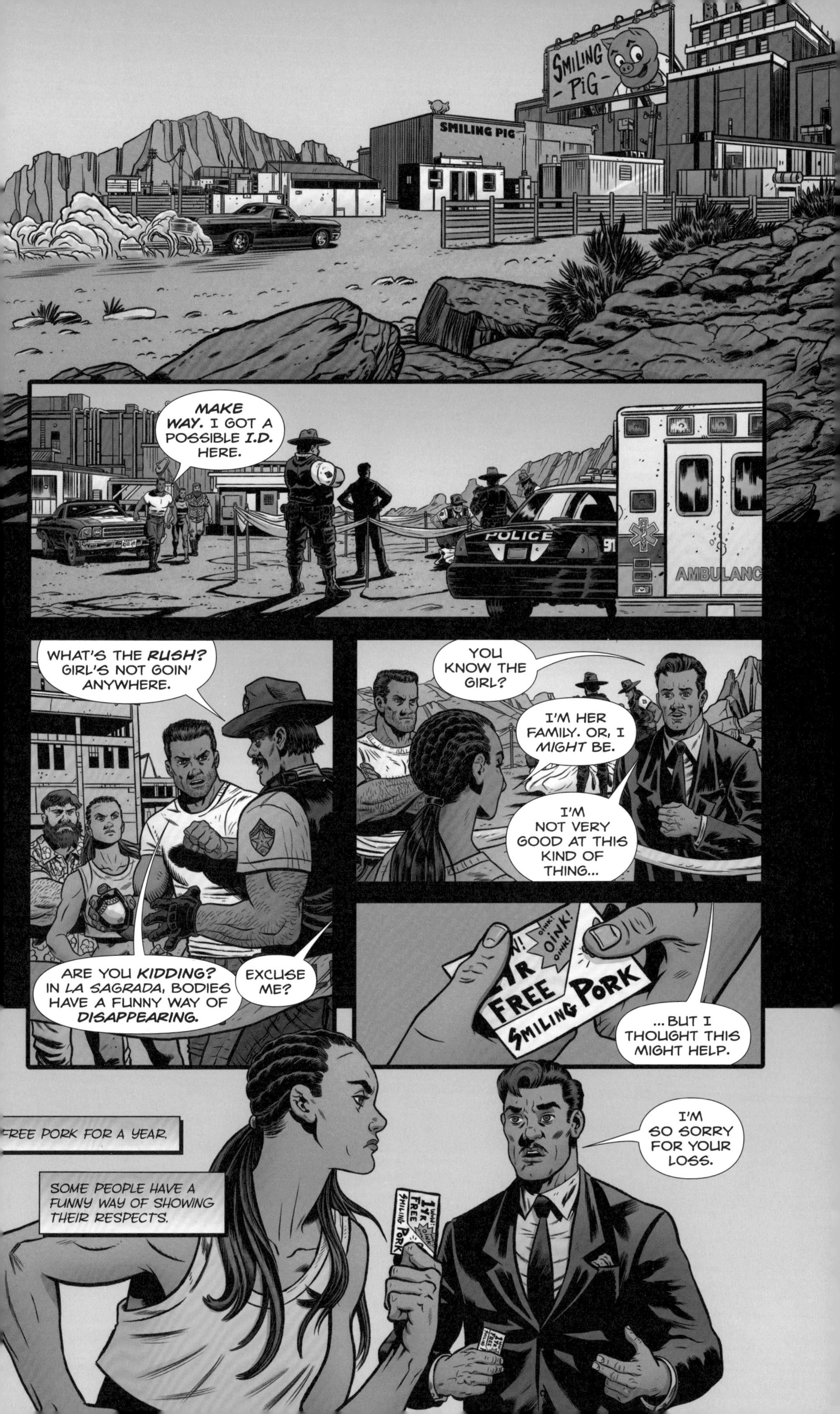

SMILING PIG
SMILING PIG
MAKE WAY. I GOT A POSSIBLE I.D. HERE.
POLICE
AMBULANC
WHAT'S THE RUSH? GIRL'S NOT GOIN' ANYWHERE.
ARE YOU KIDDING? IN LA SAGRADA, BODIES HAVE A FUNNY WAY OF DISAPPEARING.
EXCUSE ME?
YOU KNOW THE GIRL?
I'M HER FAMILY. OR, I MIGHT BE.
I'M NOT VERY GOOD AT THIS KIND OF THING...
1YR FREE SMILING PORK
OINK! OINK! OINK!
...BUT I THOUGHT THIS MIGHT HELP.
FREE PORK FOR A YEAR.
SOME PEOPLE HAVE A FUNNY WAY OF SHOWING THEIR RESPECTS.
I'M SO SORRY FOR YOUR LOSS.

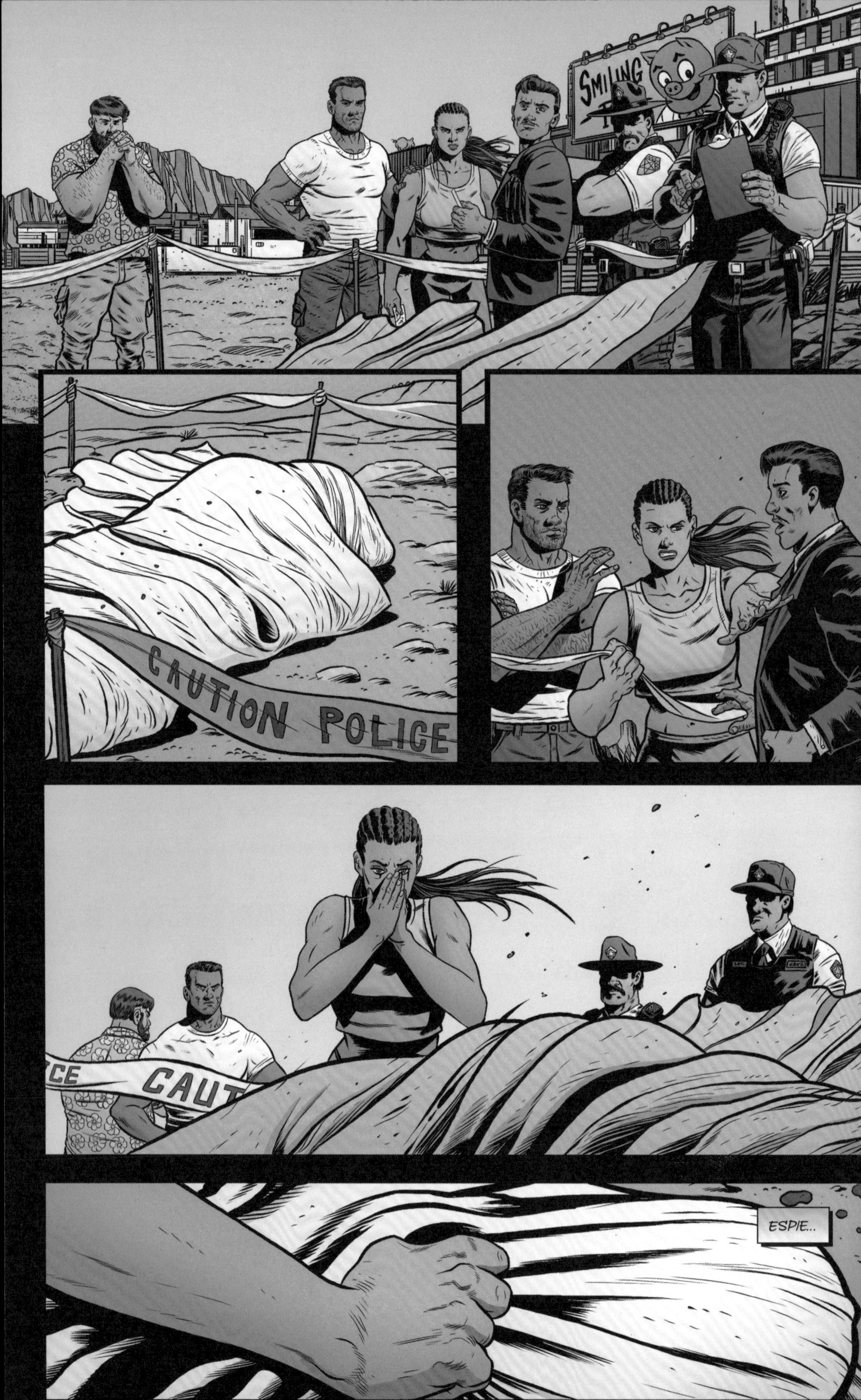
SMILING
CAUTION POLICE
ESPIE...

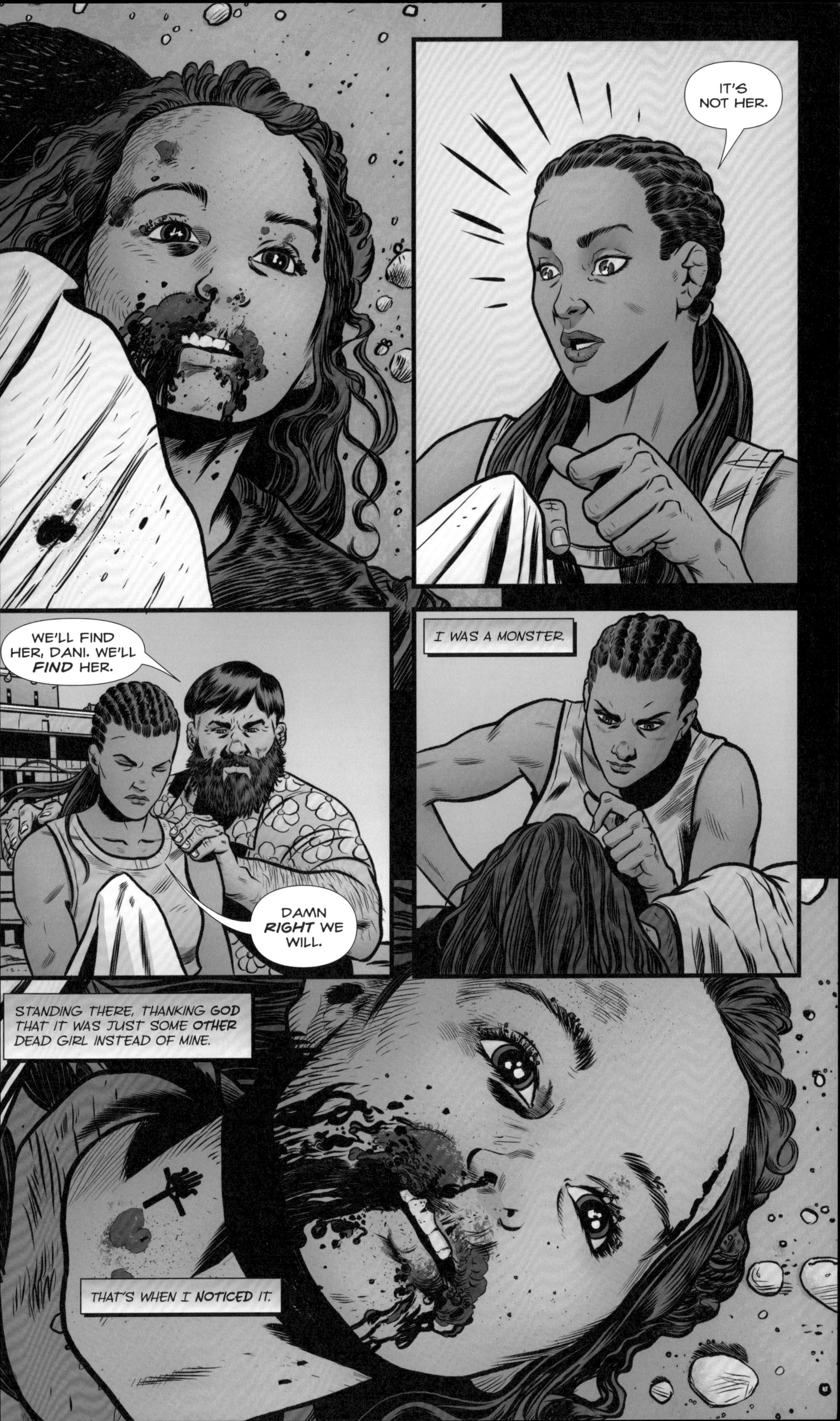
IT'S NOT HER.
WE'LL FIND HER, DANI. WE'LL FIND HER.
DAMN RIGHT WE WILL.
I WAS A MONSTER.
STANDING THERE, THANKING GOD THAT IT WAS JUST SOME OTHER DEAD GIRL INSTEAD OF MINE.
THAT'S WHEN I NOTICED IT.

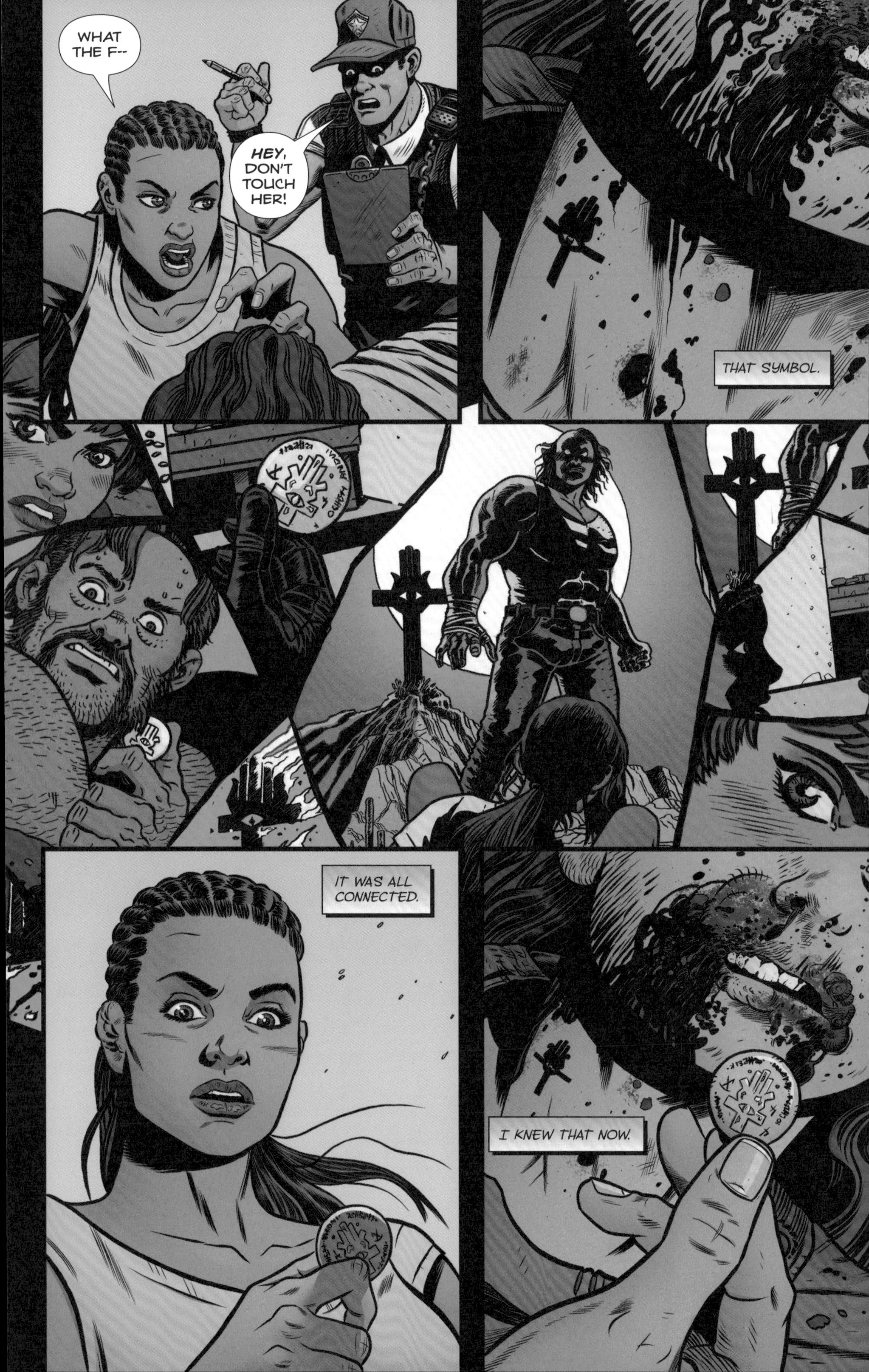
WHAT THE F--
HEY, DON'T TOUCH HER!
THAT SYMBOL.
IT WAS ALL CONNECTED.
I KNEW THAT NOW.

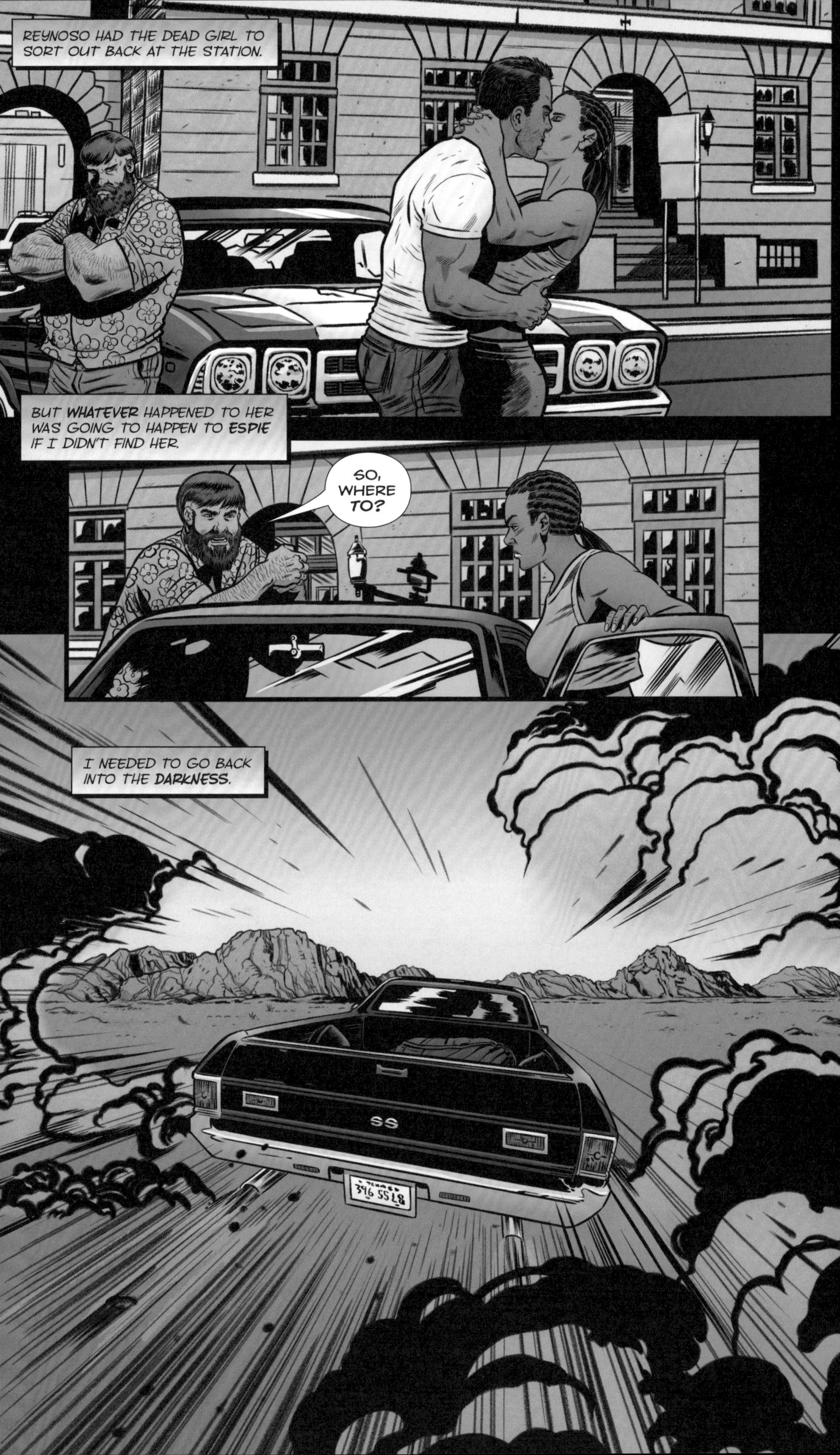
REYNOSO HAD THE DEAD GIRL TO SORT OUT BACK AT THE STATION.
BUT WHATEVER HAPPENED TO HER WAS GOING TO HAPPEN TO ESPIE IF I DIDN'T FIND HER.
SO, WHERE TO?
I NEEDED TO GO BACK INTO THE DARKNESS.
SS

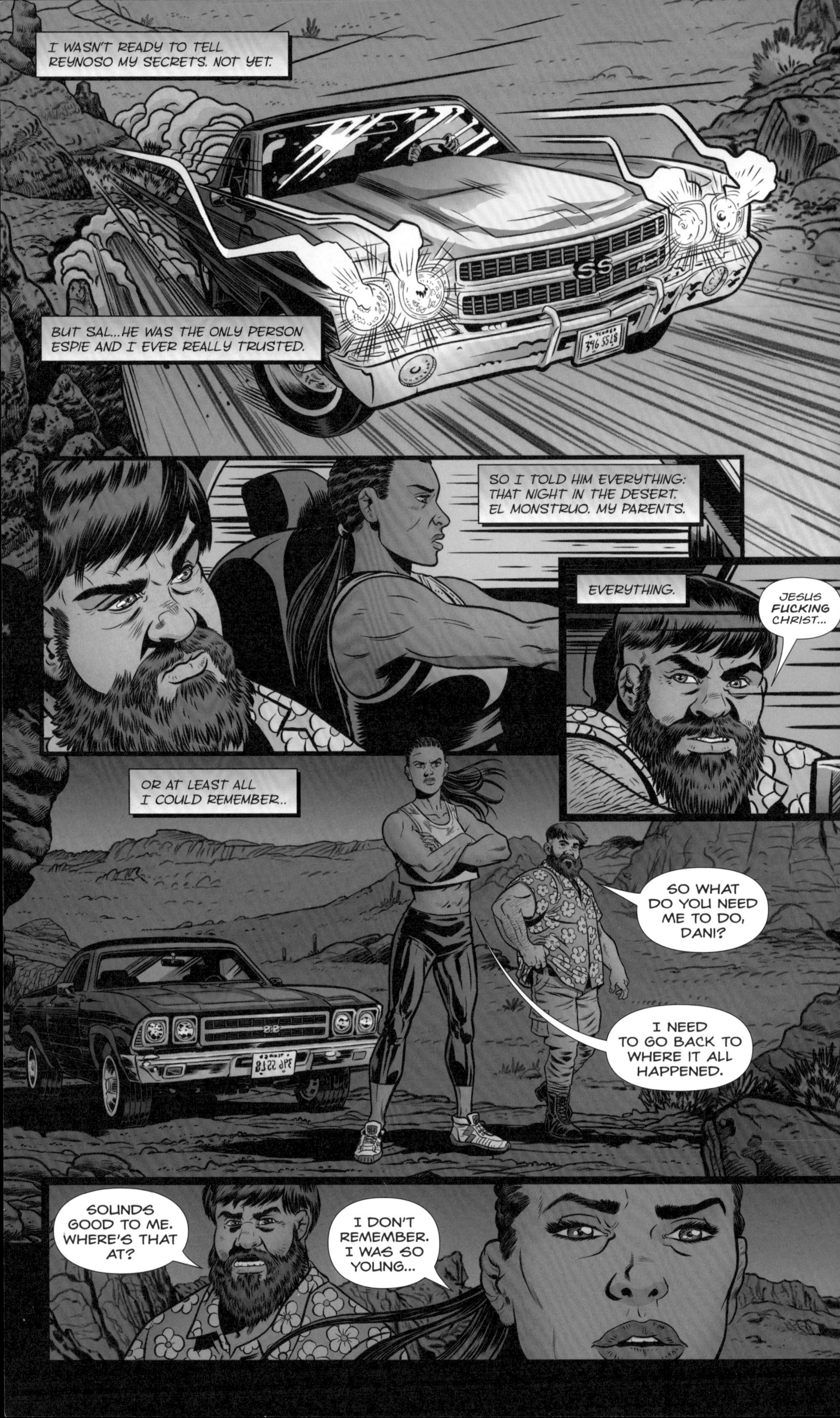

I WASN'T READY TO TELL REYNOSO MY SECRETS. NOT YET.
BUT SAL...HE WAS THE ONLY PERSON ESPIE AND I EVER REALLY TRUSTED.
SO I TOLD HIM EVERYTHING: THAT NIGHT IN THE DESERT. EL MONSTRUO. MY PARENTS.
EVERYTHING.
JESUS FUCKING CHRIST...
OR AT LEAST ALL I COULD REMEMBER...
SO WHAT DO YOU NEED ME TO DO, DANI?
I NEED TO GO BACK TO WHERE IT ALL HAPPENED.
SOUNDS GOOD TO ME. WHERE'S THAT AT?
I DON'T REMEMBER. I WAS SO YOUNG...

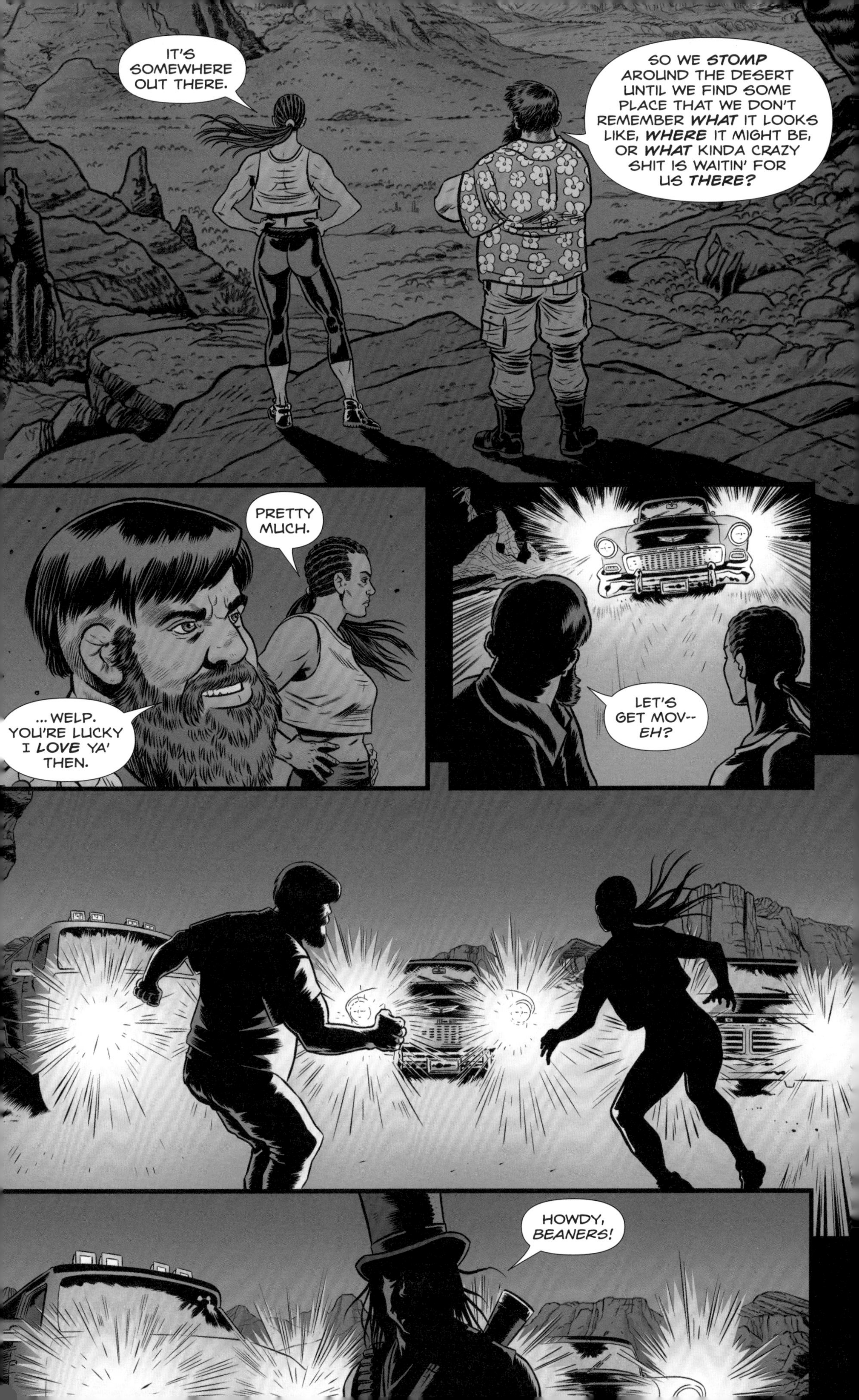
IT'S SOMEWHERE OUT THERE.
SO WE STOMP AROUND THE DESERT UNTIL WE FIND SOME PLACE THAT WE DON'T REMEMBER WHAT IT LOOKS LIKE, WHERE IT MIGHT BE, OR WHAT KINDA CRAZY SHIT IS WAITIN' FOR US THERE?
PRETTY MUCH.
...WELP. YOU'RE LUCKY I LOVE YA' THEN.
LET'S GET MOV-- EH?
HOWDY, BEANERS!

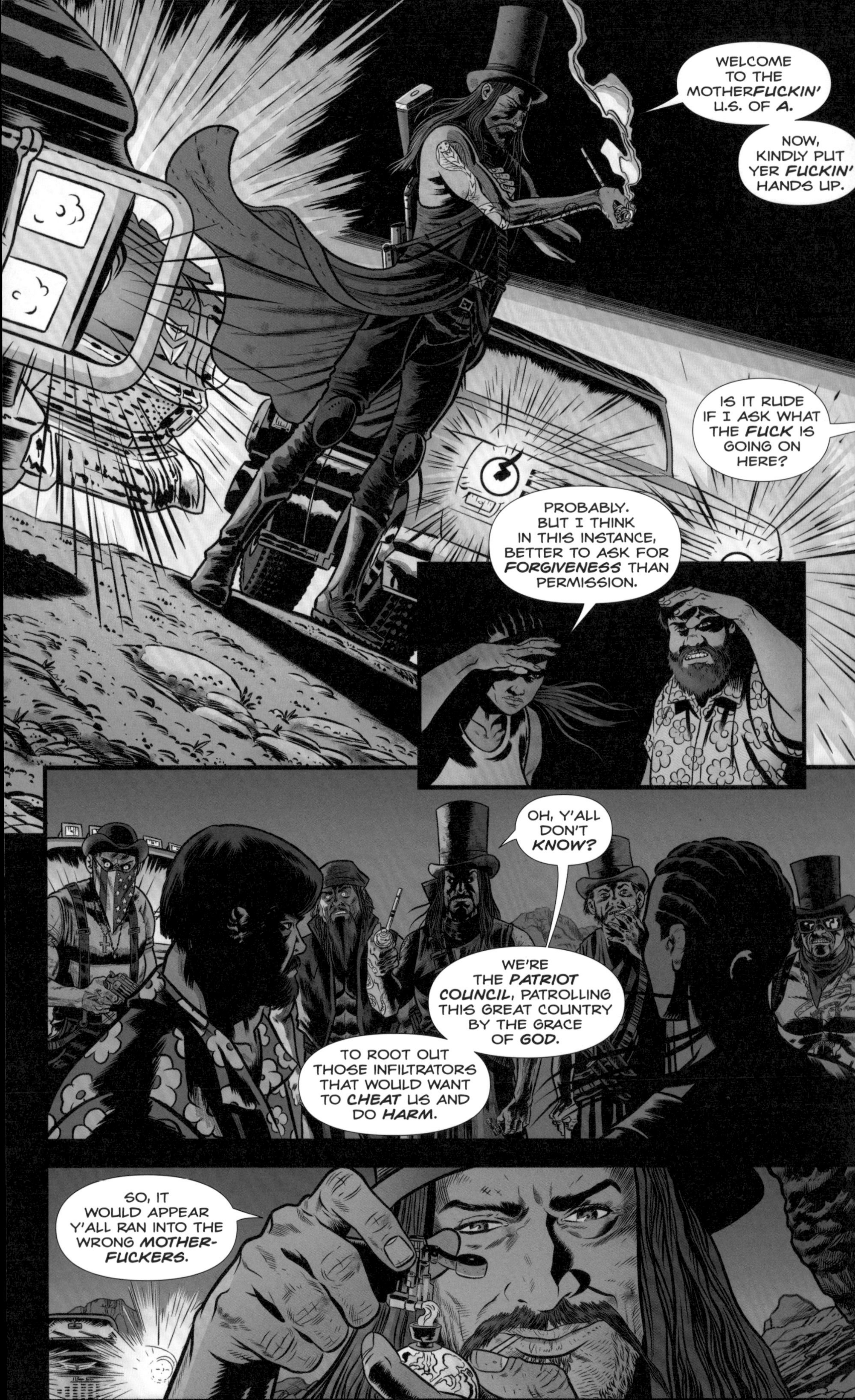
WELCOME TO THE MOTHERFUCKIN' U.S. OF A.
NOW, KINDLY PUT YER FUCKIN' HANDS UP.
IS IT RUDE IF I ASK WHAT THE FUCK IS GOING ON HERE?
PROBABLY. BUT I THINK IN THIS INSTANCE, BETTER TO ASK FOR FORGIVENESS THAN PERMISSION.
OH, Y'ALL DON'T KNOW?
WE'RE THE PATRIOT COUNCIL, PATROLLING THIS GREAT COUNTRY BY THE GRACE OF GOD.
TO ROOT OUT THOSE INFILTRATORS THAT WOULD WANT TO CHEAT US AND DO HARM.
SO, IT WOULD APPEAR Y'ALL RAN INTO THE WRONG MOTHER-FUCKERS.

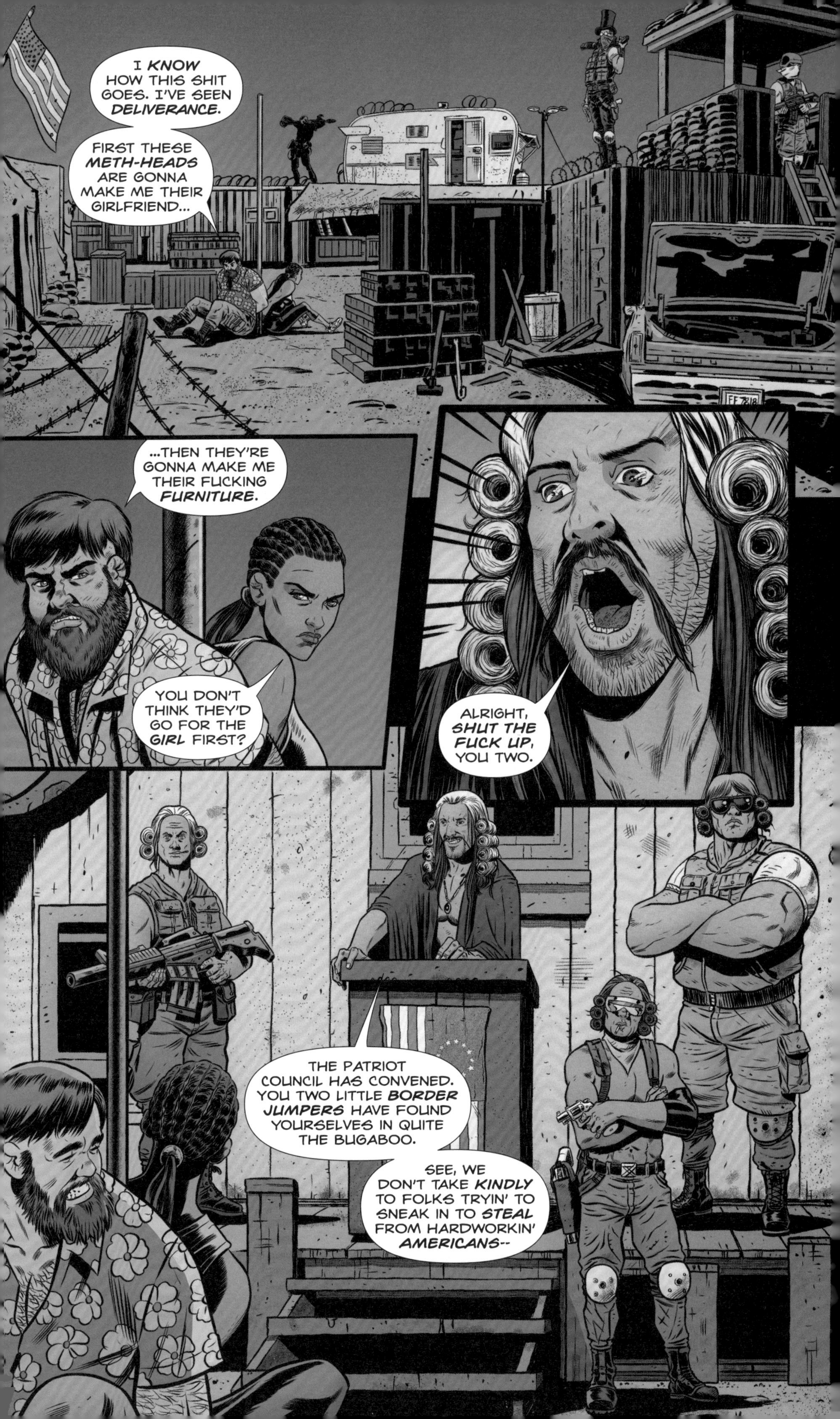
I KNOW HOW THIS SHIT GOES. I'VE SEEN DELIVERANCE.
FIRST THESE METH-HEADS ARE GONNA MAKE ME THEIR GIRLFRIEND...
...THEN THEY'RE GONNA MAKE ME THEIR FUCKING FURNITURE.
YOU DON'T THINK THEY'D GO FOR THE GIRL FIRST?
ALRIGHT, SHUT THE FUCK UP, YOU TWO.
THE PATRIOT COUNCIL HAS CONVENED. YOU TWO LITTLE BORDER JUMPERS HAVE FOUND YOURSELVES IN QUITE THE BUGABOO.
SEE, WE DON'T TAKE KINDLY TO FOLKS TRYIN' TO SNEAK IN TO STEAL FROM HARDWORKIN' AMERICANS--

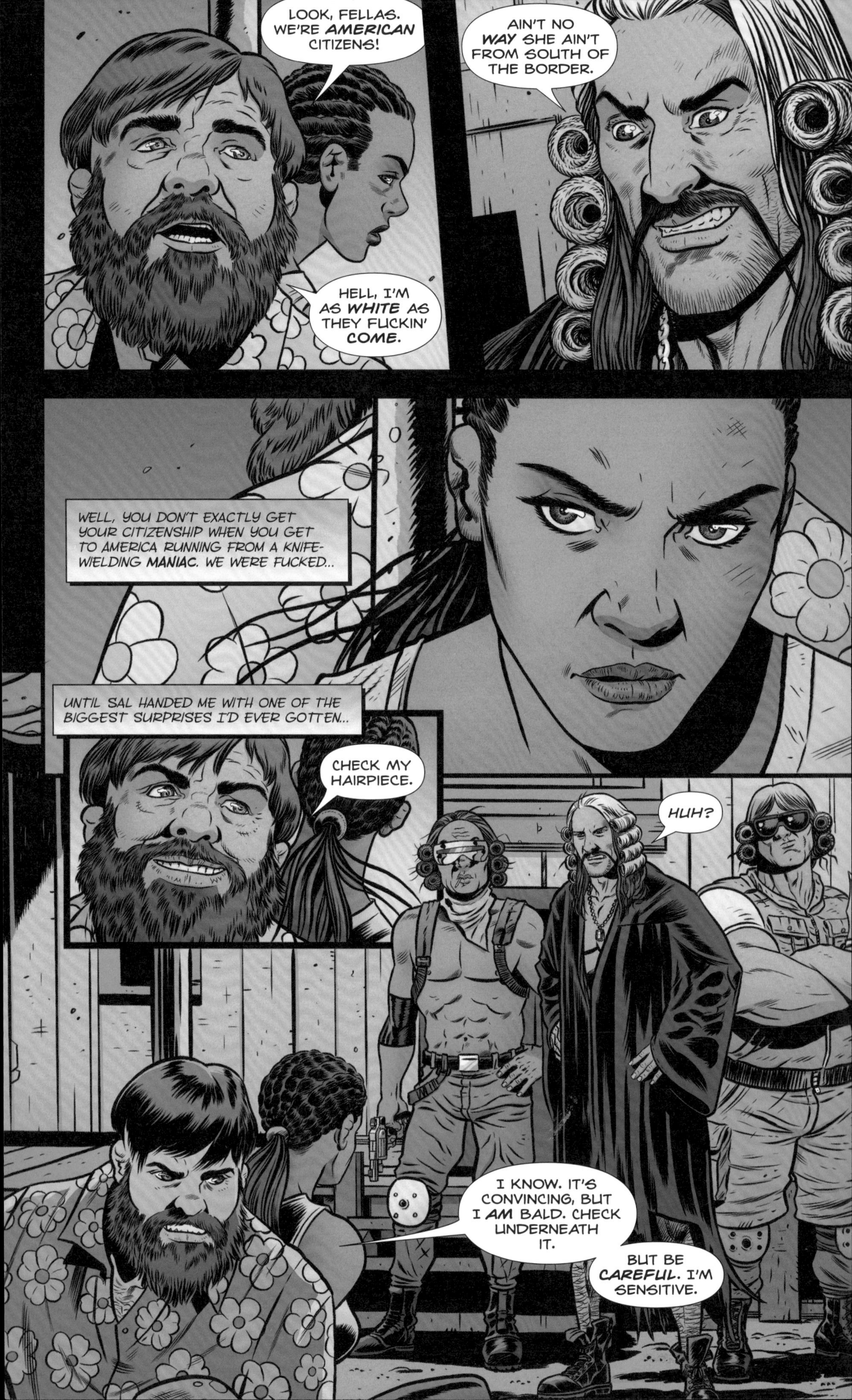

LOOK, FELLAS. WE'RE AMERICAN CITIZENS!
HELL, I'M AS WHITE AS THEY FUCKIN' COME.
AIN'T NO WAY SHE AIN'T FROM SOUTH OF THE BORDER.
WELL, YOU DON'T EXACTLY GET YOUR CITIZENSHIP WHEN YOU GET TO AMERICA RUNNING FROM A KNIFE-WIELDING MANIAC. WE WERE FUCKED...
UNTIL SAL HANDED ME WITH ONE OF THE BIGGEST SURPRISES I'D EVER GOTTEN...
CHECK MY HAIRPIECE.
HUH?
I KNOW. IT'S CONVINCING, BUT I AM BALD. CHECK UNDERNEATH IT.
BUT BE CAREFUL. I'M SENSITIVE.

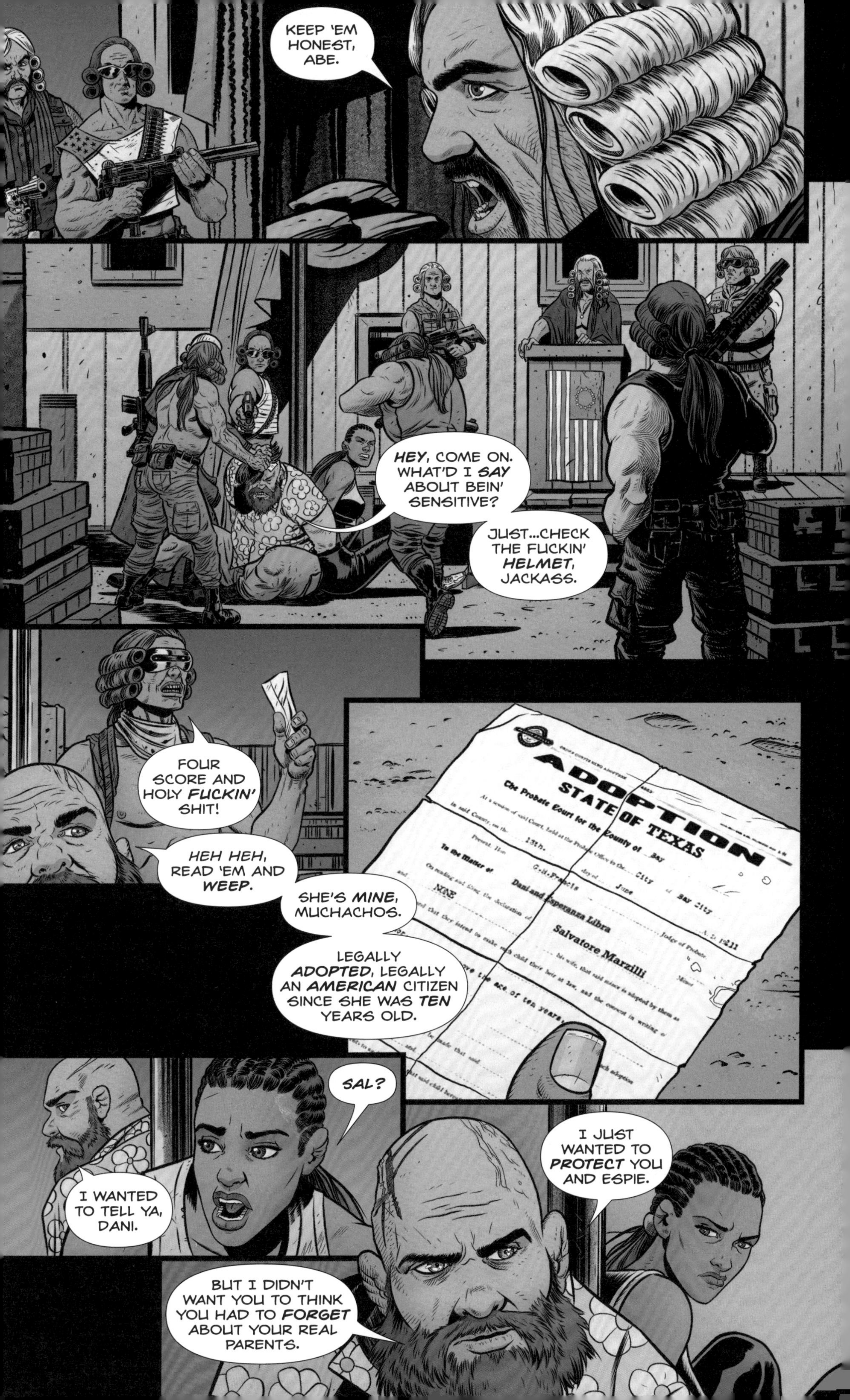
KEEP 'EM HONEST, ABE.
HEY, COME ON. WHAT'D I SAY ABOUT BEIN' SENSITIVE?
JUST...CHECK THE FUCKIN' HELMET, JACKASS.
FOUR SCORE AND HOLY FUCKIN' SHIT!
HEH HEH, READ 'EM AND WEEP.
SHE'S MINE, MUCHACHOS.
LEGALLY ADOPTED, LEGALLY AN AMERICAN CITIZEN SINCE SHE WAS TEN YEARS OLD.
ADOPTION
STATE OF TEXAS
Dani and Esperanza Libra
Salvatore Marzilli
SAL?
I WANTED TO TELL YA, DANI.
I JUST WANTED TO PROTECT YOU AND ESPIE.
BUT I DIDN'T WANT YOU TO THINK YOU HAD TO FORGET ABOUT YOUR REAL PARENTS.

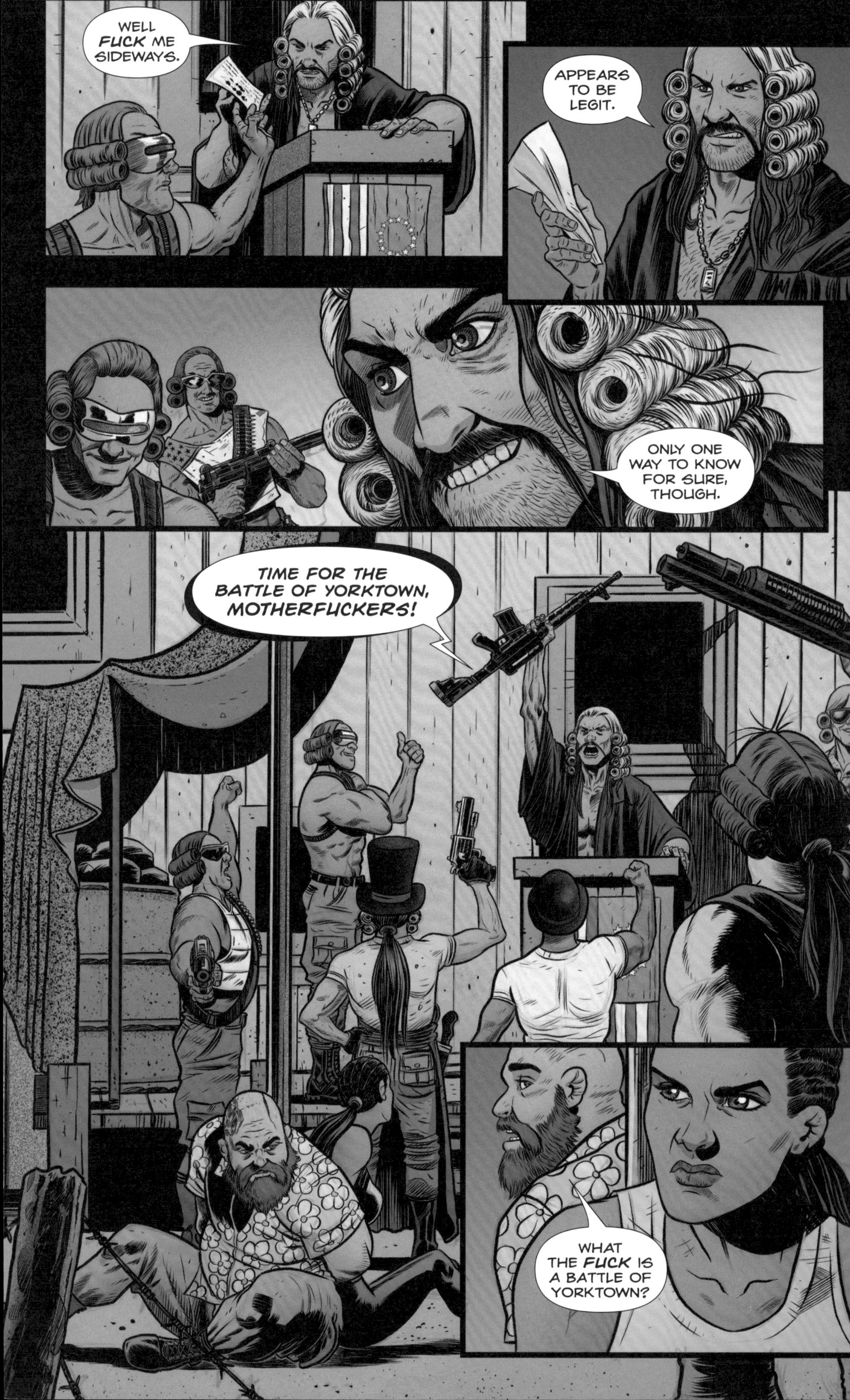
WELL FUCK ME SIDEWAYS.
APPEARS TO BE LEGIT.
ONLY ONE WAY TO KNOW FOR SURE, THOUGH.
TIME FOR THE BATTLE OF YORKTOWN, MOTHERFUCKERS!
WHAT THE FUCK IS A BATTLE OF YORKTOWN?

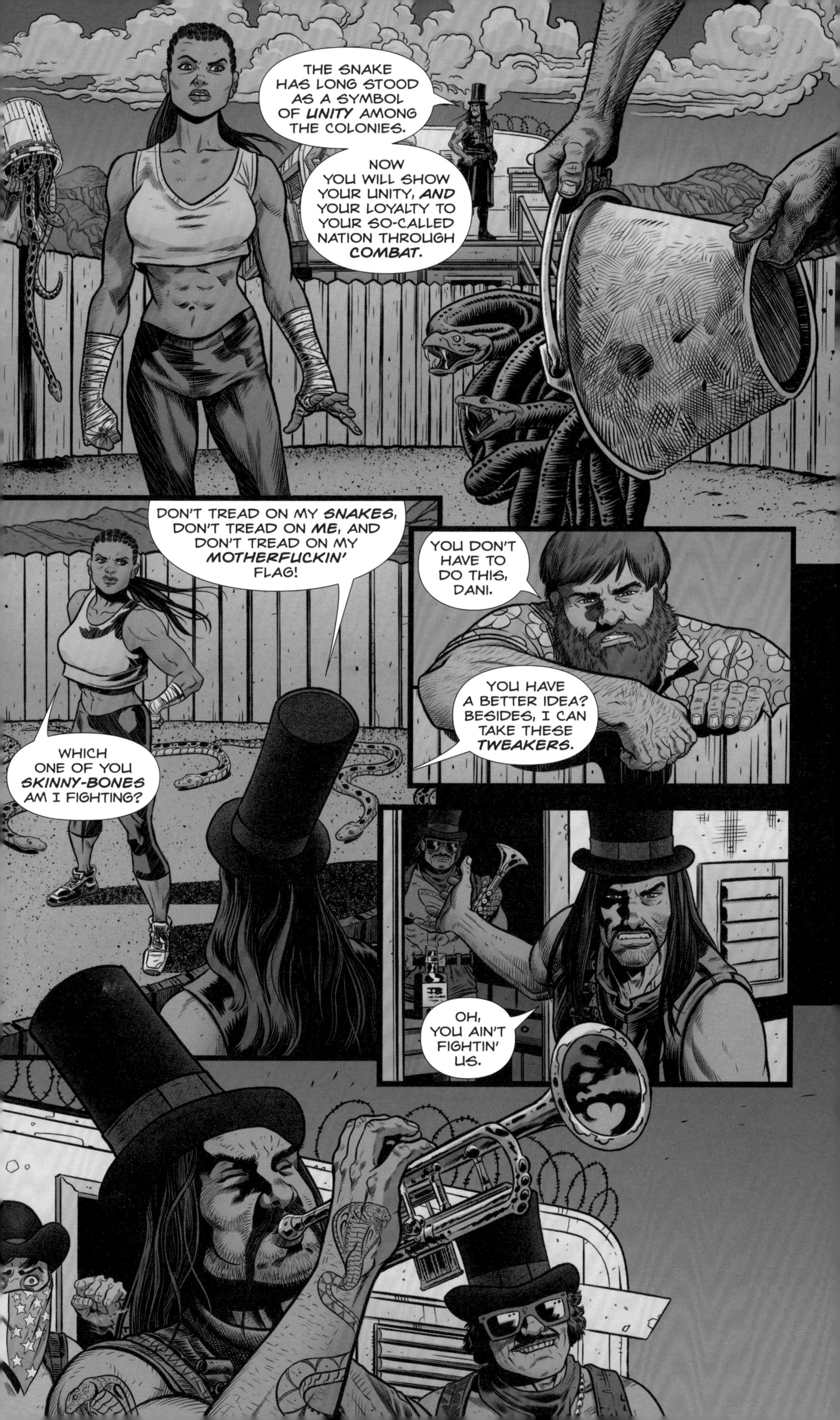
THE SNAKE HAS LONG STOOD AS A SYMBOL OF *UNITY* AMONG THE COLONIES.
NOW YOU WILL SHOW YOUR UNITY, *AND* YOUR LOYALTY TO YOUR SO-CALLED NATION THROUGH *COMBAT*.
DON'T TREAD ON MY *SNAKES*, DON'T TREAD ON *ME*, AND DON'T TREAD ON MY *MOTHERFUCKIN'* FLAG!
WHICH ONE OF YOU *SKINNY-BONES* AM I FIGHTING?
YOU DON'T HAVE TO DO THIS, DANI.
YOU HAVE A BETTER IDEA? BESIDES, I CAN TAKE THESE *TWEAKERS*.
OH, YOU AIN'T FIGHTIN' US.

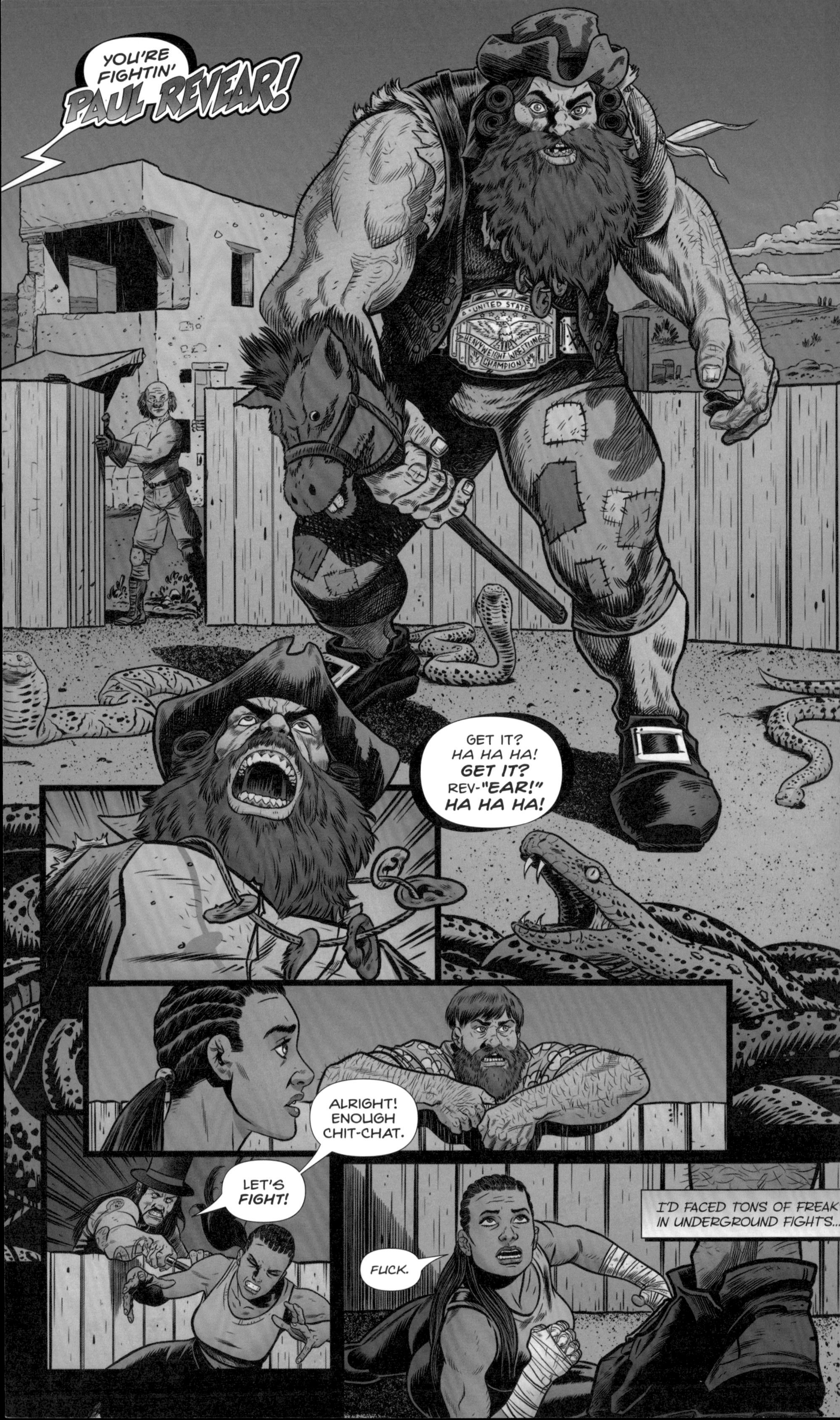
YOU'RE FIGHTIN' PAUL REVEAR!
GET IT? HA HA HA! GET IT? REV-"EAR!" HA HA HA!
ALRIGHT! ENOUGH CHIT-CHAT.
LET'S FIGHT!
FUCK.
I'D FACED TONS OF FREAK IN UNDERGROUND FIGHTS...

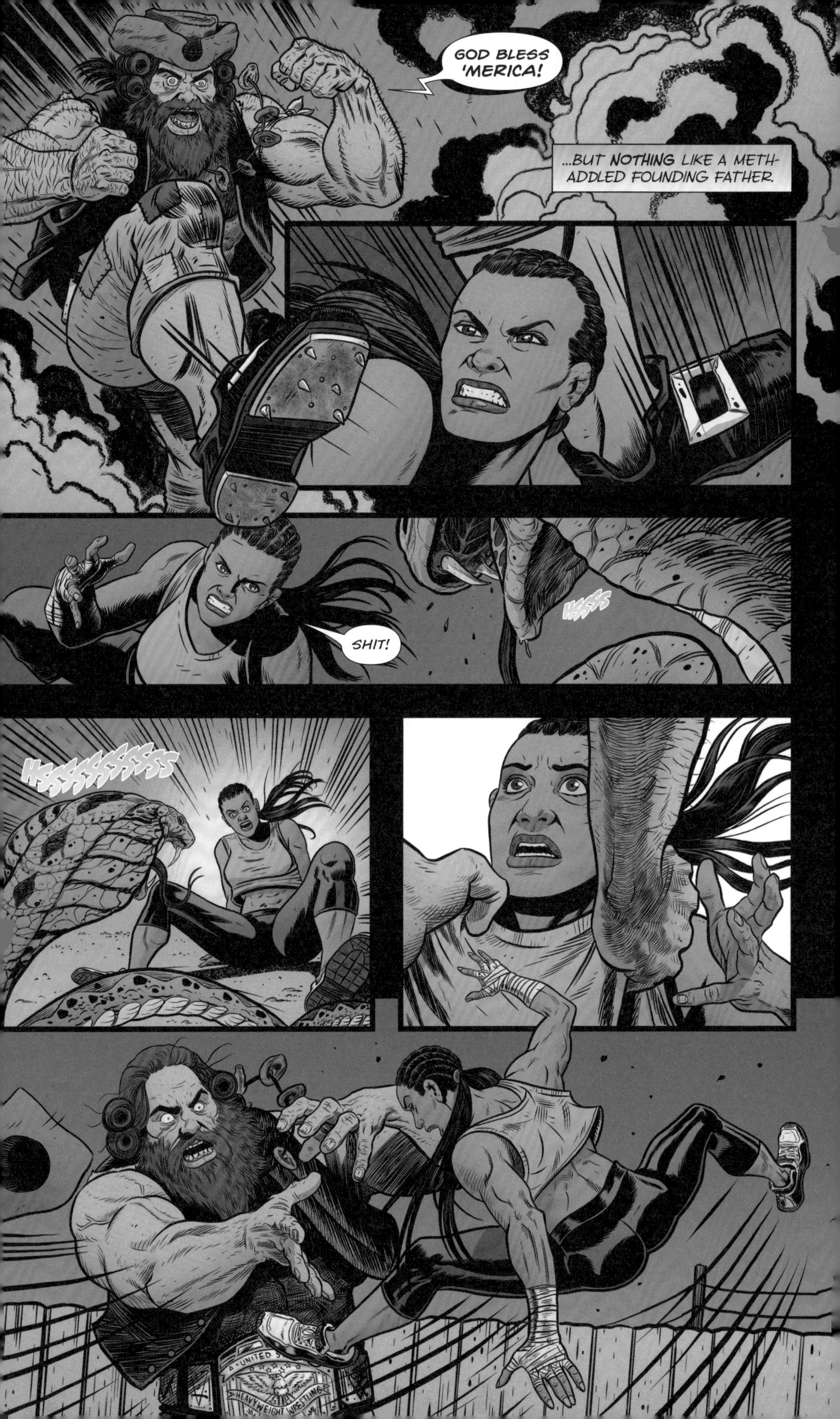
GOD BLESS 'MERICA!
...BUT NOTHING LIKE A METH-ADDLED FOUNDING FATHER.
SHIT!
HSSSS
HSSSSSSSSSSS

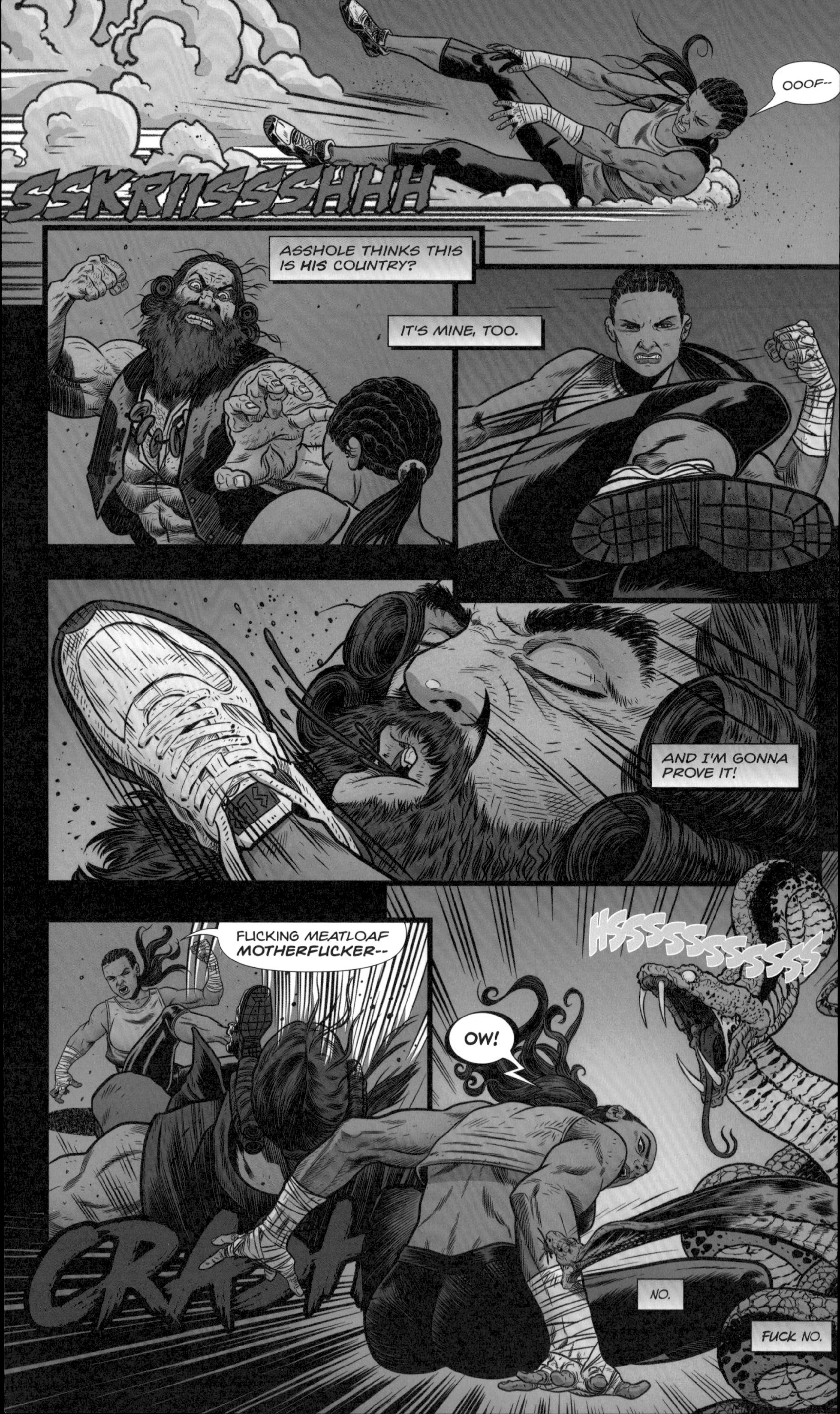
SSKRIISSSHHH
OOOF--
ASSHOLE THINKS THIS IS HIS COUNTRY?
IT'S MINE, TOO.
AND I'M GONNA PROVE IT!
FUCKING MEATLOAF MOTHERFUCKER--
CRASH
OW!
HSSSSSSSSSSS
NO.
FUCK NO.

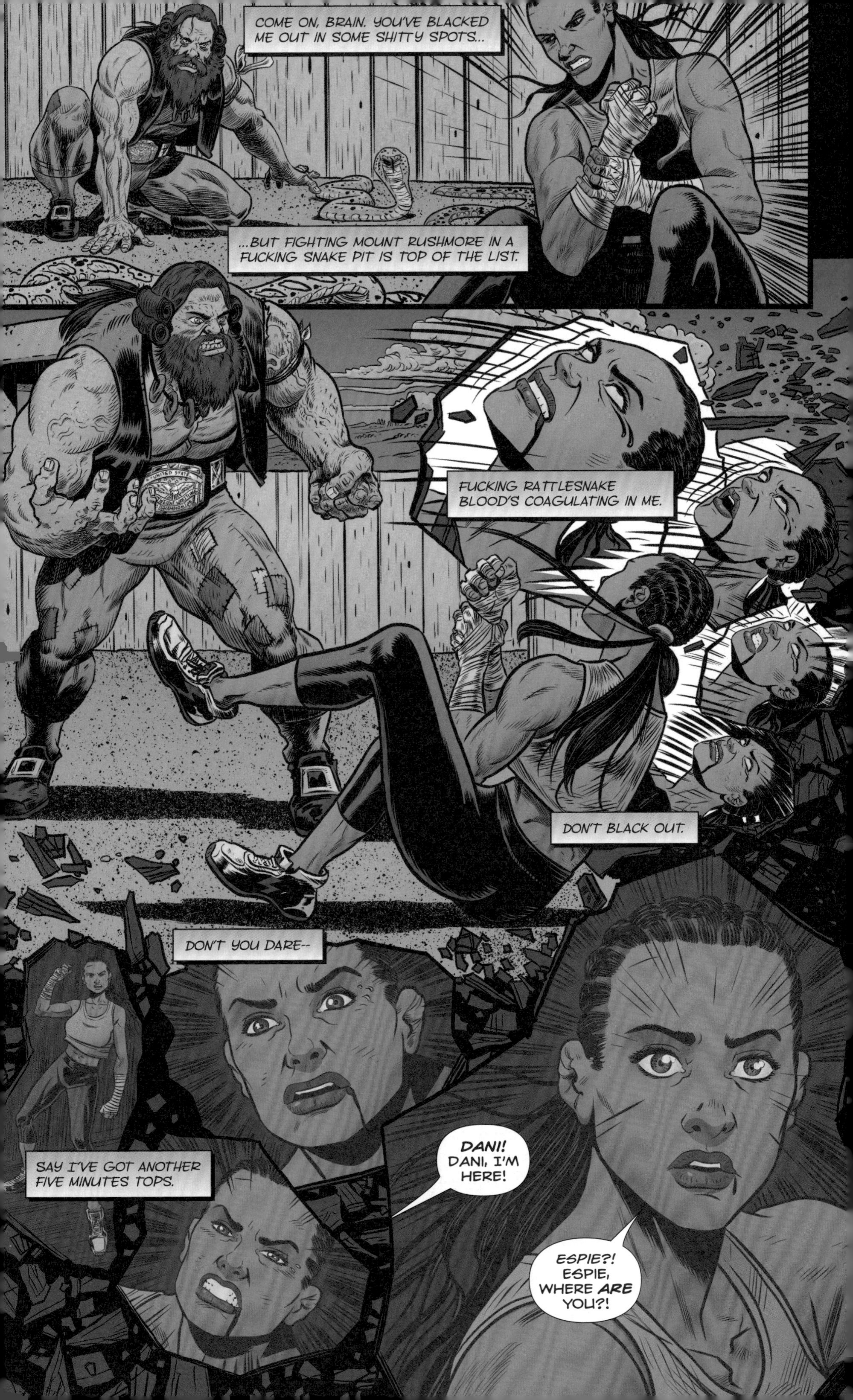
COME ON, BRAIN. YOU'VE BLACKED ME OUT IN SOME SHITTY SPOTS...
...BUT FIGHTING MOUNT RUSHMORE IN A FUCKING SNAKE PIT IS TOP OF THE LIST.
FUCKING RATTLESNAKE BLOOD'S COAGULATING IN ME.
DON'T BLACK OUT.
DON'T YOU DARE--
SAY I'VE GOT ANOTHER FIVE MINUTES TOPS.
DANI! DANI, I'M HERE!
ESPIE?! ESPIE, WHERE ARE YOU?!

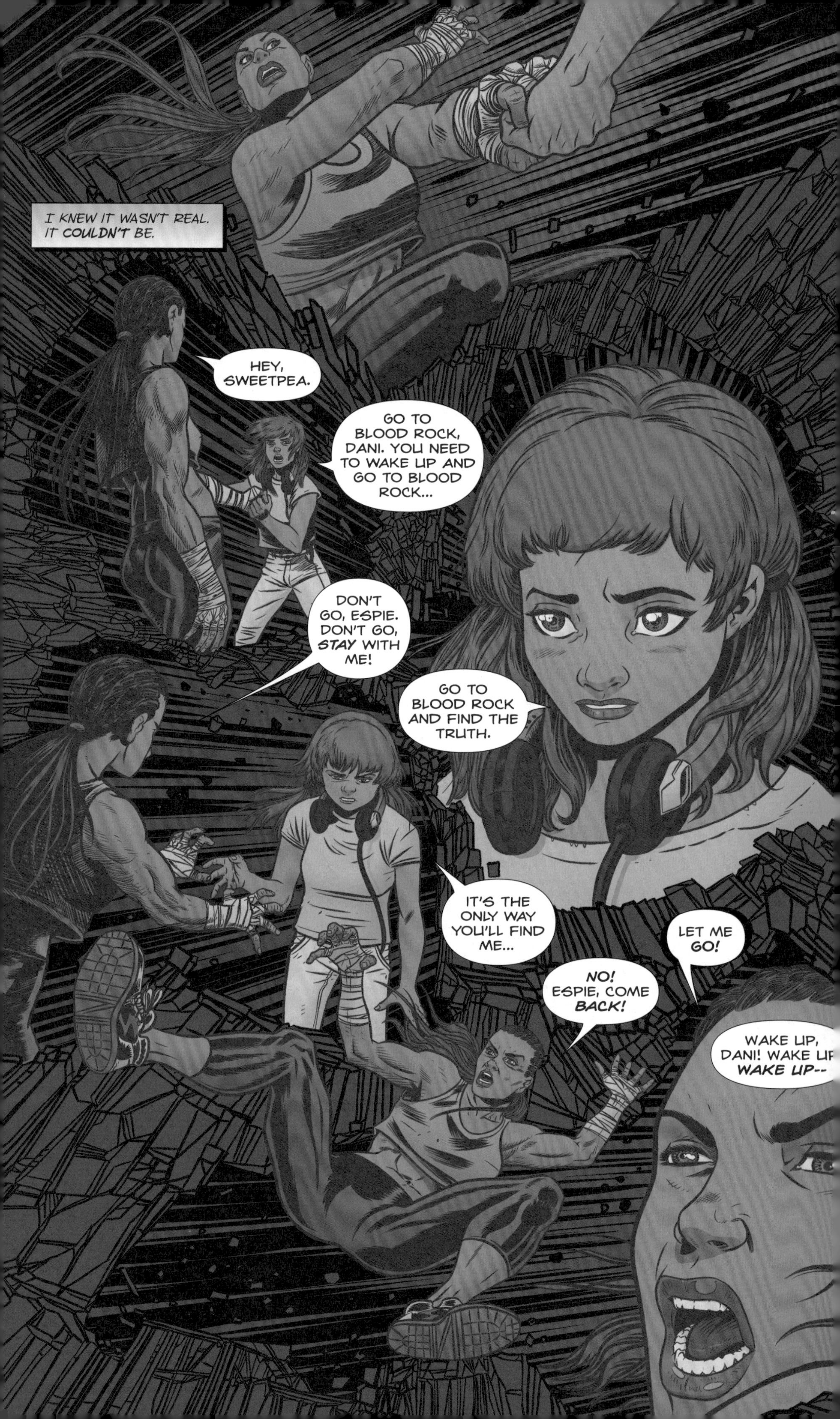
I KNEW IT WASN'T REAL. IT *COULDN'T* BE.
HEY, SWEETPEA.
GO TO BLOOD ROCK, DANI. YOU NEED TO WAKE UP AND GO TO BLOOD ROCK...
DON'T GO, ESPIE. DON'T GO, *STAY* WITH ME!
GO TO BLOOD ROCK AND FIND THE TRUTH.
IT'S THE ONLY WAY YOU'LL FIND ME...
LET ME *GO!*
NO! ESPIE, COME *BACK!*
WAKE UP, DANI! WAKE UP *WAKE UP--*

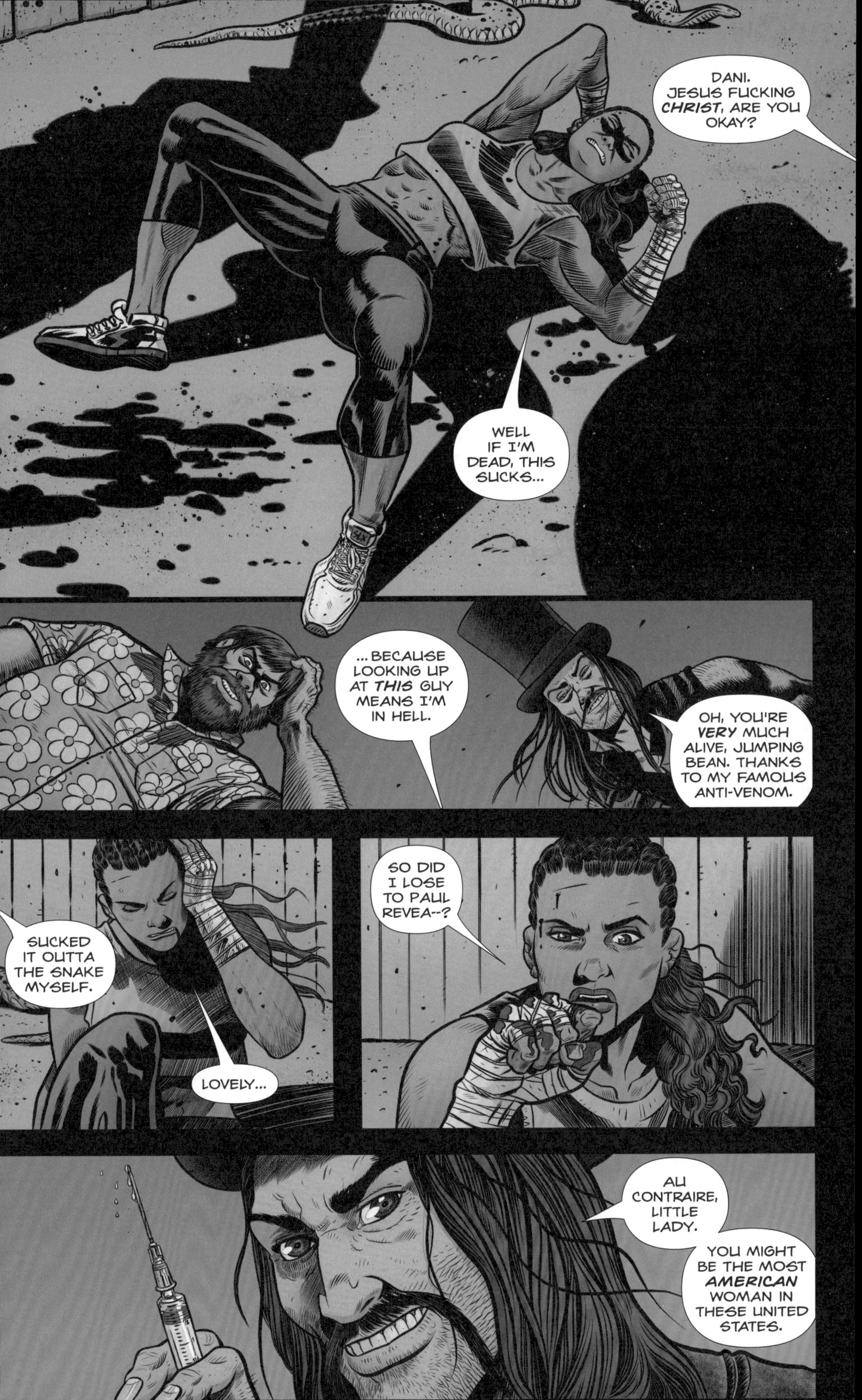
DANI. JESUS FUCKING CHRIST, ARE YOU OKAY?
WELL IF I'M DEAD, THIS SUCKS...
...BECAUSE LOOKING UP AT THIS GUY MEANS I'M IN HELL.
OH, YOU'RE VERY MUCH ALIVE, JUMPING BEAN. THANKS TO MY FAMOUS ANTI-VENOM.
SUCKED IT OUTTA THE SNAKE MYSELF.
LOVELY...
SO DID I LOSE TO PAUL REVEA--?
AU CONTRAIRE, LITTLE LADY.
YOU MIGHT BE THE MOST AMERICAN WOMAN IN THESE UNITED STATES.

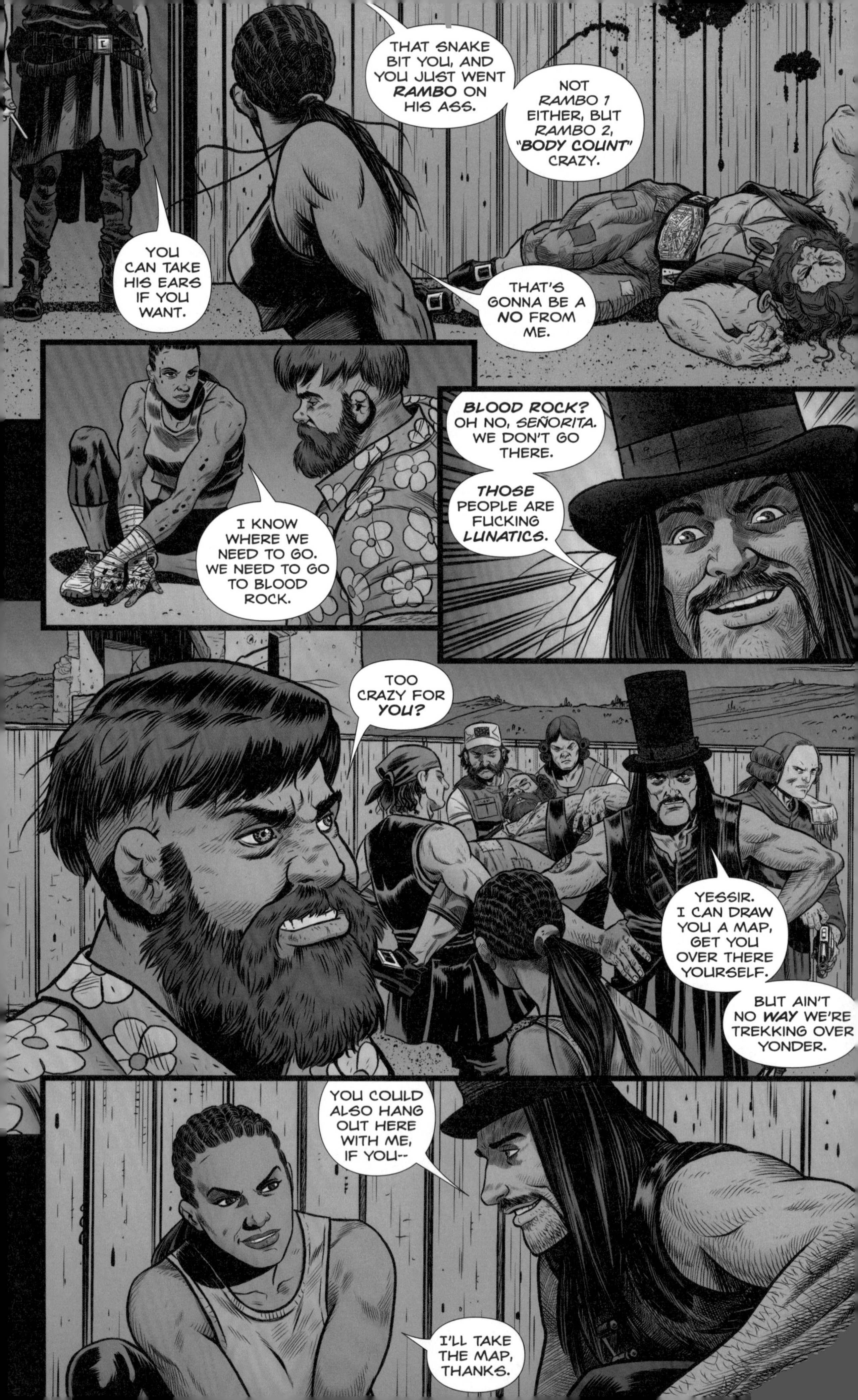
THAT SNAKE BIT YOU, AND YOU JUST WENT RAMBO ON HIS ASS.
NOT RAMBO 1 EITHER, BUT RAMBO 2, "BODY COUNT" CRAZY.
YOU CAN TAKE HIS EARS IF YOU WANT.
THAT'S GONNA BE A NO FROM ME.
I KNOW WHERE WE NEED TO GO. WE NEED TO GO TO BLOOD ROCK.
BLOOD ROCK? OH NO, SEÑORITA. WE DON'T GO THERE.
THOSE PEOPLE ARE FUCKING LUNATICS.
TOO CRAZY FOR YOU?
YESSIR. I CAN DRAW YOU A MAP, GET YOU OVER THERE YOURSELF.
BUT AIN'T NO WAY WE'RE TREKKING OVER YONDER.
YOU COULD ALSO HANG OUT HERE WITH ME, IF YOU--
I'LL TAKE THE MAP, THANKS.

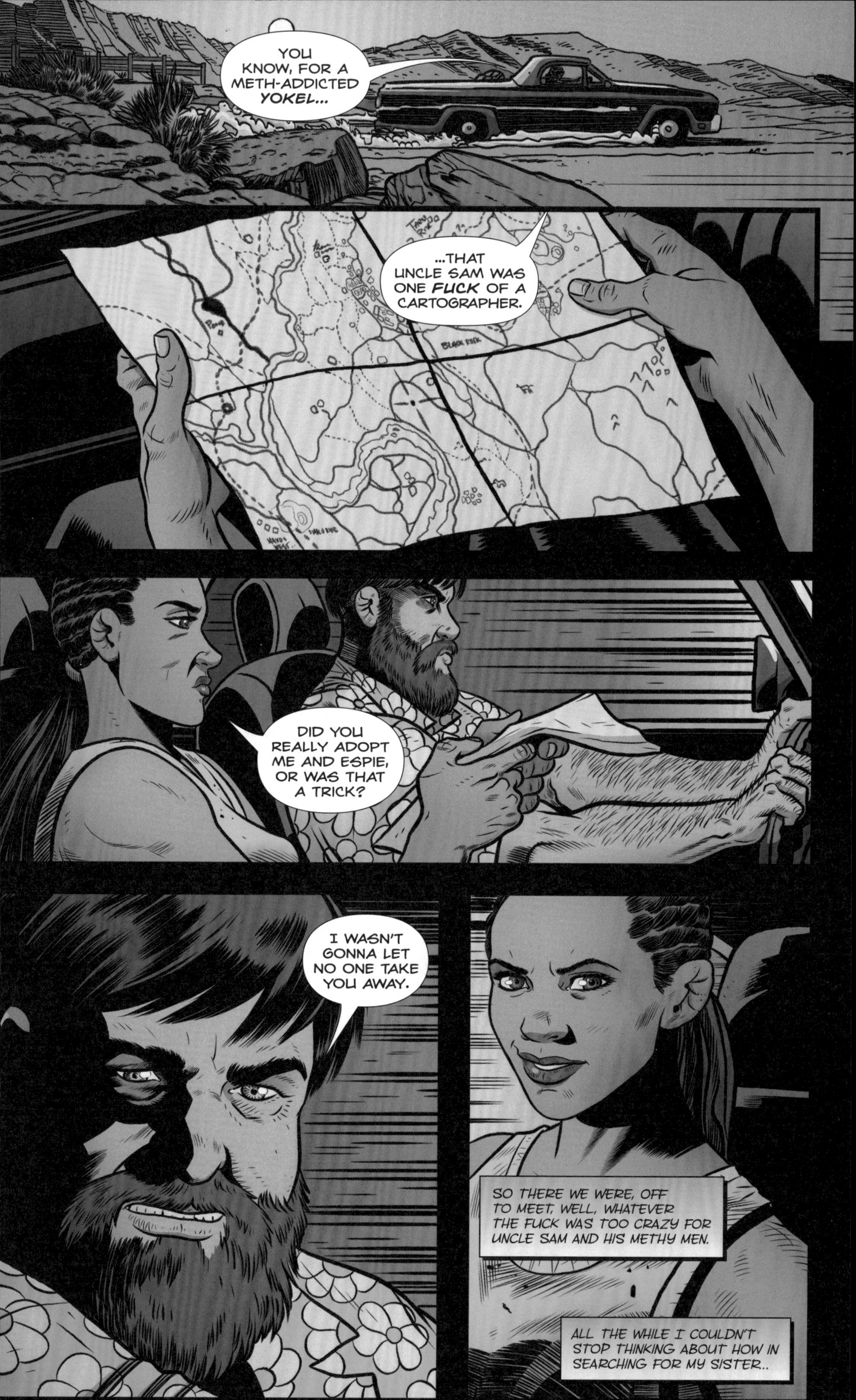
YOU KNOW, FOR A METH-ADDICTED YOKEL...
...THAT UNCLE SAM WAS ONE FUCK OF A CARTOGRAPHER.
DID YOU REALLY ADOPT ME AND ESPIE, OR WAS THAT A TRICK?
I WASN'T GONNA LET NO ONE TAKE YOU AWAY.
SO THERE WE WERE, OFF TO MEET, WELL, WHATEVER THE FUCK WAS TOO CRAZY FOR UNCLE SAM AND HIS METHY MEN.
ALL THE WHILE I COULDN'T STOP THINKING ABOUT HOW IN SEARCHING FOR MY SISTER...

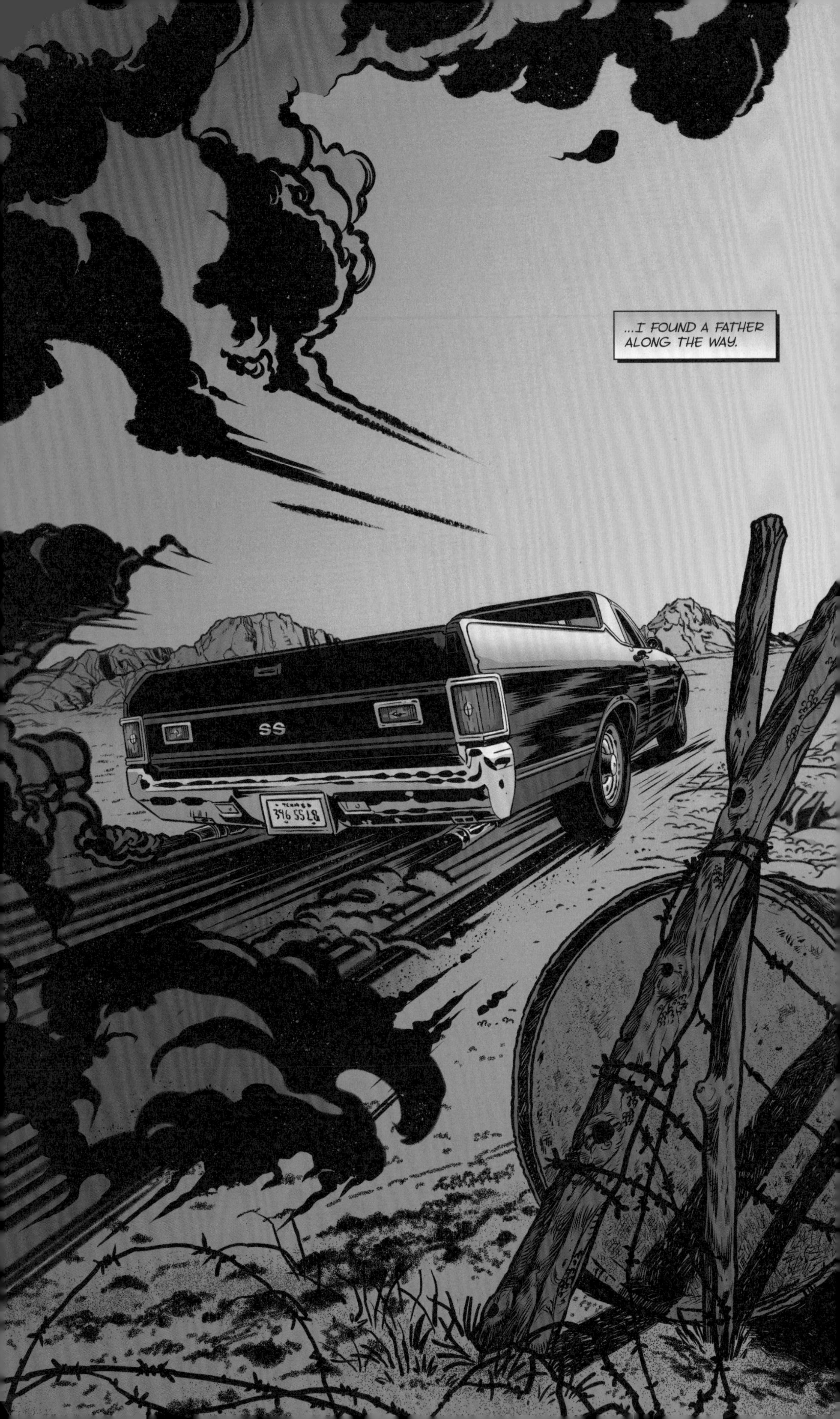
...I FOUND A FATHER ALONG THE WAY.

CHAPTER 4

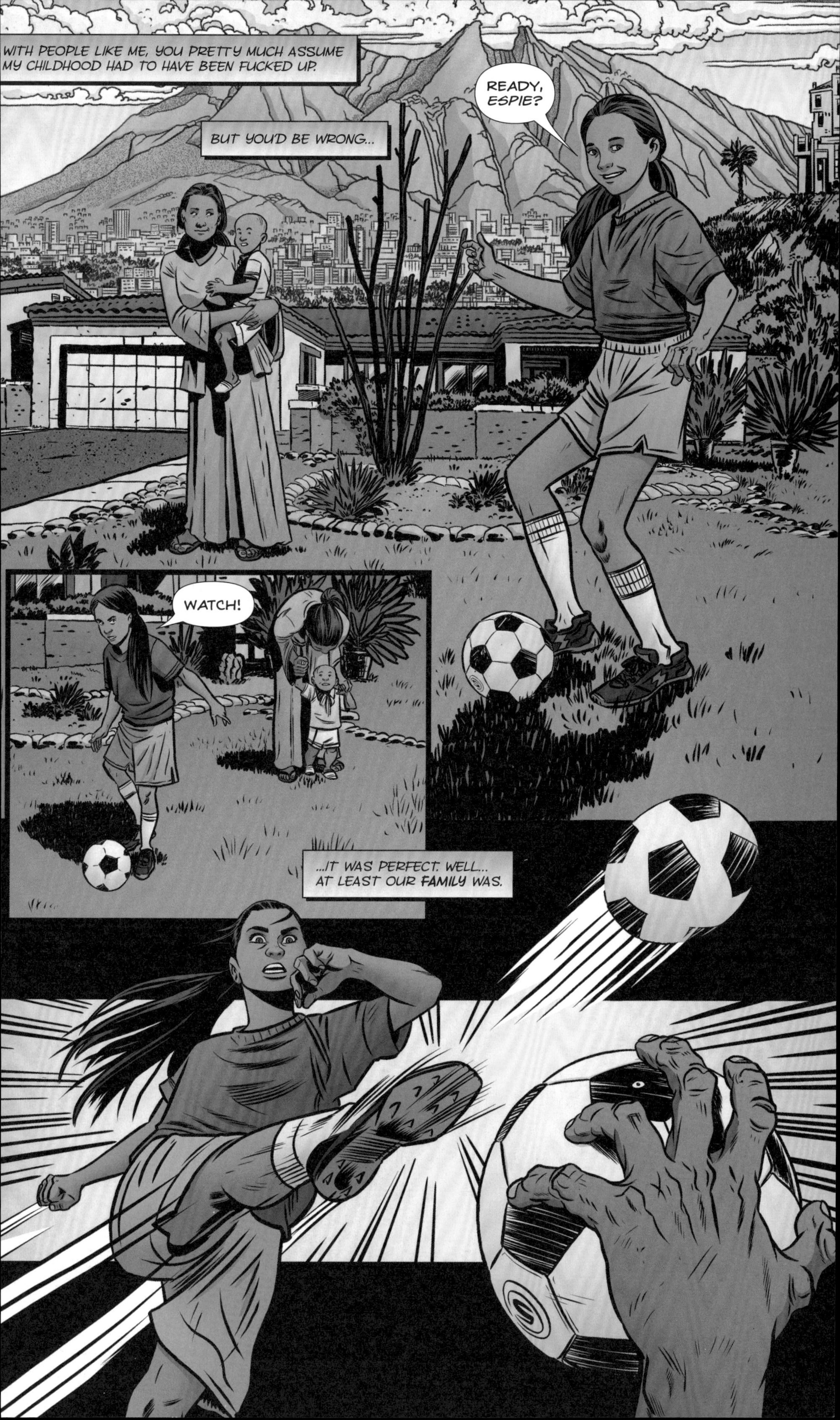
WITH PEOPLE LIKE ME, YOU PRETTY MUCH ASSUME MY CHILDHOOD HAD TO HAVE BEEN FUCKED UP.
BUT YOU'D BE WRONG...
READY, ESPIE?
WATCH!
...IT WAS PERFECT. WELL... AT LEAST OUR FAMILY WAS.

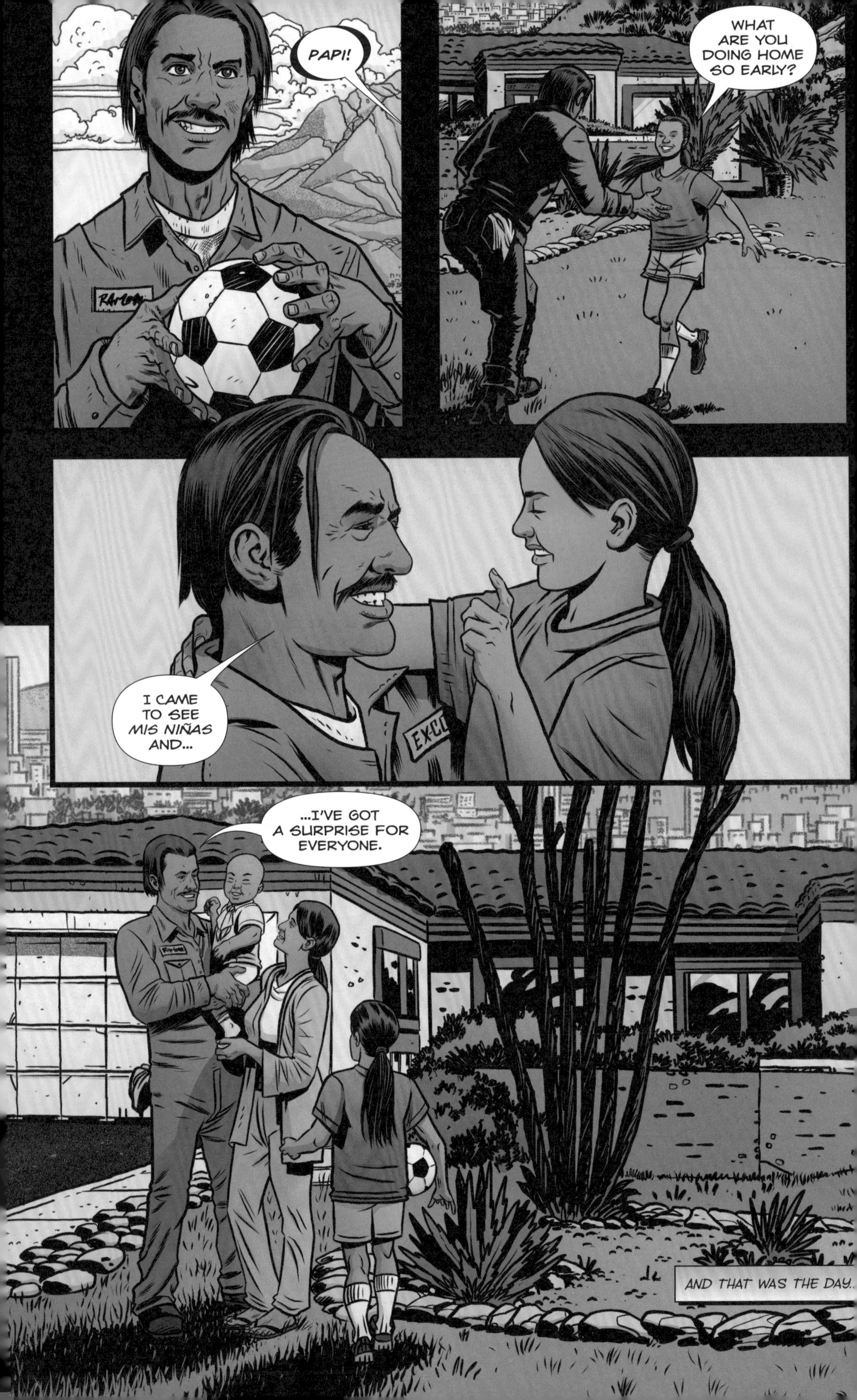
PAPI!
WHAT ARE YOU DOING HOME SO EARLY?
I CAME TO SEE MIS NIÑAS AND...
...I'VE GOT A SURPRISE FOR EVERYONE.
AND THAT WAS THE DAY.

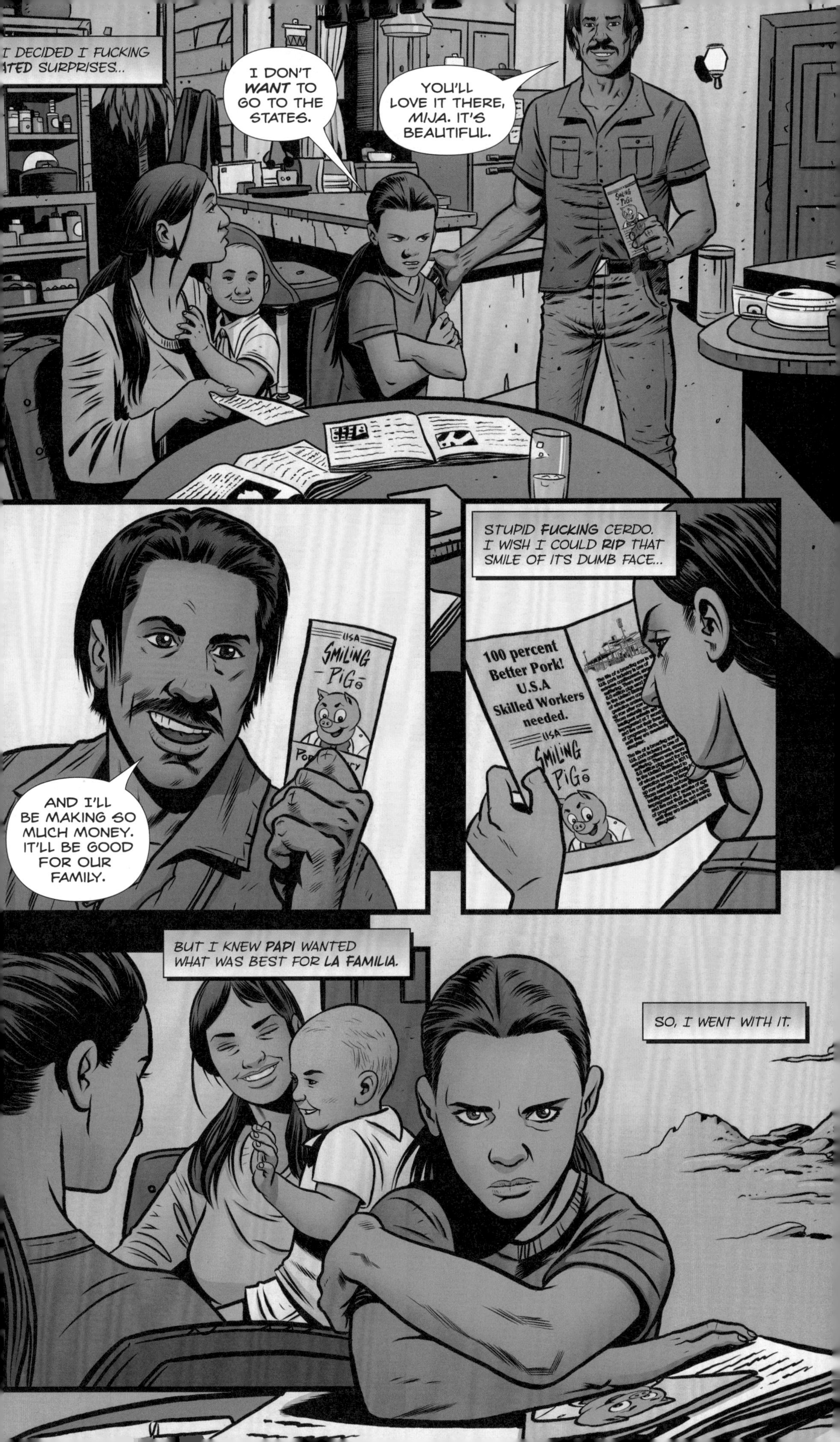

I DECIDED I FUCKING ATED SURPRISES...
I DON'T WANT TO GO TO THE STATES.
YOU'LL LOVE IT THERE, MIJA. IT'S BEAUTIFUL.
USA SMILING PIG
AND I'LL BE MAKING SO MUCH MONEY. IT'LL BE GOOD FOR OUR FAMILY.
STUPID FUCKING CERDO. I WISH I COULD RIP THAT SMILE OF ITS DUMB FACE...
100 percent Better Pork! U.S.A Skilled Workers needed.
USA SMILING PIG
BUT I KNEW PAPI WANTED WHAT WAS BEST FOR LA FAMILIA.
SO, I WENT WITH IT.

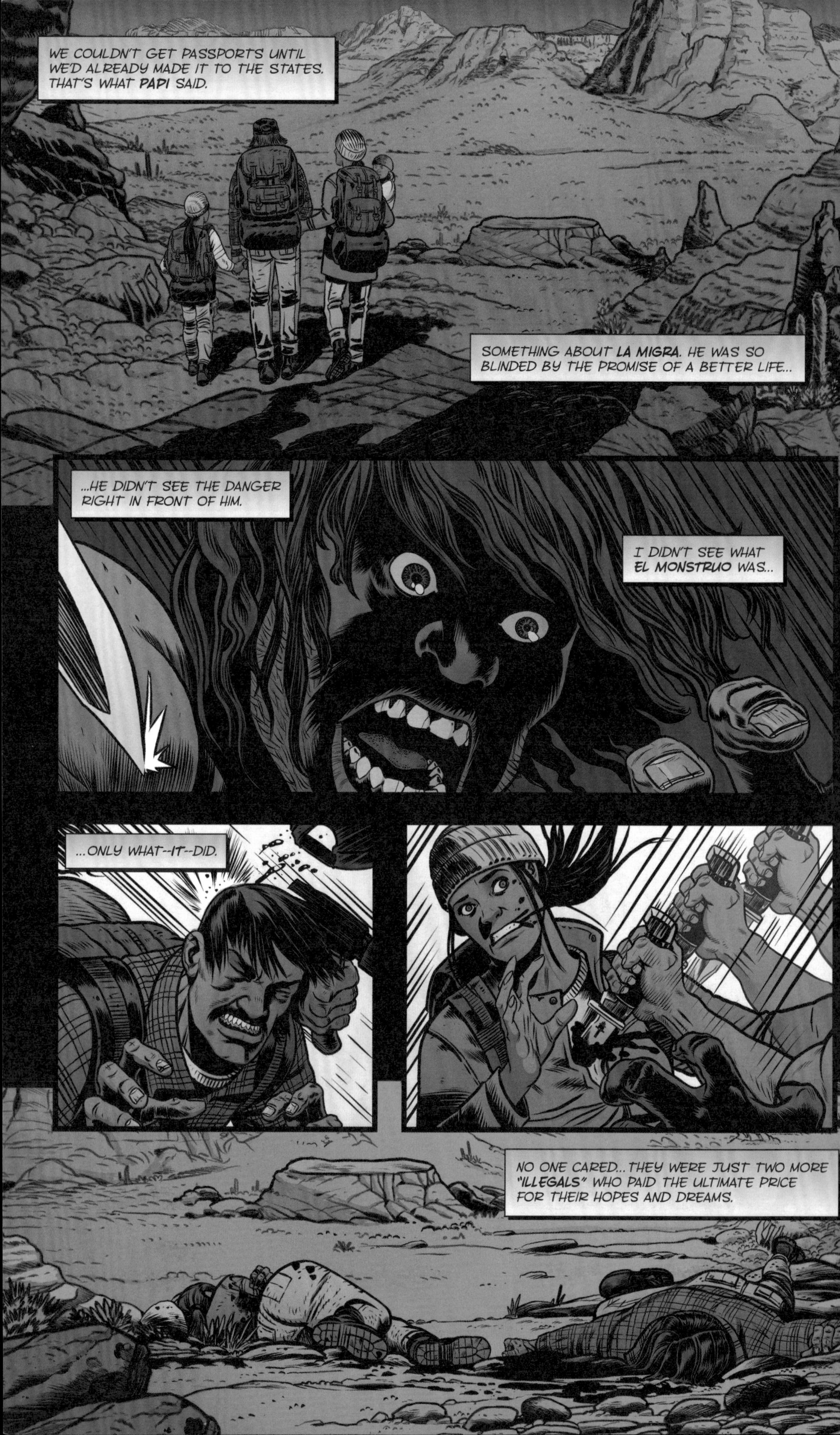
WE COULDN'T GET PASSPORTS UNTIL WE'D ALREADY MADE IT TO THE STATES. THAT'S WHAT PAPI SAID.
SOMETHING ABOUT LA MIGRA. HE WAS SO BLINDED BY THE PROMISE OF A BETTER LIFE...
...HE DIDN'T SEE THE DANGER RIGHT IN FRONT OF HIM.
I DIDN'T SEE WHAT EL MONSTRUO WAS...
...ONLY WHAT--IT--DID.
NO ONE CARED...THEY WERE JUST TWO MORE "ILLEGALS" WHO PAID THE ULTIMATE PRICE FOR THEIR HOPES AND DREAMS.

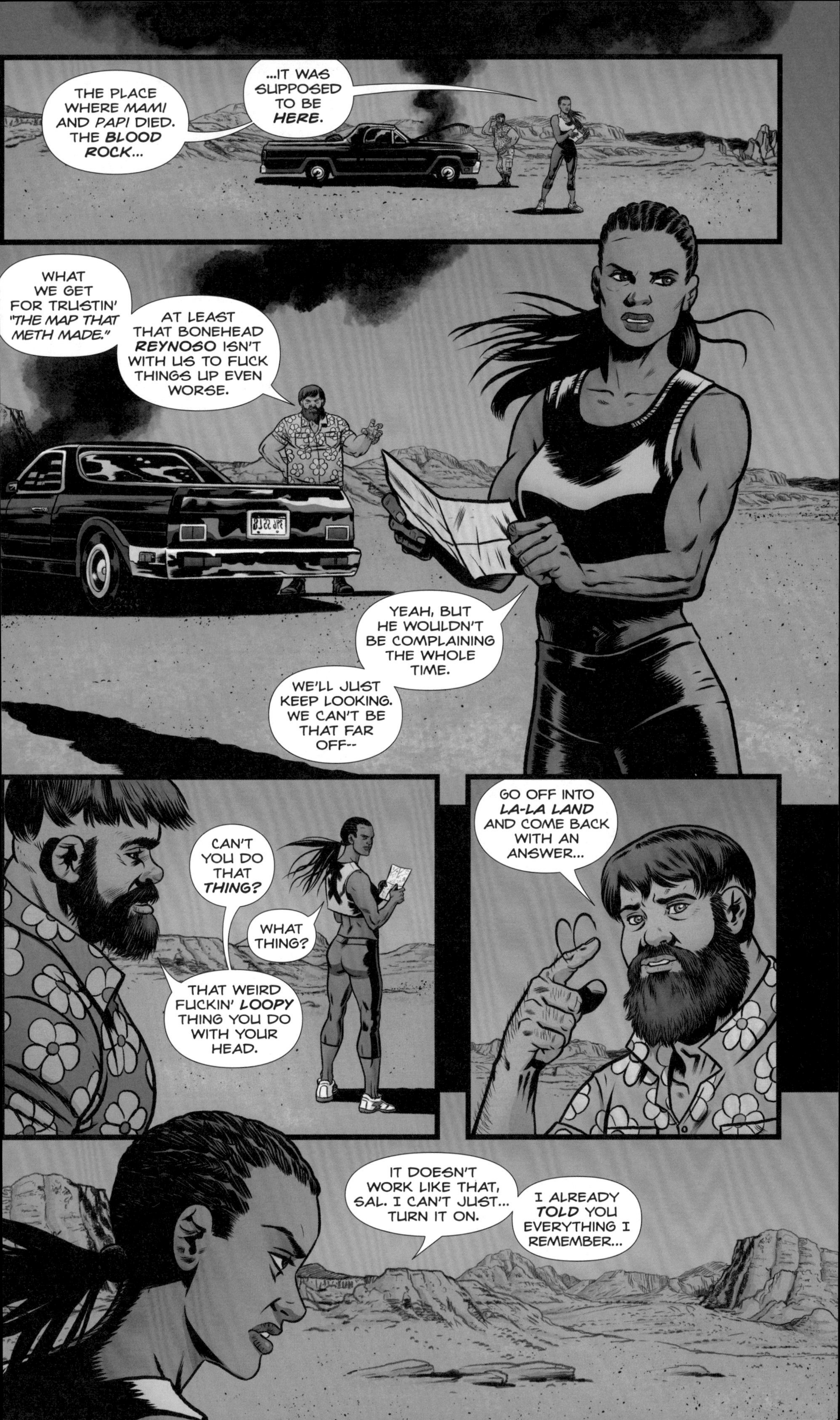
THE PLACE WHERE *MAMI* AND *PAPI* DIED. THE **BLOOD ROCK**...
...IT WAS SUPPOSED TO BE ***HERE***.
WHAT WE GET FOR TRUSTIN' *"THE MAP THAT METH MADE."*
AT LEAST THAT BONEHEAD **REYNOSO** ISN'T WITH US TO FUCK THINGS UP EVEN WORSE.
YEAH, BUT HE WOULDN'T BE COMPLAINING THE WHOLE TIME.
WE'LL JUST KEEP LOOKING. WE CAN'T BE THAT FAR OFF--
CAN'T YOU DO THAT ***THING?***
WHAT THING?
THAT WEIRD FUCKIN' ***LOOPY*** THING YOU DO WITH YOUR HEAD.
GO OFF INTO ***LA-LA LAND*** AND COME BACK WITH AN ANSWER...
IT DOESN'T WORK LIKE THAT, SAL. I CAN'T JUST... TURN IT ON.
I ALREADY ***TOLD*** YOU EVERYTHING I REMEMBER...

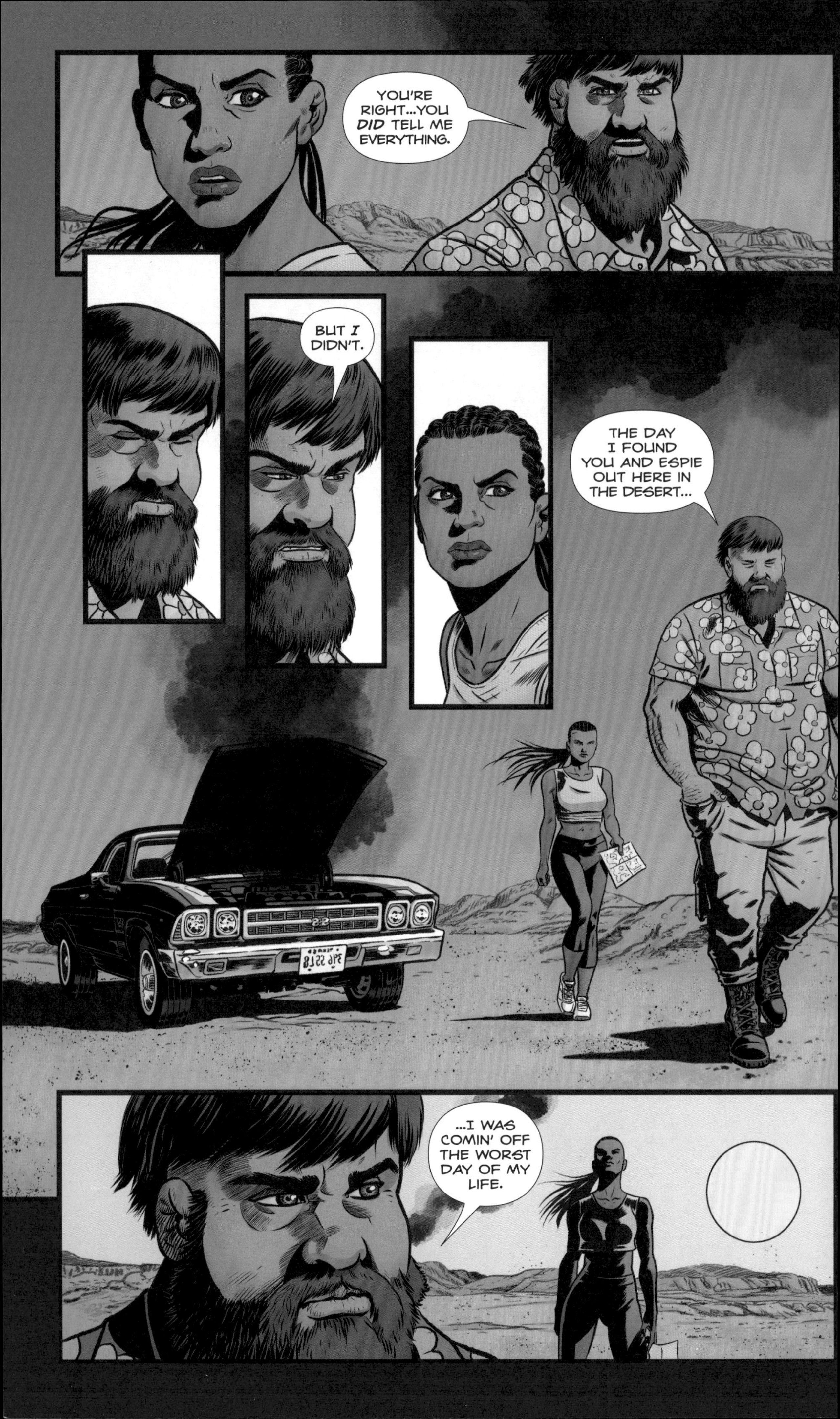
YOU'RE RIGHT...YOU DID TELL ME EVERYTHING.
BUT I DIDN'T.
THE DAY I FOUND YOU AND ESPIE OUT HERE IN THE DESERT...
...I WAS COMIN' OFF THE WORST DAY OF MY LIFE.

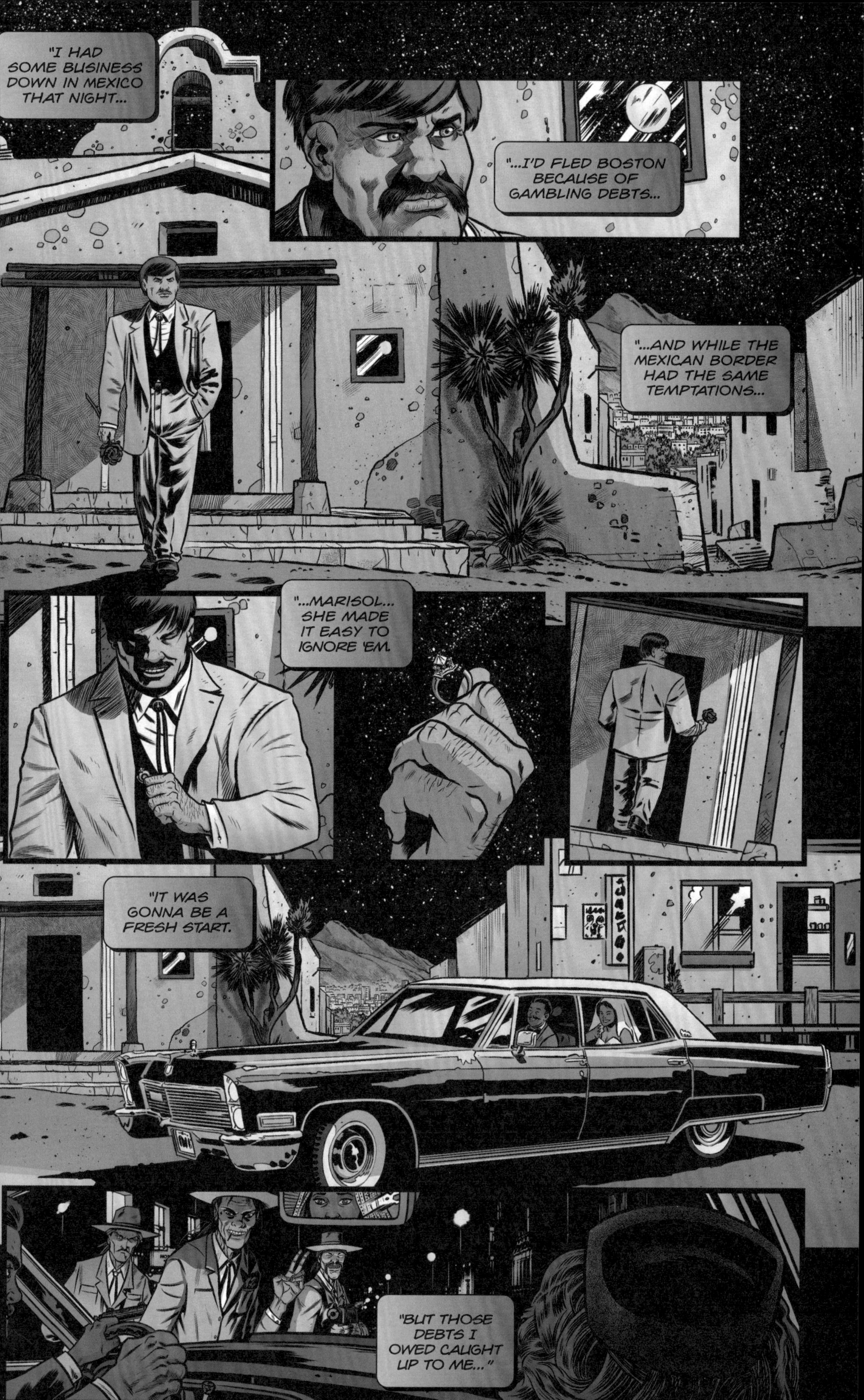
"I HAD SOME BUSINESS DOWN IN MEXICO THAT NIGHT...
"...I'D FLED BOSTON BECAUSE OF GAMBLING DEBTS...
"...AND WHILE THE MEXICAN BORDER HAD THE SAME TEMPTATIONS...
"...MARISOL... SHE MADE IT EASY TO IGNORE 'EM.
"IT WAS GONNA BE A FRESH START.
"BUT THOSE DEBTS I OWED CAUGHT UP TO ME..."

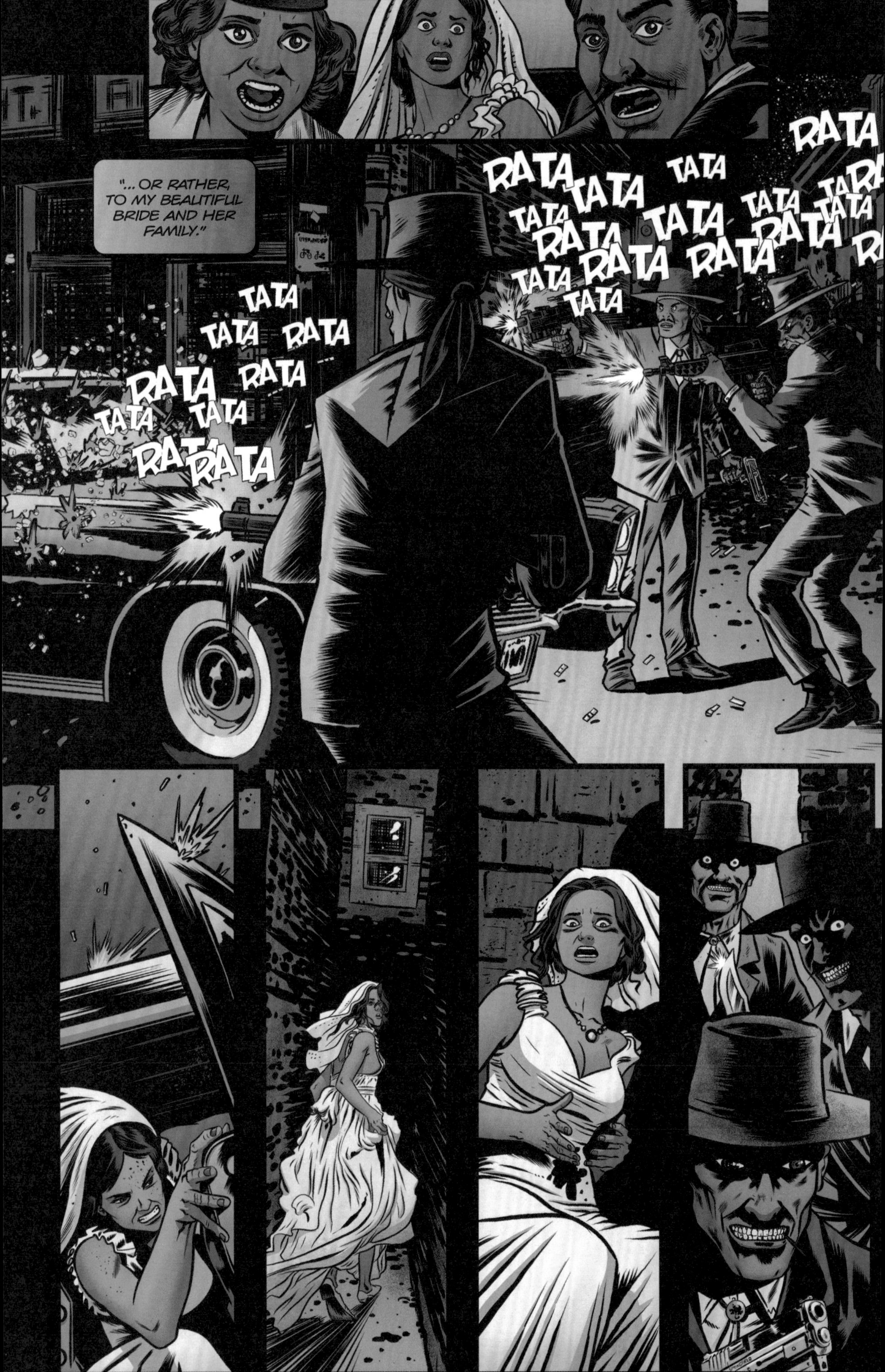
"...OR RATHER, TO MY BEAUTIFUL BRIDE AND HER FAMILY."
RATA TATA TATA RATA
TATA TATA TATA TARA
RATA TATA RATA TATA
TATA RATA RATA
TATA
TATA
TATA RATA
RATA RATA
TATA TATA
RATA RATA

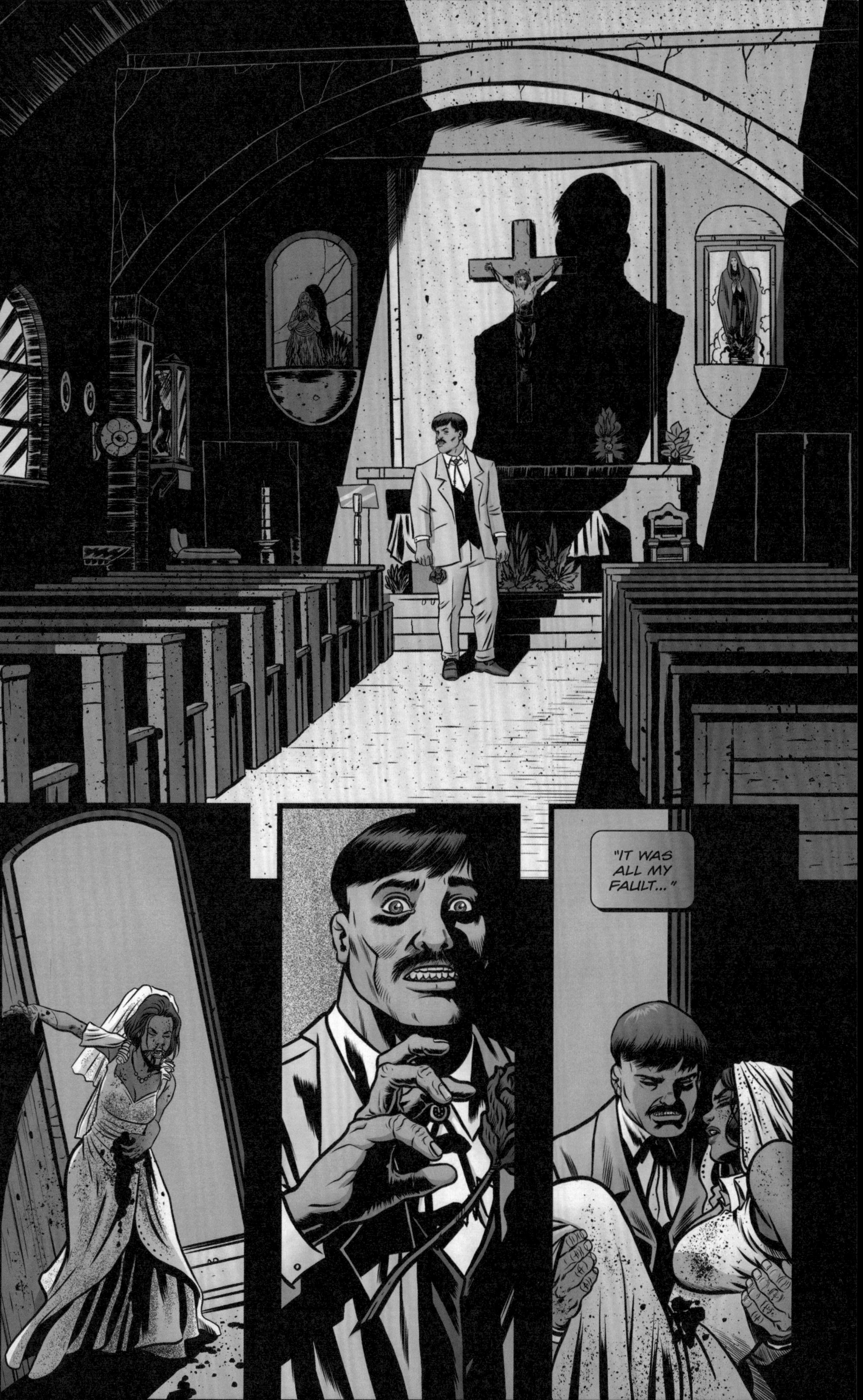
"IT WAS ALL MY FAULT..."

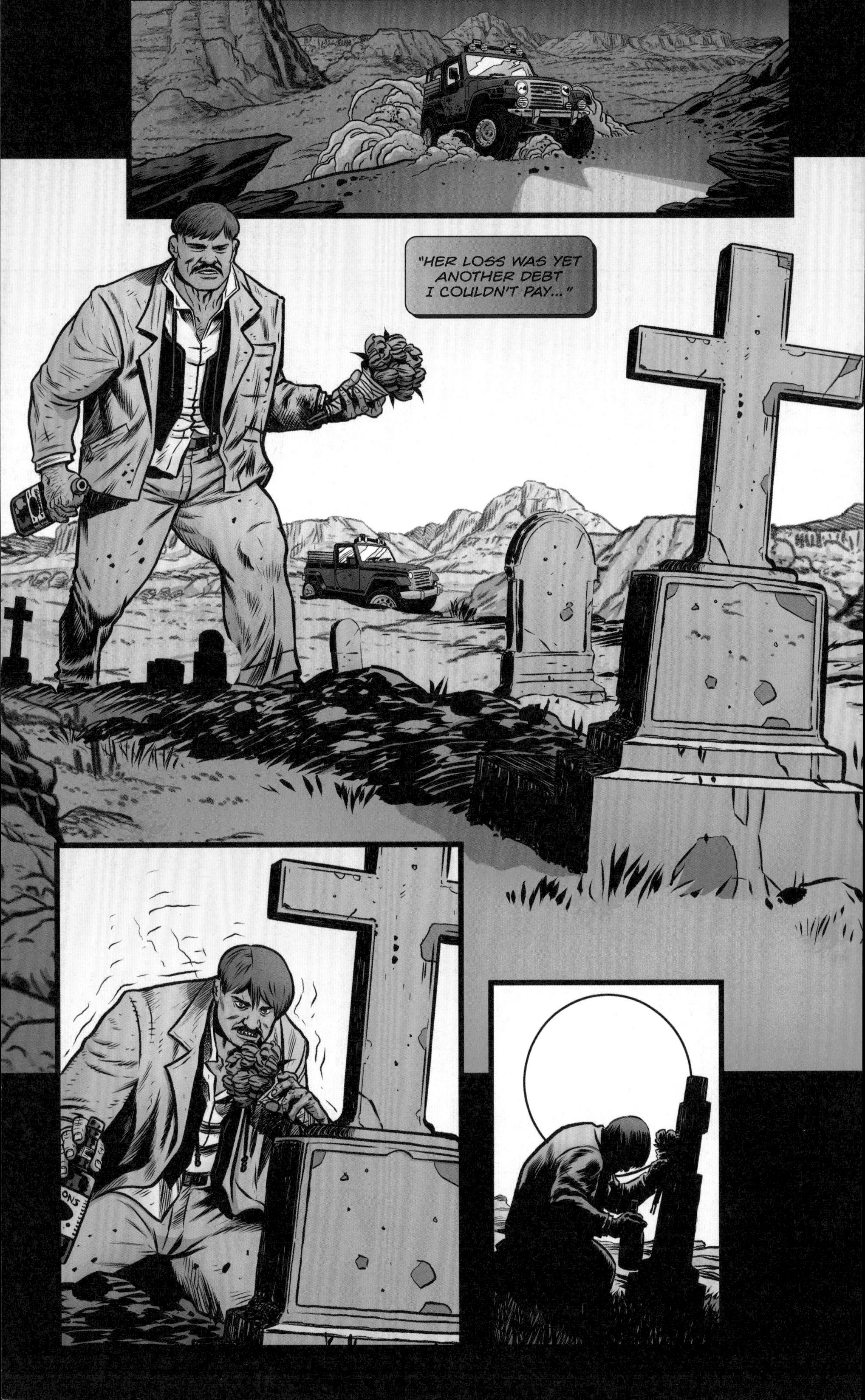
"HER LOSS WAS YET ANOTHER DEBT I COULDN'T PAY..."

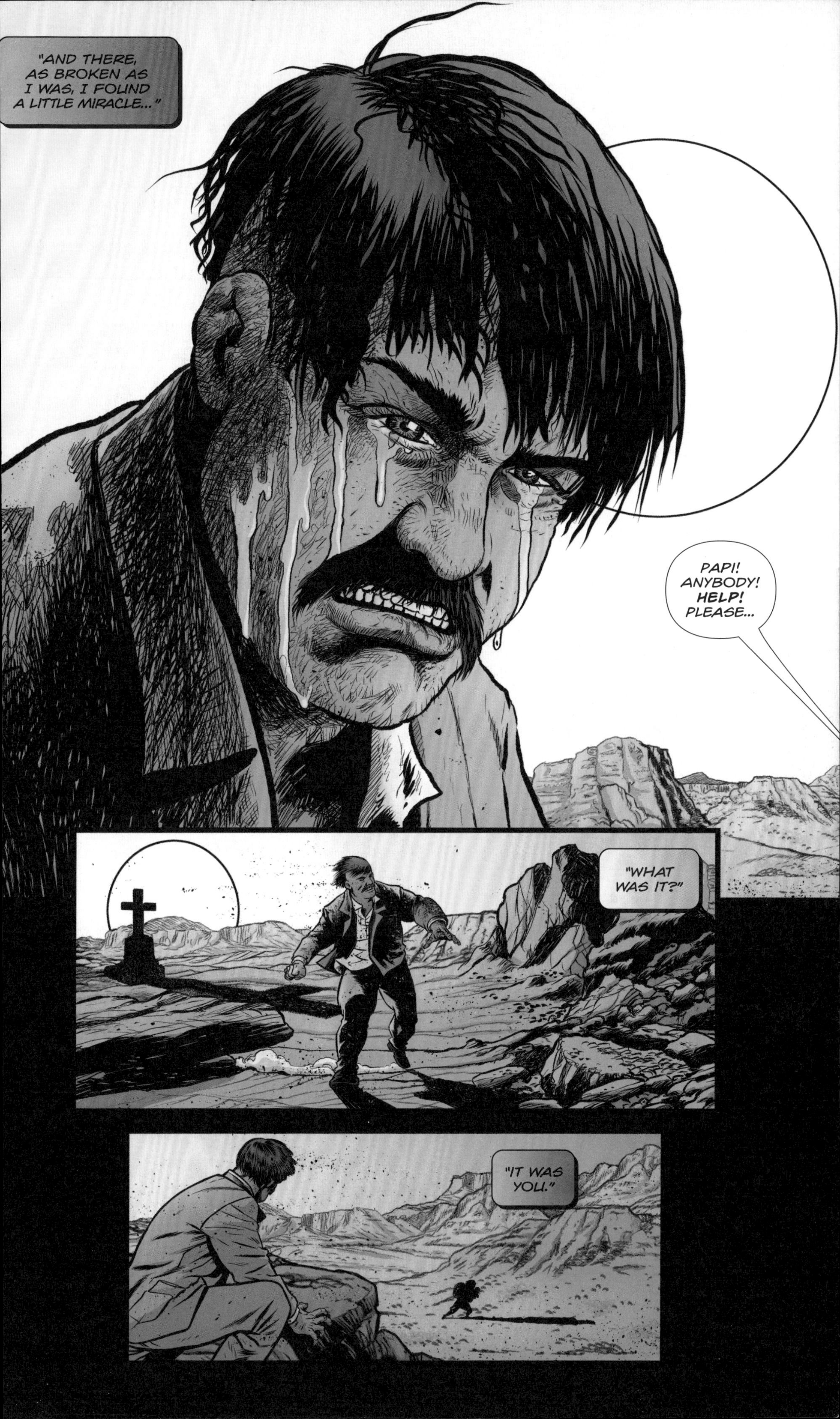
"AND THERE, AS BROKEN AS I WAS, I FOUND A LITTLE MIRACLE..."
PAPI! ANYBODY! **HELP!** PLEASE...
"WHAT WAS IT?"
"IT WAS YOU."

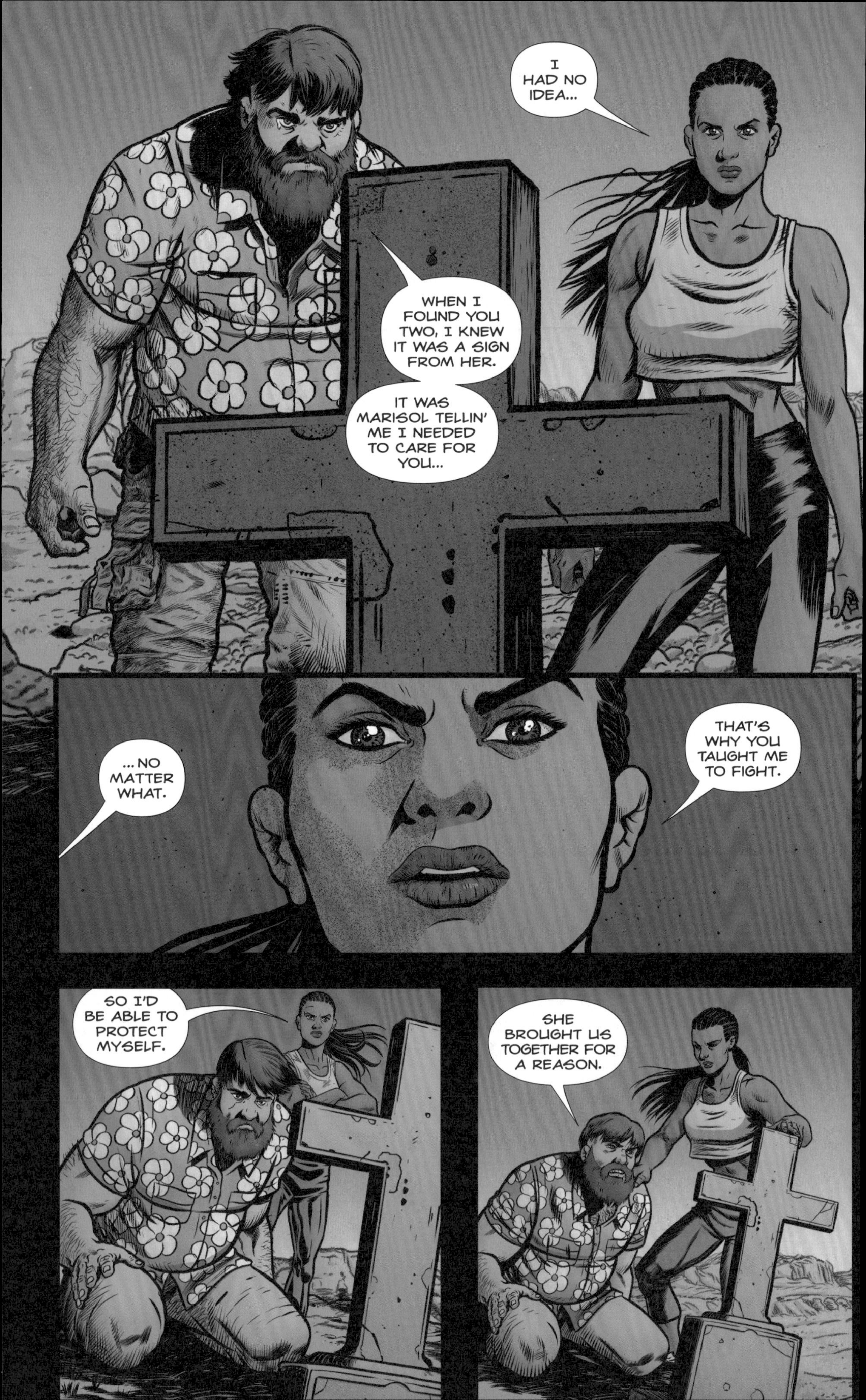
I HAD NO IDEA...
WHEN I FOUND YOU TWO, I KNEW IT WAS A SIGN FROM HER.
IT WAS MARISOL TELLIN' ME I NEEDED TO CARE FOR YOU...
...NO MATTER WHAT.
THAT'S WHY YOU TAUGHT ME TO FIGHT.
SO I'D BE ABLE TO PROTECT MYSELF.
SHE BROUGHT US TOGETHER FOR A REASON.

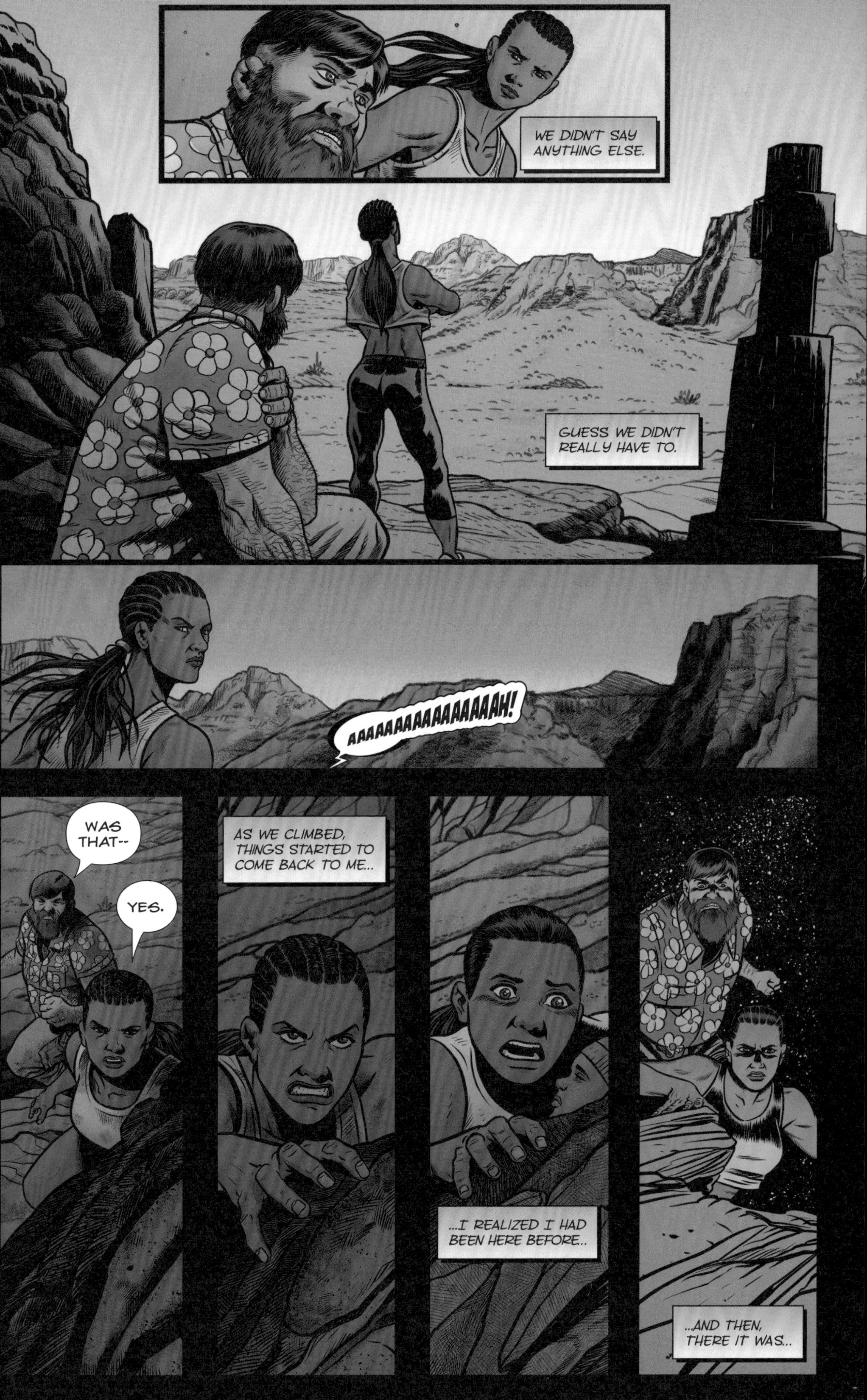
WE DIDN'T SAY ANYTHING ELSE.
GUESS WE DIDN'T REALLY HAVE TO.
AAAAAAAAAAAAAAAH!
WAS THAT--
YES.
AS WE CLIMBED, THINGS STARTED TO COME BACK TO ME...
...I REALIZED I HAD BEEN HERE BEFORE...
...AND THEN, THERE IT WAS...

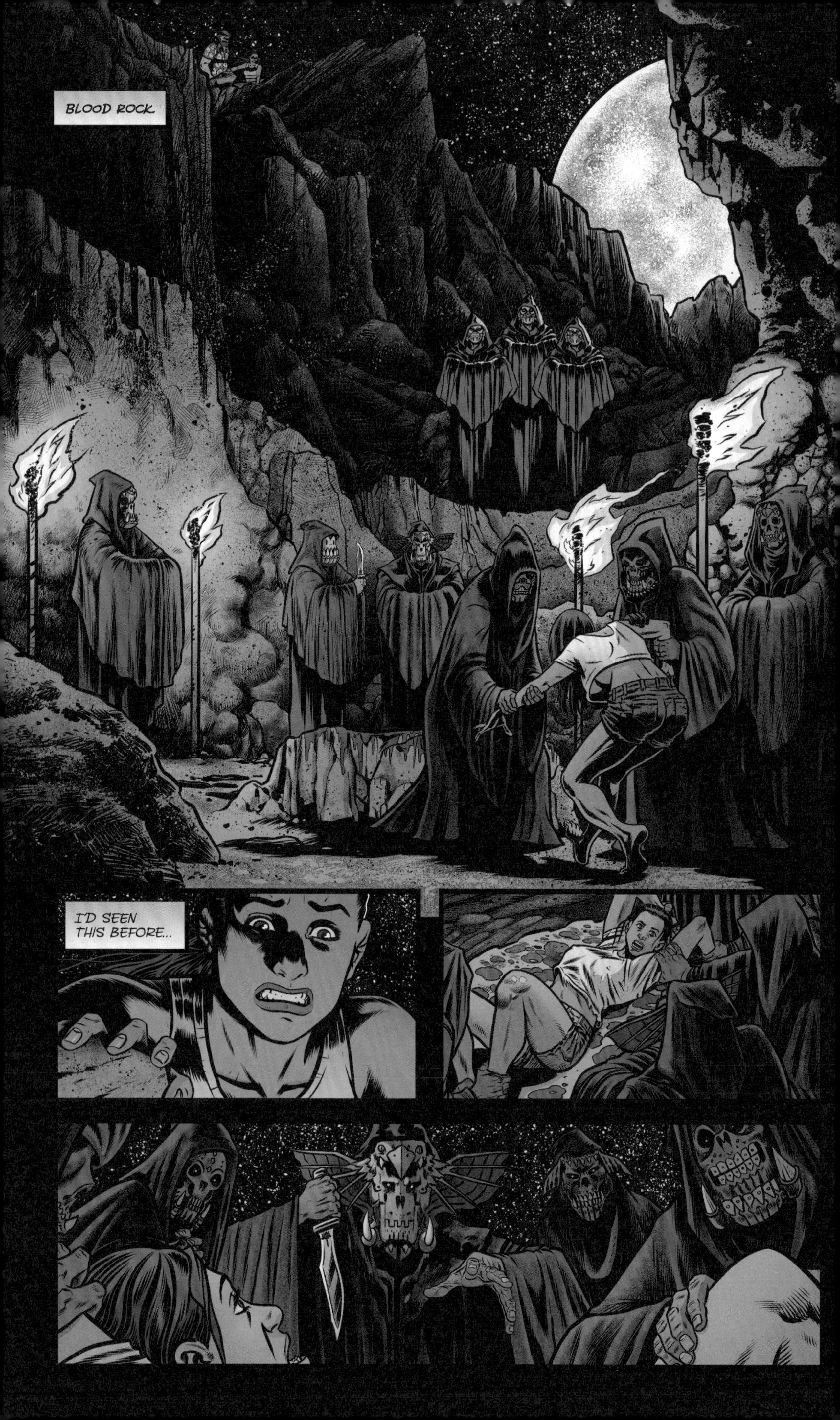
BLOOD ROCK.
I'D SEEN THIS BEFORE...

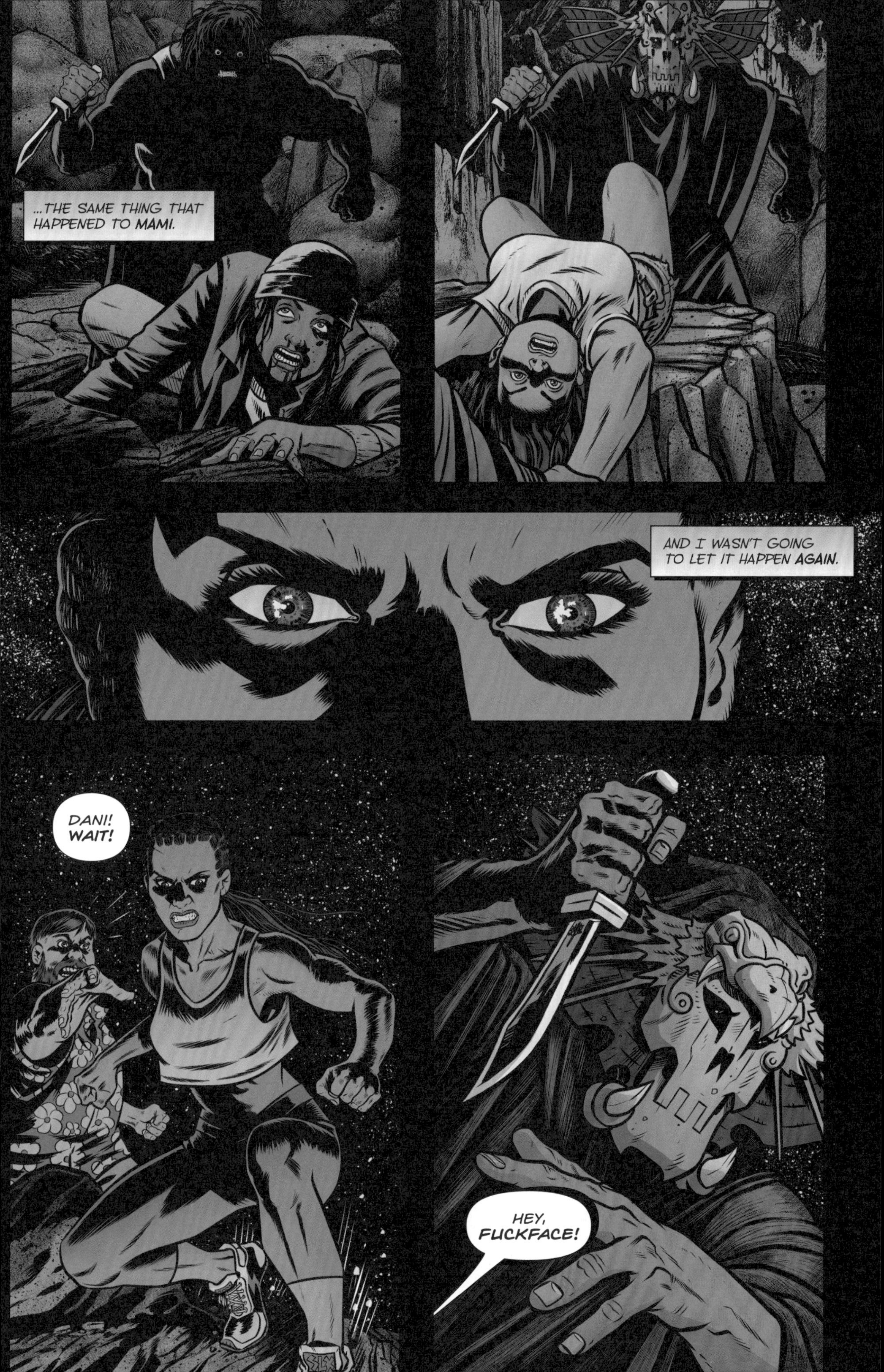
...THE SAME THING THAT HAPPENED TO MAMI.
AND I WASN'T GOING TO LET IT HAPPEN AGAIN.
DANI! WAIT!
HEY, FUCKFACE!

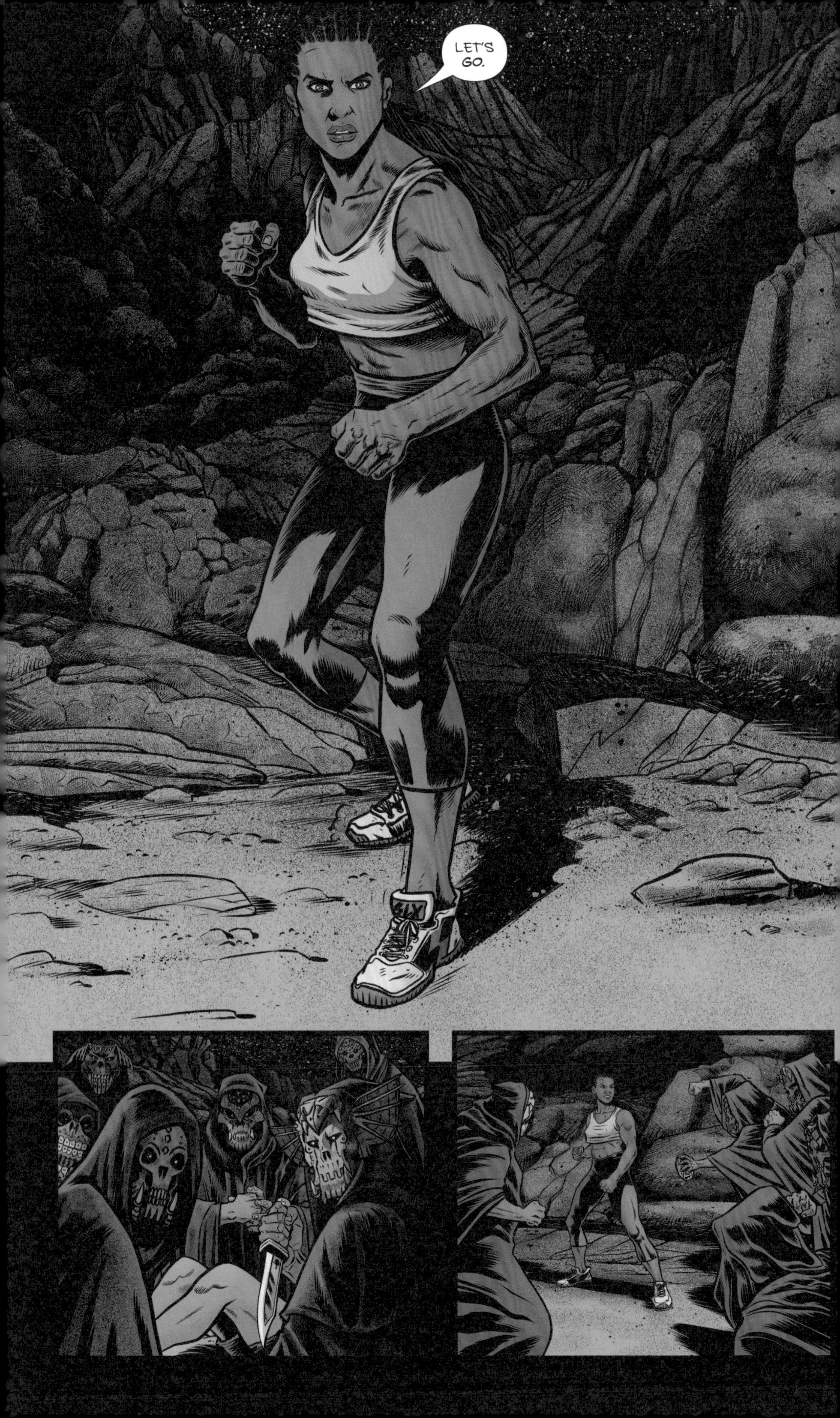
LET'S GO.

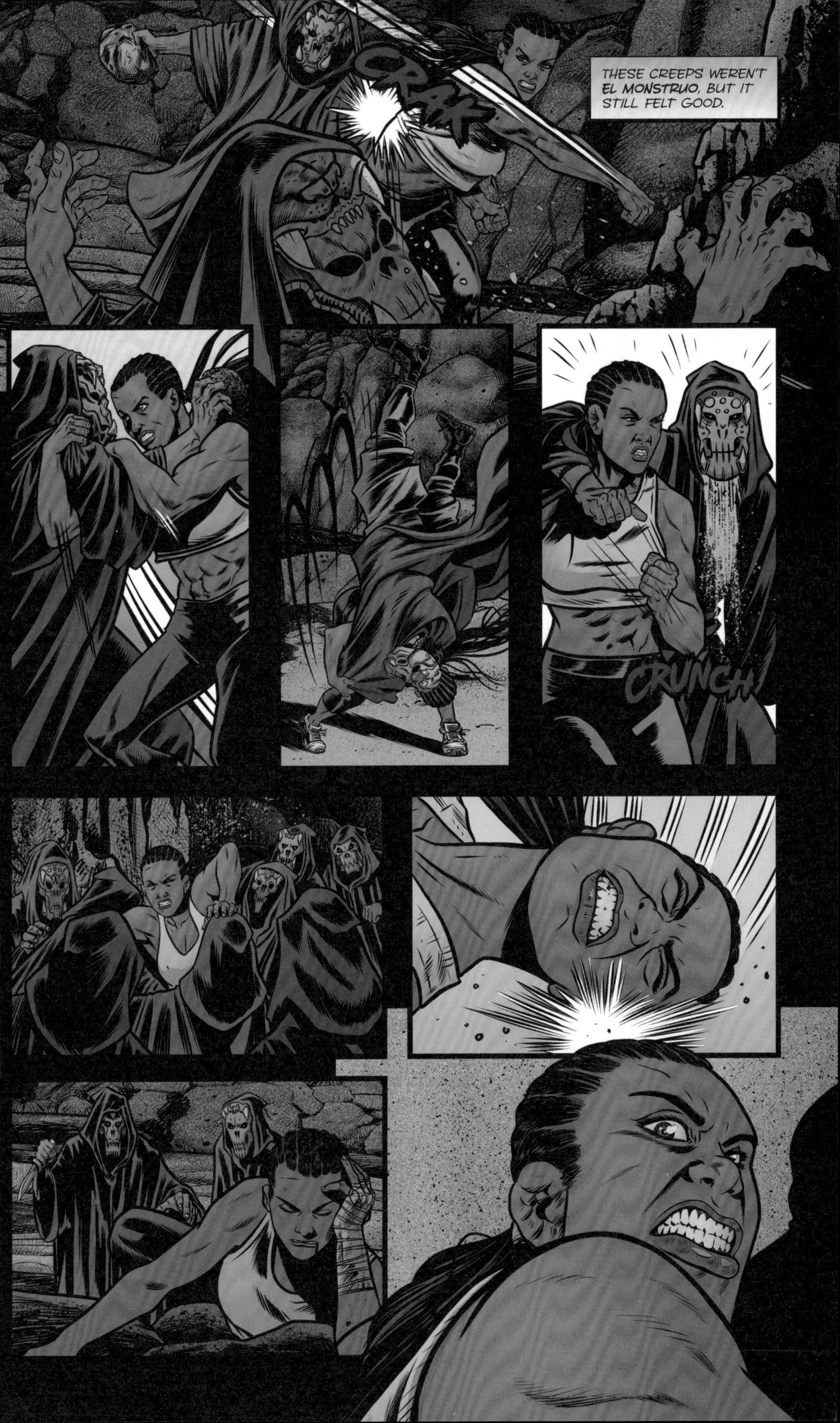
THESE CREEPS WEREN'T EL MONSTRUO, BUT IT STILL FELT GOOD.
CRAK
CRUNCH

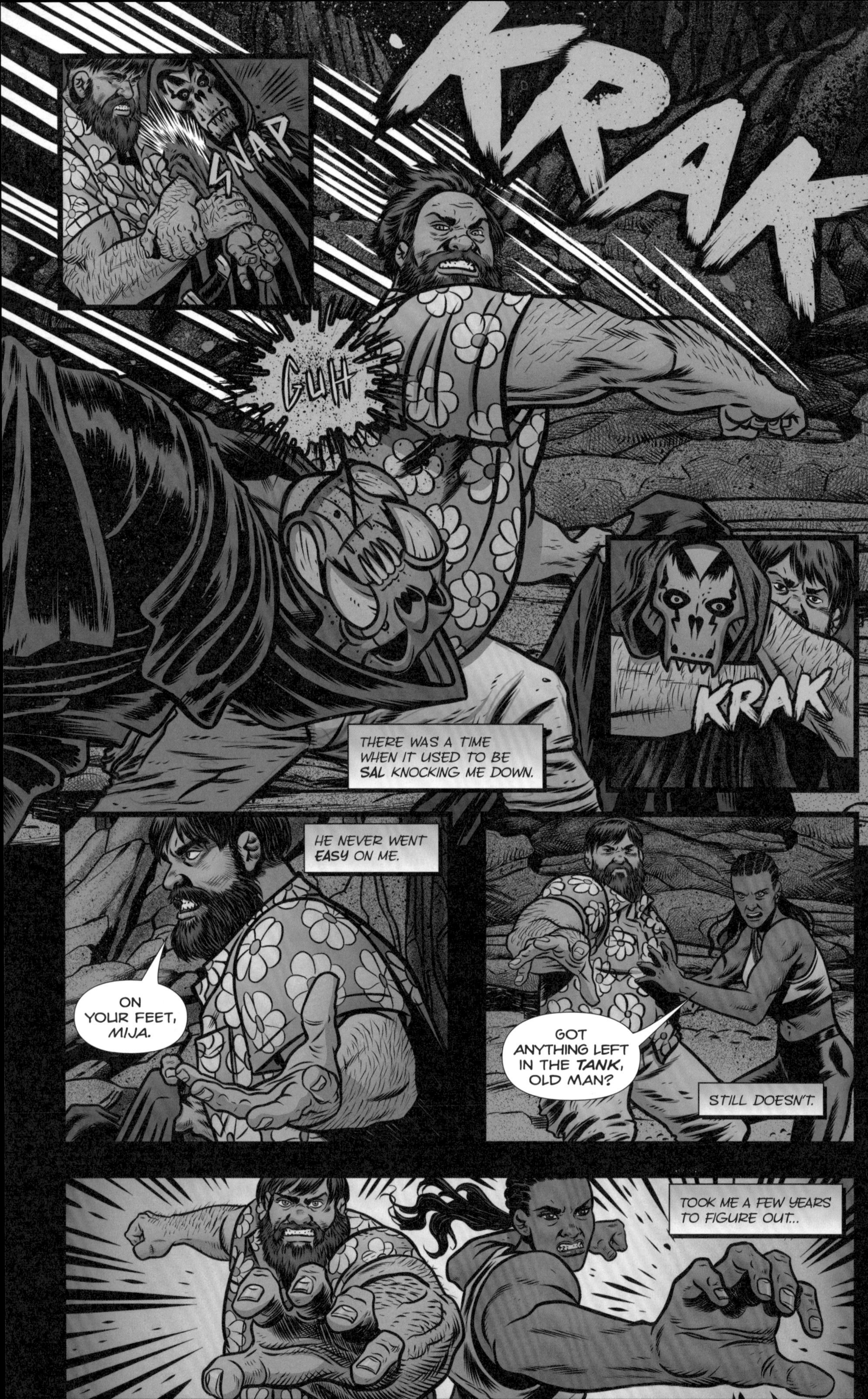
SNAP
KRAK
GUH
KRAK
THERE WAS A TIME WHEN IT USED TO BE SAL KNOCKING ME DOWN.
HE NEVER WENT EASY ON ME.
ON YOUR FEET, MIJA.
GOT ANYTHING LEFT IN THE TANK, OLD MAN?
STILL DOESN'T.
TOOK ME A FEW YEARS TO FIGURE OUT...

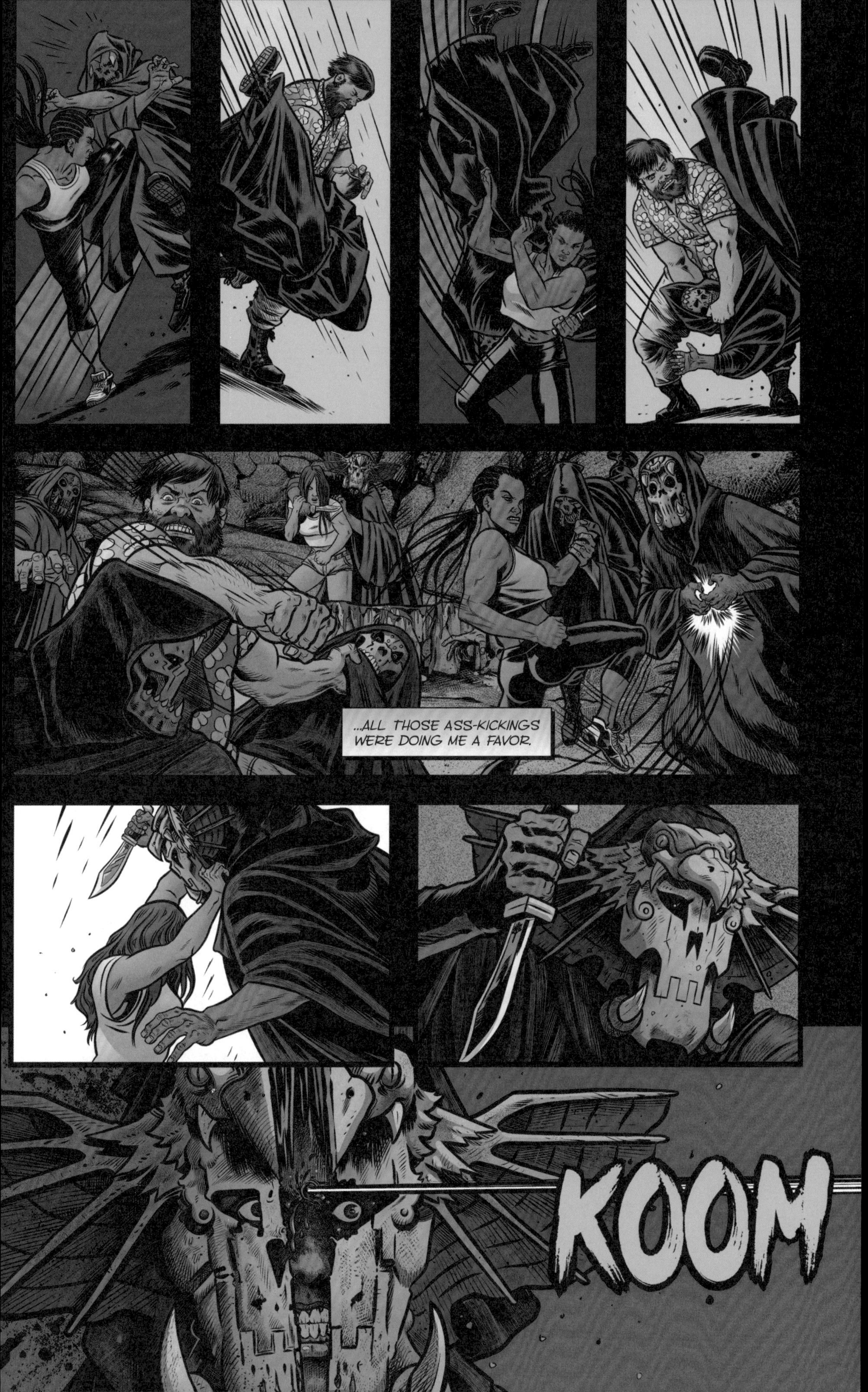
...ALL THOSE ASS-KICKINGS WERE DOING ME A FAVOR.
KOOM

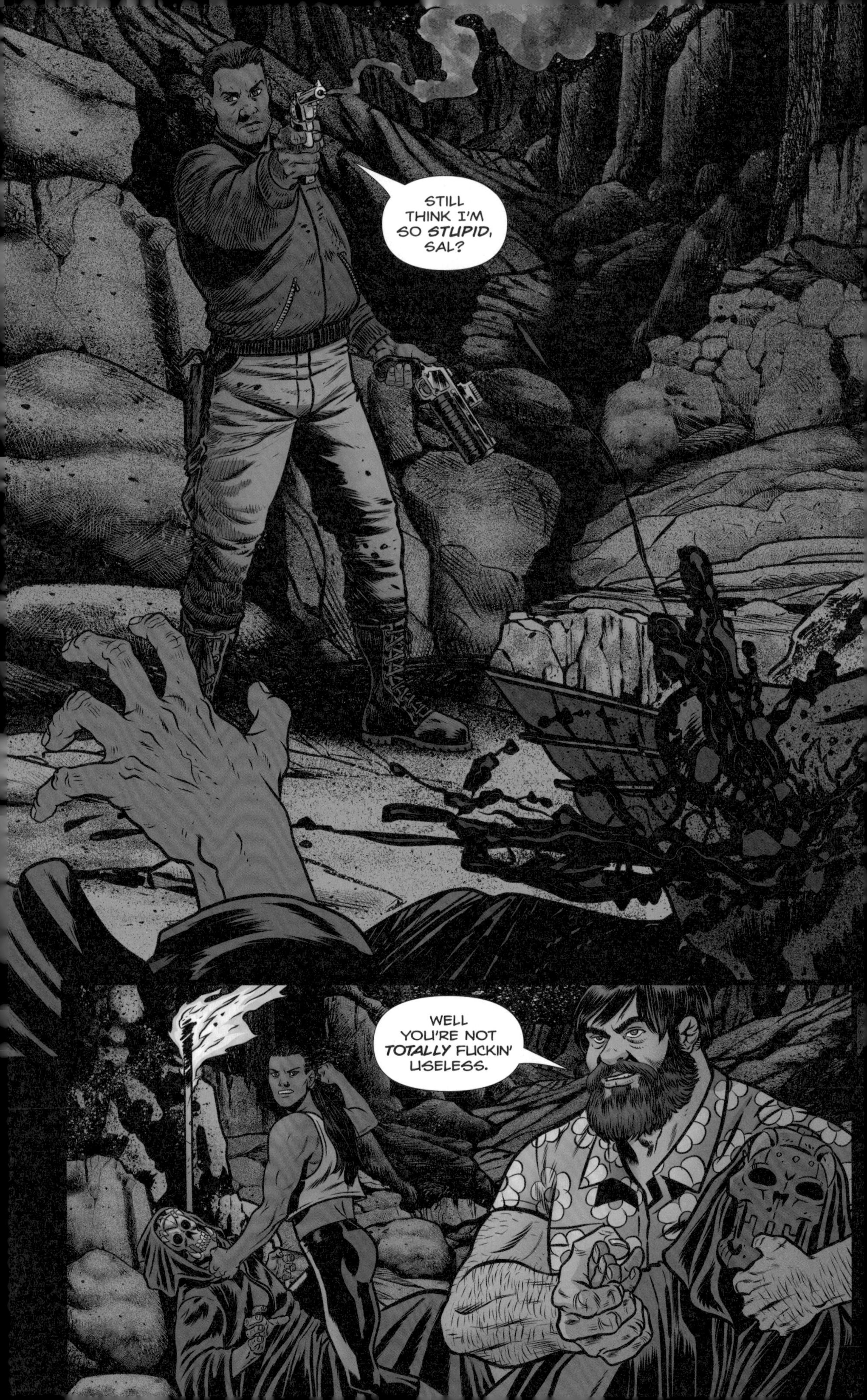
STILL THINK I'M SO STUPID, SAL?
WELL YOU'RE NOT TOTALLY FUCKIN' USELESS.

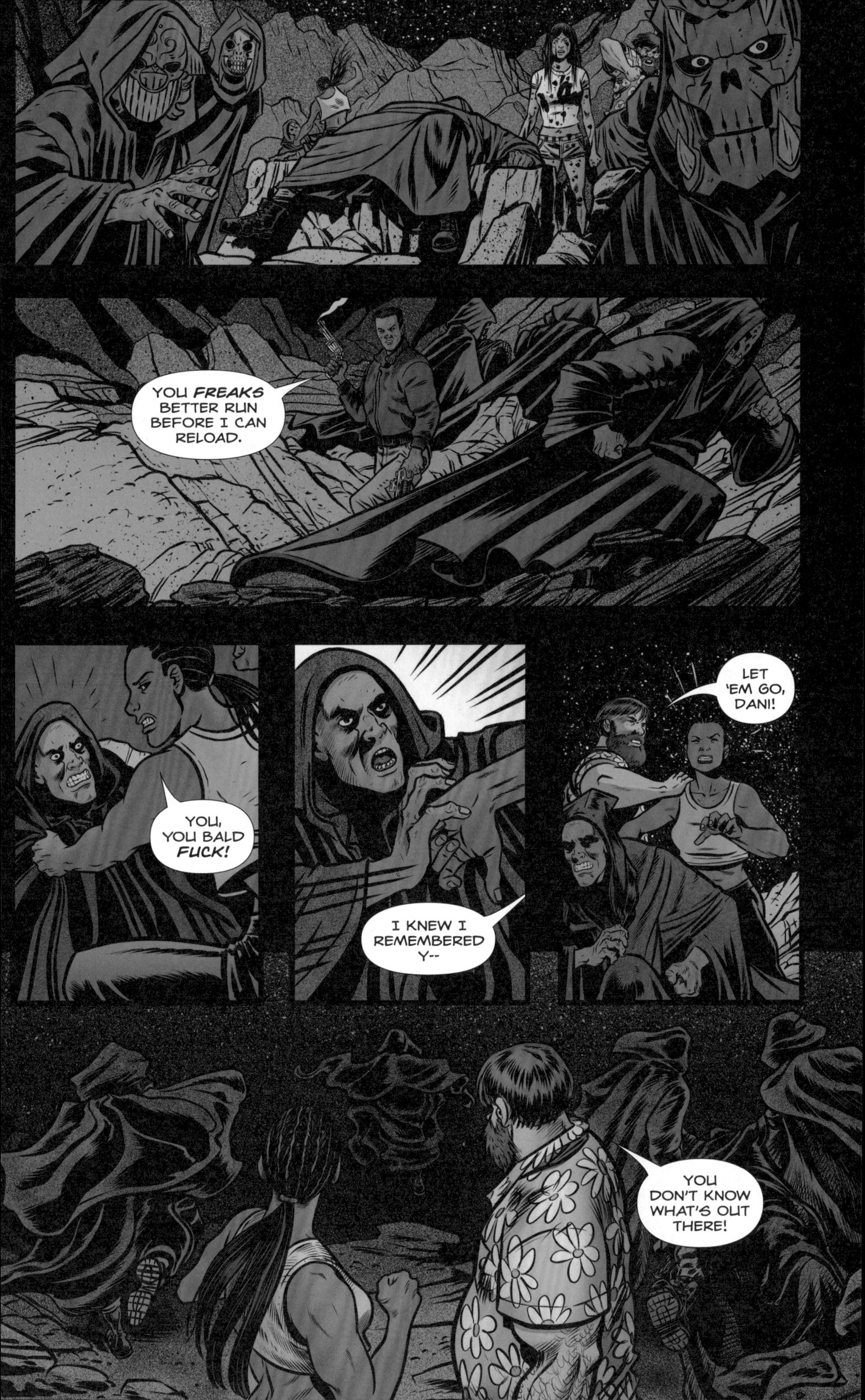
YOU FREAKS BETTER RUN BEFORE I CAN RELOAD.
YOU, YOU BALD FUCK!
I KNEW I REMEMBERED Y--
LET 'EM GO, DANI!
YOU DON'T KNOW WHAT'S OUT THERE!

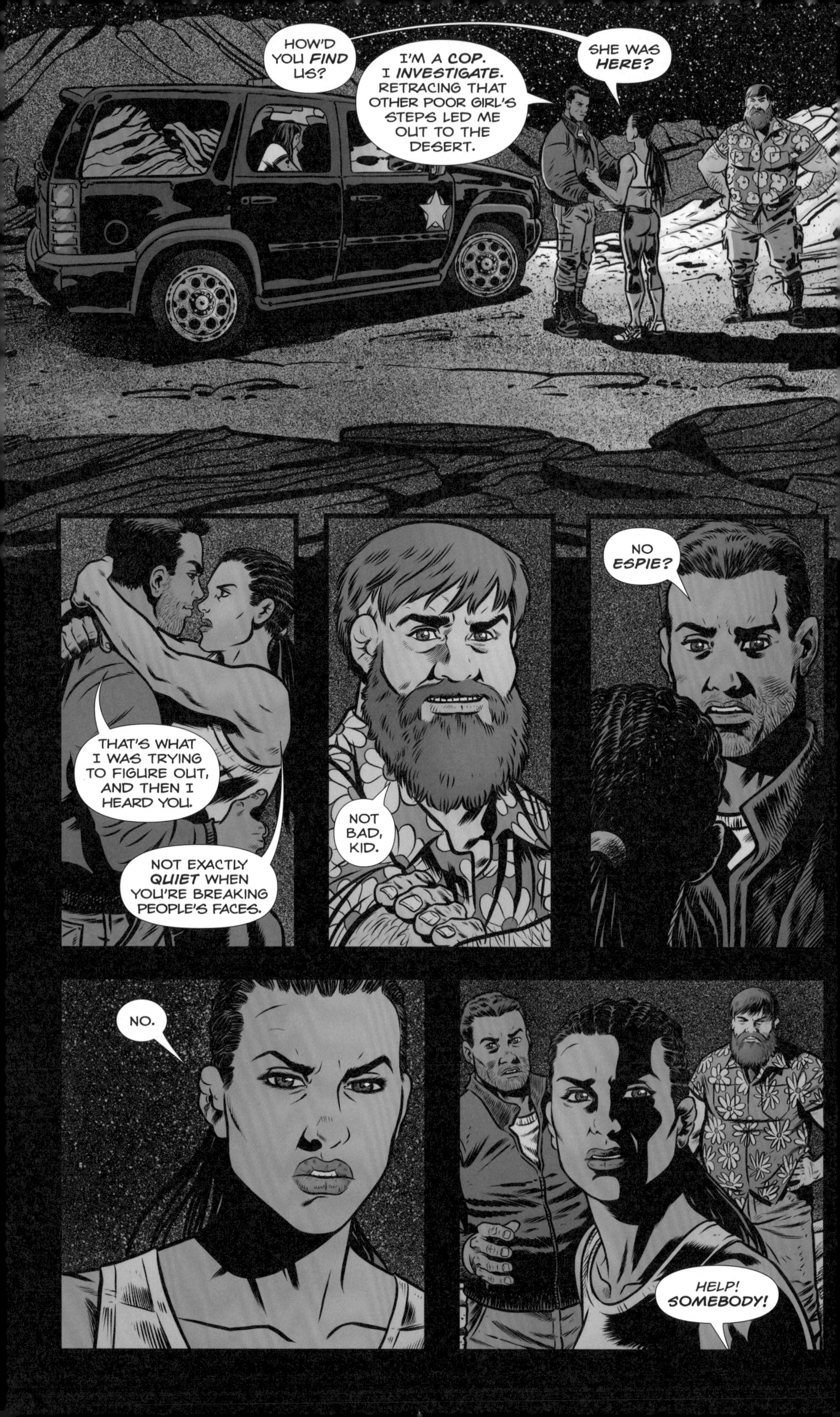
HOW'D YOU *FIND* US?
I'M A **COP.** I *INVESTIGATE.* RETRACING THAT OTHER POOR GIRL'S STEPS LED ME OUT TO THE DESERT.
SHE WAS *HERE?*
THAT'S WHAT I WAS TRYING TO FIGURE OUT, AND THEN I HEARD YOU.
NOT EXACTLY *QUIET* WHEN YOU'RE BREAKING PEOPLE'S FACES.
NOT BAD, KID.
NO *ESPIE?*
NO.
HELP! **SOMEBODY!**

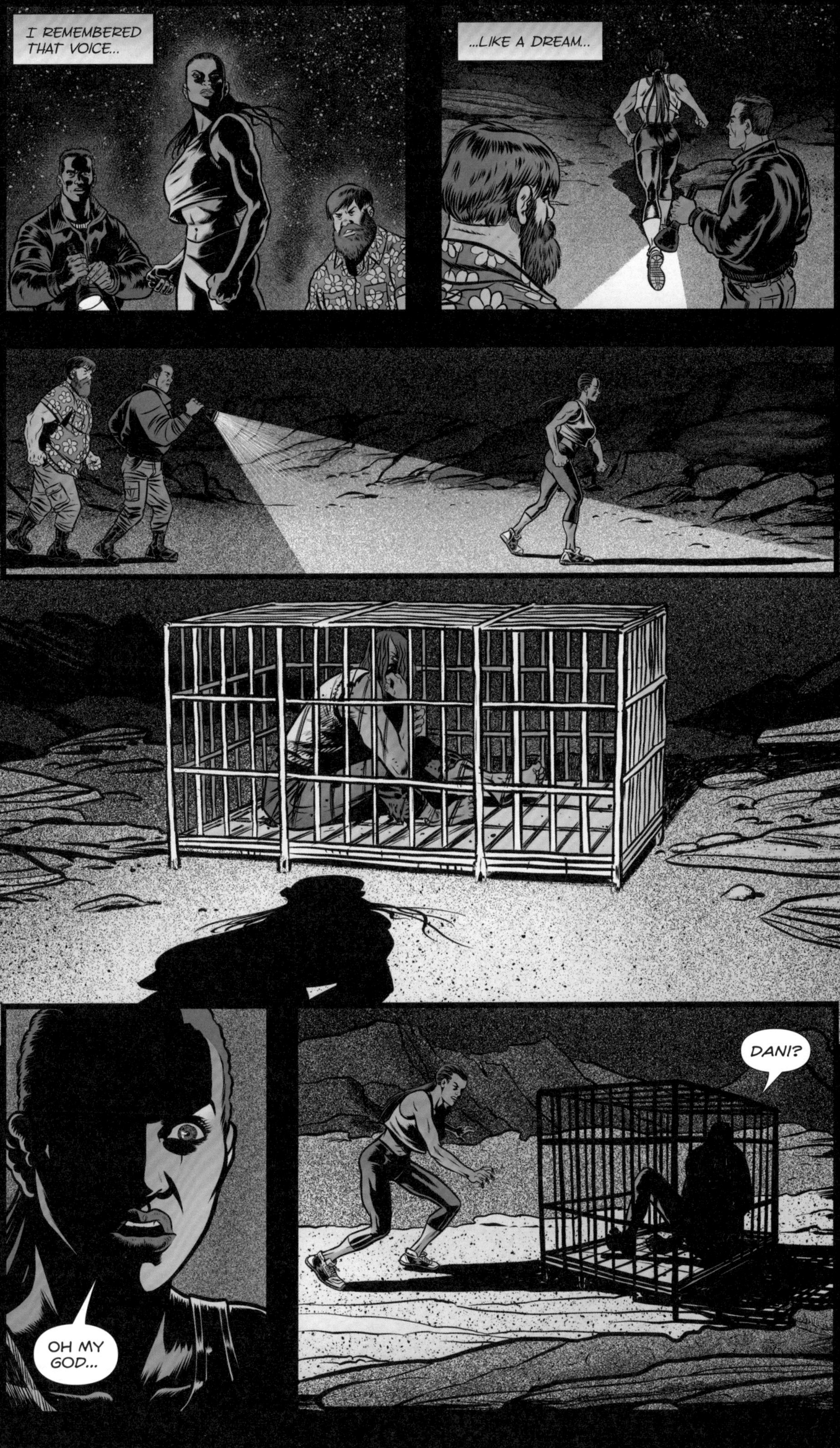
I REMEMBERED THAT VOICE...
...LIKE A DREAM...
OH MY GOD...
DANI?

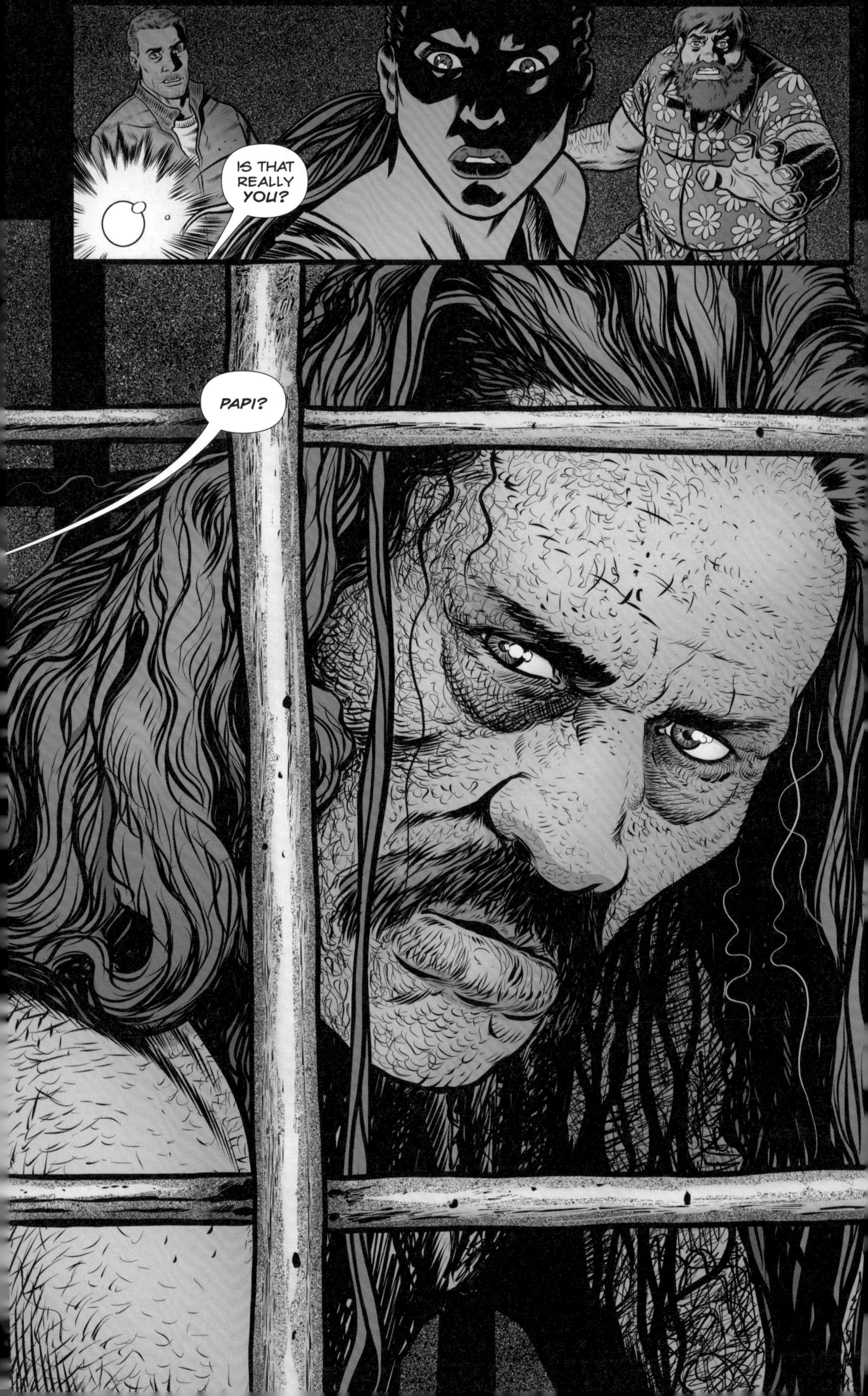
IS THAT REALLY YOU?
PAPI?

CHAPTER 5

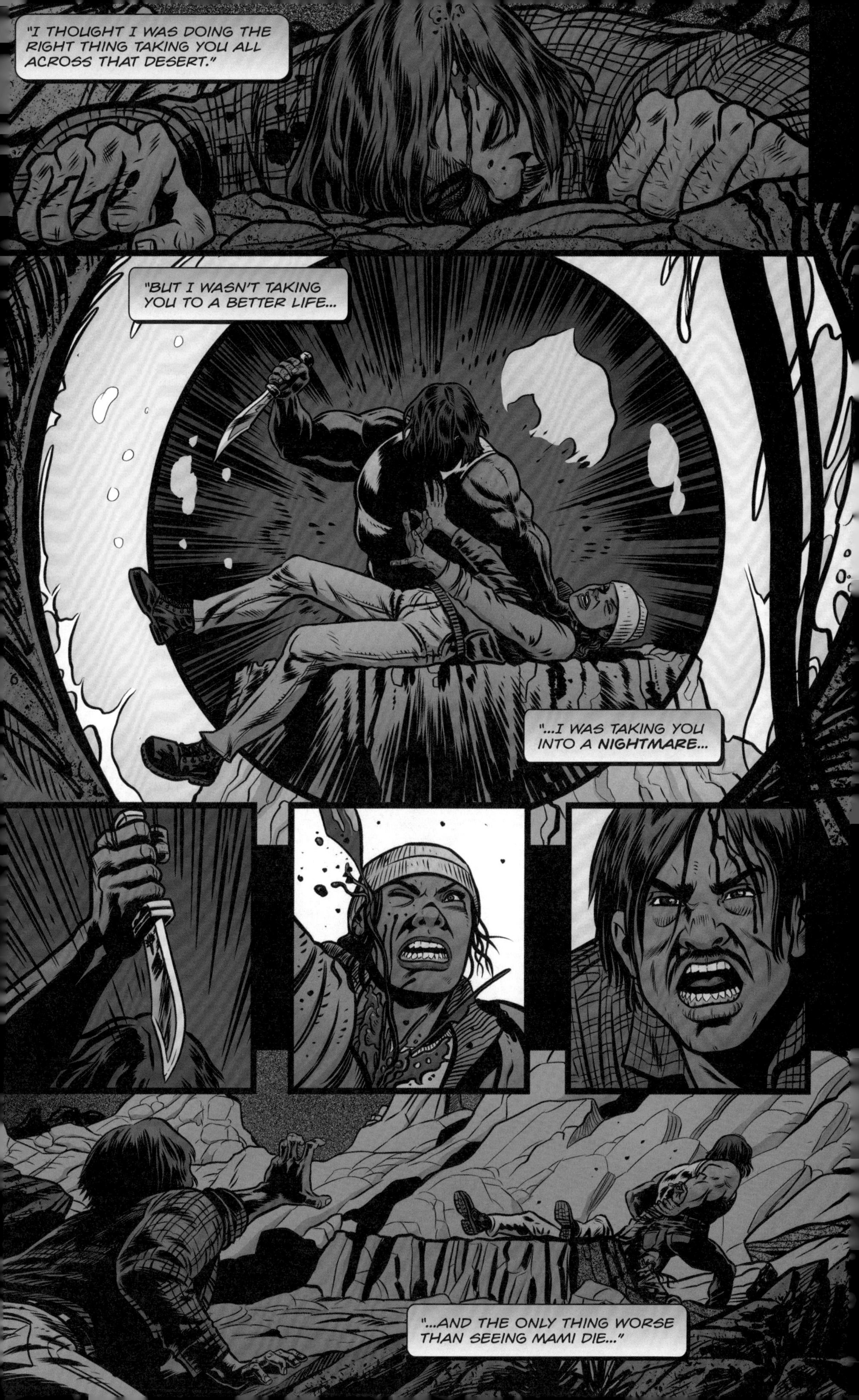
"I THOUGHT I WAS DOING THE RIGHT THING TAKING YOU ALL ACROSS THAT DESERT."
"BUT I WASN'T TAKING YOU TO A BETTER LIFE...
"...I WAS TAKING YOU INTO A NIGHTMARE...
"...AND THE ONLY THING WORSE THAN SEEING MAMI DIE..."

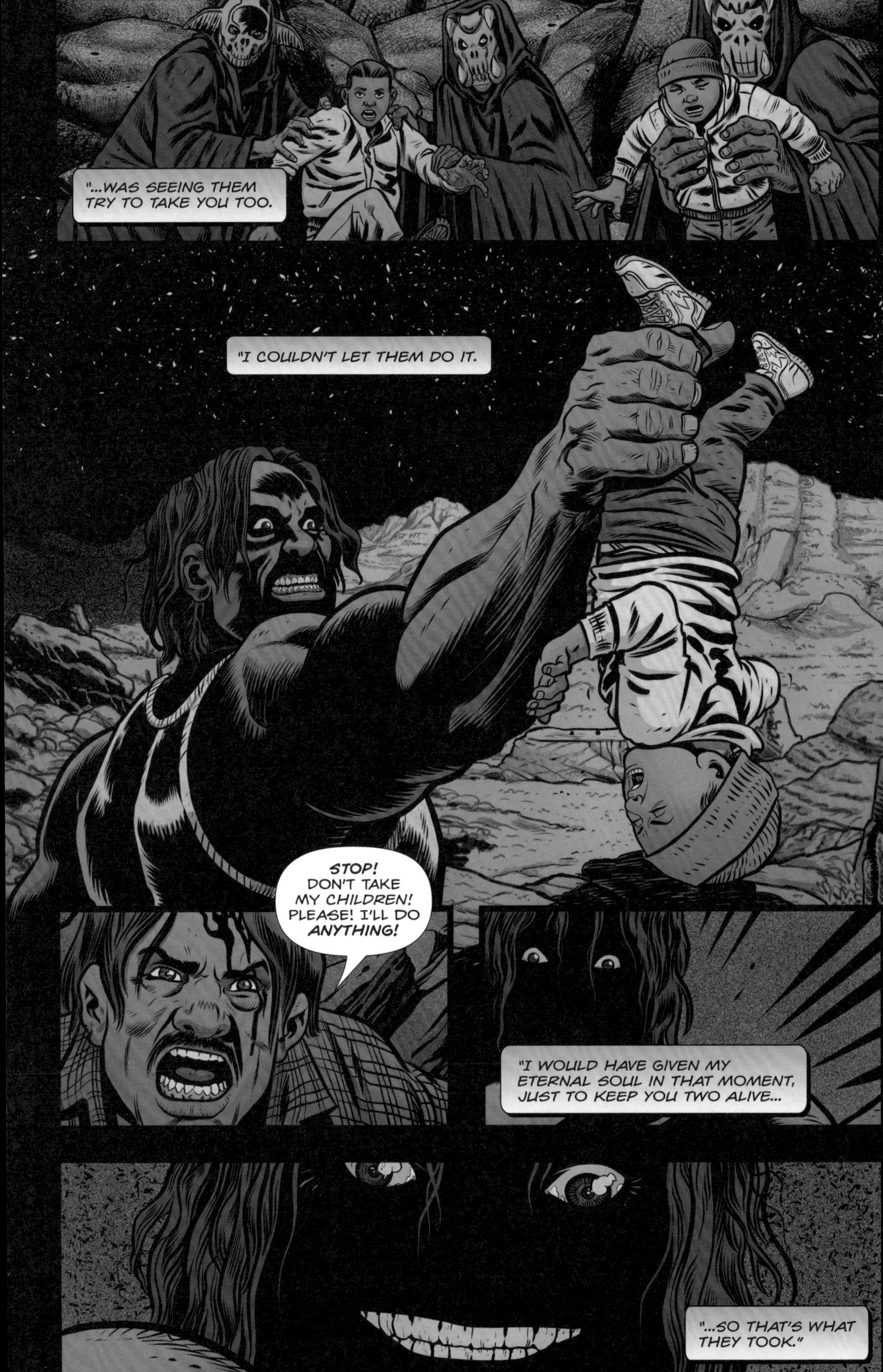
"...WAS SEEING THEM TRY TO TAKE YOU TOO.
"I COULDN'T LET THEM DO IT.
STOP! DON'T TAKE MY CHILDREN! PLEASE! I'LL DO ANYTHING!
"I WOULD HAVE GIVEN MY ETERNAL SOUL IN THAT MOMENT, JUST TO KEEP YOU TWO ALIVE...
"...SO THAT'S WHAT THEY TOOK."

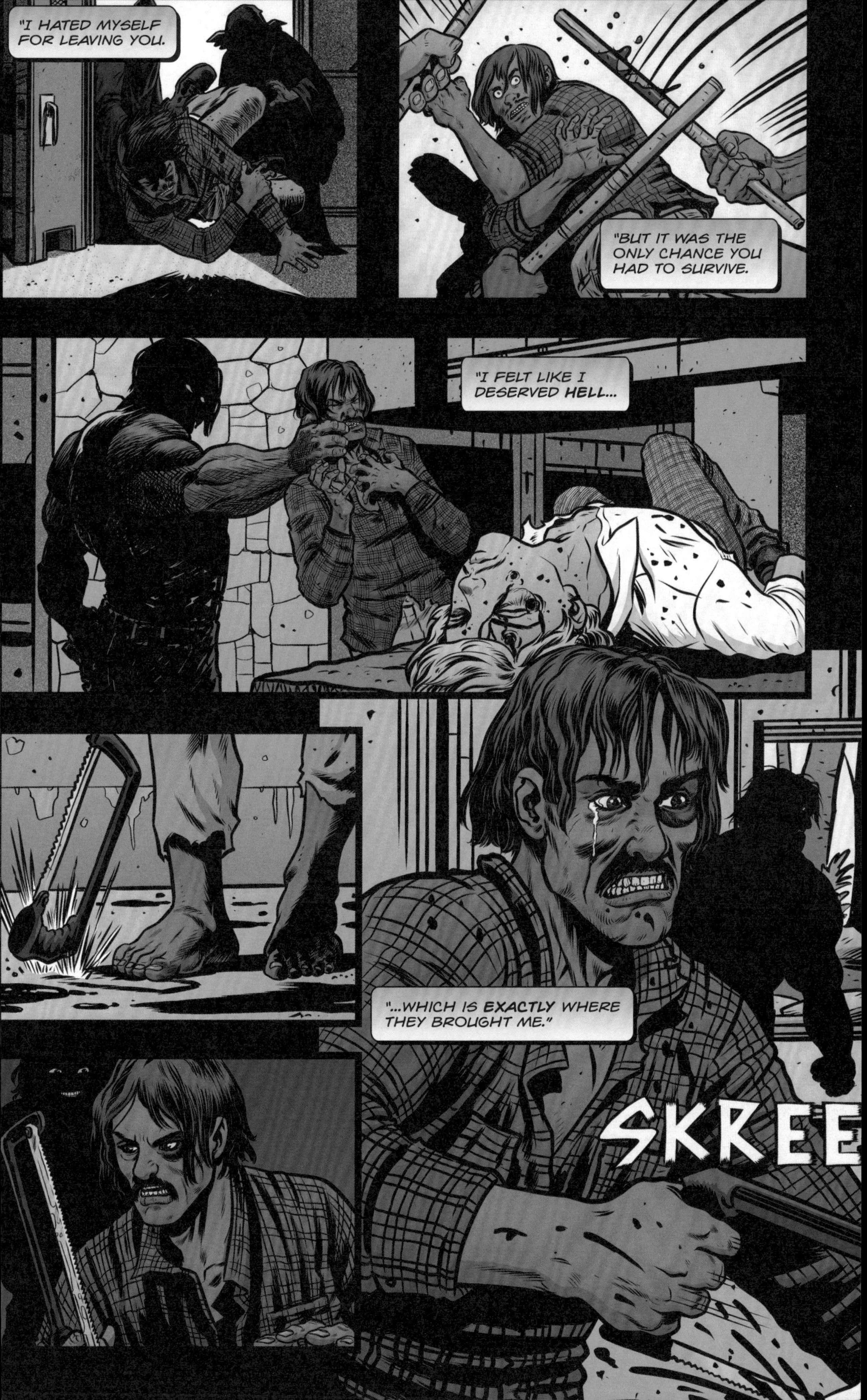
"I HATED MYSELF FOR LEAVING YOU.
"BUT IT WAS THE ONLY CHANCE YOU HAD TO SURVIVE.
"I FELT LIKE I DESERVED HELL...
"...WHICH IS EXACTLY WHERE THEY BROUGHT ME."
SKREE

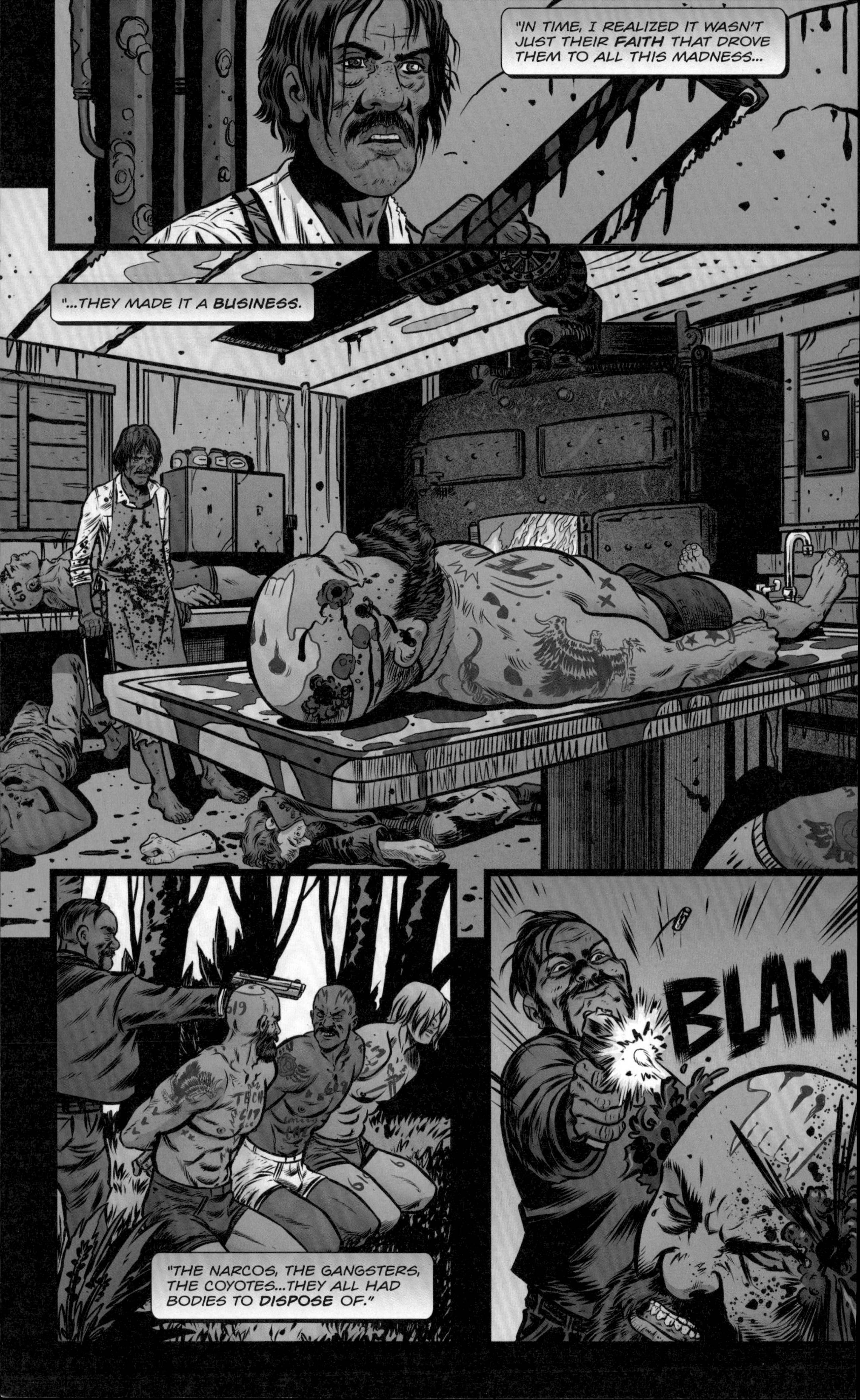
"IN TIME, I REALIZED IT WASN'T JUST THEIR FAITH THAT DROVE THEM TO ALL THIS MADNESS...
"...THEY MADE IT A BUSINESS.
"THE NARCOS, THE GANGSTERS, THE COYOTES...THEY ALL HAD BODIES TO DISPOSE OF."
BLAM

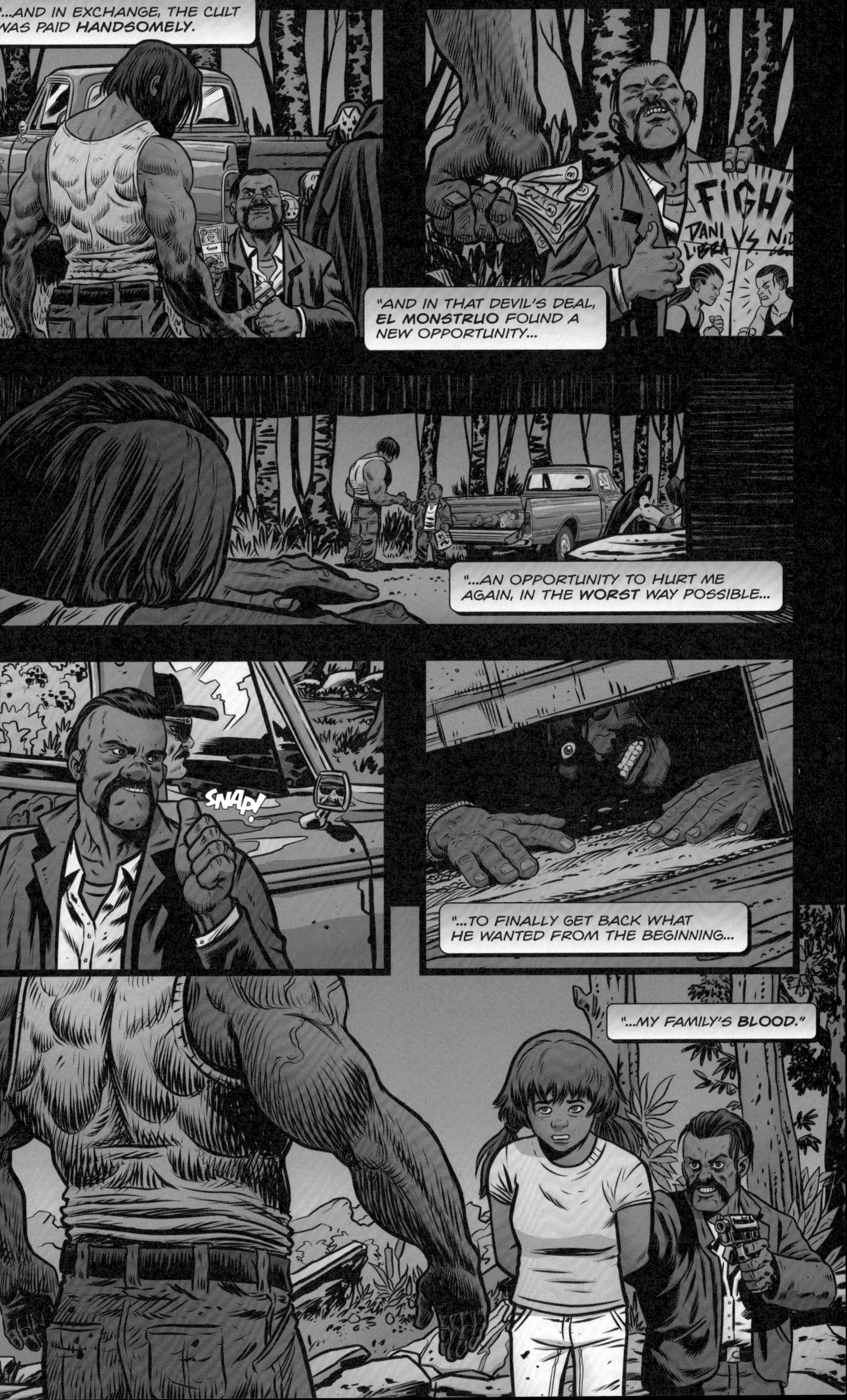
"...AND IN EXCHANGE, THE CULT WAS PAID HANDSOMELY.
"AND IN THAT DEVIL'S DEAL, EL MONSTRUO FOUND A NEW OPPORTUNITY...
"...AN OPPORTUNITY TO HURT ME AGAIN, IN THE WORST WAY POSSIBLE...
SNAP!
"...TO FINALLY GET BACK WHAT HE WANTED FROM THE BEGINNING...
"...MY FAMILY'S BLOOD."

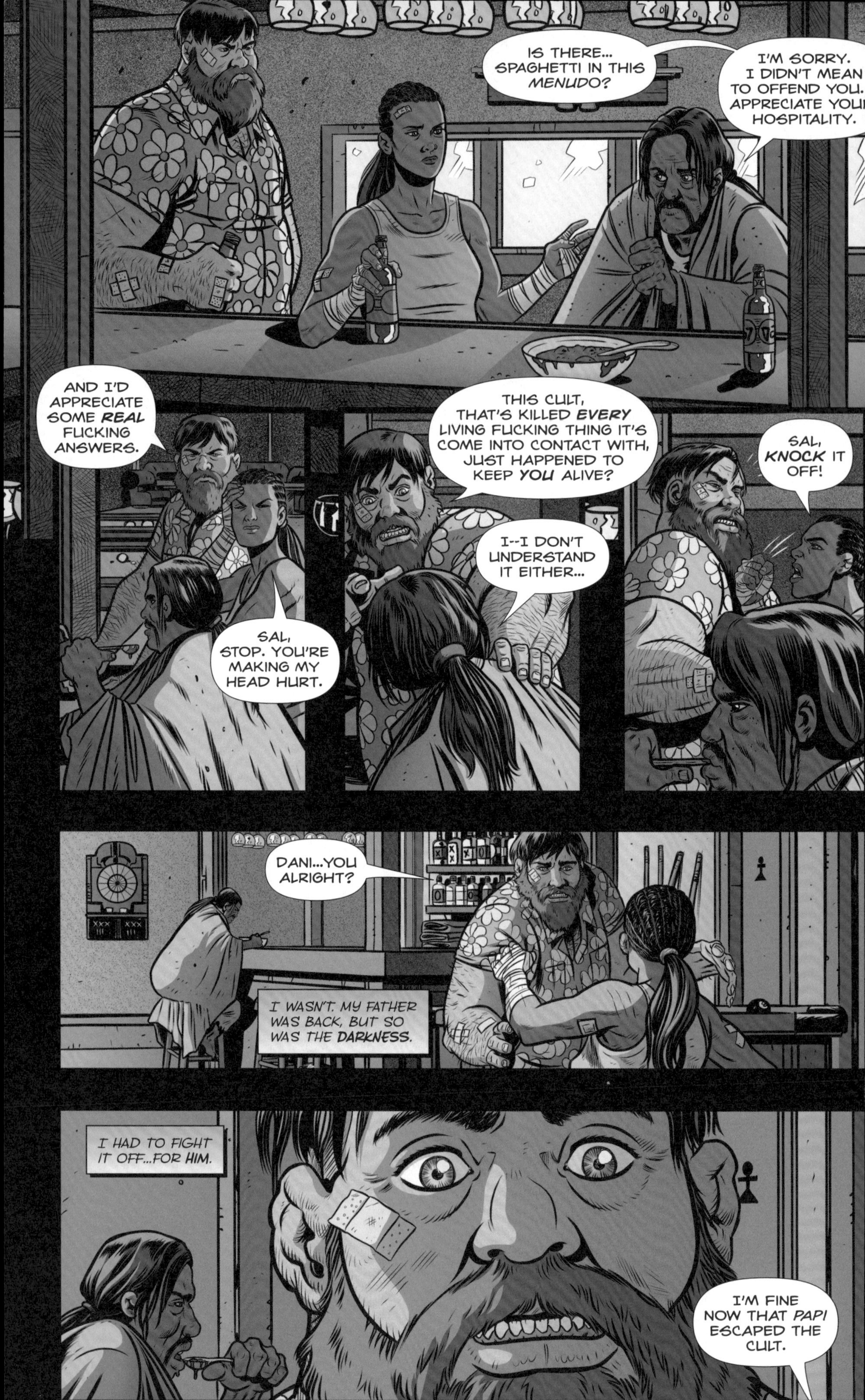
IS THERE... SPAGHETTI IN THIS MENUDO?
I'M SORRY. I DIDN'T MEAN TO OFFEND YOU. APPRECIATE YOUR HOSPITALITY.
AND I'D APPRECIATE SOME REAL FUCKING ANSWERS.
SAL, STOP. YOU'RE MAKING MY HEAD HURT.
THIS CULT, THAT'S KILLED EVERY LIVING FUCKING THING IT'S COME INTO CONTACT WITH, JUST HAPPENED TO KEEP YOU ALIVE?
I--I DON'T UNDERSTAND IT EITHER...
SAL, KNOCK IT OFF!
DANI...YOU ALRIGHT?
I WASN'T. MY FATHER WAS BACK, BUT SO WAS THE DARKNESS.
I HAD TO FIGHT IT OFF...FOR HIM.
I'M FINE NOW THAT PAPI ESCAPED THE CULT.

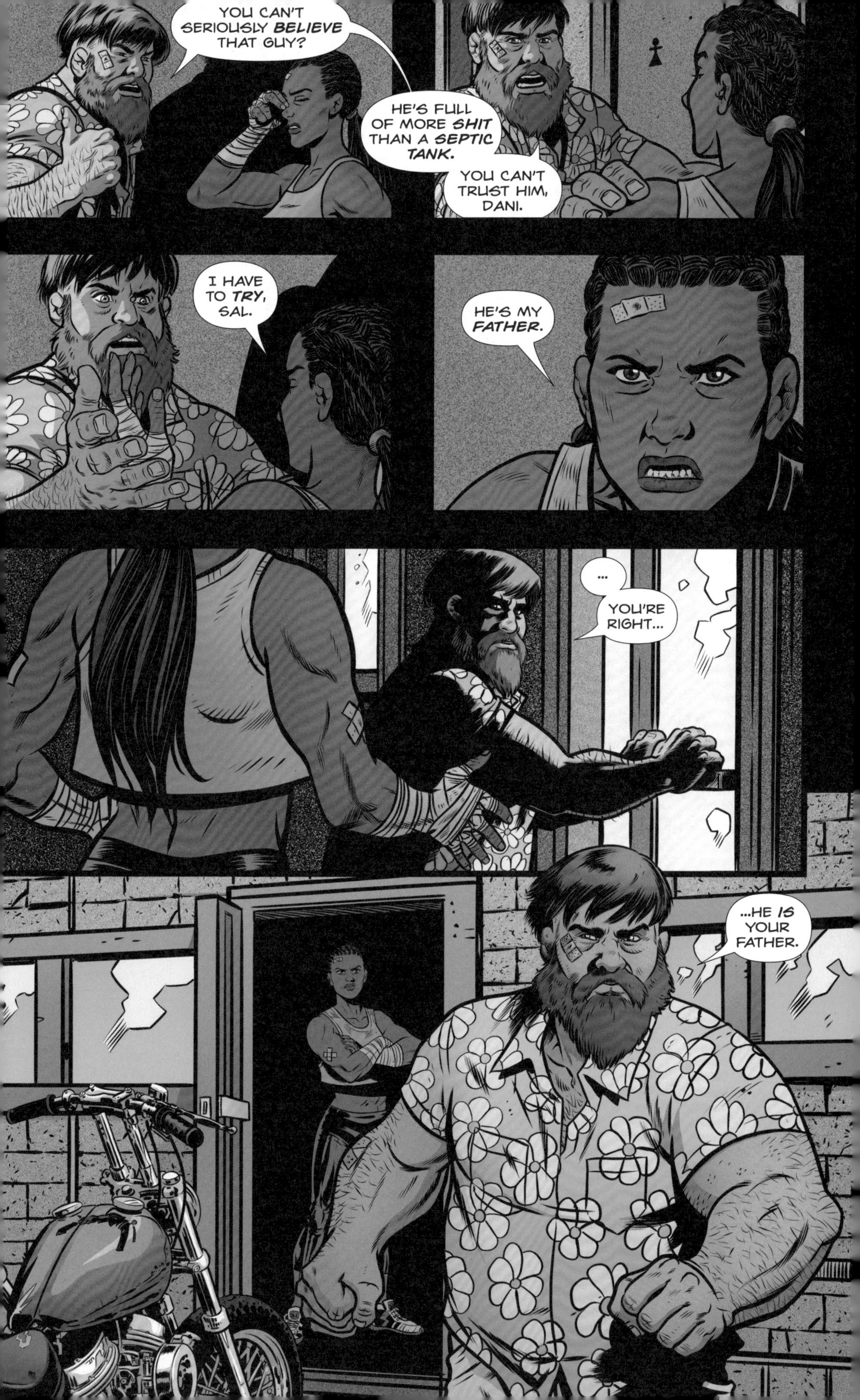
YOU CAN'T SERIOUSLY BELIEVE THAT GUY?
HE'S FULL OF MORE SHIT THAN A SEPTIC TANK.
YOU CAN'T TRUST HIM, DANI.
I HAVE TO TRY, SAL.
HE'S MY FATHER.
...
YOU'RE RIGHT...
...HE IS YOUR FATHER.

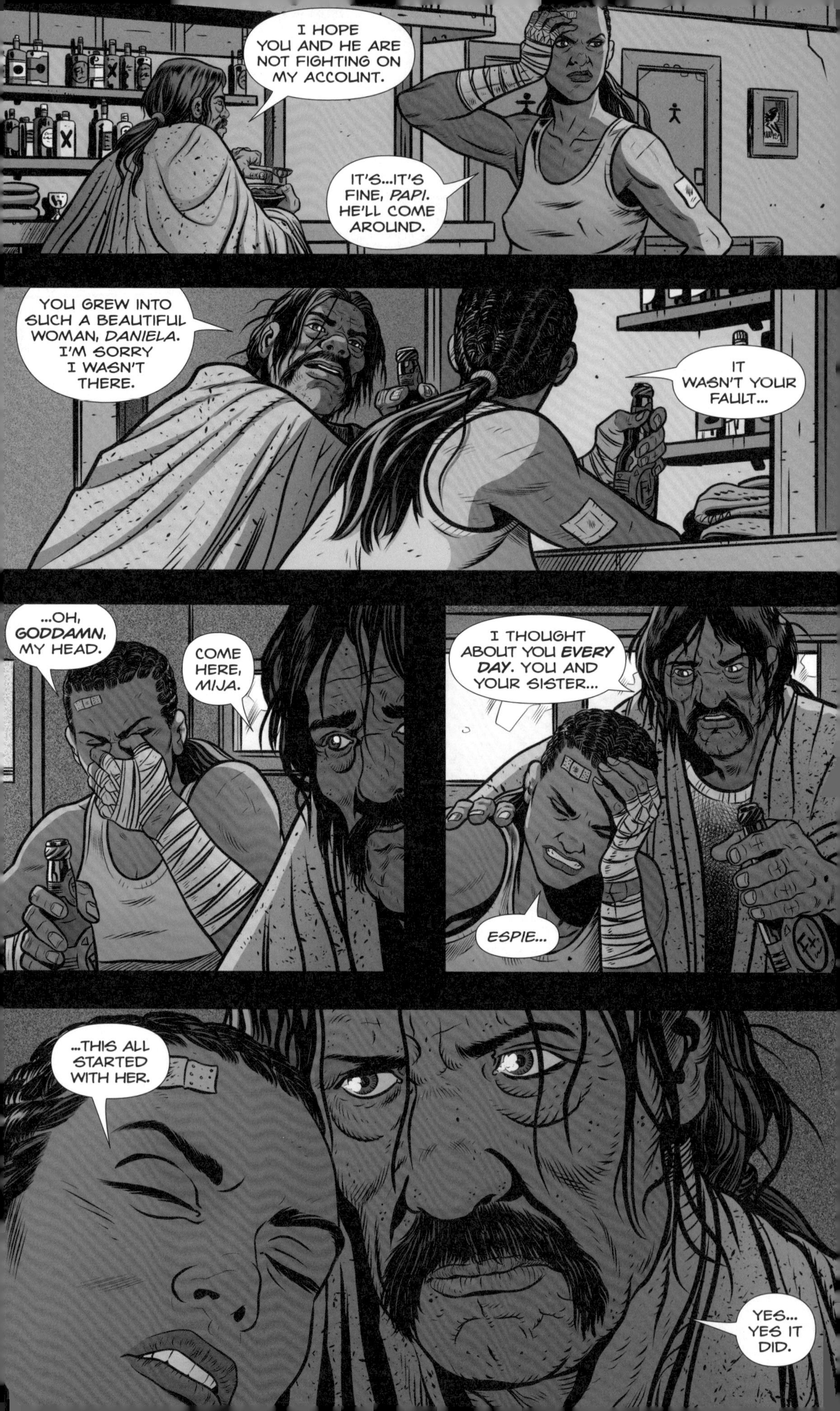
I HOPE YOU AND HE ARE NOT FIGHTING ON MY ACCOUNT.
IT'S...IT'S FINE, *PAPI*. HE'LL COME AROUND.
YOU GREW INTO SUCH A BEAUTIFUL WOMAN, *DANIELA*. I'M SORRY I WASN'T THERE.
IT WASN'T YOUR FAULT...
...OH, **GODDAMN**, MY HEAD.
COME HERE, *MIJA*.
I THOUGHT ABOUT YOU **EVERY DAY**. YOU AND YOUR SISTER...
ESPIE...
...THIS ALL STARTED WITH HER.
YES... YES IT DID.

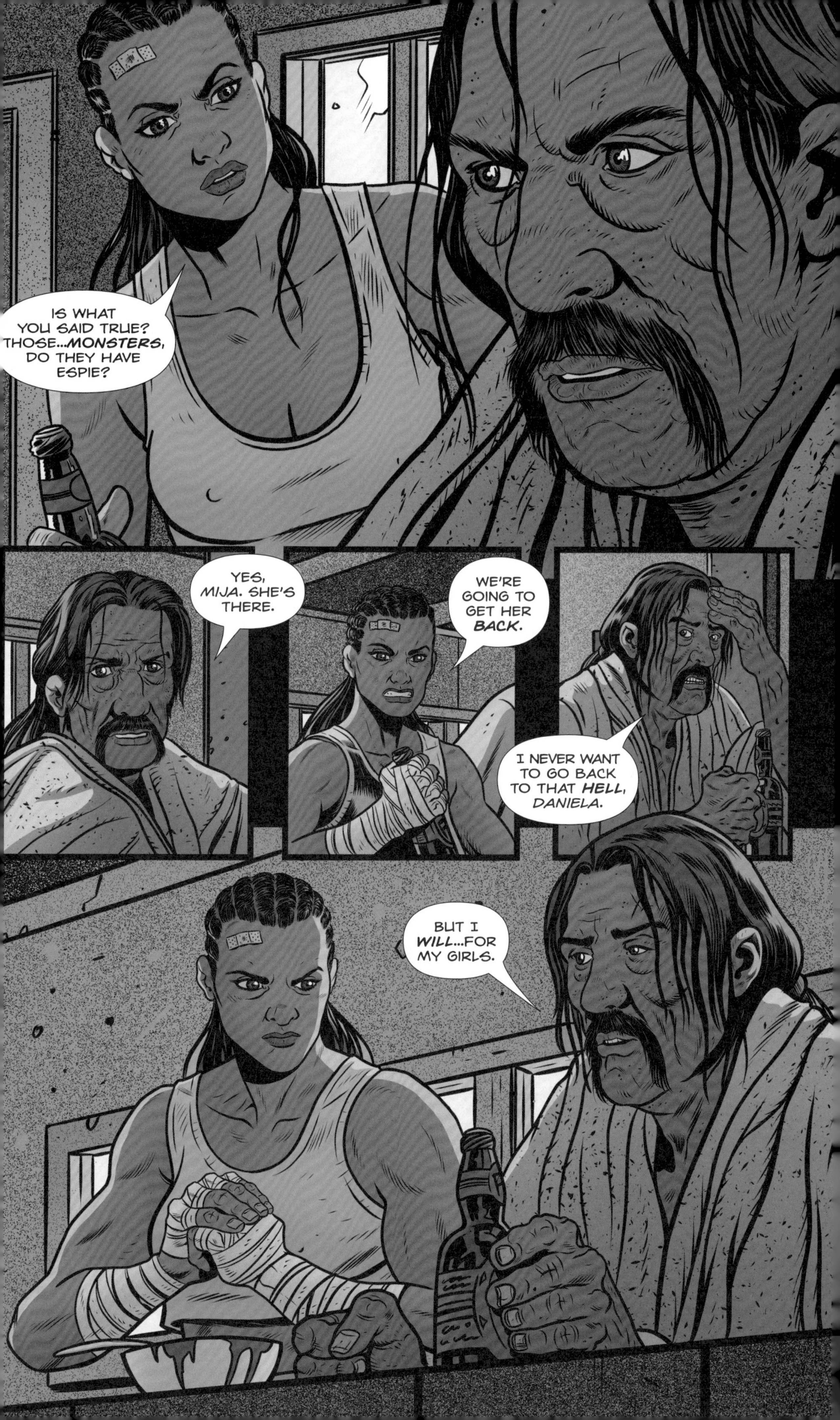
IS WHAT YOU SAID TRUE? THOSE...MONSTERS, DO THEY HAVE ESPIE?
YES, MIJA. SHE'S THERE.
WE'RE GOING TO GET HER BACK.
I NEVER WANT TO GO BACK TO THAT HELL, DANIELA.
BUT I WILL...FOR MY GIRLS.

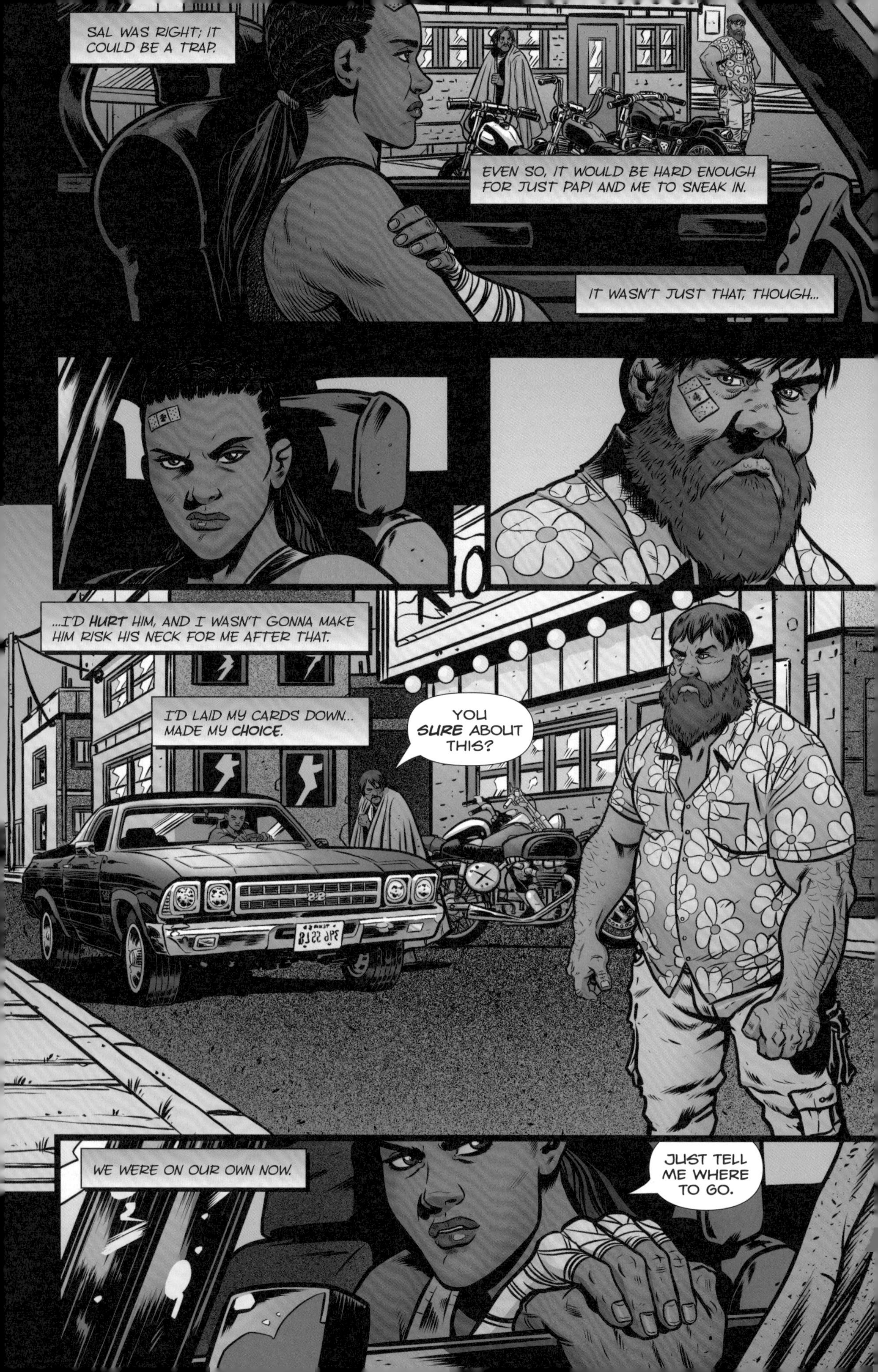

SAL WAS RIGHT; IT COULD BE A TRAP.
EVEN SO, IT WOULD BE HARD ENOUGH FOR JUST PAPI AND ME TO SNEAK IN.
IT WASN'T JUST THAT, THOUGH...
...I'D HURT HIM, AND I WASN'T GONNA MAKE HIM RISK HIS NECK FOR ME AFTER THAT.
I'D LAID MY CARDS DOWN... MADE MY CHOICE.
YOU SURE ABOUT THIS?
WE WERE ON OUR OWN NOW.
JUST TELL ME WHERE TO GO.

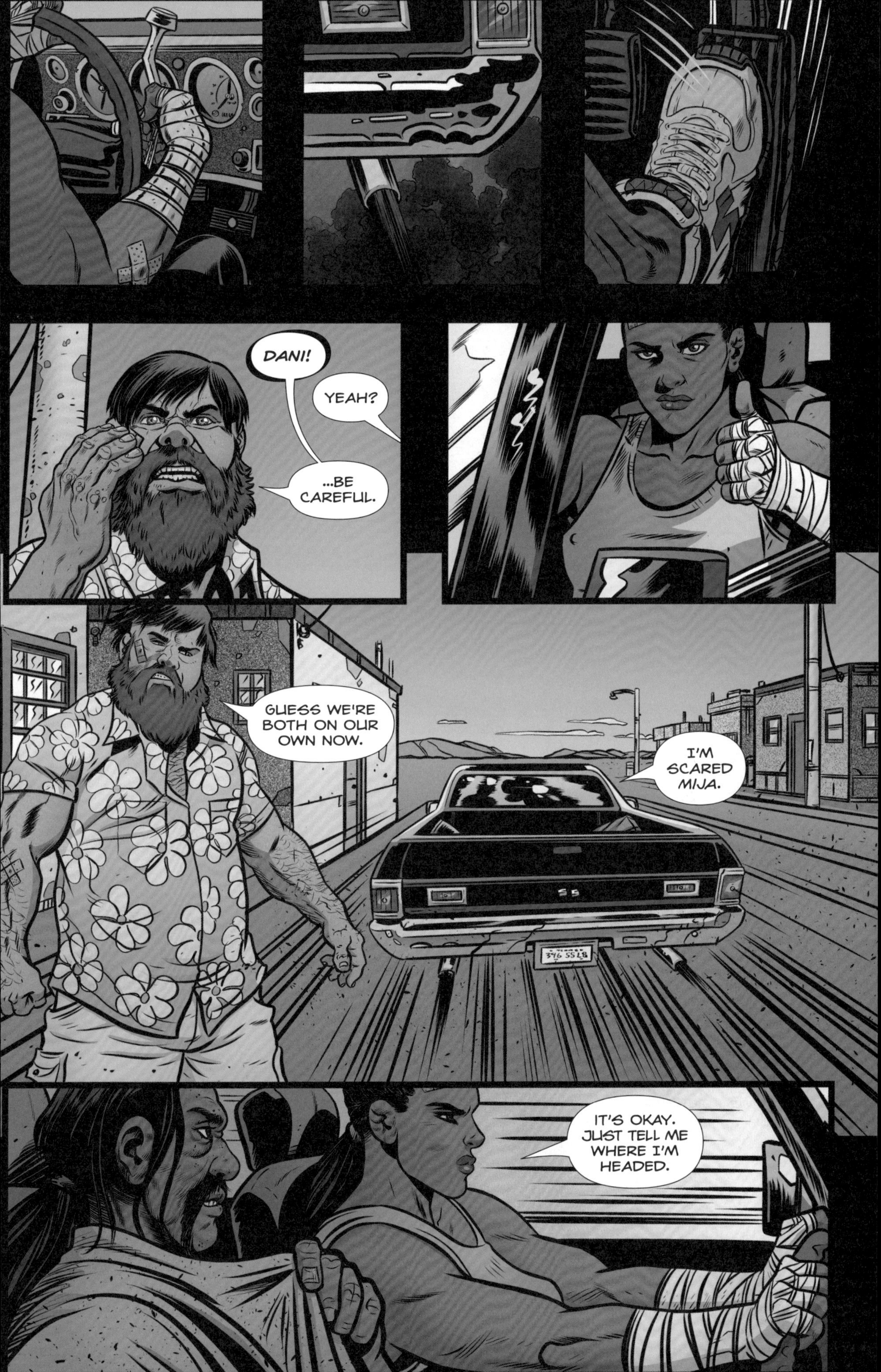
DANI!
YEAH?
...BE CAREFUL.
GUESS WE'RE BOTH ON OUR OWN NOW.
I'M SCARED MIJA.
IT'S OKAY. JUST TELL ME WHERE I'M HEADED.

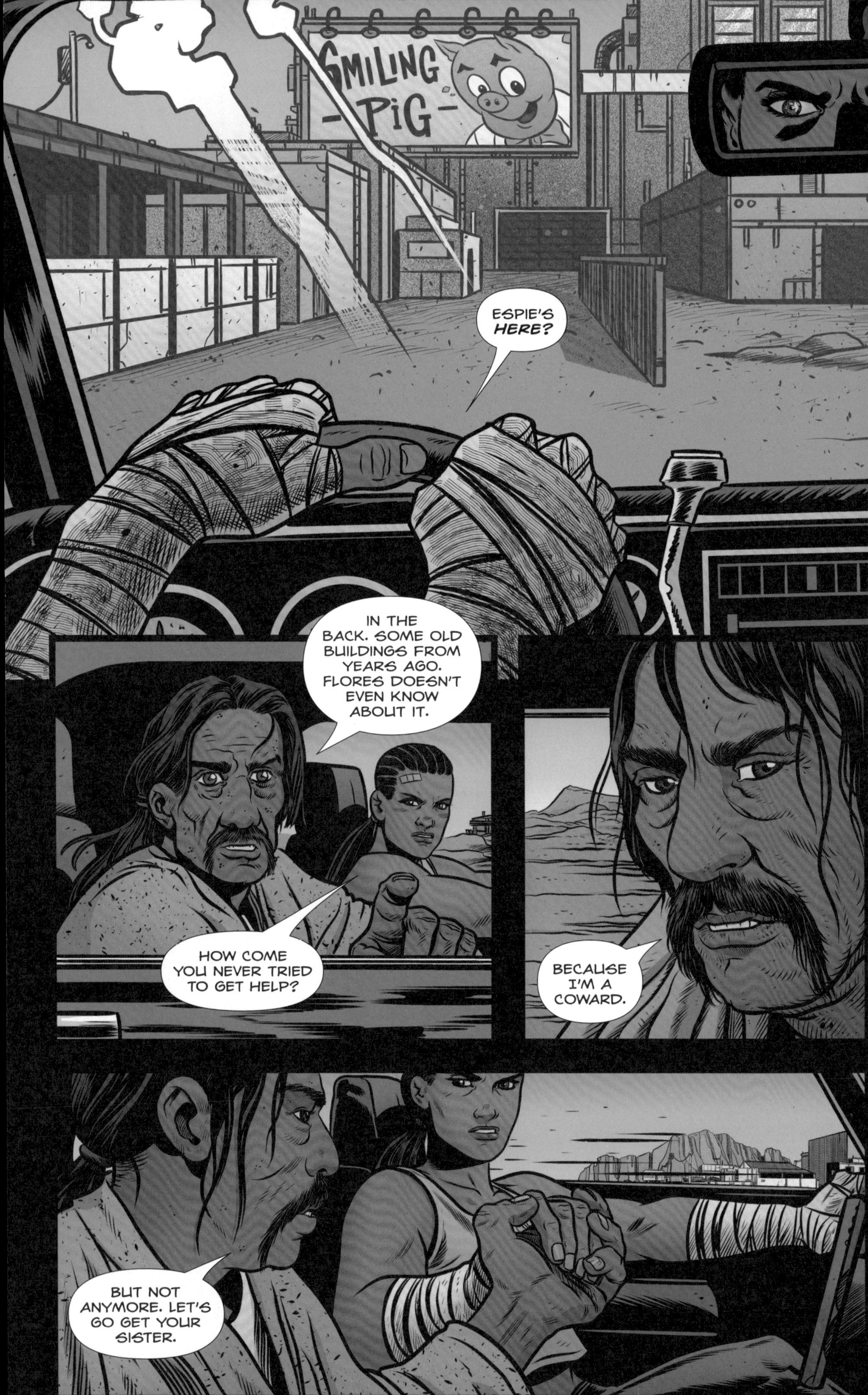
SMILING PIG
ESPIE'S *HERE?*
IN THE BACK. SOME OLD BUILDINGS FROM YEARS AGO. FLORES DOESN'T EVEN KNOW ABOUT IT.
HOW COME YOU NEVER TRIED TO GET HELP?
BECAUSE I'M A COWARD.
BUT NOT ANYMORE. LET'S GO GET YOUR SISTER.

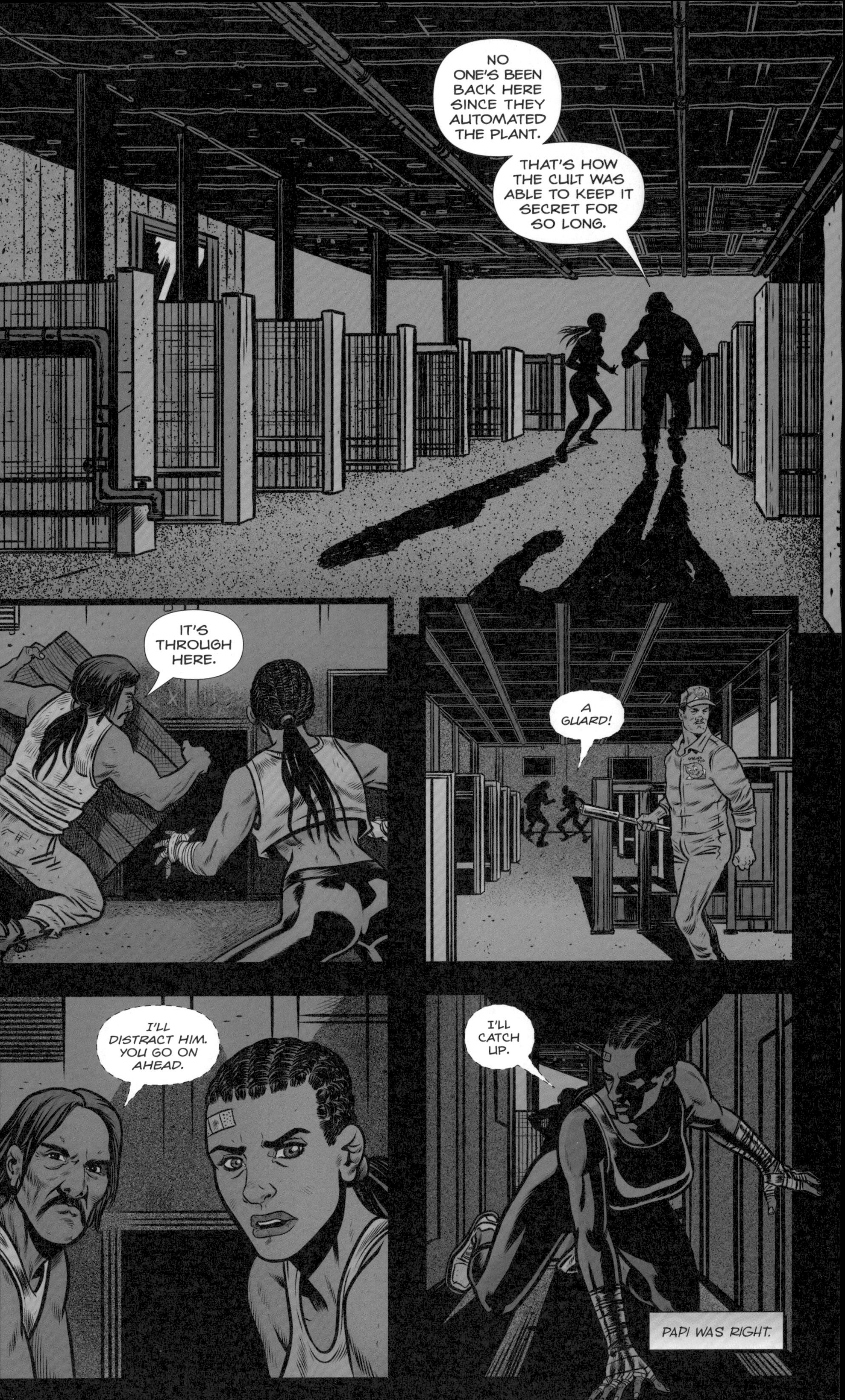
NO ONE'S BEEN BACK HERE SINCE THEY AUTOMATED THE PLANT.
THAT'S HOW THE CULT WAS ABLE TO KEEP IT SECRET FOR SO LONG.
IT'S THROUGH HERE.
A GUARD!
I'LL DISTRACT HIM. YOU GO ON AHEAD.
I'LL CATCH UP.
PAPI WAS RIGHT.

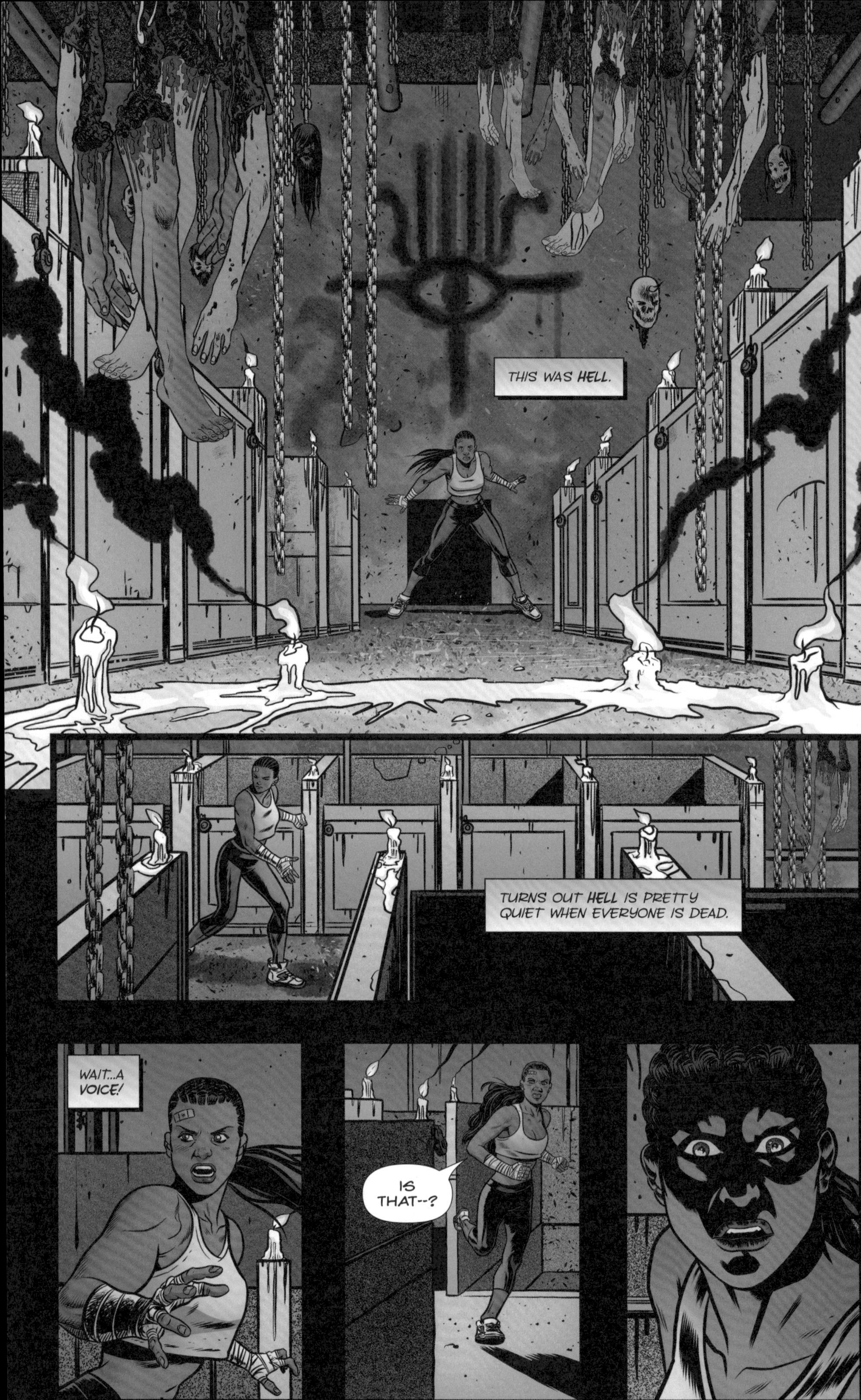
THIS WAS HELL.
TURNS OUT HELL IS PRETTY QUIET WHEN EVERYONE IS DEAD.
WAIT...A VOICE!
IS THAT--?

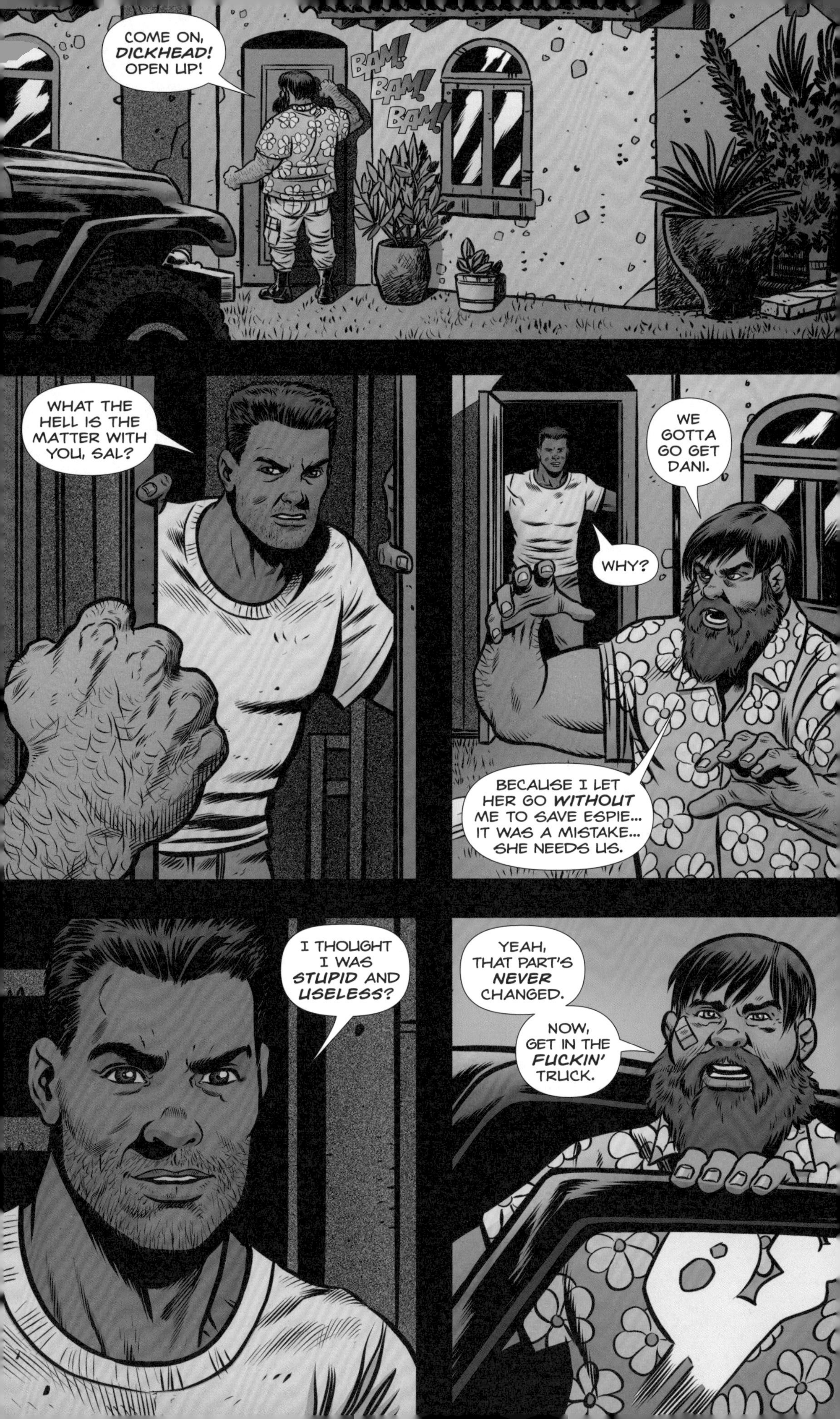
COME ON, DICKHEAD! OPEN UP!
BAM! BAM! BAM!
WHAT THE HELL IS THE MATTER WITH YOU, SAL?
WE GOTTA GO GET DANI.
WHY?
BECAUSE I LET HER GO WITHOUT ME TO SAVE ESPIE... IT WAS A MISTAKE... SHE NEEDS US.
I THOUGHT I WAS STUPID AND USELESS?
YEAH, THAT PART'S NEVER CHANGED.
NOW, GET IN THE FUCKIN' TRUCK.

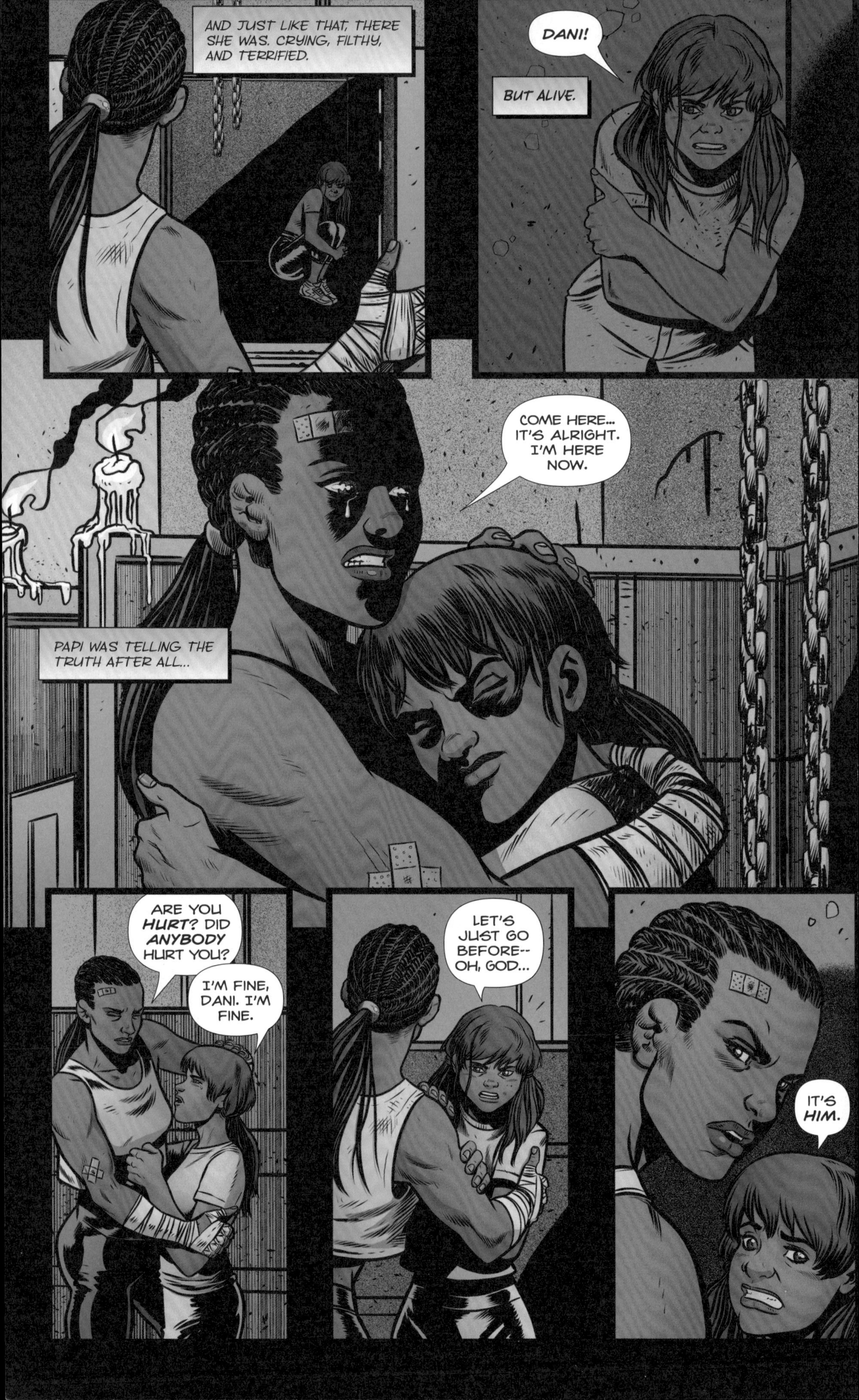
AND JUST LIKE THAT, THERE SHE WAS. CRYING, FILTHY, AND TERRIFIED.
DANI!
BUT ALIVE.
COME HERE... IT'S ALRIGHT. I'M HERE NOW.
PAPI WAS TELLING THE TRUTH AFTER ALL...
ARE YOU HURT? DID ANYBODY HURT YOU?
I'M FINE, DANI. I'M FINE.
LET'S JUST GO BEFORE-- OH, GOD...
IT'S HIM.

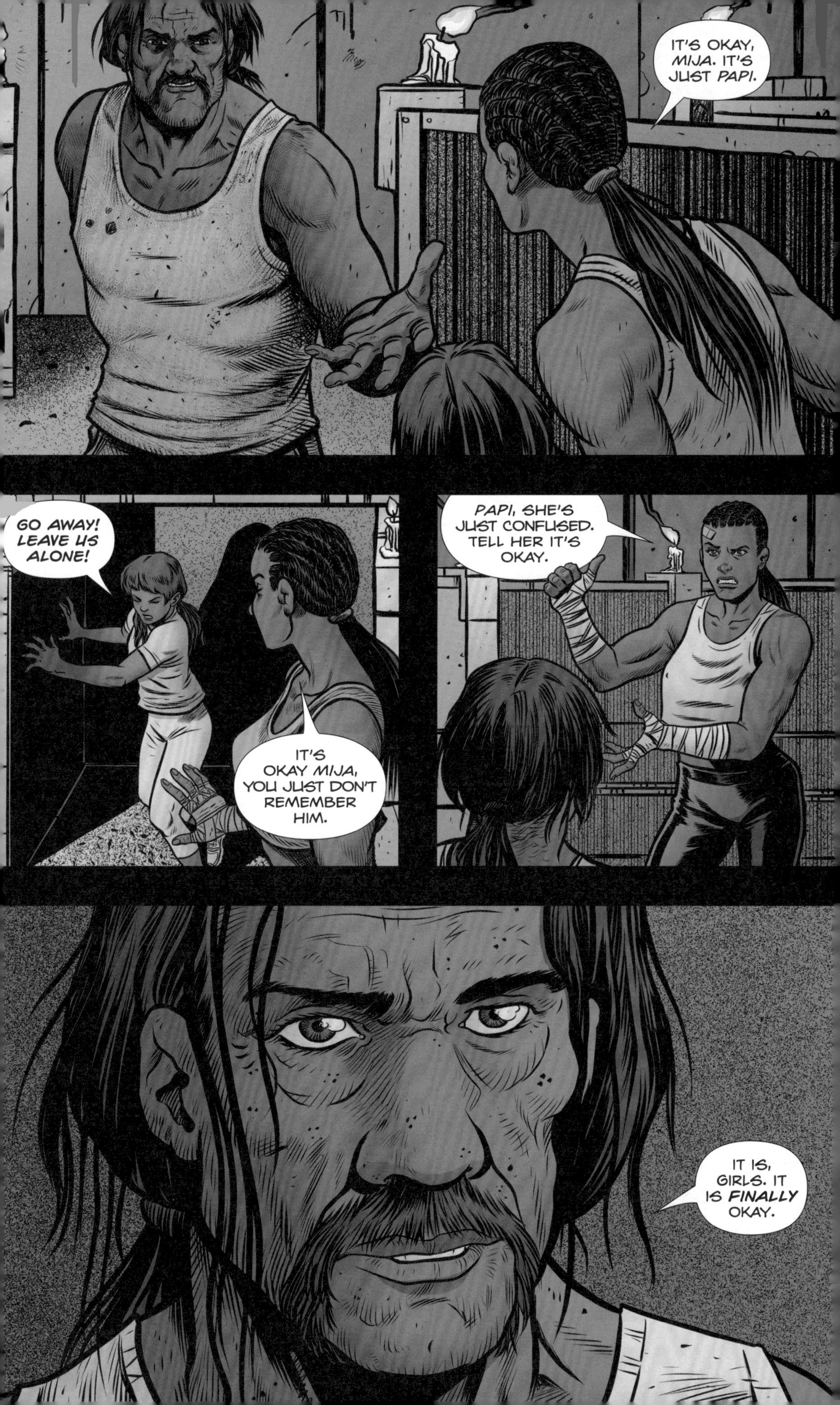
IT'S OKAY, MIJA. IT'S JUST PAPI.
GO AWAY! LEAVE US ALONE!
IT'S OKAY MIJA, YOU JUST DON'T REMEMBER HIM.
PAPI, SHE'S JUST CONFUSED. TELL HER IT'S OKAY.
IT IS, GIRLS. IT IS FINALLY OKAY.

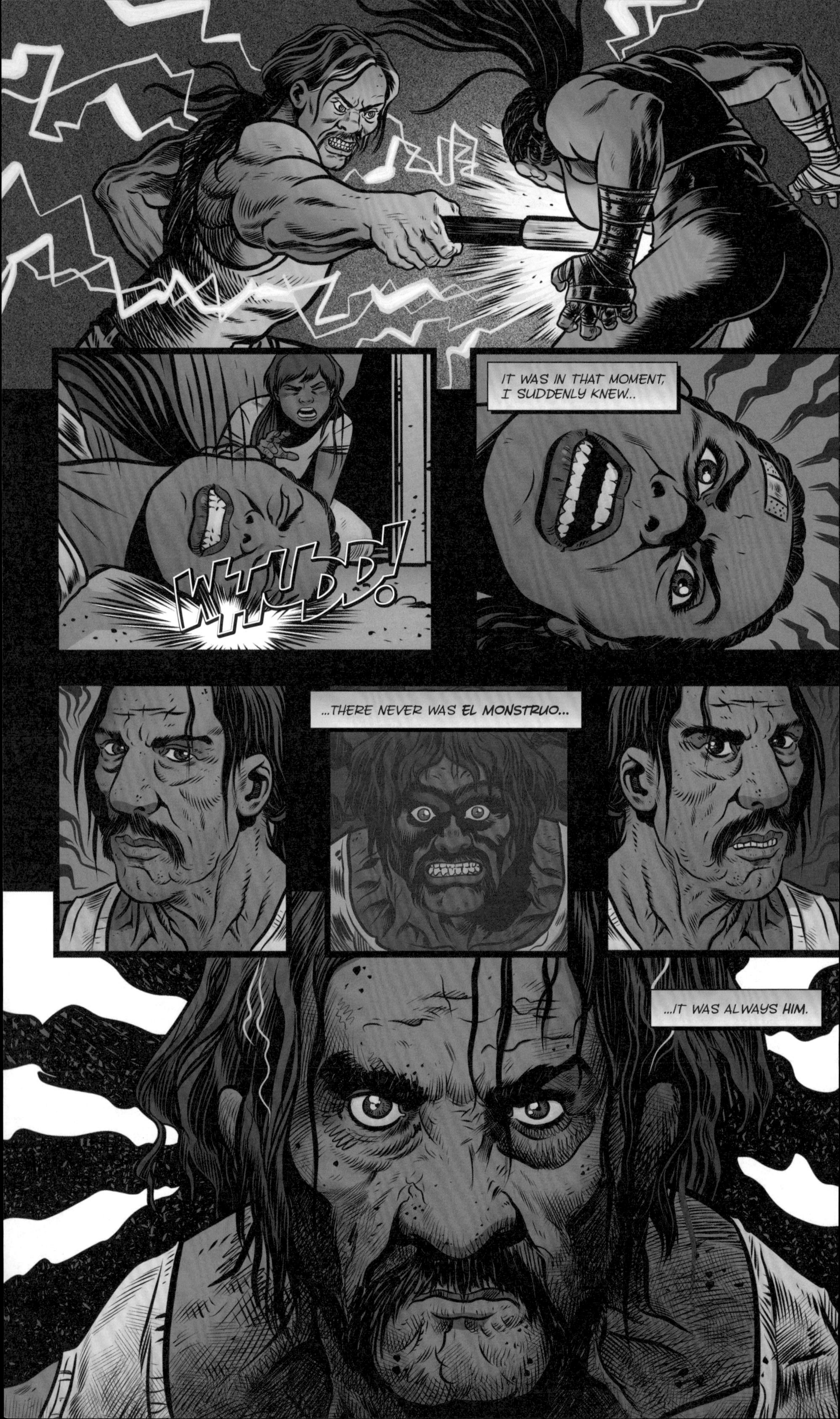
WHUDD!
IT WAS IN THAT MOMENT, I SUDDENLY KNEW...
...THERE NEVER WAS EL MONSTRUO...
...IT WAS ALWAYS HIM.

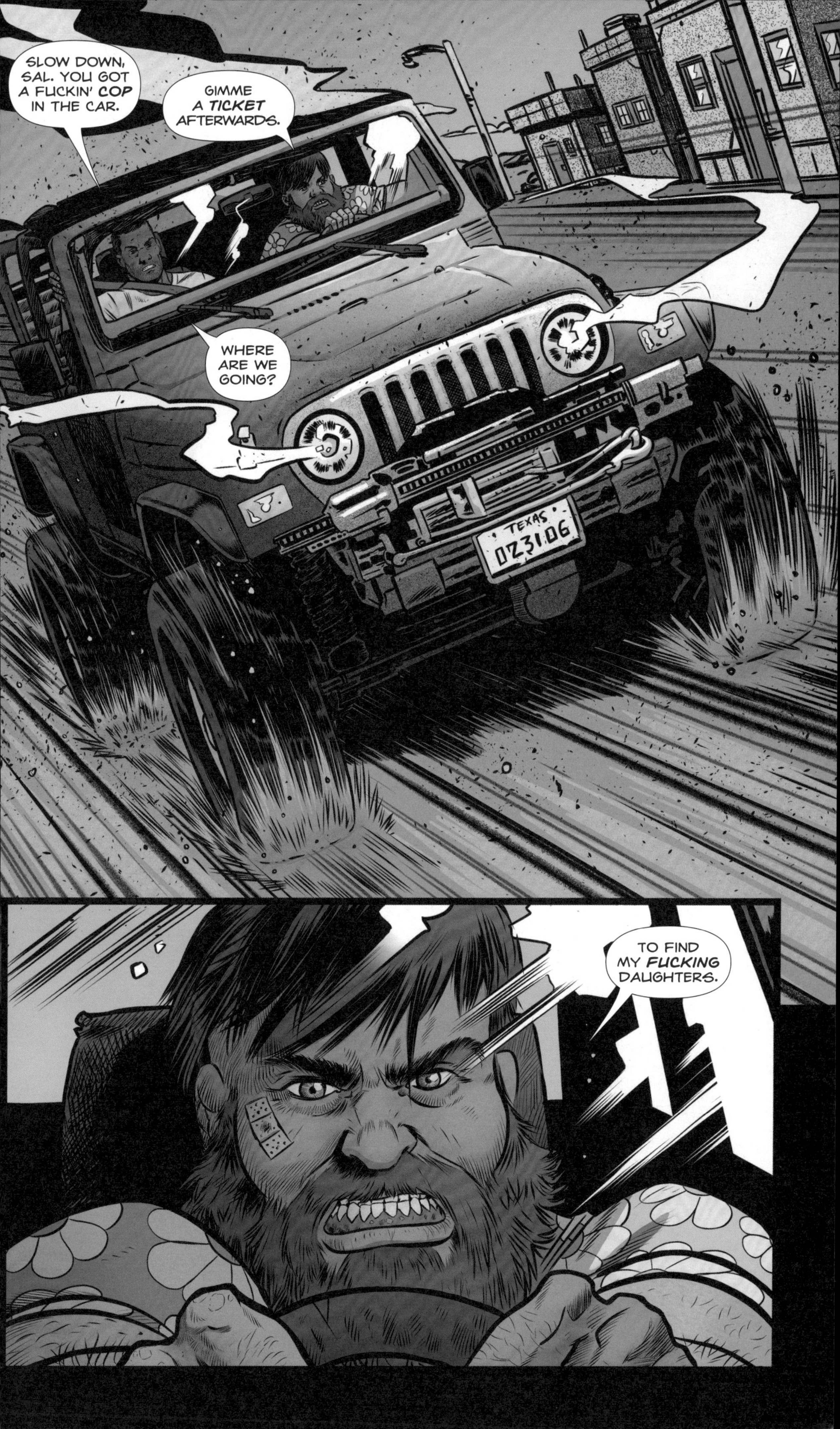
SLOW DOWN, SAL. YOU GOT A FUCKIN' COP IN THE CAR.
GIMME A TICKET AFTERWARDS.
WHERE ARE WE GOING?
TEXAS 0Z31 DG
TO FIND MY FUCKING DAUGHTERS.

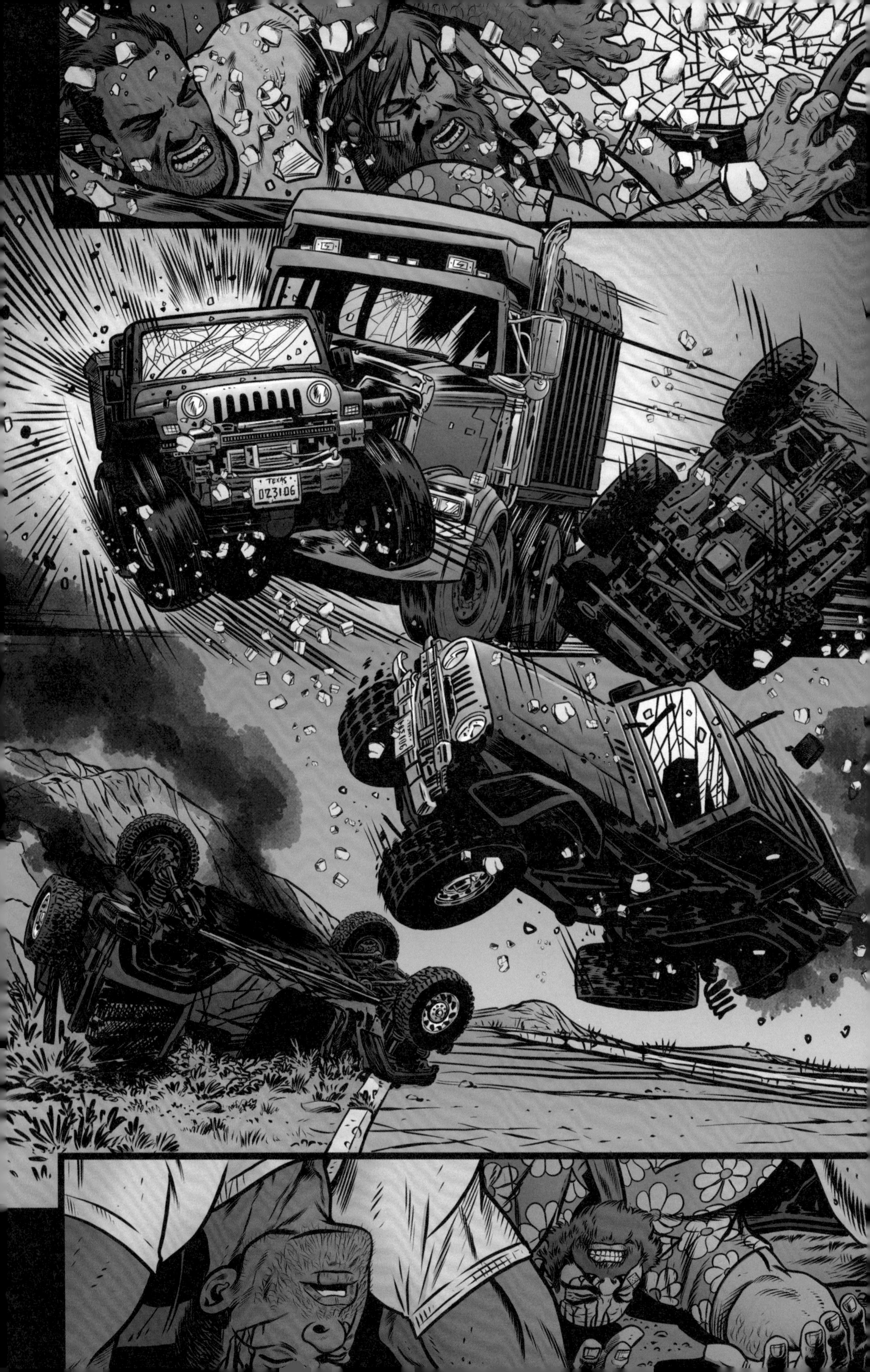
TEXAS
0Z31.06

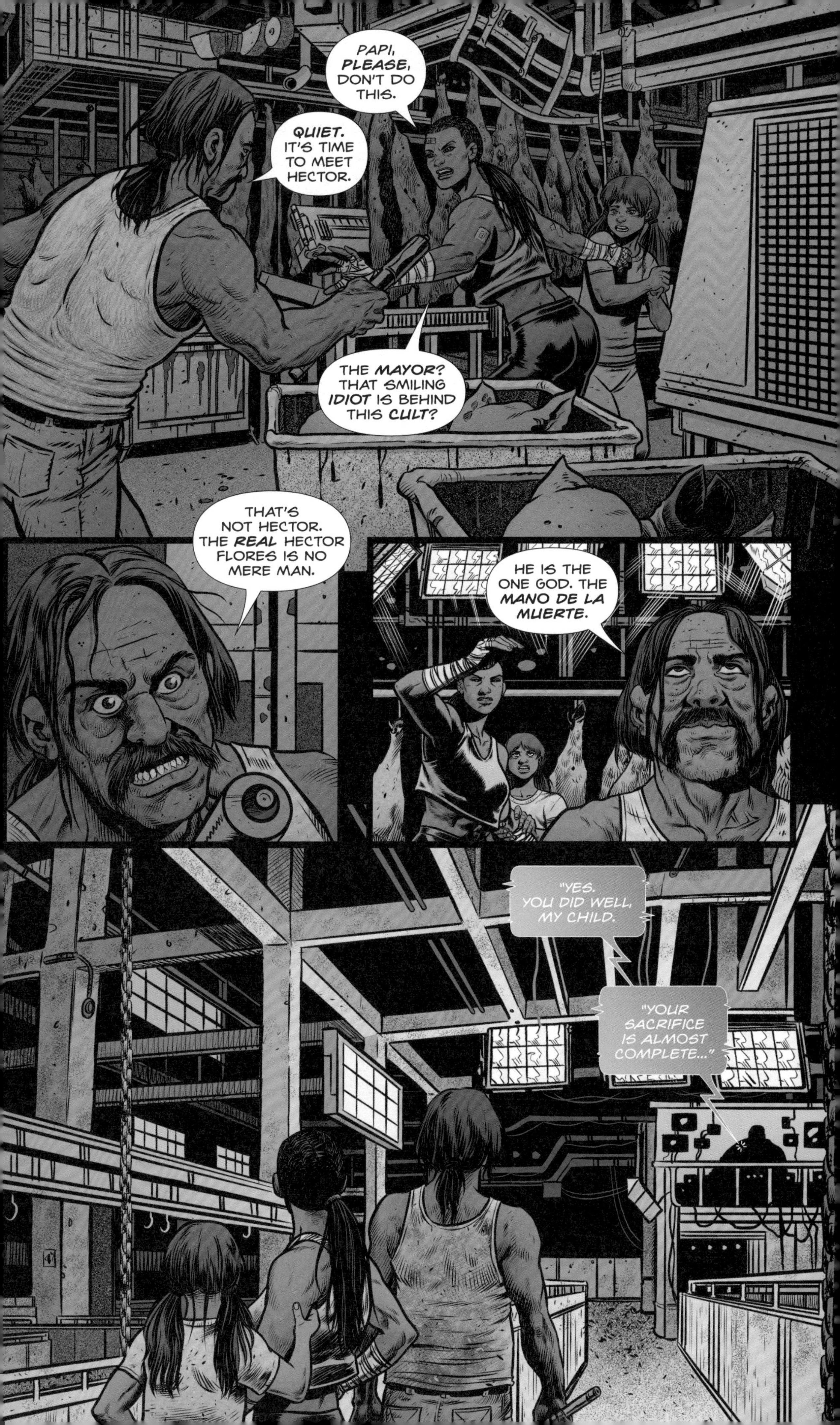
PAPI, PLEASE, DON'T DO THIS.
QUIET. IT'S TIME TO MEET HECTOR.
THE MAYOR? THAT SMILING IDIOT IS BEHIND THIS CULT?
THAT'S NOT HECTOR. THE REAL HECTOR FLORES IS NO MERE MAN.
HE IS THE ONE GOD. THE MANO DE LA MUERTE.
"YES. YOU DID WELL, MY CHILD.
"YOUR SACRIFICE IS ALMOST COMPLETE..."

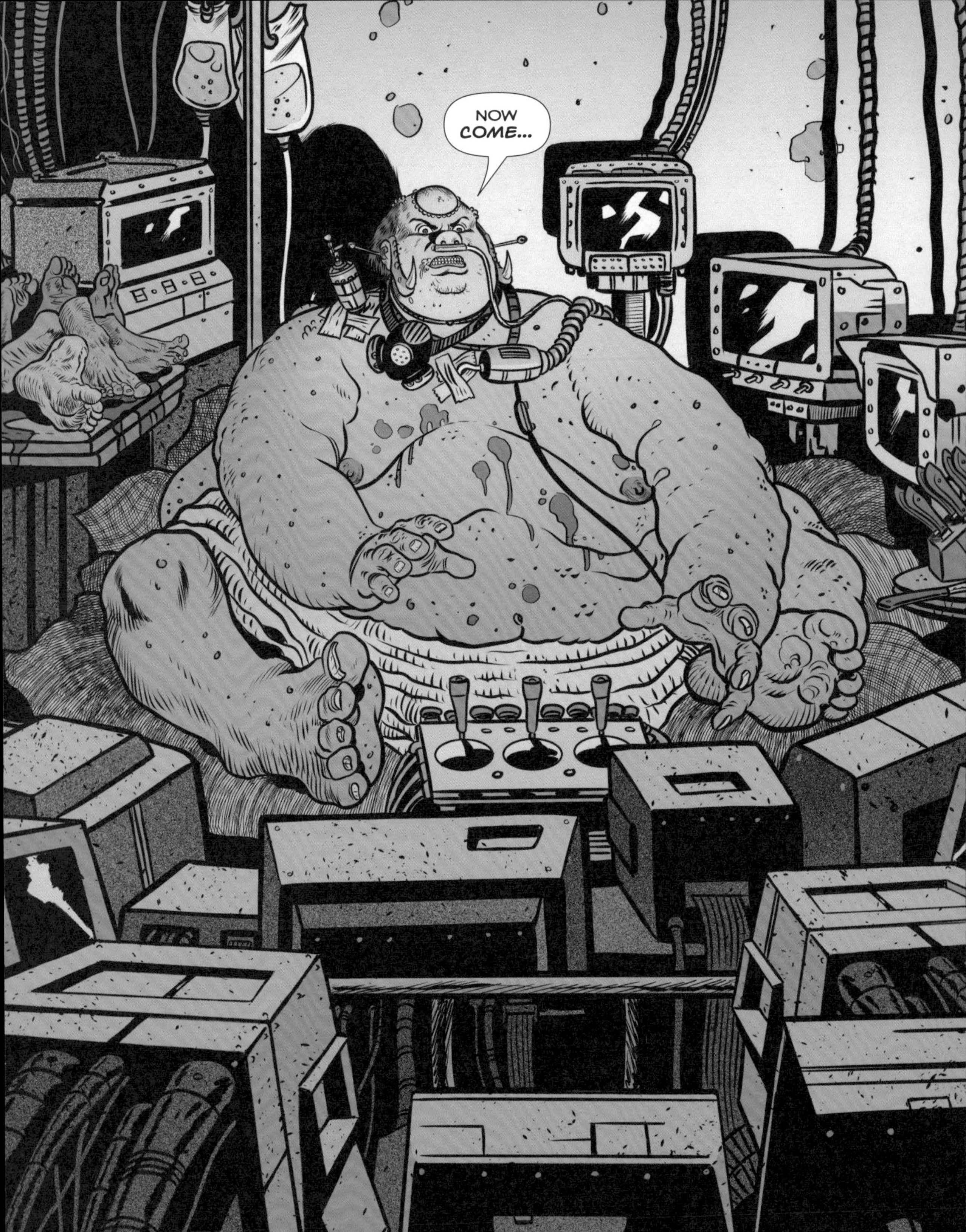
NOW COME...
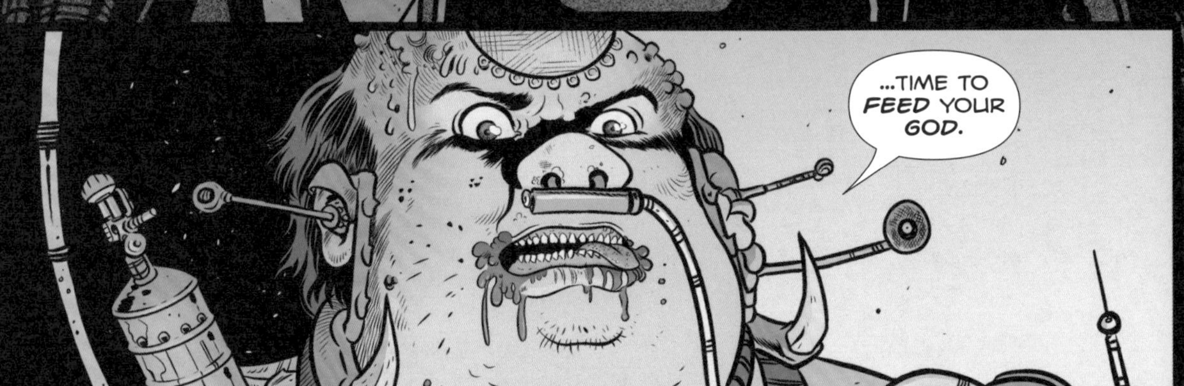
...TIME TO FEED YOUR GOD.

CHAPTER 6

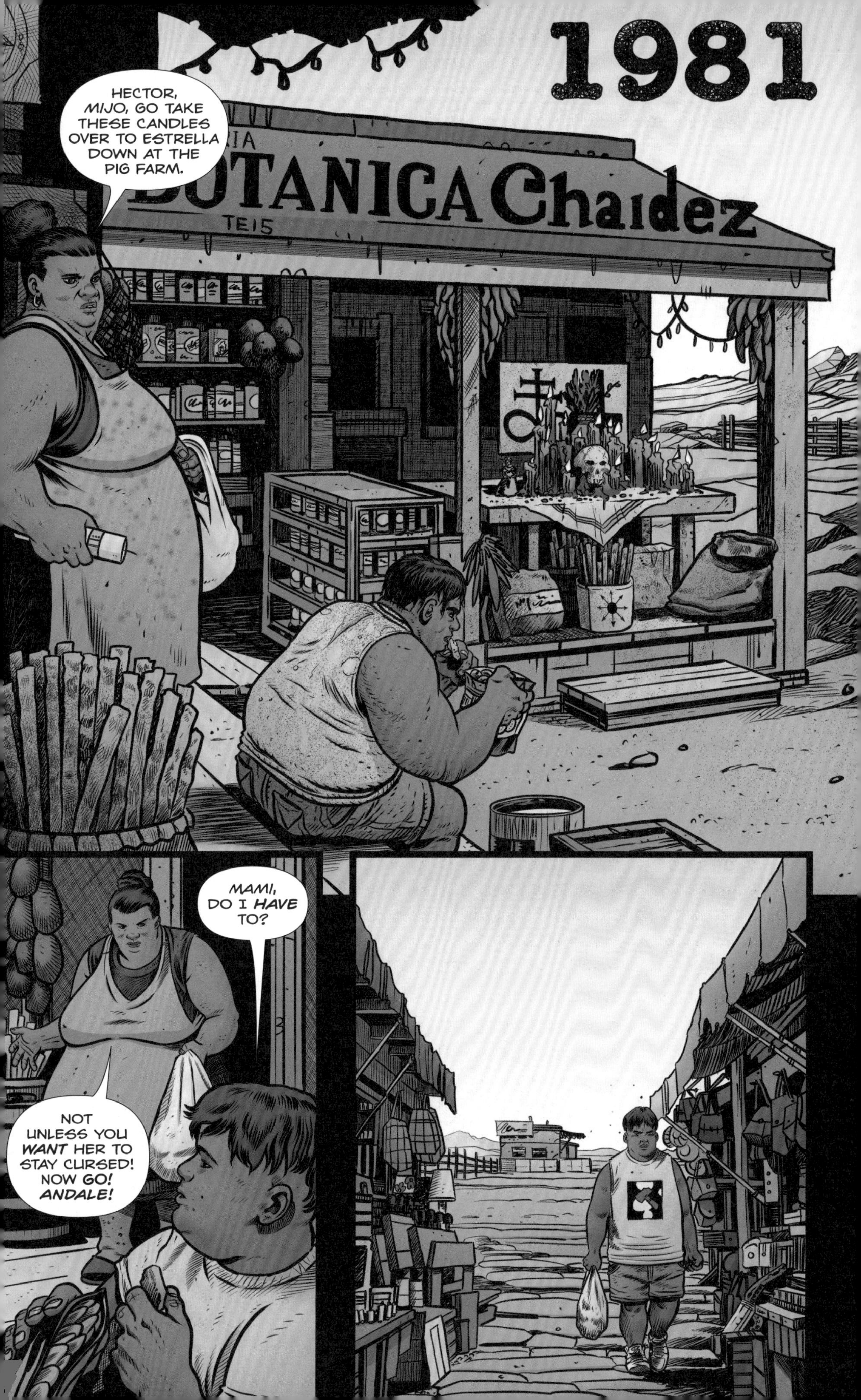
1981
HECTOR, MIJO, GO TAKE THESE CANDLES OVER TO ESTRELLA DOWN AT THE PIG FARM.
BOTANICA Chaidez
MAMI, DO I *HAVE* TO?
NOT UNLESS YOU *WANT* HER TO STAY CURSED! NOW *GO! ANDALE!*

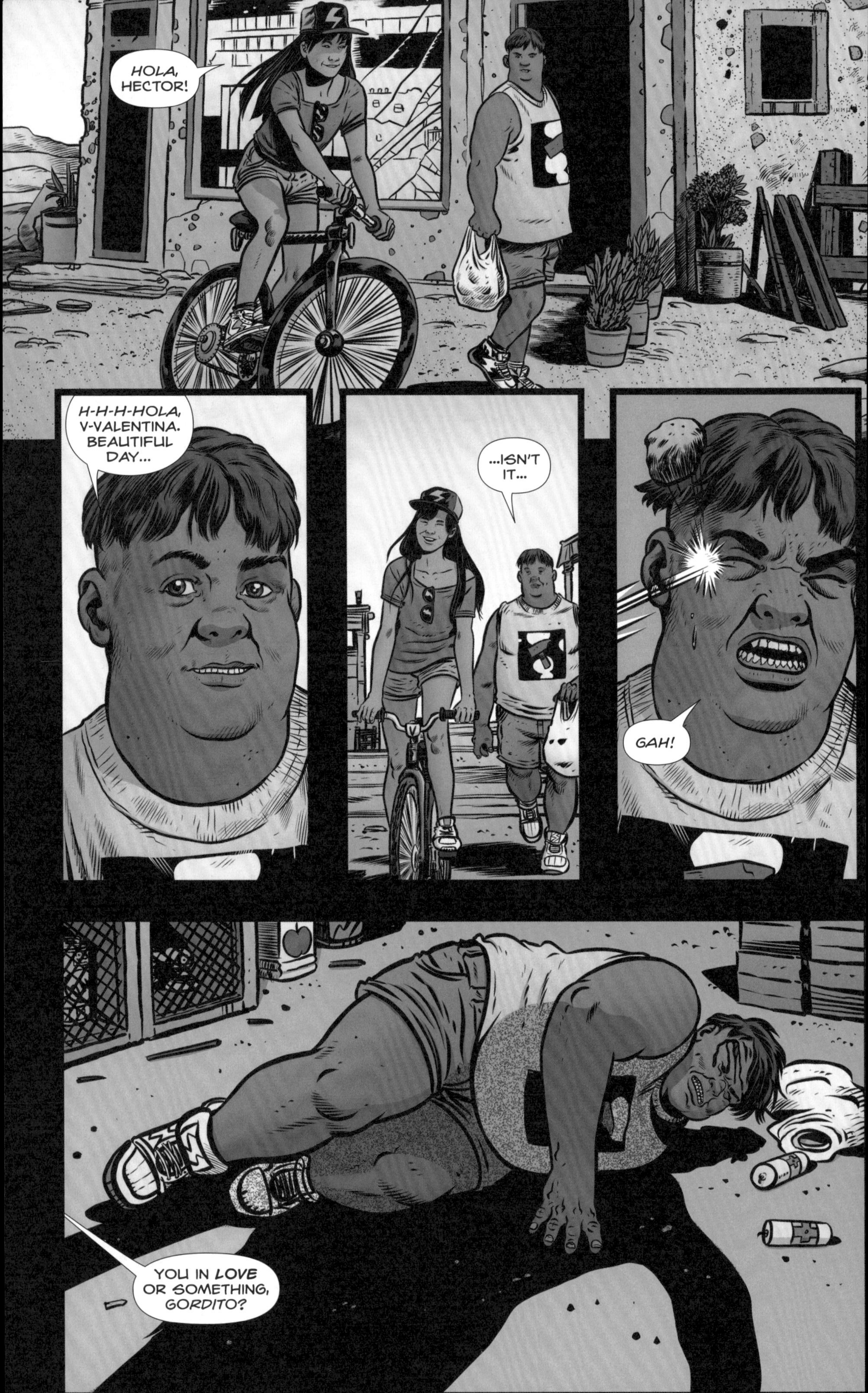
HOLA, HECTOR!
H-H-H-HOLA, V-VALENTINA. BEAUTIFUL DAY...
...ISN'T IT...
GAH!
YOU IN LOVE OR SOMETHING, GORDITO?

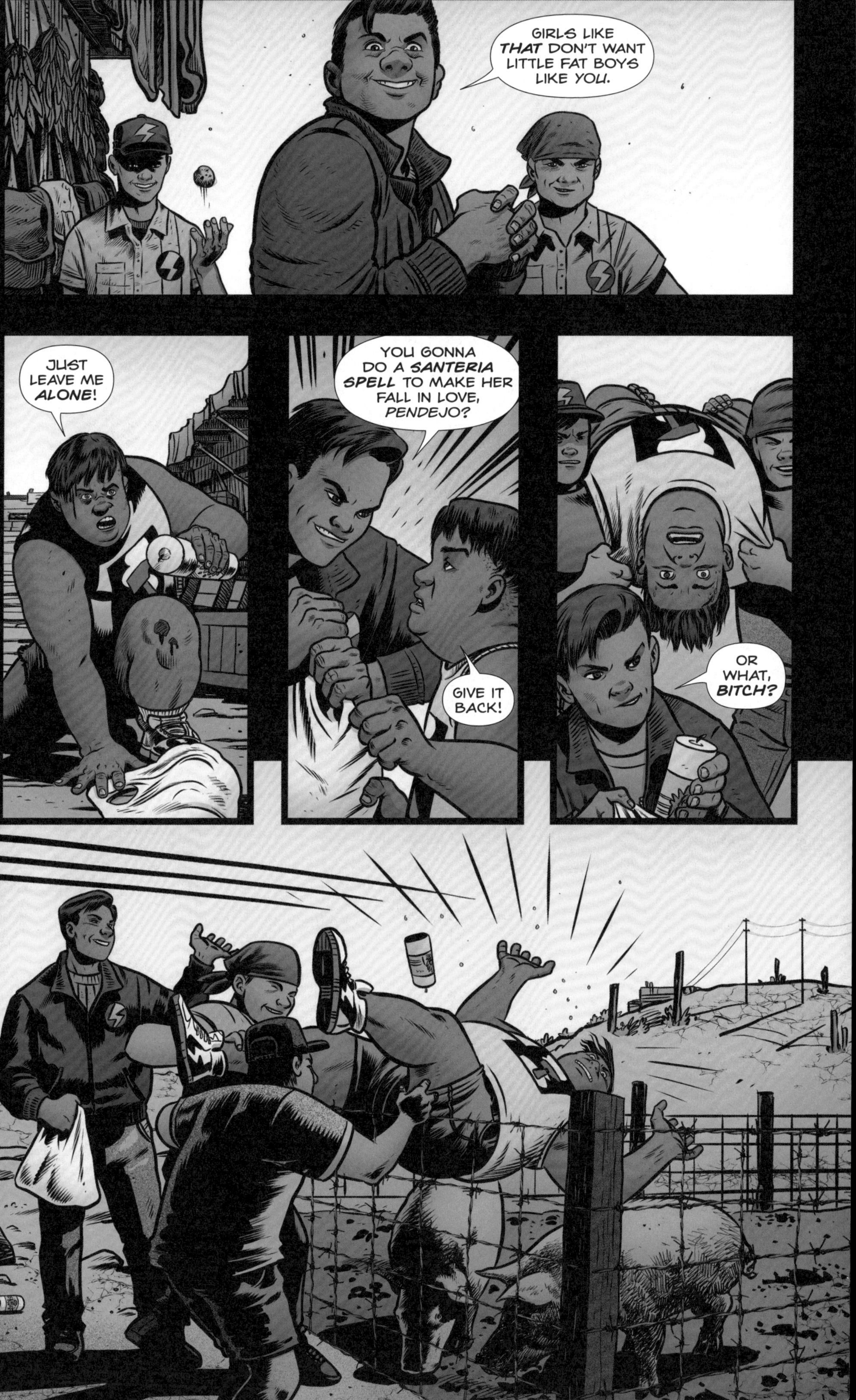
GIRLS LIKE THAT DON'T WANT LITTLE FAT BOYS LIKE YOU.
JUST LEAVE ME ALONE!
YOU GONNA DO A SANTERIA SPELL TO MAKE HER FALL IN LOVE, PENDEJO?
GIVE IT BACK!
OR WHAT, BITCH?

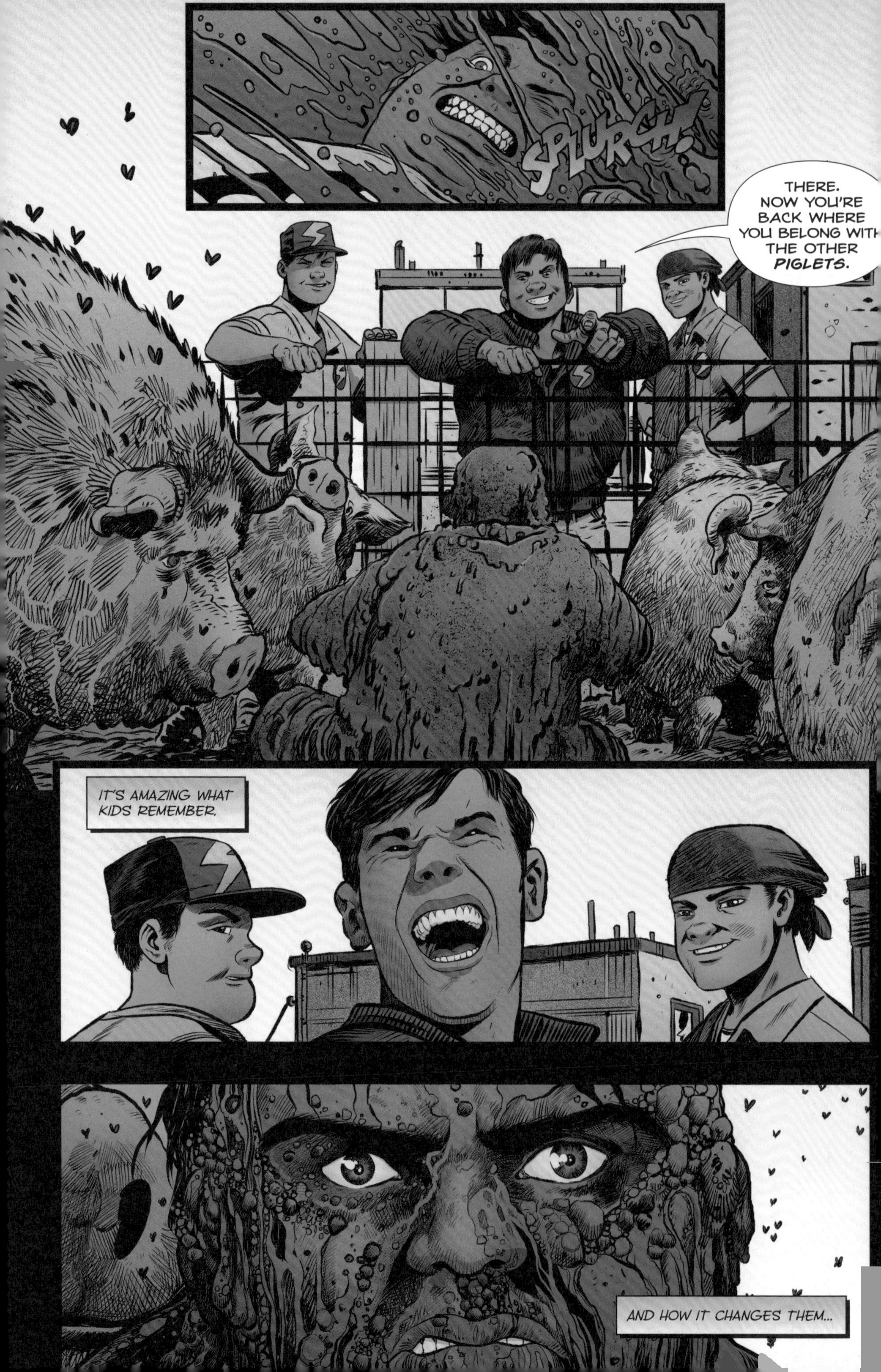
SPLURCH!
THERE. NOW YOU'RE BACK WHERE YOU BELONG WITH THE OTHER *PIGLETS*.
IT'S AMAZING WHAT KIDS REMEMBER.
AND HOW IT CHANGES THEM...

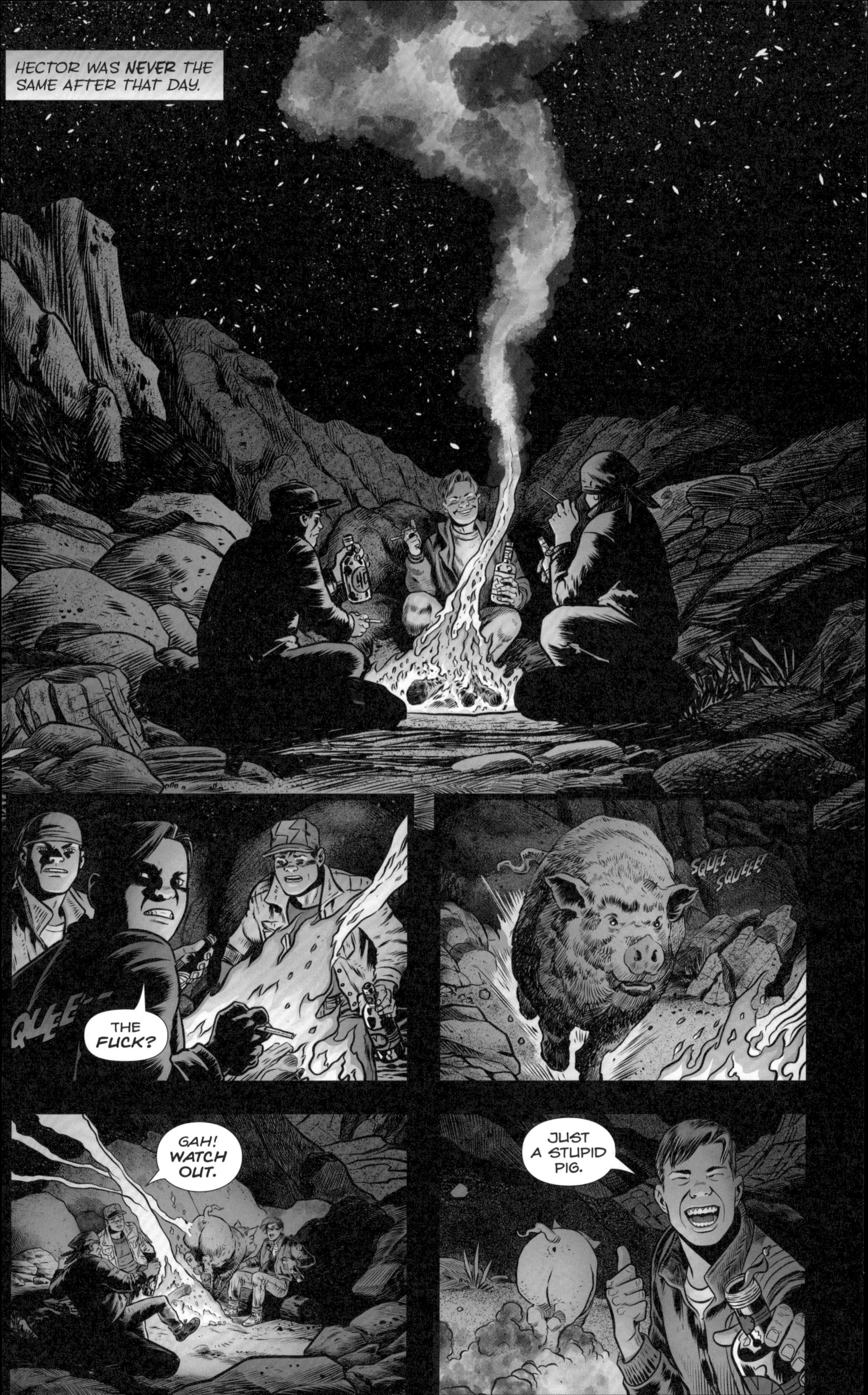
HECTOR WAS NEVER THE SAME AFTER THAT DAY.
QUEE--
THE FUCK?
SQUEE SQUEEE!
GAH! WATCH OUT.
JUST A STUPID PIG.

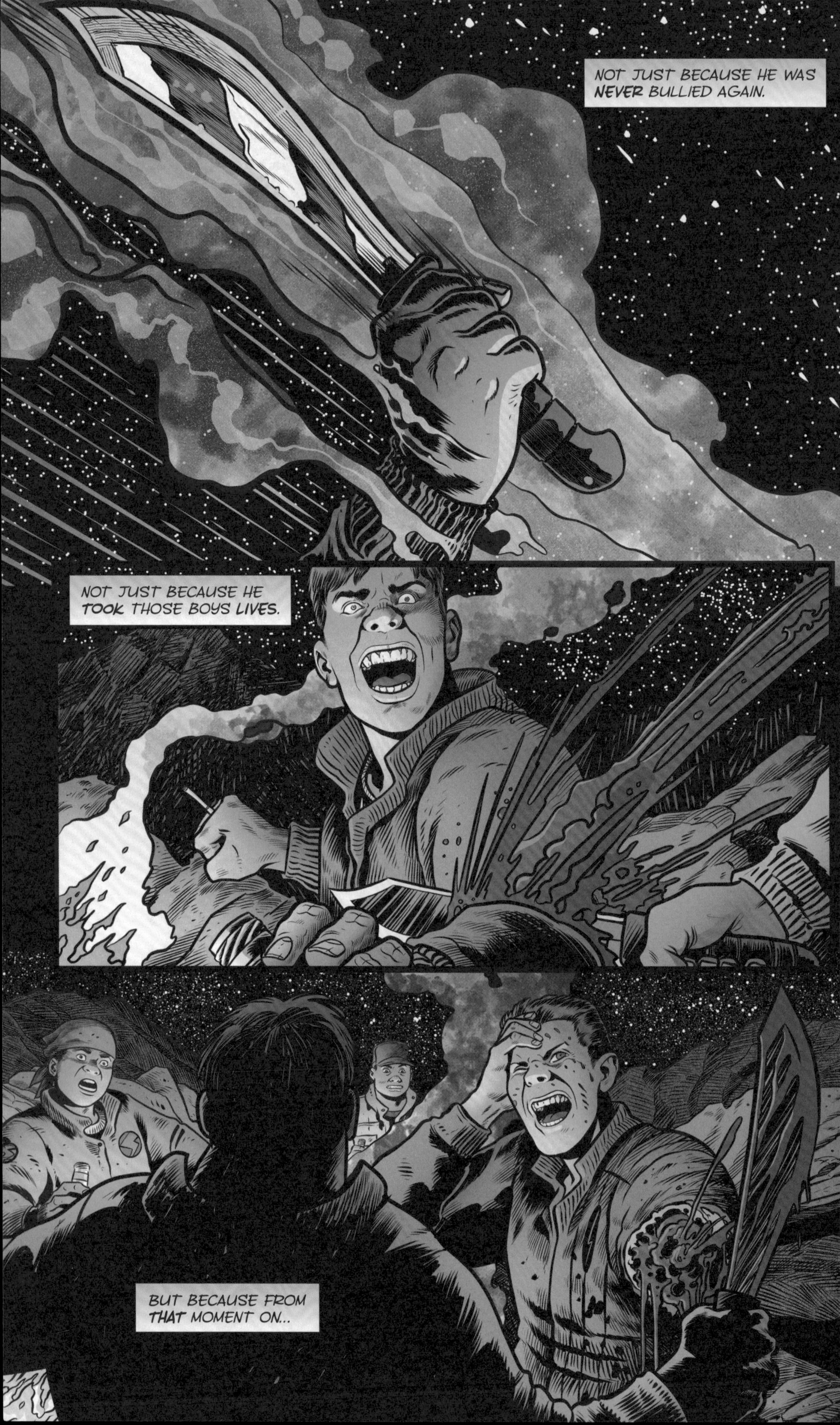
NOT JUST BECAUSE HE WAS NEVER BULLIED AGAIN.
NOT JUST BECAUSE HE TOOK THOSE BOYS LIVES.
BUT BECAUSE FROM THAT MOMENT ON...

...HECTOR HAD A TASTE FOR A DIFFERENT KIND OF MEAT.
MAYBE IF HECTOR HAD WHAT I HAD...THE DARKNESS...
...IF HE COULD'VE JUST FORGOTTEN THE THINGS THAT HAPPENED TO HIM...

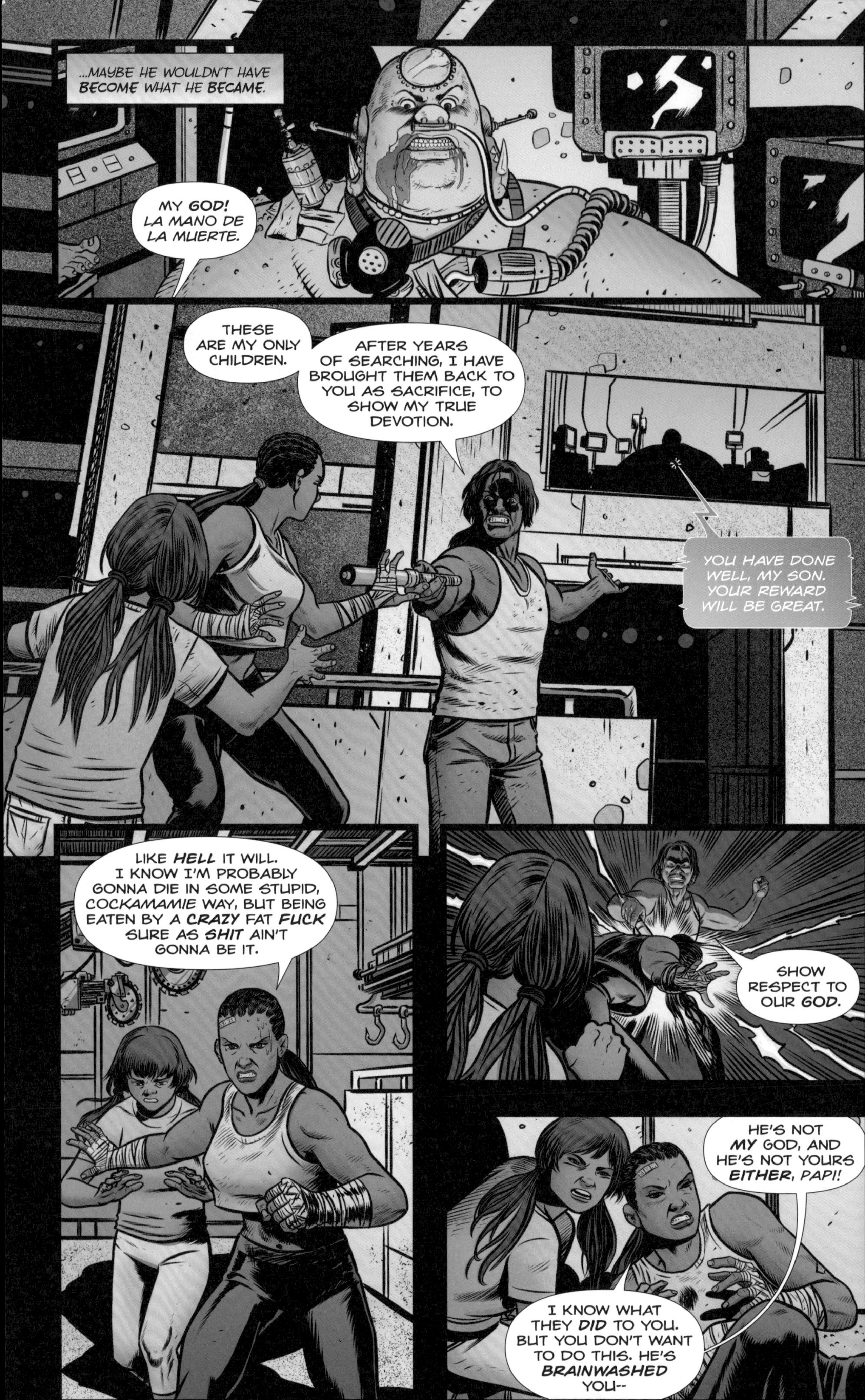
...MAYBE HE WOULDN'T HAVE BECOME WHAT HE BECAME.
MY GOD! LA MANO DE LA MUERTE.
THESE ARE MY ONLY CHILDREN.
AFTER YEARS OF SEARCHING, I HAVE BROUGHT THEM BACK TO YOU AS SACRIFICE, TO SHOW MY TRUE DEVOTION.
YOU HAVE DONE WELL, MY SON. YOUR REWARD WILL BE GREAT.
LIKE HELL IT WILL. I KNOW I'M PROBABLY GONNA DIE IN SOME STUPID, COCKAMAMIE WAY, BUT BEING EATEN BY A CRAZY FAT FUCK SURE AS SHIT AIN'T GONNA BE IT.
SHOW RESPECT TO OUR GOD.
HE'S NOT MY GOD, AND HE'S NOT YOURS EITHER, PAPI!
I KNOW WHAT THEY DID TO YOU. BUT YOU DON'T WANT TO DO THIS. HE'S BRAINWASHED YOU--

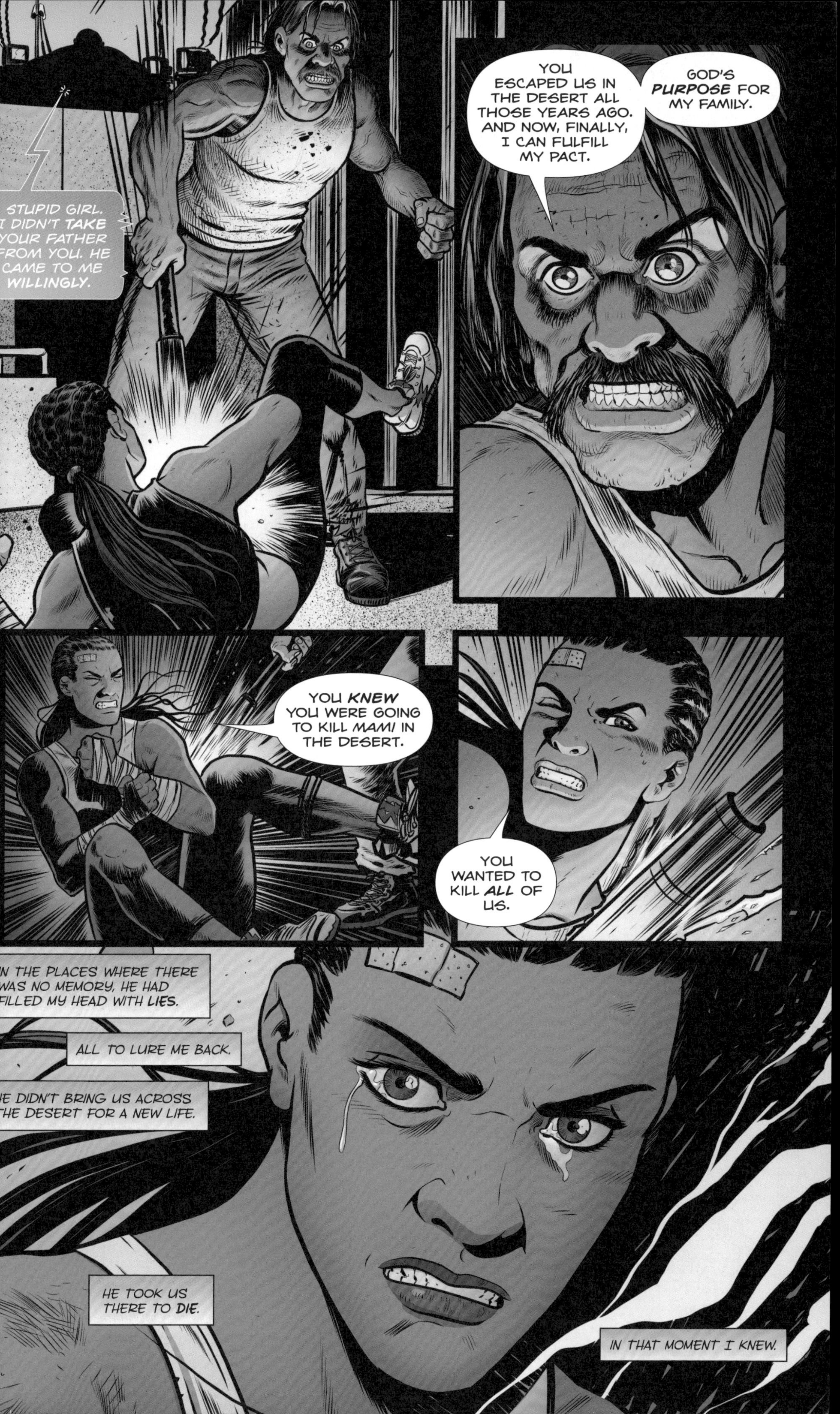
STUPID GIRL. I DIDN'T TAKE YOUR FATHER FROM YOU. HE CAME TO ME WILLINGLY.
YOU ESCAPED US IN THE DESERT ALL THOSE YEARS AGO. AND NOW, FINALLY, I CAN FULFILL MY PACT.
GOD'S PURPOSE FOR MY FAMILY.
YOU KNEW YOU WERE GOING TO KILL MAMI IN THE DESERT.
YOU WANTED TO KILL ALL OF US.
IN THE PLACES WHERE THERE WAS NO MEMORY, HE HAD FILLED MY HEAD WITH LIES.
ALL TO LURE ME BACK.
HE DIDN'T BRING US ACROSS THE DESERT FOR A NEW LIFE.
HE TOOK US THERE TO DIE.
IN THAT MOMENT I KNEW.

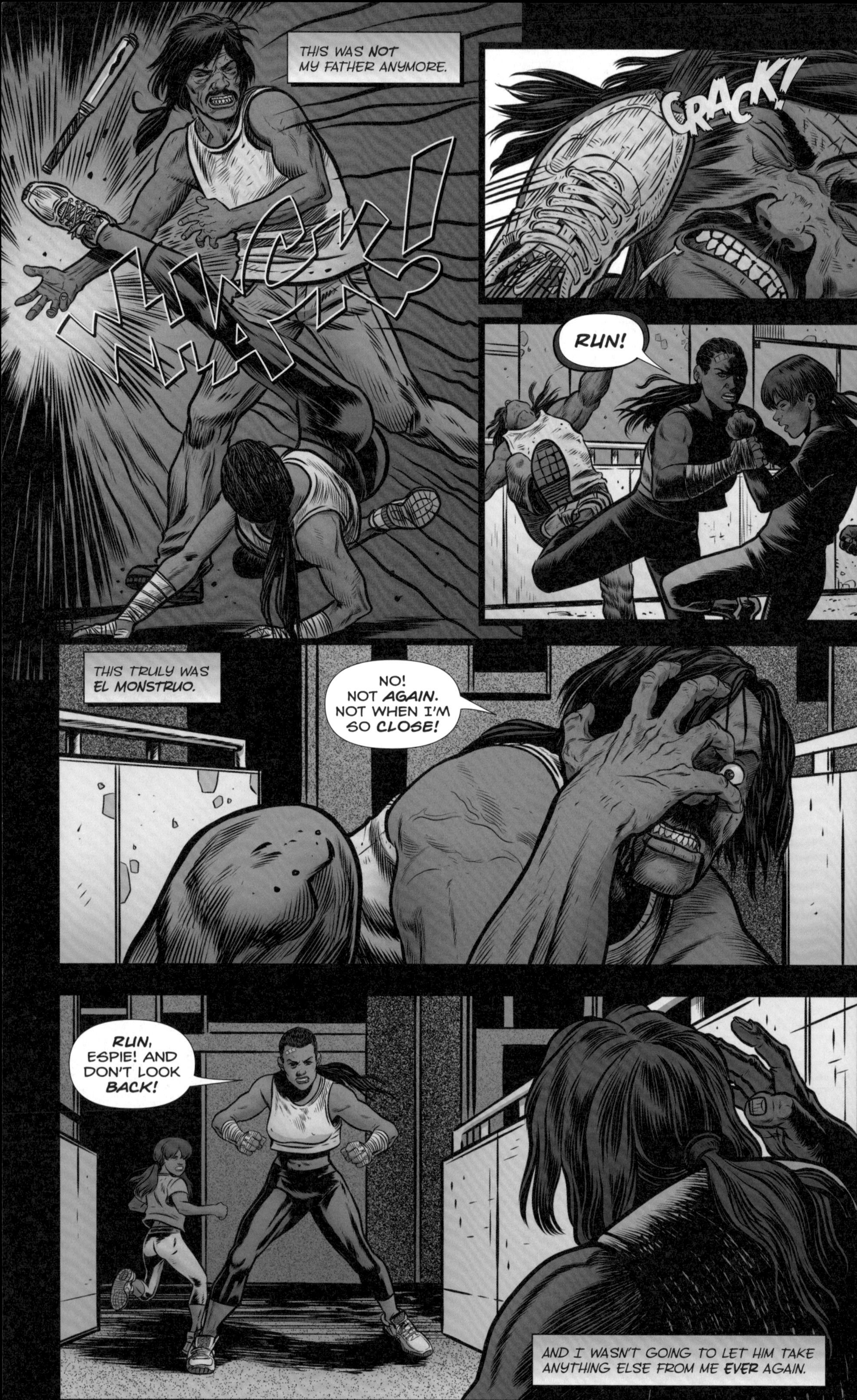
THIS WAS NOT MY FATHER ANYMORE.
WHACK!
CRACK!
RUN!
THIS TRULY WAS EL MONSTRUO.
NO! NOT AGAIN. NOT WHEN I'M SO CLOSE!
RUN, ESPIE! AND DON'T LOOK BACK!
AND I WASN'T GOING TO LET HIM TAKE ANYTHING ELSE FROM ME EVER AGAIN.

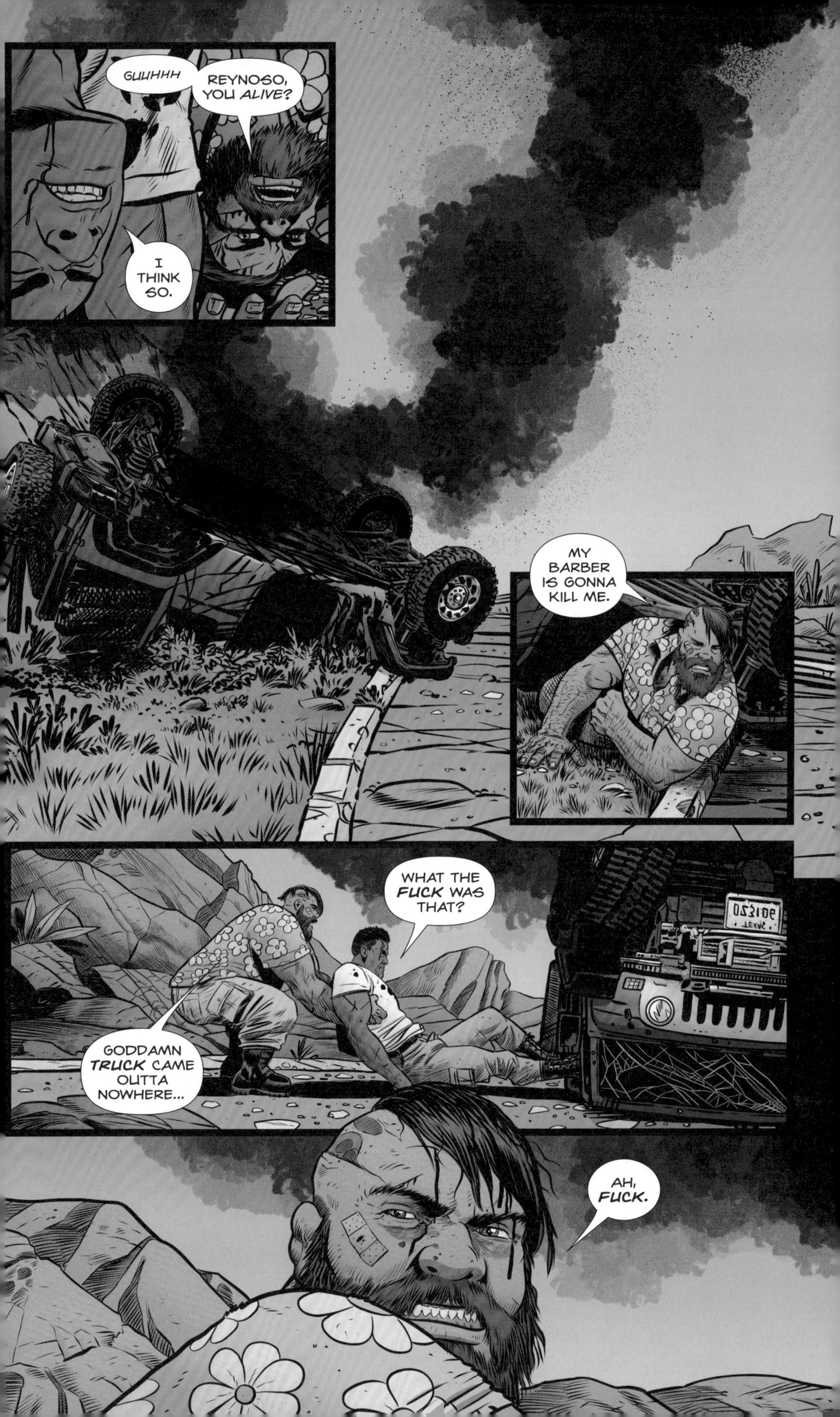
GUUHHH
REYNOSO, YOU *ALIVE?*
I THINK SO.
MY BARBER IS GONNA KILL ME.
WHAT THE ***FUCK*** WAS THAT?
GODDAMN ***TRUCK*** CAME OUTTA NOWHERE...
AH, ***FUCK.***

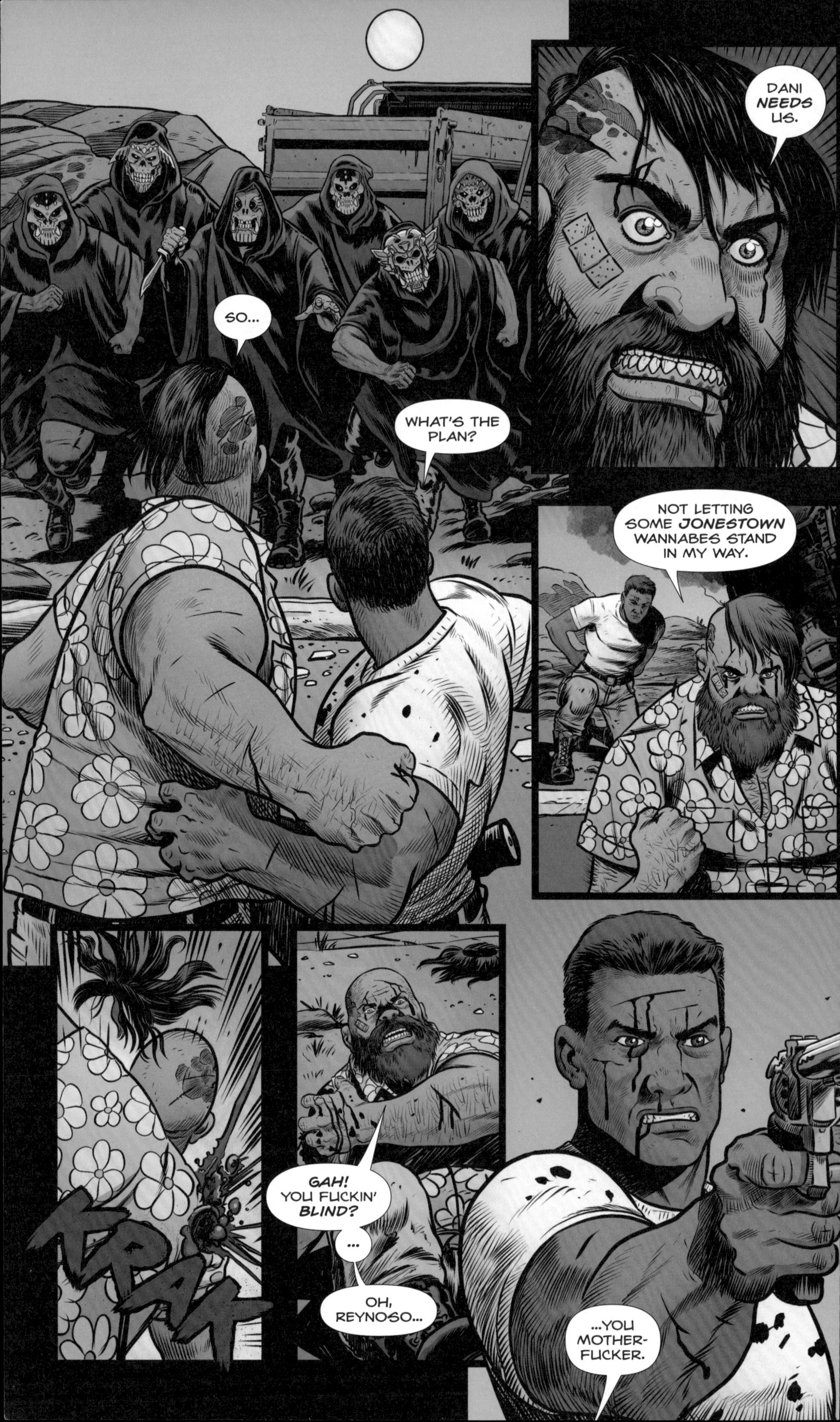
SO...
WHAT'S THE PLAN?
DANI NEEDS US.
NOT LETTING SOME JONESTOWN WANNABES STAND IN MY WAY.
KRAAK
GAH! YOU FUCKIN' BLIND?
...
OH, REYNOSO...
...YOU MOTHER-FUCKER.

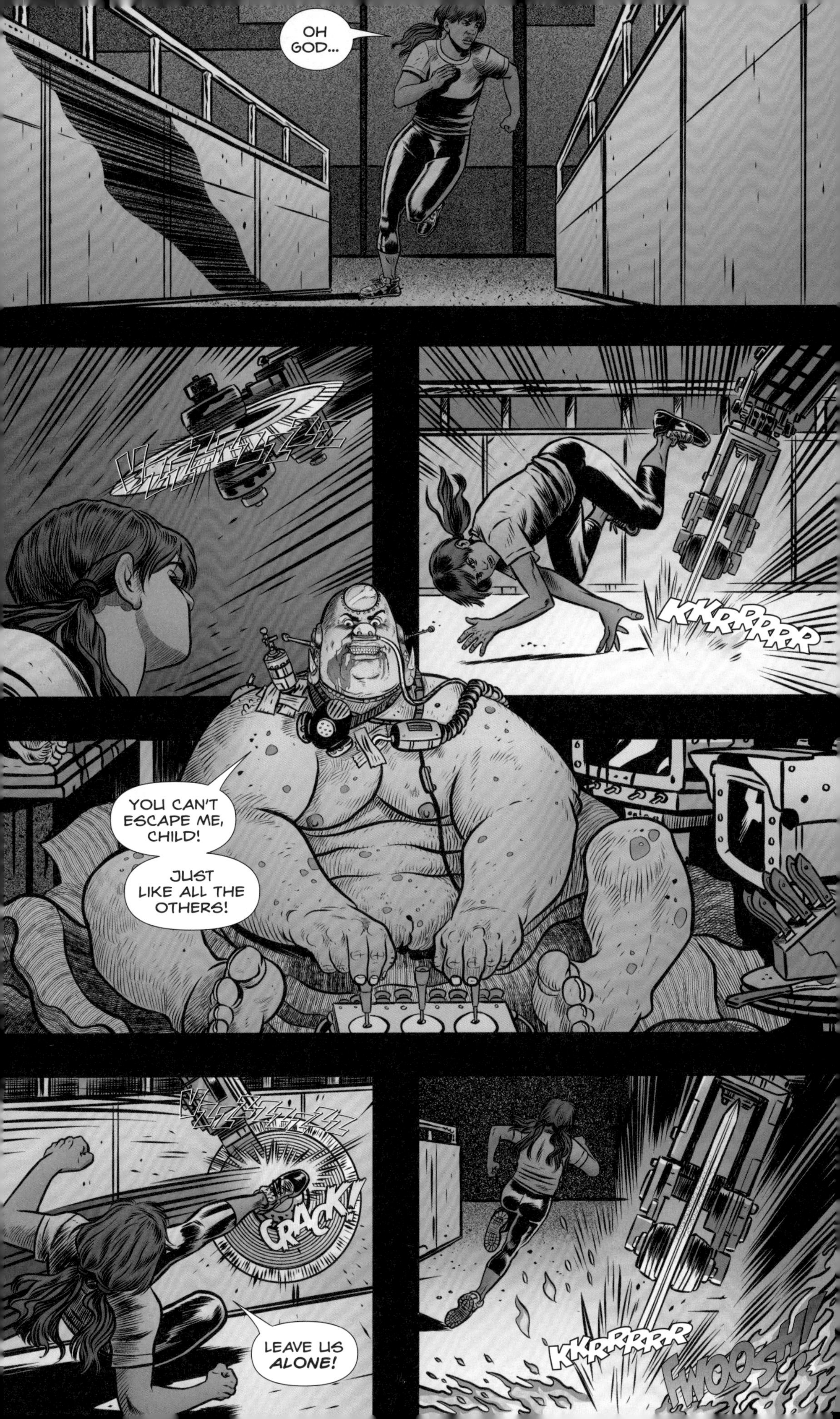
OH GOD...
KKRRRRRRR
YOU CAN'T ESCAPE ME, CHILD!
JUST LIKE ALL THE OTHERS!
CRACK!
LEAVE US ALONE!
KKRRRRRRR
FWOOSH!

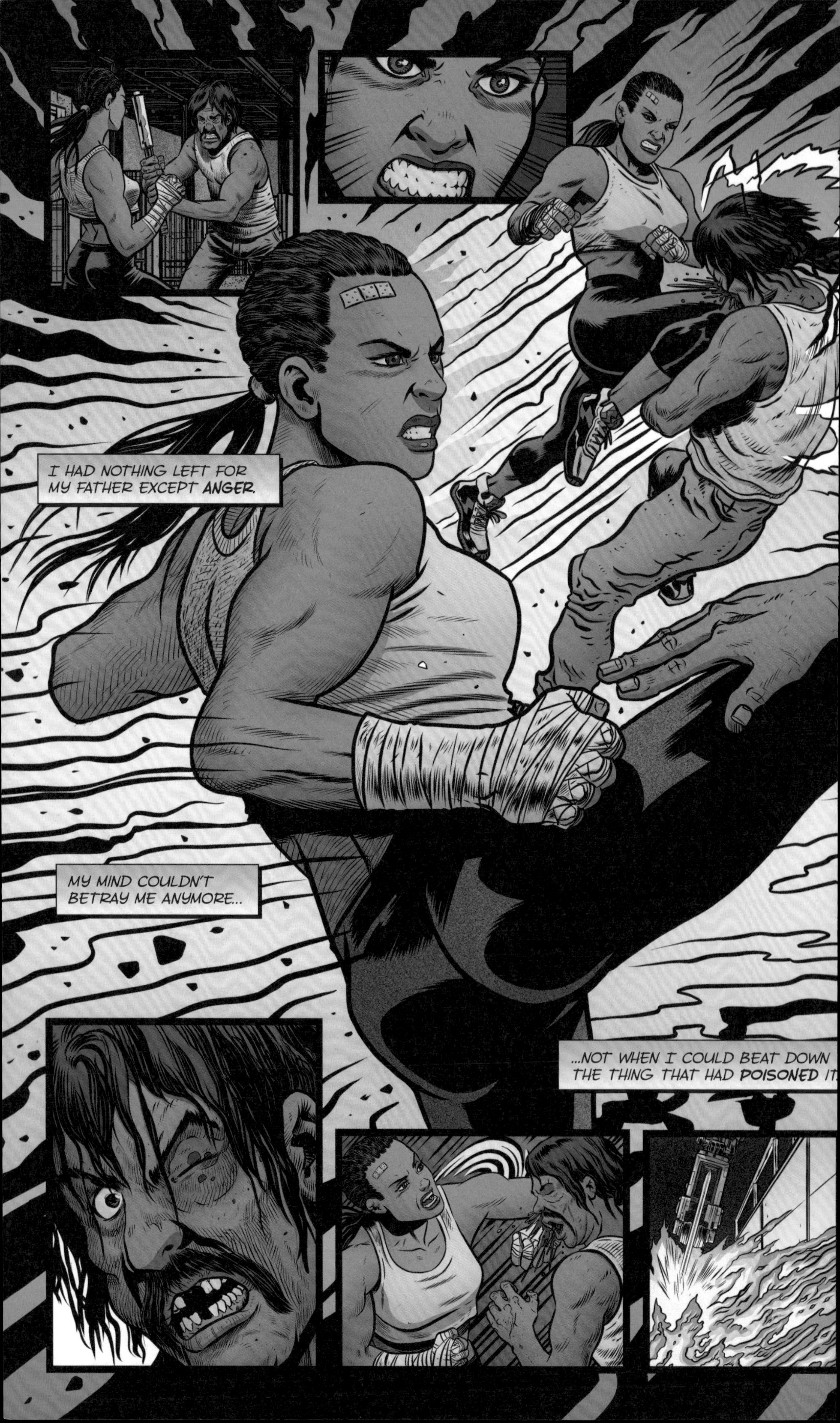
I HAD NOTHING LEFT FOR MY FATHER EXCEPT ANGER.
MY MIND COULDN'T BETRAY ME ANYMORE...
...NOT WHEN I COULD BEAT DOWN THE THING THAT HAD POISONED IT.

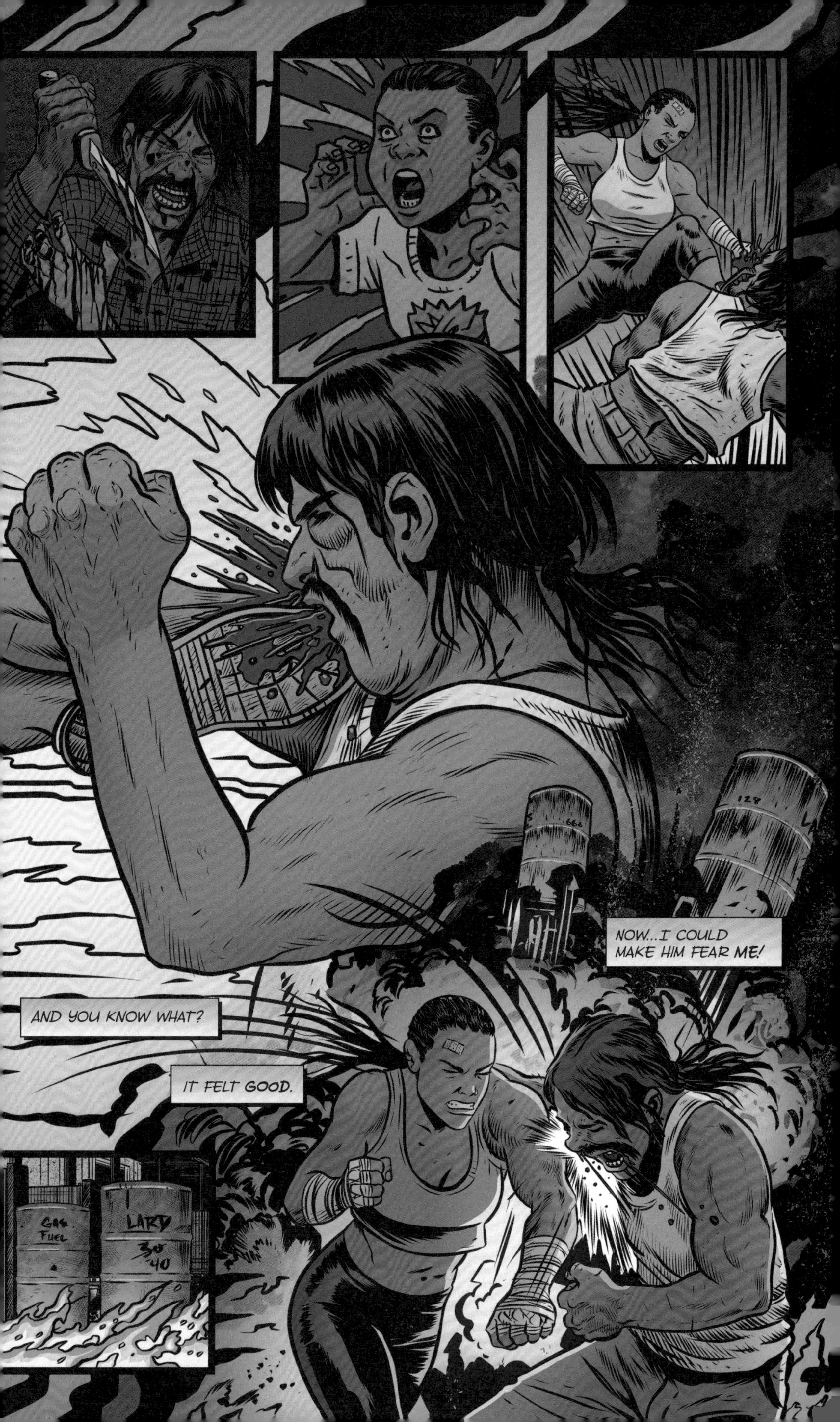

NOW...I COULD MAKE HIM FEAR ME!
AND YOU KNOW WHAT?
IT FELT GOOD.
GAS FUEL
LARD

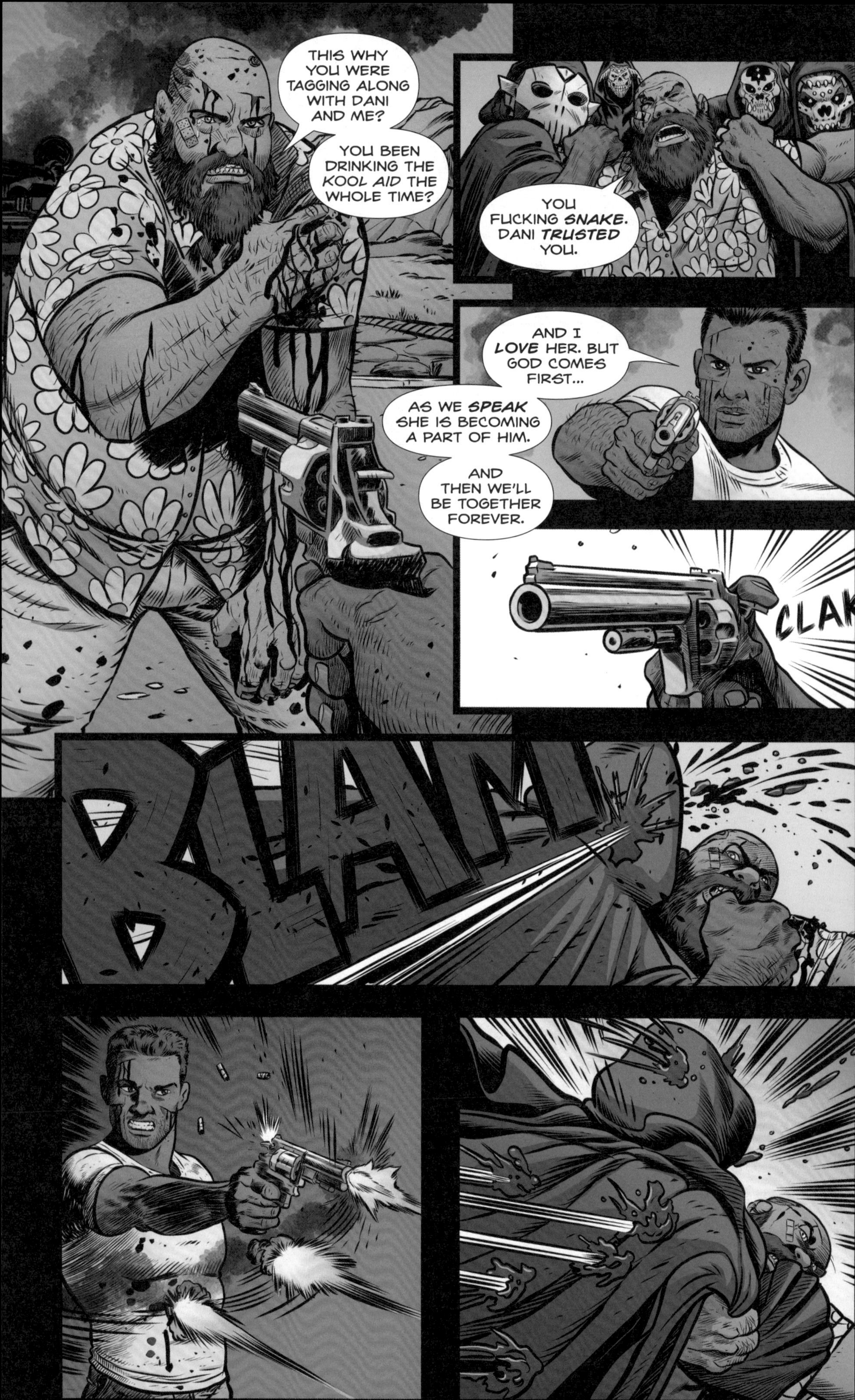
THIS WHY YOU WERE TAGGING ALONG WITH DANI AND ME?
YOU BEEN DRINKING THE *KOOL AID* THE WHOLE TIME?
YOU FUCKING **SNAKE**. DANI ***TRUSTED*** YOU.
AND I ***LOVE*** HER. BUT GOD COMES FIRST...
AS WE ***SPEAK*** SHE IS BECOMING A PART OF HIM.
AND THEN WE'LL BE TOGETHER FOREVER.
CLAK
BLAM

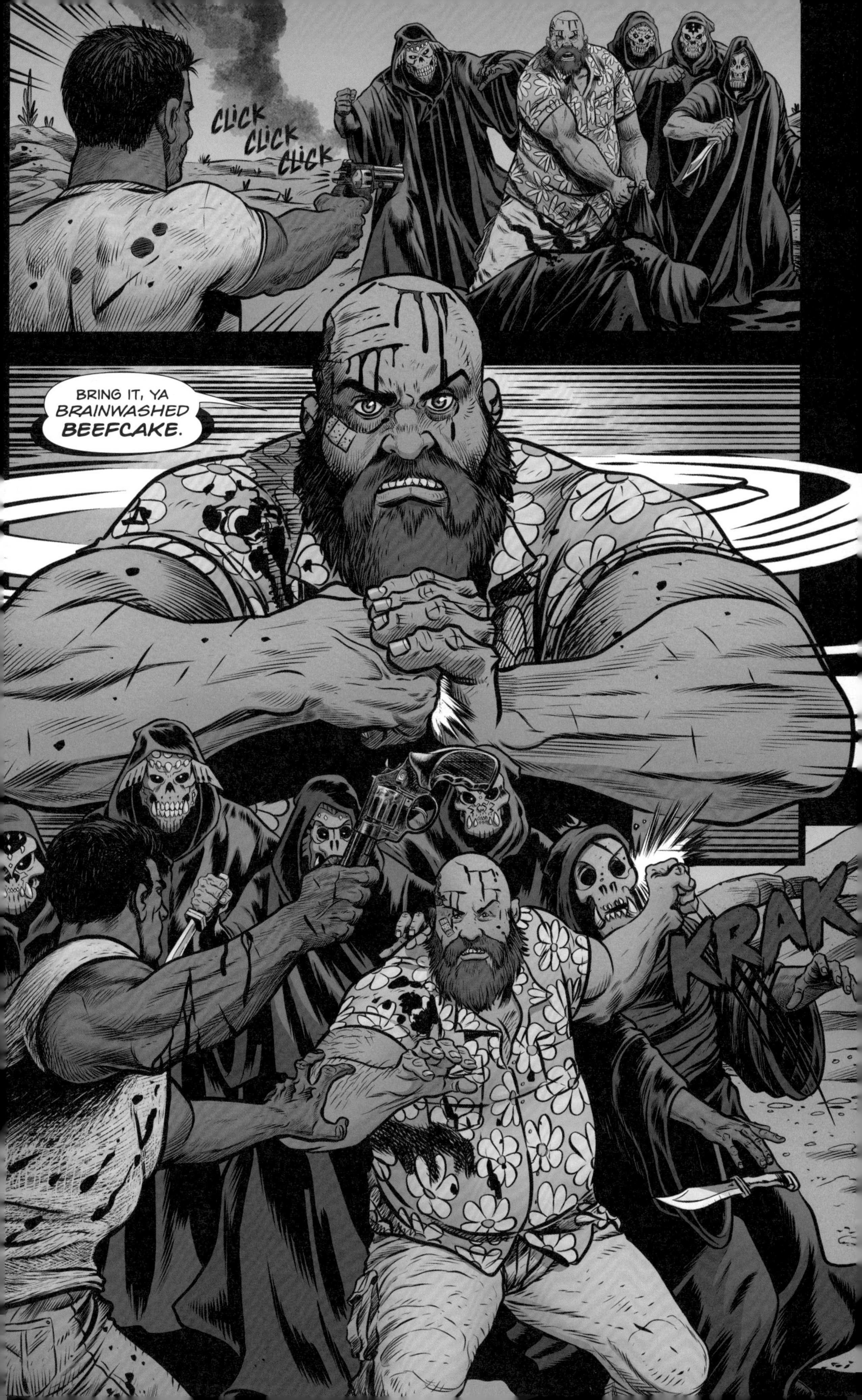
CLICK
CLICK
CLICK
BRING IT, YA BRAINWASHED BEEFCAKE.
KRAK

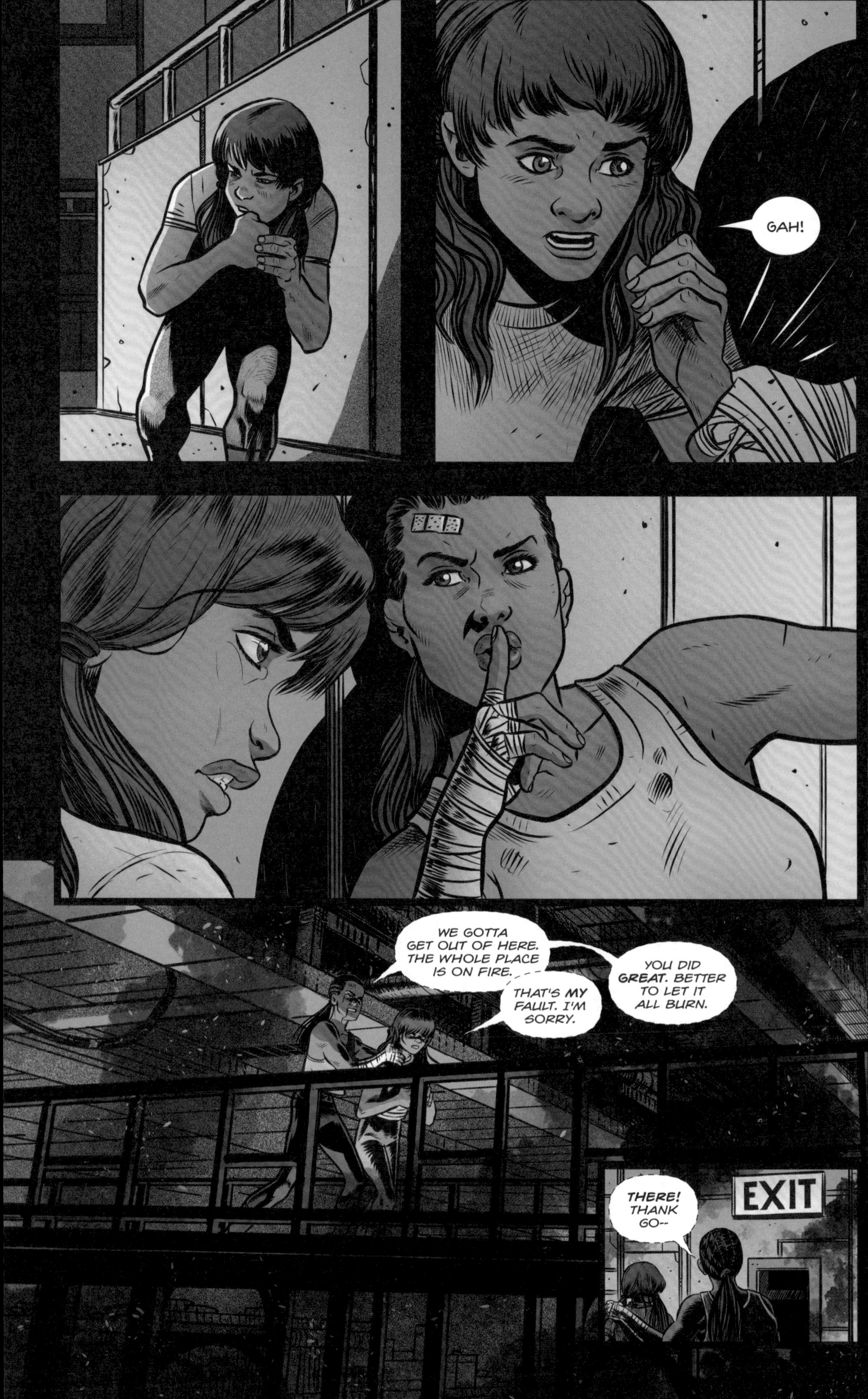
GAH!
WE GOTTA GET OUT OF HERE. THE WHOLE PLACE IS ON FIRE.
THAT'S MY FAULT. I'M SORRY.
YOU DID GREAT. BETTER TO LET IT ALL BURN.
THERE! THANK GO--
EXIT

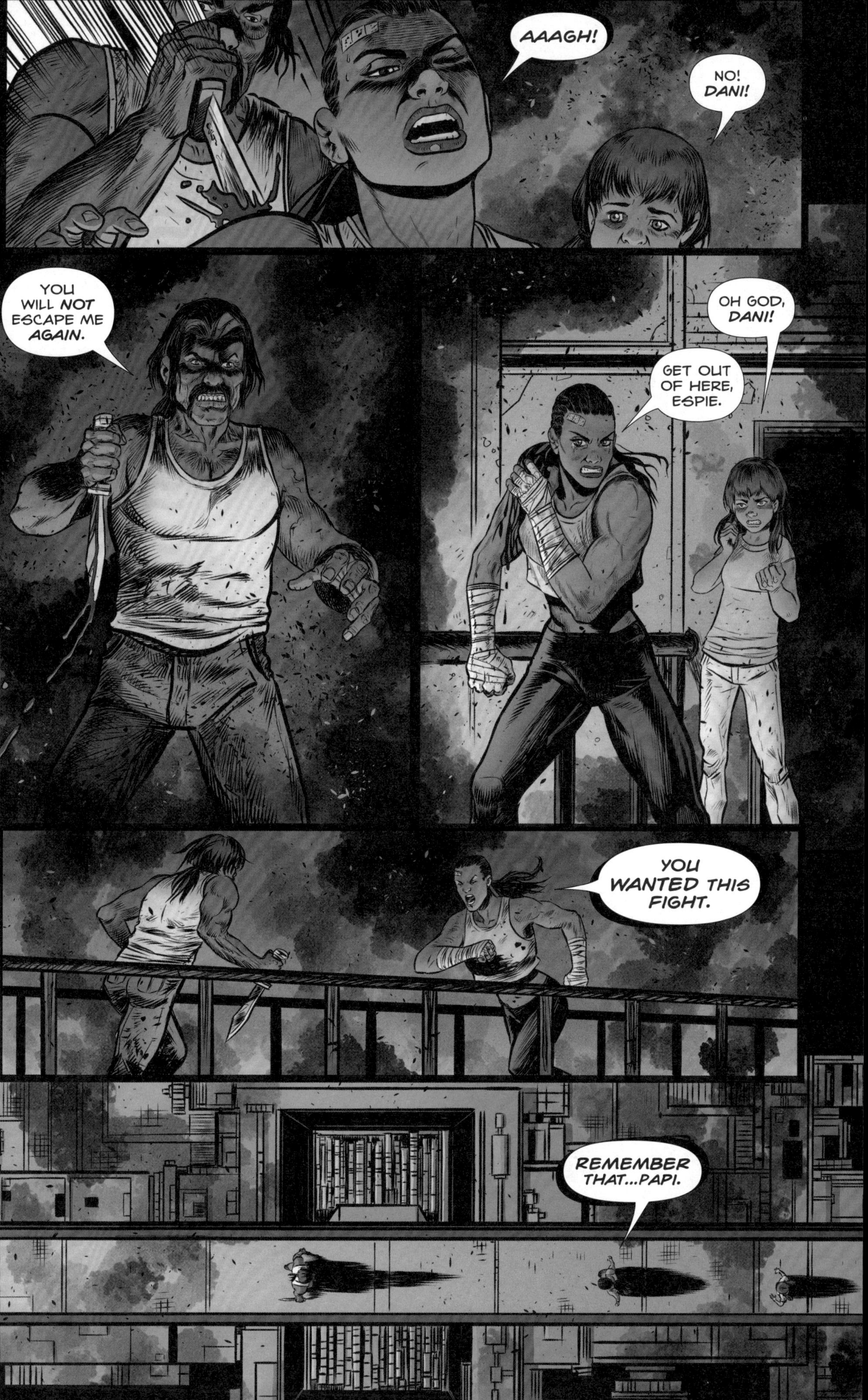
AAAGH!
NO! DANI!
YOU WILL NOT ESCAPE ME AGAIN.
OH GOD, DANI!
GET OUT OF HERE, ESPIE.
YOU WANTED THIS FIGHT.
REMEMBER THAT...PAPI.

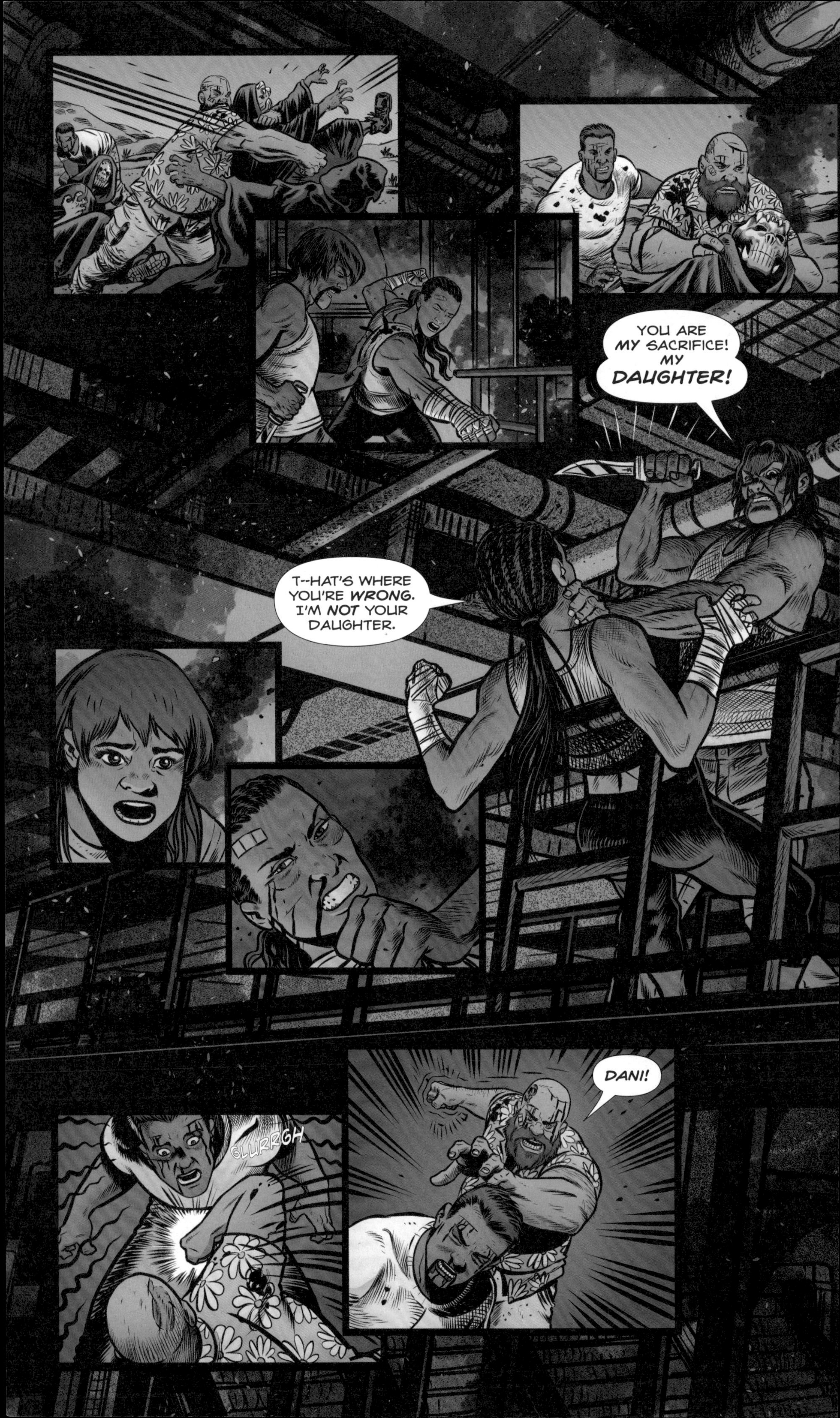
YOU ARE MY SACRIFICE! MY DAUGHTER!
T--HAT'S WHERE YOU'RE WRONG. I'M NOT YOUR DAUGHTER.
GLURRGH
DANI!

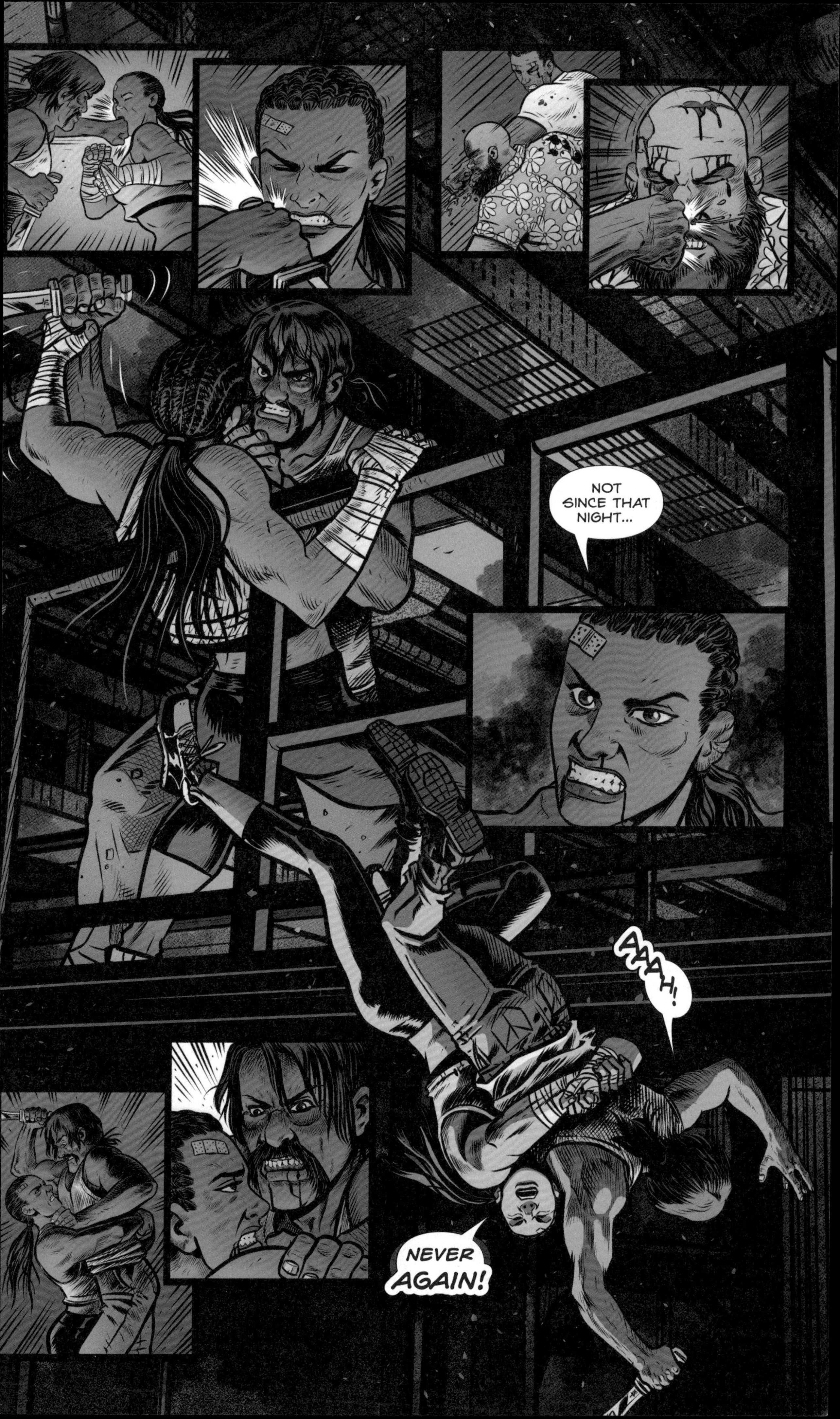
NOT SINCE THAT NIGHT...
AAAAH!
NEVER AGAIN!

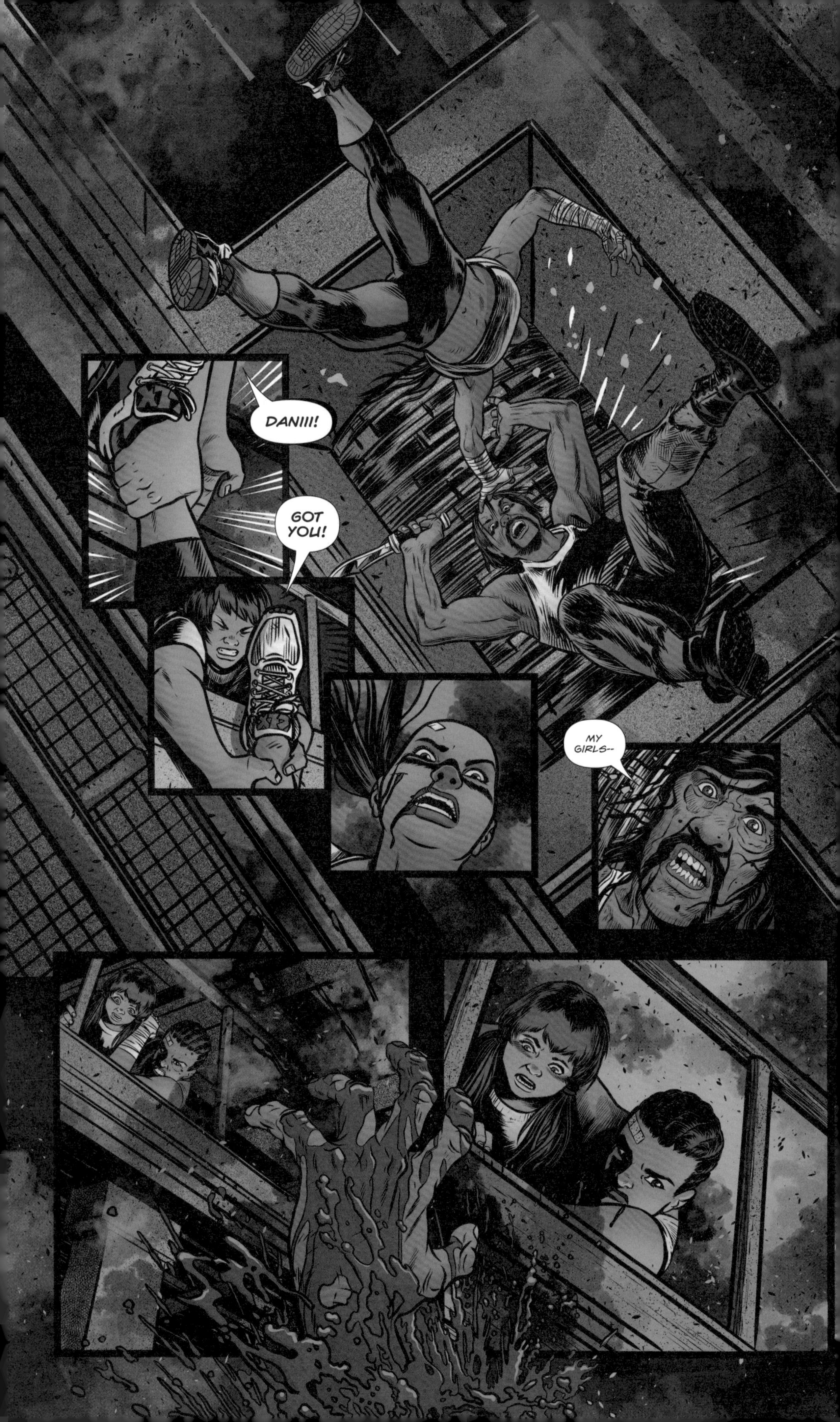
DANIII!
GOT YOU!
MY GIRLS--

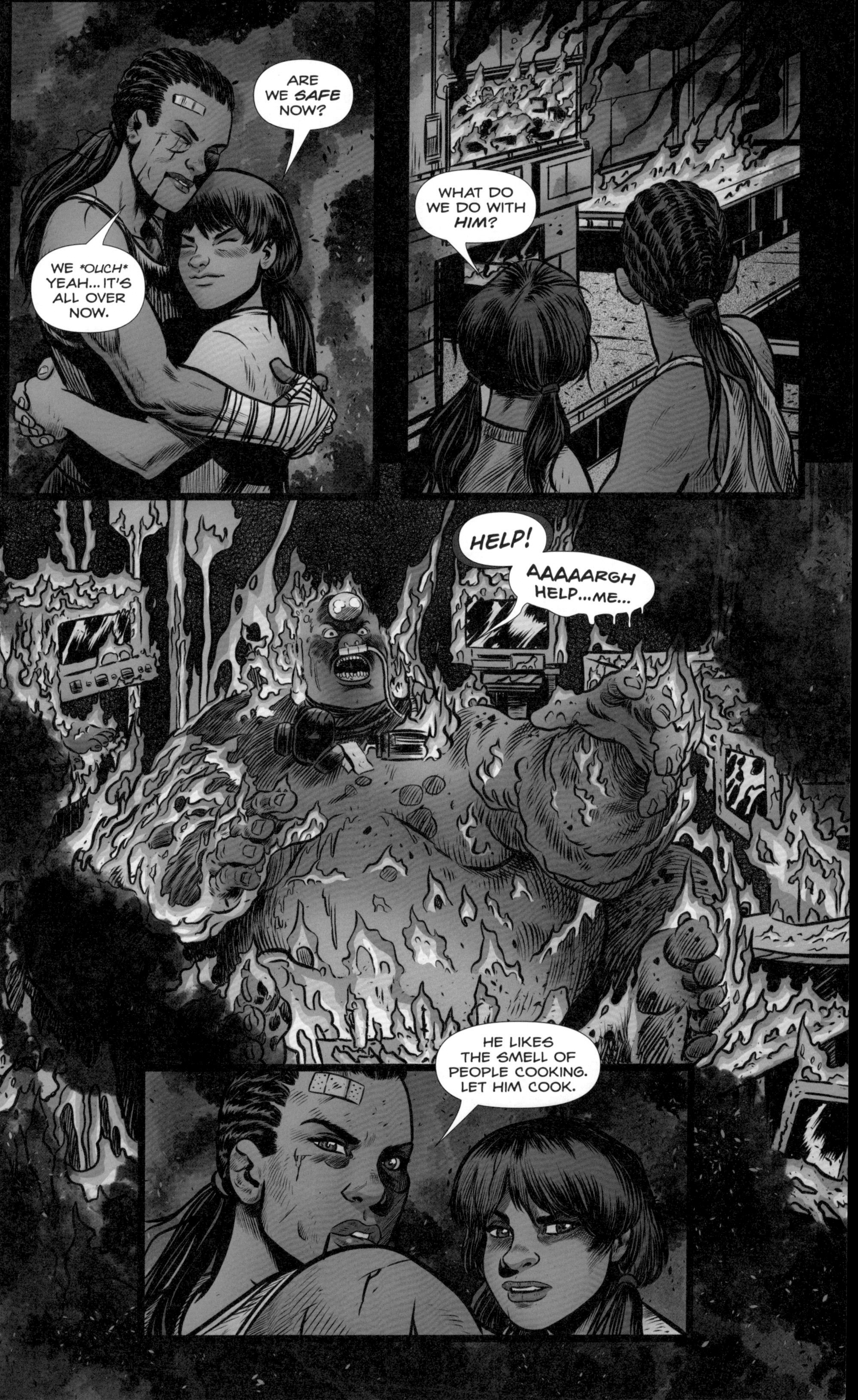
ARE WE SAFE NOW?
WE *OUCH* YEAH... IT'S ALL OVER NOW.
WHAT DO WE DO WITH HIM?
HELP!
AAAAARGH HELP...ME...
HE LIKES THE SMELL OF PEOPLE COOKING. LET HIM COOK.

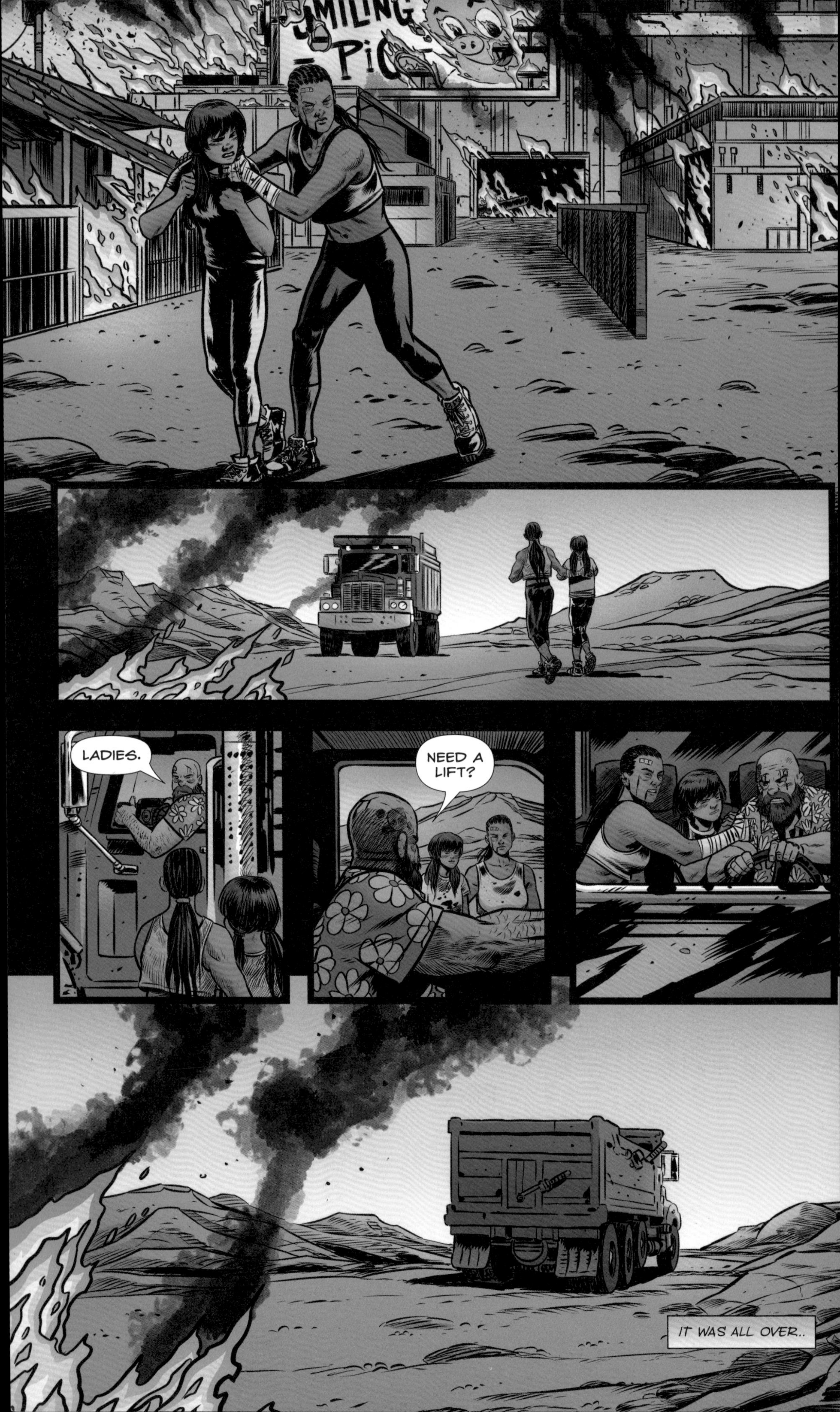
SMILING PIG
LADIES.
NEED A LIFT?
IT WAS ALL OVER..

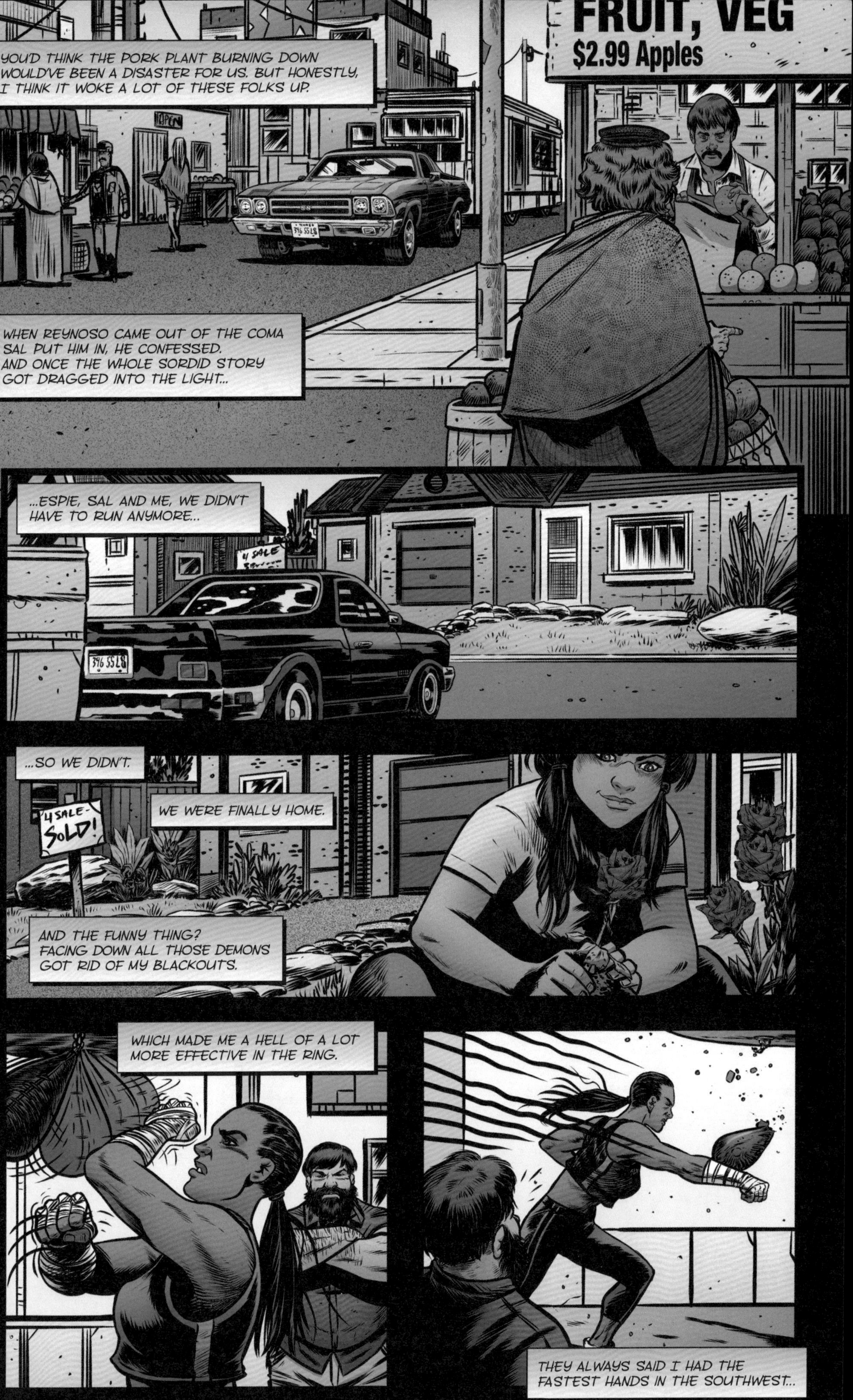
FRUIT, VEG
$2.99 Apples
YOU'D THINK THE PORK PLANT BURNING DOWN WOULD'VE BEEN A DISASTER FOR US. BUT HONESTLY, I THINK IT WOKE A LOT OF THESE FOLKS UP.
OPEN
WHEN REYNOSO CAME OUT OF THE COMA SAL PUT HIM IN, HE CONFESSED. AND ONCE THE WHOLE SORDID STORY GOT DRAGGED INTO THE LIGHT...
...ESPIE, SAL AND ME, WE DIDN'T HAVE TO RUN ANYMORE...
4 SALE
...SO WE DIDN'T.
4 SALE- SOLD!
WE WERE FINALLY HOME.
AND THE FUNNY THING? FACING DOWN ALL THOSE DEMONS GOT RID OF MY BLACKOUTS.
WHICH MADE ME A HELL OF A LOT MORE EFFECTIVE IN THE RING.
THEY ALWAYS SAID I HAD THE FASTEST HANDS IN THE SOUTHWEST...

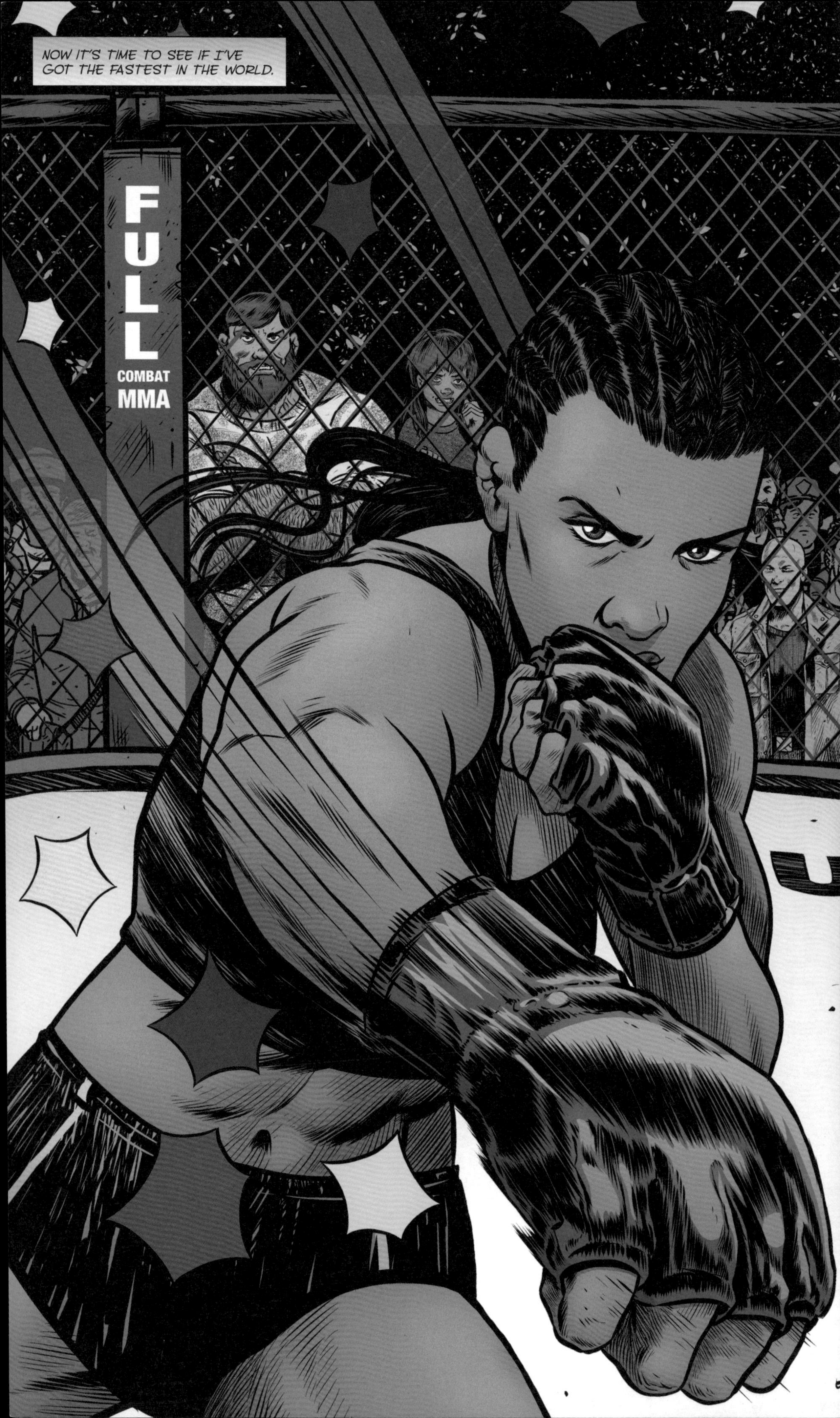
NOW IT'S TIME TO SEE IF I'VE GOT THE FASTEST IN THE WORLD.
FULL COMBAT MMA

ORIGINAL COVER ART BY
ANY BELANGER

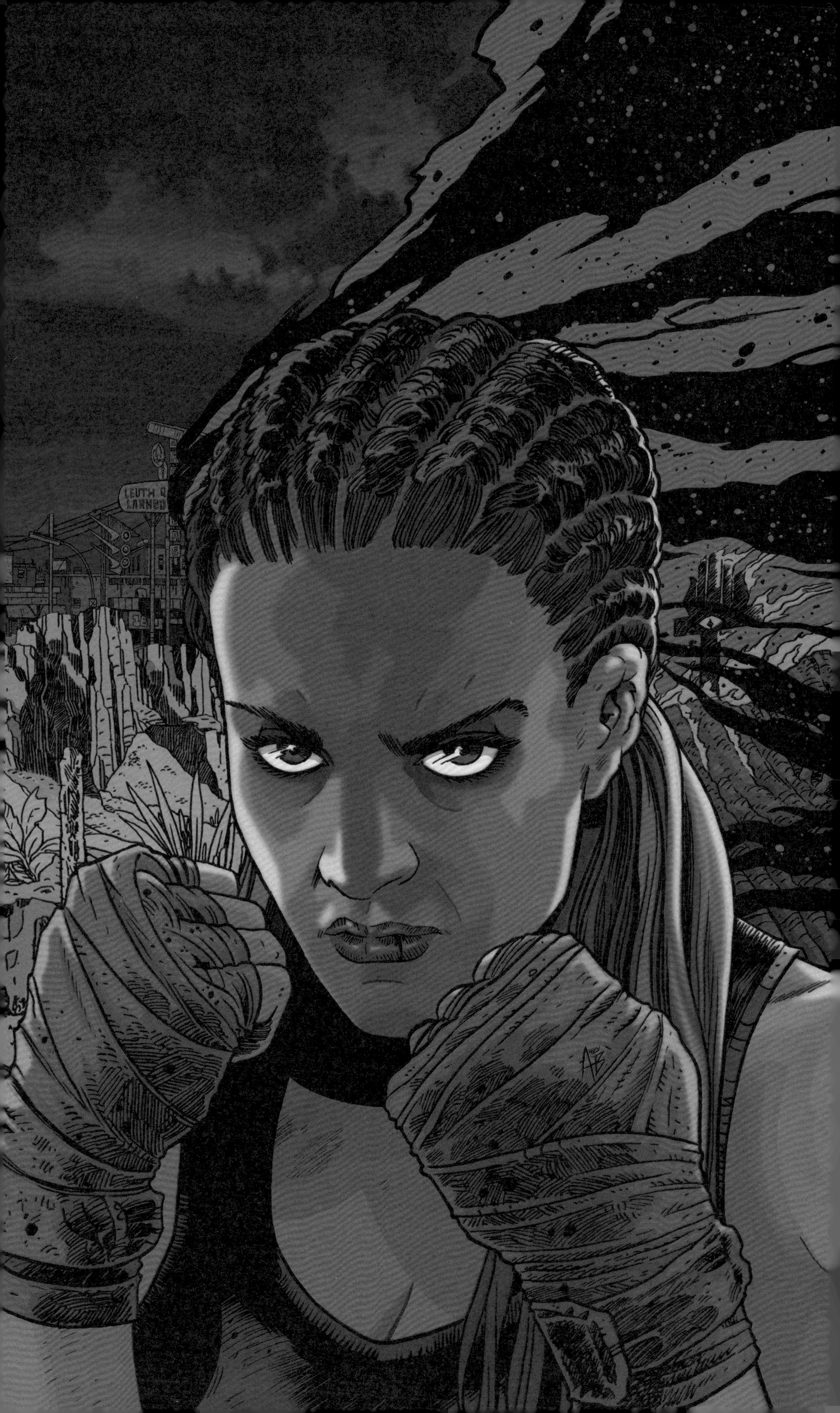
LEUTH
LARNED

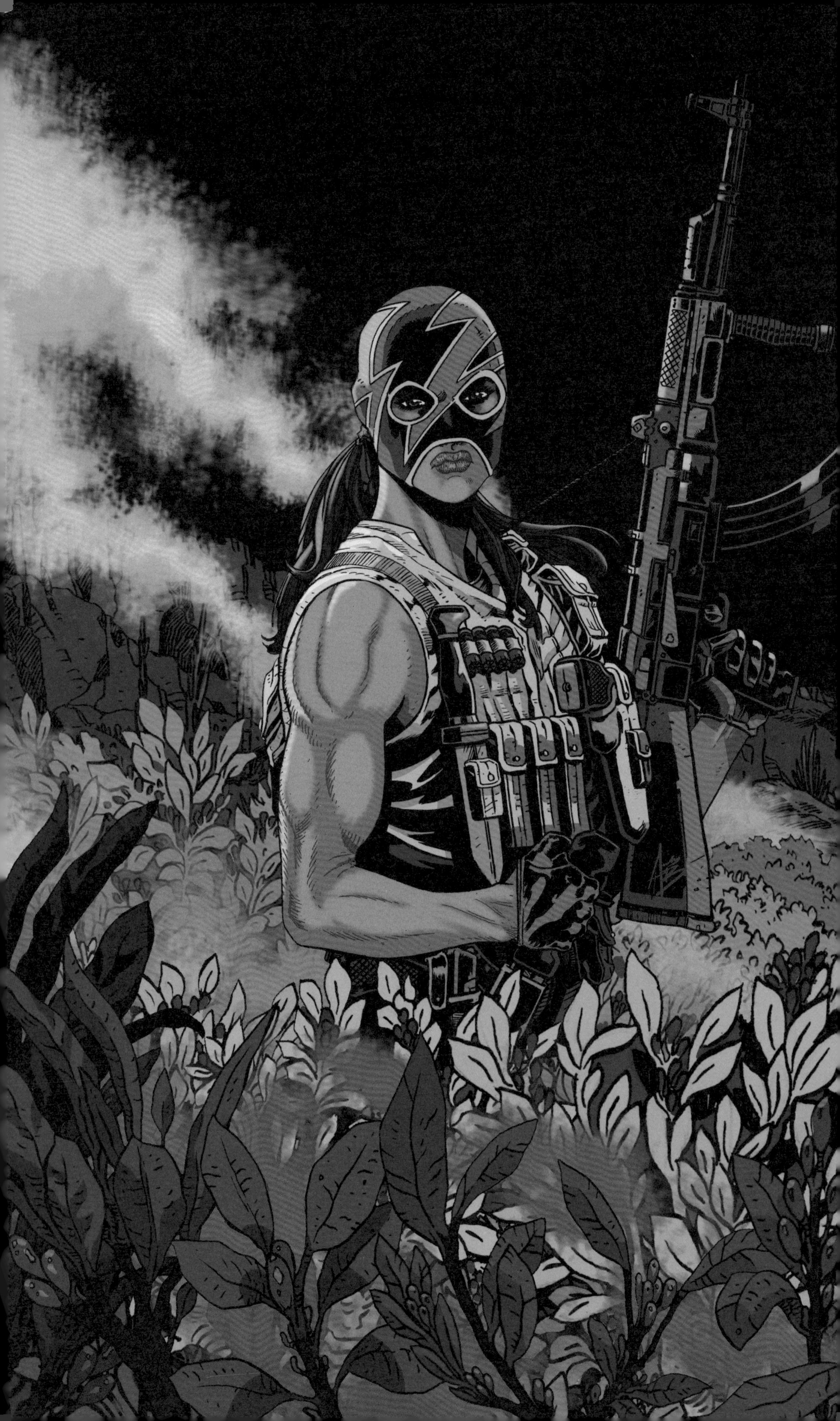

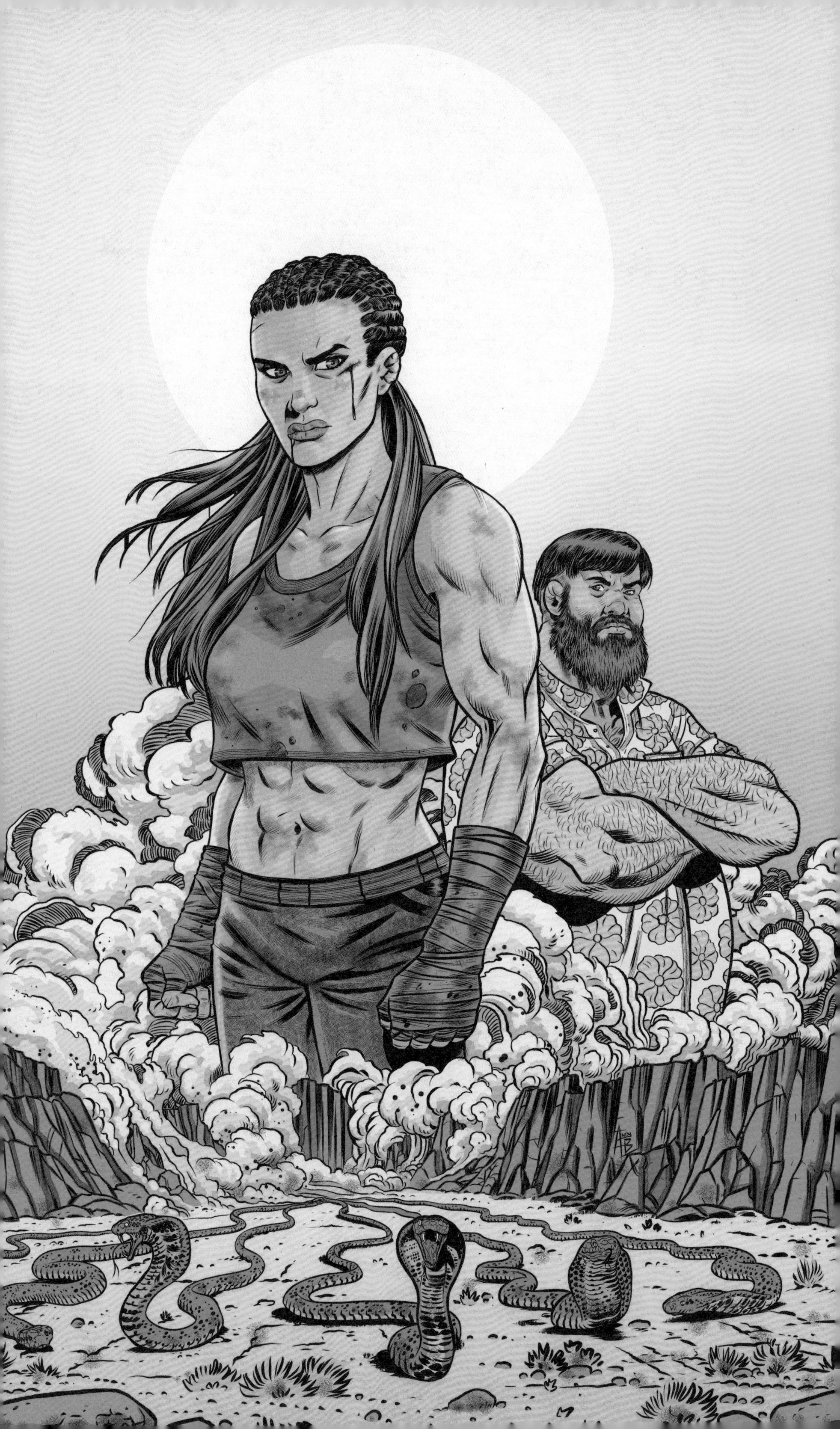

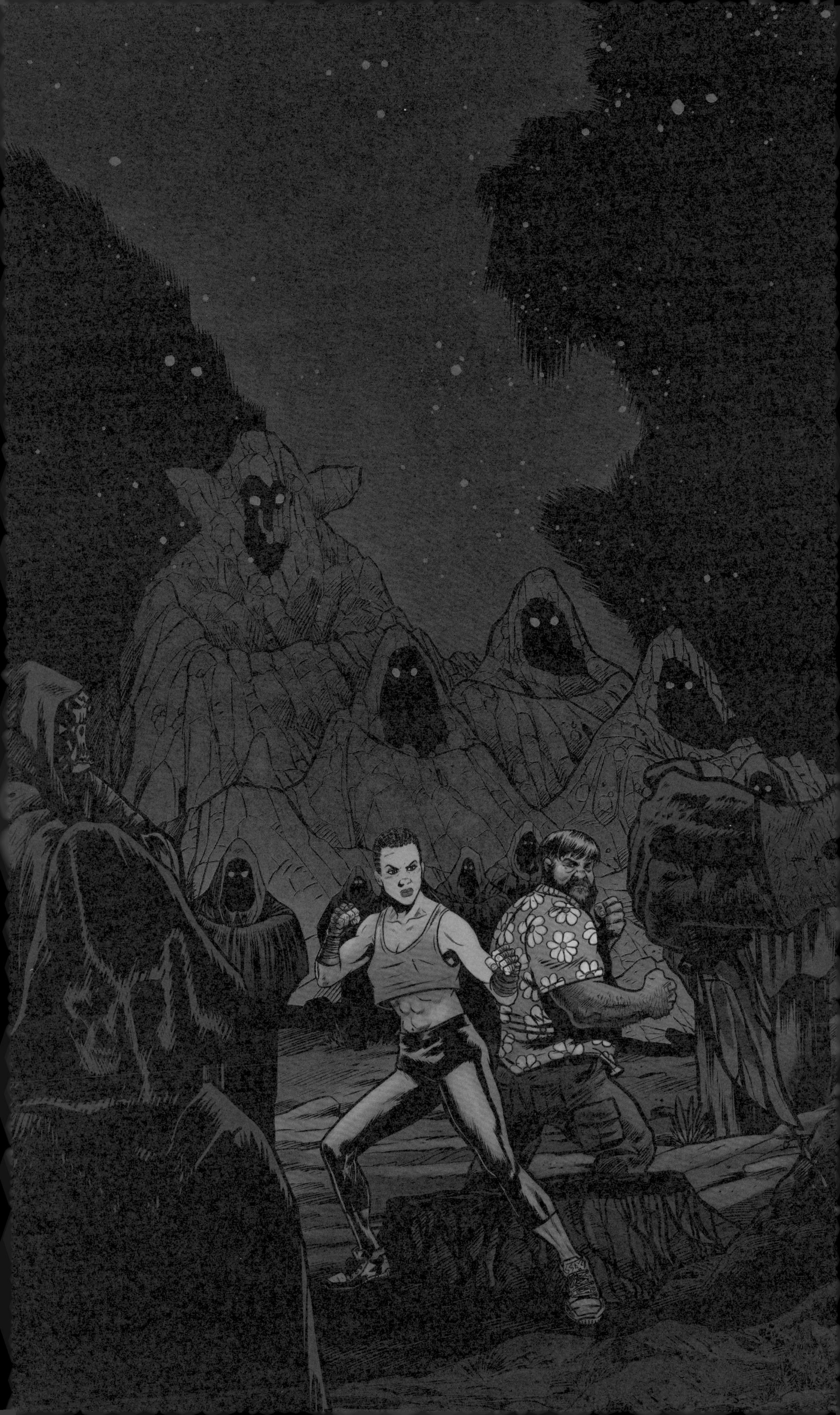

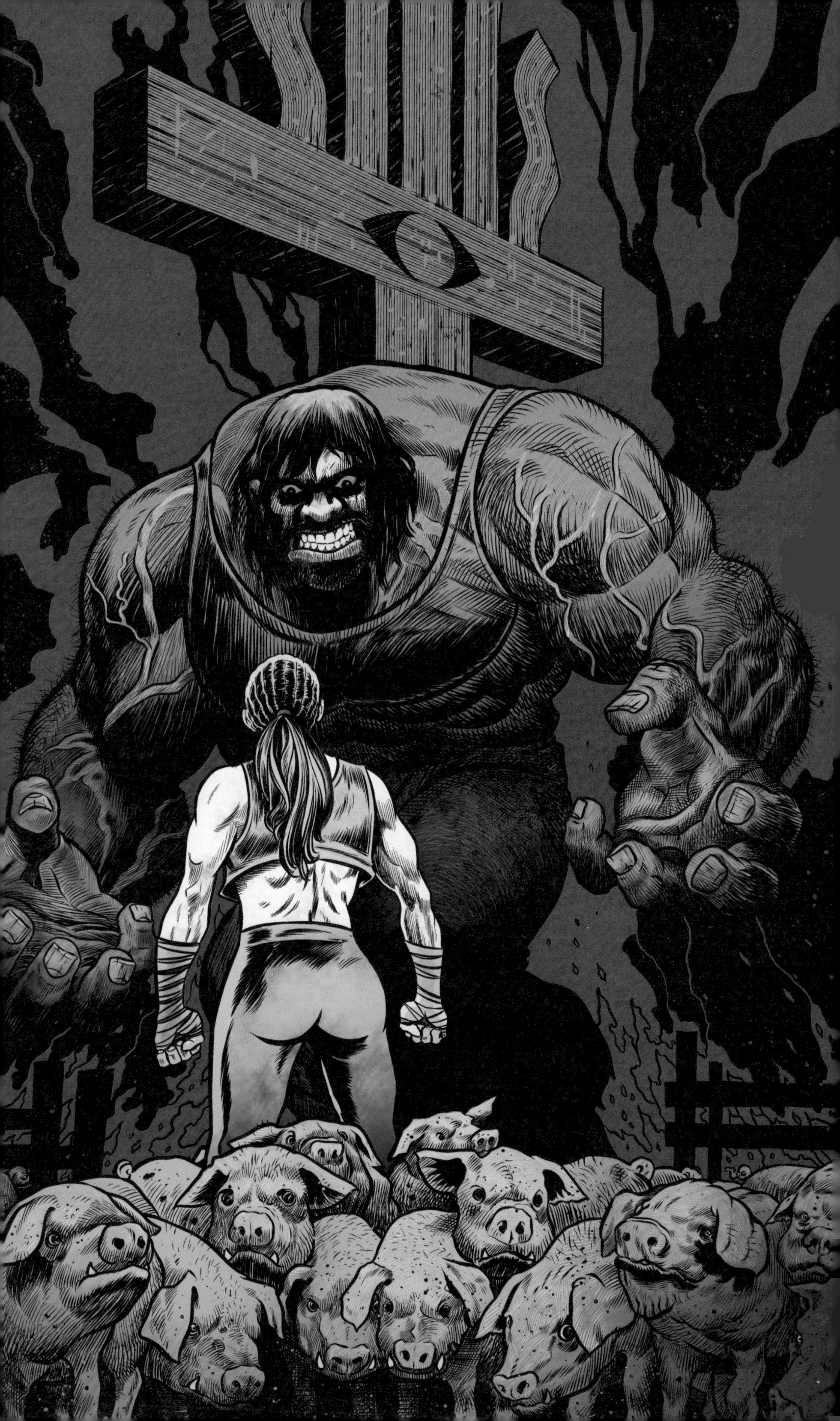

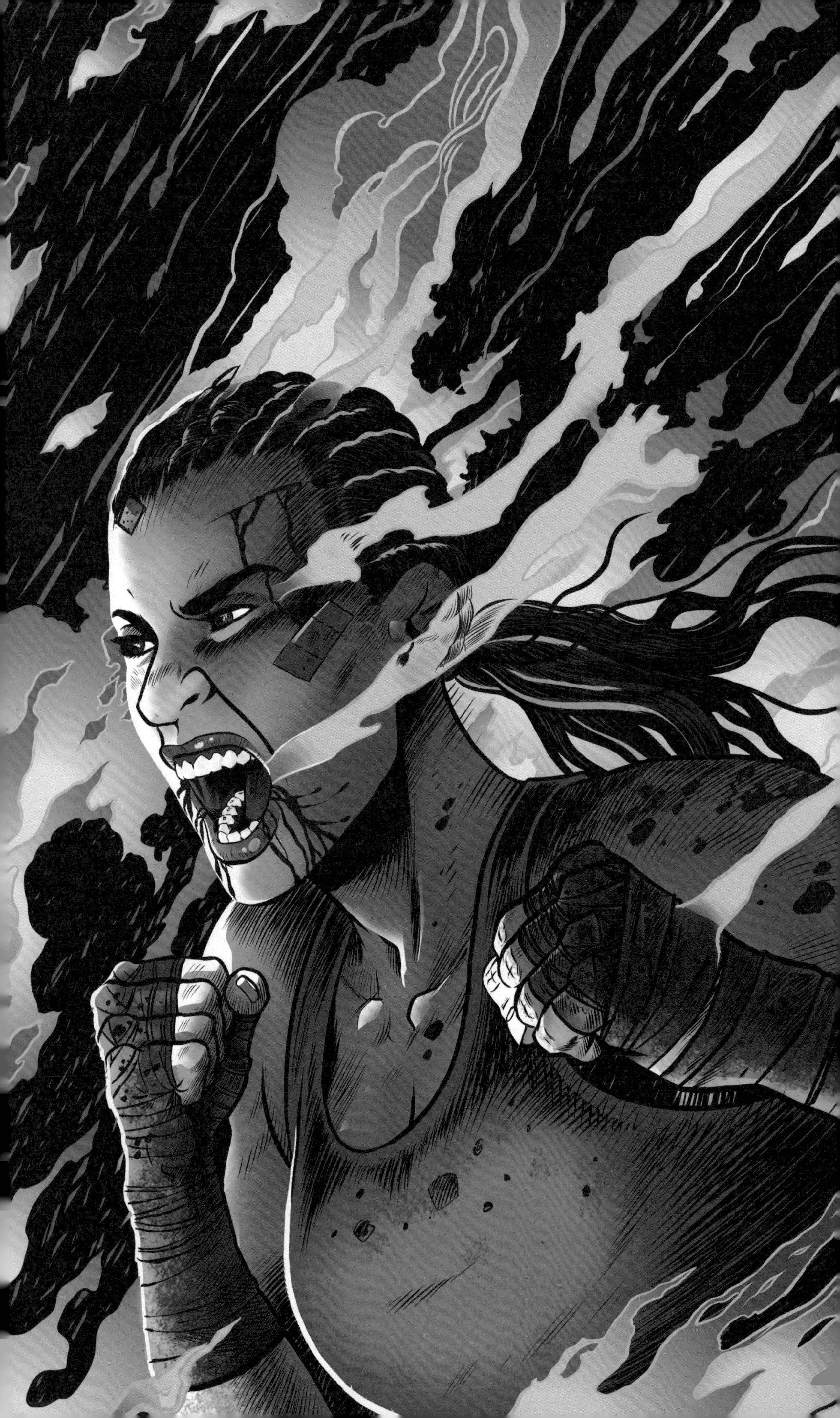

CREATORS

NATALIE CHAIDEZ | WRITER

Born and raised in Los Angeles, Natalie Chaidez is a graduate of UCLA film
school. After film school, she was a participant in the prestigious Disney Writers'
Fellowship. Natalie was recently the Executive Producer/ Showrunner on USA's
hit drama, QUEEN OF THE SOUTH. Previously, she created and ran the SyFy series
HUNTERS and was the Executive Producer/Showrunner on 12 MONKEYS.

ANDY BELANGER | ARTIST

Andy Belanger works as a freelance cartoonist/illustrator based in Montreal. He does
work in the mainstream comic market, plus a wide variety of work for the Canadian
Film, Television and Video Game industries. Other works include SWAMP THING with
Scott Snyder and Jeff Lemire. Andy was also lead Trailer Animator on the video game
FARCRY 3 BLOOD DRAGON for UbiSoft. In Montreal Andy moonlights as a Pro Wrestler
for IWS (the International Wrestling Syndicate) and wrestles under the name
Bob "The Animal" Anger.

DANIELA MIWA | COLOR ARTIST

Daniela is a Brazilian comic book artist who has been coloring comic books since
2013. Some of her works include THE FEARSOME DR. FANG, THE OLD GUARD and most
recently, GHOST IN THE SHELL; GLOBAL NEURAL NETWORK.

SERGE LAPOINTE | LETTERER

Serge has worked in the comic book and entertainment industry for the last 20
years. After first breaking in as an inker in the late 90's, he has since added to his
arsenal the jobs of letterer and colorist, as well as editor (ASSASSIN'S CREED and
SPLINTER CELL graphic novels for Ubi Workshop) and art director (various creative
projects, through his own studio: Studio Lounak)..

SEBASTIAN GIRNER | EDITOR

Sebastian Girner is a German-born, American-raised comic editor and writer.
His editing includes such series as DEADLY CLASS, SOUTHERN BASTARDS and THE
PUNISHER. He lives and works in Brooklyn with his wife.